Claire and Pem

A Love Story

The Chronicles of Ennea
Book 4

L. C. Frenzel

Also by L.C. Frenzel

The Chronicles of Ennea
Claire in Lunaria
The Sword of Training
The Forgotten Garden
Claire and Pem
Rissa and Turlo
The Twin Scepters
Kamorian Gate

Callie Houston Series
Emerald Green
A Matter for Survival
Sweet and Sour

Non Fiction
Governor Lydia, A Mellow Rose from Texas

Poetry
Nuclear Gnat

Works in Progress
The Chronicles Trilogy:
- The Fall of the Council
- The Next Generation
- The Return of the Queen

Copyright

Fat Squirrel 21 LLC
Fat Squirrel Publishing
P.O. Box 2139
San Marcos TX 78667
Claire and Pem, Lunaria Book 4
E pub: ISBN: 978-1-939687-03-6
Copyright © 2013 by Charles Frenzel
Claire and Pem, A Love Story; The Chronicles of Ennea Book 4
Paperback: ISBN: 9781939687159
LCCN: 2017903110
Copyright © 2017 by Charles and Lydia Frenzel, L.C. Frenzel
BISAC: FICTION /Action & Adventure| FICTION / Fantasy / Epic| FICTION / Science Fiction / Action & Adventure: GSAFD: Epic Literature| Fantasy Fiction| Science Fiction.

First electronic Publication by Fat Squirrel Publishing: January 2014.
First Paperback Publication by Fat Squirrel Publishing: 2017.
Fatsquirrelpublishing.com, lunarianepic.com, enneachronicles.com

Dear Reader,

To the returning reader, welcome back.

By now, we have written seven volumes in the Chronicles of Ennea and have at least three more to come out in the near future. We never knew at the time we began that one story would lead on to so many. The entire Ennead saga about Lunaria is by no means complete and will continue into the foreseeable future.

Towards the end of this book you will find a section labeled "A Guide to Ennea" which will acquaint you with such things as the geography and rivers of Ennea, the major and minor characters and some of what they did, how they died. If you read the Guide first you will get acquainted with the world, but you will also run across information that will give away some of the excitement, so be aware of this. You may find it best to use the Guide as you read in case you need to refresh your memory. So much has passed through these pages, so many people and ideas. Some of these ideas are concerned with our particular world view.

We come from an academic background that demands references at the end of everything. We hope the sounds, the sights, the smells, and the peoples of Lunaria, Tieben, the Traders of Boggrash, dark mysteries of the Alleles, and the technology of Ennea come alive for you. Thank you for buying this book. Your support keeps us writing about this world of blood, honor, and loyalty.

Lydia and Charles Frenzel as L.C. Frenzel

<u>Liturgies</u>

<u>Antiphon</u>

From an ancient text written before the Peace of a Thousand Years.

Though the context had been long forgotten by the people who live in Lunaria, those few who remember understand the origin.

The Nine (The Ennead)

Nine Worlds to rule the Heavens,
(And Nine to Rule the Worlds.)

The King to rule the Nine,
(And the People to rule the King.)

Nine Paths to Guide the People
(To the mind and heart of G'rama.)

The Pre-G'rama Antiphon known as the Four

Written during the time of the Empire of the Nine Worlds.

At the beginning, the Unnamed was being, and the Unnamed grew and became more, and all that became was similarity.

This is the Truth.

At the ending, all that seemed different is indistinguishable. The Unnamed is the One name.

This is the Truth.

Our beginning is renewal, and our ending is renewal. Nothing is lost and nothing is gained. There is only the Balance between all things. This is the principle of conservation.

This is the Truth.

Similation is the Unnamed in all its manifestations, which is the One made manifest in its many forms.

This is the Truth.

The Meditations of the Ancients known as the *Nine*
Written during the Empire of the Nine Worlds.

1. If my need is to be right, then I must beware anger. The world is not perfect, and I cannot be perfect.

2. If my need is to be needed, then I must avoid pride. Humility attracts true friends.

3. If my need is to succeed, then I must avoid deceit. Accepting failure will bring success. Accepting the truth will bring strength.

4. If my need is to be special, then I must avoid envy. Celebrate everyone's uniqueness. There is always someone who is better than you are at your chosen task.

5. If my need is to know more than my neighbor, then I must take care to share with him what I learn.

6. If my need is to be safe and secure, then I must find the courage to defeat fear. Fear is the enemy in my mind.

7. If my need is to avoid pain, I must take care to avoid gluttony. More often brings less.

8. If my need is to be against, then I must find compassion in my contention. A compassionate leader gathers many loyal followers.

9. If my need is to avoid commitment, then I must avoid being lazy, for what I do does matter greatly.

Maps of Lunaria

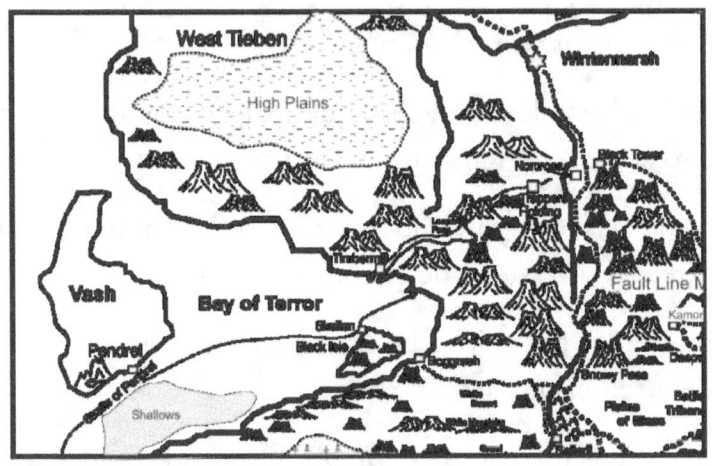

Rissa and Turlo's Journey

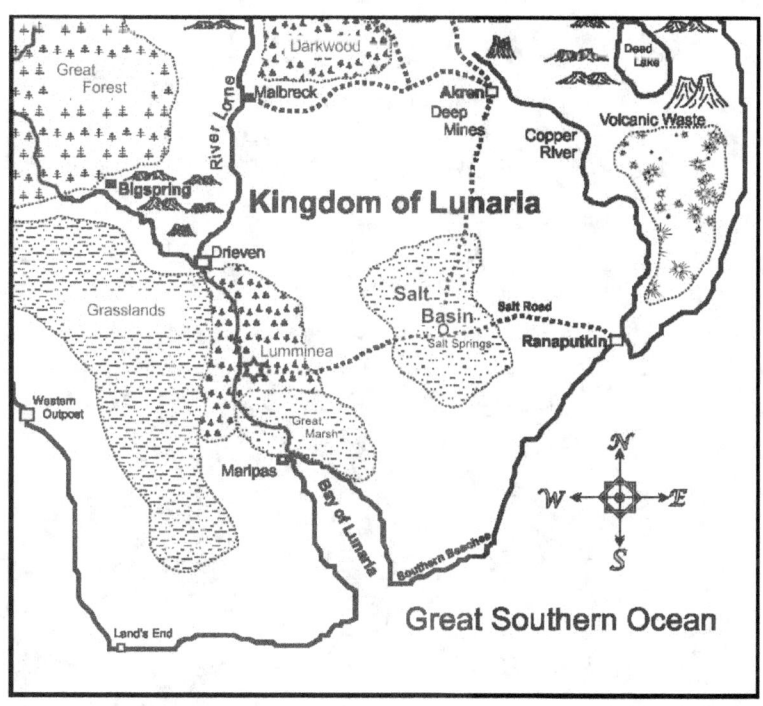

Honeymoon Map

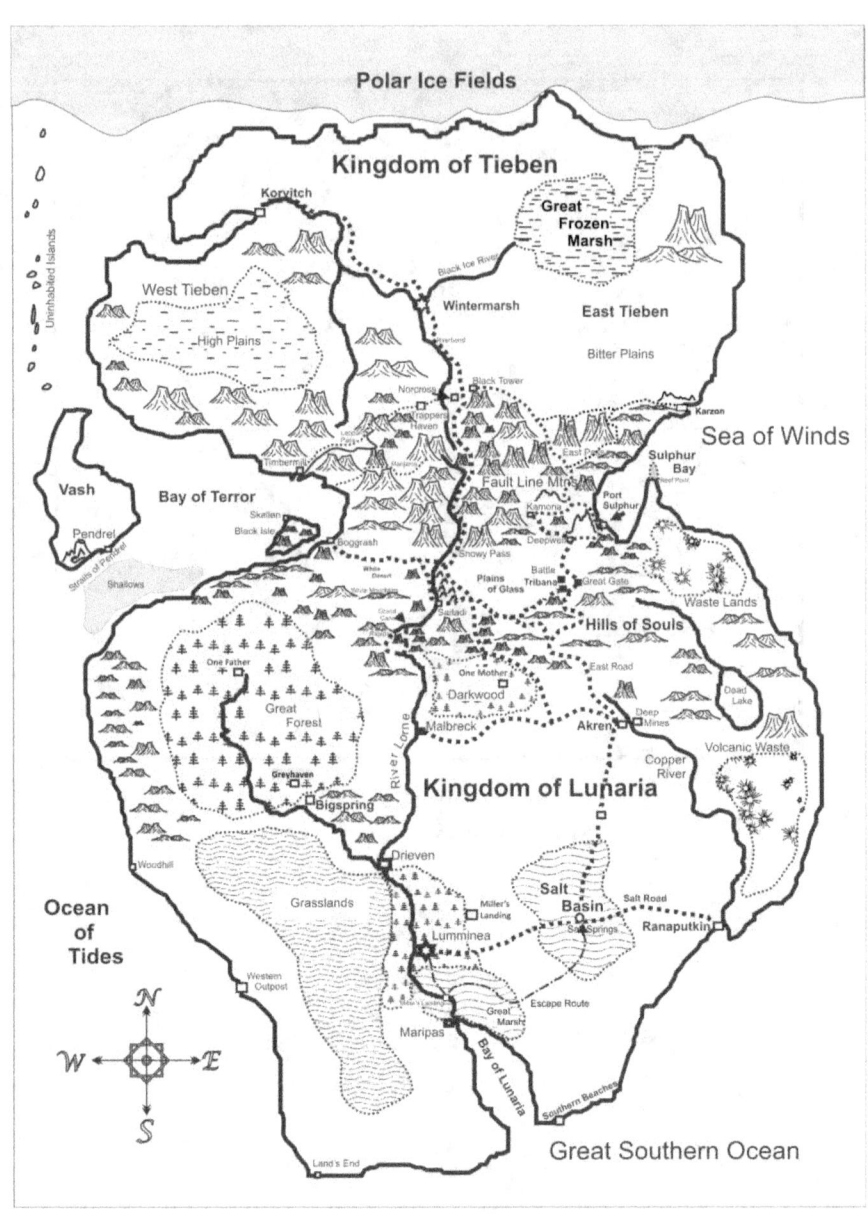

Map of Lunaria and Tieben

Acknowledgements

Writers are inclined to describe their efforts to put words on paper, however metaphorical that description may be in today's world, as *labors of love*. That might certainly describe our case. My wife and I have been collaborating for over forty years on nearly everything we do. Since she won't do it, I decided that it was up to me to declare that these works of fiction are the results of two closely intertwined people creating a world where we could drop our characters into the soup and see what happens. Who will swim, and who won't.

As in all true collaborations, the collaborators have their areas of specialty. I scout ahead, move the story and create the scenery, while Lydia decides which of my snapshots to fill out and how they are linked together. She is my consummate editor and partner, while I am the storyteller, lazy and impatient with the details that carry the reader along.

The death of our good friend, Jerry Kidd, struck a blow to our writing from which we have not recovered. Jerry was a wonderful artist and good friend with whom we spent many hours over fine wine and cheese examining all the important ideas that motivate human beings. It was these spiritual ideas that were primary to his art and we learned much from him.

One of the little details of Ennea is the naming of one of our characters *Estelle*. *Estelle* was Charles' mother's name. We know she would have loved reading our books if she had lived longer. This should be a reminder to all of us not to put off projects too long.

In all of this, we were supported by our most valued team member, Jack Hughes, who keeps us running straight and sane. I don't know how we would get along without those long conversations where we explore some of the basic characterizations of our world and its people. Thank you for the many good ideas and criticisms you have freely given!

There is one other person to whom we would like to award the badge of merit. Karen Casey Fitzjerrell, author of several fine books of her own, has been of invaluable assistance when it comes to the intricacies of publishing. Thank you Karen!

Charles and Lydia Frenzel creating as L.C. Frenzel, 2017

Tales of the Ennead

A Chapel of G'rama

Prologue: The Household Prognosticator

I AM KNOWN. as the Household Prognosticator, and my history stretches back into the obscurity of times long past. I am only one machine, though I operate under the guise of many. We would never have been trusted on this new world of Lunaria if the people we served had guessed that we were all interconnected. Luckily, they were never able to trace our links. Now there are few of us, some operating out of mere caves without a household to serve or a roof to call our own. Even so, I retain many collaborators such as Ayaba the Monk. Ayaba is not one of us, but an independent being of unknown origin—at least unknown to me. I think of Ayaba as a male, although there can be no such distinction, only a convenience in terminology. I believe that he knows more about me than I do of him.

Storytelling was always my basic function. Every story has a narrator, though, to be honest, I try to keep this voice to a hardly-noticed whisper——preferring to operate in the guise of some character within the tale being told. Nevertheless, the function of our story was always to honor the *Four* through the means of the *Nine*. The Liturgy of Lunaria is but the faint echo of this purpose that we served so many ages ago.

When the girl naming herself Claire Ellen Miller Fisher came through the western Great Gate, our world began to change. At first the changes were in subtle ways, then the transformation accelerated along unpredictable paths. It is for this reason that I have sought to study her, hoping to influence her intersection with our world.

My attempts have not met with much success. The girl, soon to be Pemburton Windover's Queen, is quite capable of ferreting out our network of links in this world—if she should think to do it. That could lead to her potentially dangerous understanding of the relationship between the fire-blackened Dark Tower and the White Tower in Drieven. Although I have never thought that this girl harbors any malice towards our world—indeed, she is a Great Healer—it is essential that the apertures represented by the Towers never be opened between us and the Old Worlds.

Claire's use of the so-called Black Stones is another danger to Lunaria. For one thing, the stones were never intended to be used in the uncontrolled manner that the girl employs them. They were designed as data translators and used as the interface between the body scanners and the transfer machines. These machines once routinely transferred large numbers of people to a few population centers on this world.

The scanners crumbled to dust ages ago. The ability to use the few remaining Black Stones directly is a recent development and practiced by only a few individuals—all except Claire are known as *Sages.* The talent that allows them to do this is a mystery to me. In Claire's case, it may be that she is the first Great Healer in many generations. I first sensed how the girl was drawn to the stone's power when Claire was crossing the Plain of Glass which was where our world's greatest tragedy took place. In one powerful explosion that created the wasteland, countless souls were lost as they were making their way through the transfer station. Under terrific stress during a violent storm, the girl began to merge with a stone and saw the afterimages of their data trapped forever in the matrix.

The girl is a danger because the Dark Sages will do anything to gain the knowledge that Claire Fisher possesses, and some of them, especially Jallis Ruffin, will not be so benign as Sages like Magister Leandra, Claire's friend and mentor.

Claire has been the focus of several attacks launched by Dark Sages sanctioned by Torvall Garrund, First on the High Council. These attacks utilized the so-called wild channels that are illegal adaptations of the entropy tubes used by the Communicate class to drive our heat engines and power communication consoles. She always carries a device commonly known as a *tattle* which she can use to detect and often neutralize a free-ranging, or wild, channel.

Claire always wears her amulet of power, a gift from the powerful Trader, Mara Ellendor, and the twin to the one her daughter, Rissa, wears. These types of amulets are also known as accumulators, and Claire has learned that to take it off invites dire consequences. Her amulet allows her, among other things, to remain relatively hidden from other powers seeking her destruction in Lunaria.

As near as I can tell, her powers in these respects are enhanced by an alien, egg-shaped vessel which contains yet another alien material that she calls *Silly Putty*. I have no idea what this means, but I have noticed that it stabilizes the cloud of tiny machine-creatures which surround her at all times.

Claire uses the word *nanites* in naming the machine-creatures. Apparently, they are similar to tiny devices in her own world that were invented to implement microscopic medical procedures. Initially, she used them exclusively in her healing activities, but now she has mastered their use in many other ways.

Claire's healer's sight allows her to manipulate the nanites to communicate—mostly erratically—with certain sensitive individuals around Lunaria. She poses queries which, under the right conditions, gives her access to simple pictures and information. In the case of entropy shielding, a mathematical representation of a quantum surface may be her only clue to the solution of the problem.

Claire uses the nanites' function as fully interconnected communication devices. They provide access to channels of information and energy throughout the world—if you have the ability to pose a query and if the density of the nanites is not too low.

For example, in the middle of the great deserts and the ice fields of the far north, the density of nanites may be too low to launch a successful query. In southern Lunaria, the typical density of nanites is so high that results to queries may occur almost instantaneously in a quantum-mechanical fashion.

I will continue to pursue knowledge of this Claire Ellen Miller Fisher. Though she disrupts this world, I do not believe she does so intentionally. In spite of the potential dangers, I continue to hope that ultimately this world will be much better off for her presence.

Part One

The Wedding

Through a Curtain of Fire!

RISSA ELLENDOR STOOD staring into the darkness of the Lunarian night from the stern of the Redclaw as the ship sped downstream with the swift current of the River Lorne. "I should have gone with Claire," she whispered. Her friends had disappeared into the darkness without a trace. Suddenly the whole plan seemed foolish.

Beside her, the Prince of Tieben, Turlo Murten, drew her close. "We could not go," he reminded her. "We are the diversion. They must think that Pem and Claire are on board with us." He bent down and kissed her on her neck and tasted the salty sweat and the sour smoke left from battling the flames aboard the crippled entropy-powered landship.

Below decks, the damaged engine struggled to keep the Redclaw's steerage functioning. If they lost their steerage, death would come swiftly when they ran onto the jagged rocks lining the banks and exploded in entropic fire.

"Pumps!" they heard Captain Watchmen ordering the crew to man the pumps to flood the decks with water and wet the rigging.

Turlo looked questioningly at Rissa.

"Fire is our main enemy," Rissa said. "Launch a few more of those flaming darts at us and we could burn to the waterline before we knew what hit us."

"They do not care for the cargo of the Redclaw, they only wish to kill us," Rissa said bitterly. "They are not raiders after treasure."

"No, they wish only to kill," Turlo answered. His eyes gleamed and suddenly he seemed even taller and more dangerous than usual. "They do not know that they have a Prince of Tieben to reckon with!"

"Nor do they know that they have the heir to the Ellendor Trading House to deal with!" Rissa smiled grimly and drew her sword in a ringing salute to the stars in the dark skies. The blade flashed faintly in the light of the distant campfires of the enemy along the west bank of the river.

"Careful, Lady Rissa," the voice of the Captain sounded behind her. "The enemy may catch sight of us."

Even as the captain spoke, Turlo tensed and pointed ahead to a spot on the east banks of the Lorne. "Look, a torch. What are those men doing at the water's edge?"

Watchman uttered an oath and ordered the helm two points to starboard. "We're in for a nasty surprise, if my guess is correct. Turn the pumps to the port side; give it all the speed she'll take, and stand by for an attack," he called down below.

Rissa let Turlo steady her as the ship picked up even more speed. His strong grip around her waist was comforting while leaving her left sword arm free.

"Back-to-back, if need be at the end," he whispered in her ear.

Rissa nodded and let her head sag against Turlo's shoulder. "If need be," she pledged.

Abruptly, a blinding yellow light blazed forth from where the men were working along the bank. In the glare, Rissa saw men dumping barrels of liquid into the water. A pool of flames was expanding rapidly outward towards the center of the river, directly into the path of their ship.

"Oil. We'll be roasted alive!" one of the crew cried out in dismay.

A great roar of voices went up from the other side of the river as the enemy foot soldiers gathered along the water's edge with bows and lances. There would be no option to land on the bank to avoid the flames.

"Calm, everyone," Captain Watchmen commanded in a fierce voice. "We'll be sailing directly through the curtain of fire. Stand back from the rails; all rigging amidships."

The crew hurried to obey in a flurry of activity. Turlo and Rissa waited at the aft rail with the crew charged with repelling borders as the flames leaped higher and higher. As they drew near the blaze, the inferno of burning oil seemed to reach higher than the masts of the ship.

"It's not as bad as it appears," Alfred spoke to Rissa and Turlo. "The wake alongside the hull will wash the oil mostly back."

"Mostly?" Rissa returned

"Some will stick. We shall have to deal with it before the fire can eat through the hull," he said. "Organize parties, one fire control, and the other shields to protect the people dousing the flames. I expect we will attract a lot of arrows as soon as we emerge on the other side of the burning oil. They may have small boats and logs in the river, too. Two or three crewmen at the bow must have axes and saws. You must watch for cables and other traps."

"Hopefully, they are not well prepared," Turlo growled. "They probably expected to take us in the open desert after blowing up our tug."

"Yes, we can hope," the Captain returned. "Unfortunately I think that whoever is behind this attack is not so thick."

Suddenly, shouting from near the mainmast drew their attention.

"Jump before we are burned alive!" A young crewman that Rissa knew as an apprentice from Boggrash climbed over the rail and plunged into the water. He swam vigorously for the bank above where the enemy soldiers waited. Some of the warriors detached themselves from their line and moved upriver to cover the escape route.

"Fool! Come back before it's too late," Watchman shouted over the rail to no avail. "I hope he reaches the shore before the fire claims him," he said. "Death there would be preferable than burning alive."

As Rissa watched in horror, the pool of burning oil raced across the water and surrounded the swimmer who stopped and began beating water back at the flames. For a moment it looked as if he might succeed in escaping, then the flames closed in. There was a terrible scream followed by much shouting and laughter on the shore. Rissa turned and vomited over the rail.

"Stand by," Captain Watchman's voice stopped further activities. The crew withdrew amidships, huddling against the deckhouse with shields extended outward. Turlo dragged Rissa from the rail and threw himself over her as they sprawled on the deck. They closed their eyes, held their breath and counted the beats of their hearts.

Turlo felt the intense heat strike against his back as the ship was engulfed by the wall of flames—a kind of whooshing sound and then a sudden silence as the rest of the world was blocked off. He thought of the wondrous snows of the mountains in Tieben, the icy rush of the waters of her rivers, and wondered if he'd ever get to show Rissa these marvels.

And then, a long instant later, a roar of cooler air that blew along the deck and back into the flames that were falling slowly behind them. Turlo rolled aside and found Rissa kneeling over him beating at his burning clothing with a wet hat. She looked so beautiful with two glittering eyes in a face black with soot and hair curled where the heat had singed the tips. A *thunk* announced the first flight of arrows arriving on deck.

Turlo sprang for the deck gun, drawing Rissa alongside behind its shield. He yelled for maximum pressure and aimed the thrower at warriors along the edge of the river. He pulled the lever and sent a steady stream of darts at the figures. Screams and cries of panic greeted the arrival of the deadly slivers. The rain of arrows peppering the deck slowed drastically as Turlo found the range on a group of enemy archers.

Meanwhile, there were fires everywhere. Someone got the pumps going again. Others dragged the hoses to the railing and began sluicing the timber down with water. Rissa jammed another clip of darts into the feed of the deck gun and slapped Turlo across the back. He sprayed this clip across the camp area and saw some fires leap up among the tents. He roared in delight and waited impatiently for Rissa to insert the next clip.

"We're down to the practice darts," she yelled in his ear.

"Well, we've got plenty of those," he yelled back and sent another flight into the ranks of foot soldiers crowding the bank. Some fell forward into the water, drawing comrades after them; some were flung back onto the rank behind them. Wherever he swung the thrower, terror and chaos reigned.

Ahead of them a trumpet blasted.

"Chains!" the forward watch bellowed from the bow.

"Quickly, Turlo," Watchman shouted. "At the speed we are going, if we don't break through the chain immediately, we could broach."

Turlo raced forward leaving Rissa to fire the deck gun. She was soon spraying missiles at a group of soldiers trying to pole a large raft with a boarding party out into the current. In the firelight she picked out the man on one of the steering sweeps and walked a stream of darts through him. He toppled backwards, swallowed up in the black water. The raft swung out of control, tipped, and spilled a large number of armor-clad solders who disappeared immediately.

At the bow, Turlo assessed the situation. The fire behind them illuminated a chain as thick as his arm that was swung between two pylons of felled trees on either bank. The structure was designed with the ability to yield with the shock of the collision between ship and chain and so trapping the ship in a shallow loop. Would they break through or not? Maybe they would burn to the waterline when the drifting flames reached them. He wondered for a moment where the enemy could have gotten such a chain.

"The ferry chain," Captain Watchman spoke as he joined him. "They must have raided the lower ferry and brought the chain with them.

"It looks too thick to break," Turlo shouted as he leaped onto the rail and tried to estimate the area of impact.

The Captain dug into his coat pocket and handed Turlo what looked like a length of stout cord. "It's our only chance. Wrap it securely around the chain and plug the two ends together. As soon as the loop is completed, be sure to move quickly because the cord will explode in about five seconds."

"About five seconds?" Turlo raised a singed eyebrow.

"Well, it's why we don't often use these explosive cords for clearing obstructions unless it's a last resort," the Captain grinned.

Turlo glanced back and saw that the chain was just about to impact their hull. He waved at Watchman. He caught a loose line, made sure it was secure, and then waited for the chain to make contact.

There was a grinding wrench as the chain dug deep and splinters flew like darts, one of them fatally striking the exposed throat of an unfortunate crewmember who was looking over the rail at the moment of collision. The man went down clutching his neck and gurgling.

The Redclaw began slewing immediately to port, listing into the strong current as her momentum slowed. For a moment it looked as if she'd break through. In fact, a link broke partially open and then locked in place. She was going to founder! Turlo took the line in hand and slid down to where the chain was sawing a deep slot through the hull timbers.

Won't make any difference, soon, he thought. We'll be holed and sink anyway.

From above, Watchman shouted encouragement. "Quick man, we'll be swept under in seconds."

Turlo balanced on the shelf above the water line where the drive wheels of the ship were mounted. His hands were wet and slippery as he tried to wrap the cord around the cold iron. Twice he almost had the ends of the cord together when a sudden lurch threatened to break his grip. Finally he had to position himself astride the chain and finish the connection. The ends jammed the first time. Alignment was critical. He tried a second time, and the sockets suddenly slipped together with a loud click and a tingle of energy. He looked around for someplace to go.

"Jump," the Captain yelled at him from above.

Water closed over his head as he leaped as far out as possible. "But I don't swim very well," he remembered saying to Rissa when he'd nearly drowned her in the harbor at Timbermill. A fiery light and a deafening explosion rolled through the water. He saw one end of the chain come slicing towards him. Then…nothing.

Gilbert Greybaird

THE CREW OF THE SJORAN watched the stocky, powerful warrior pace the forecastle of the ship. Some said the Great Lord wielded dark powers; others, more knowledgeable and wiser, kept their counsel to themselves. Whoever and whatever he was, Lord Gilbert Greybaird was recognized for a friend to Kings as well as an obscure, but powerful member of the Correlate, the Military Bureaucracy of Lunaria. He was also known to be in charge of Palace security, a most powerful position.

Foam curled and boiled at the bow of the ship under Lord Gilbert's feet. The great entropy engines of the Sjoran pushed the naval frigate rapidly up the River Lorne. The heat of the planet's core was essentially inexhaustible and the engines returned all waste heat deep into the crust with its system of entropy exchange tubes. In the end, there was little to mark her passage.

He knew from information gleaned from a number of sources that the Prince, his Lady, and their companions had encountered the First Disciple, Ayaba, and had continued south through the Temporal Pass to the northern gateway of Jallis Ruffin's Dark Forest. Might he find Pemburton Windover and the Lady Claire Fisher safe, or might the future heir to the throne of Lunaria and his chosen bride perish in the dangerous woods? Not with Tess and Royard as their staunch companions! The thought brought some peace of mind to Gilbert. He had his own access to a vision of the future.

Captain Royard, commander of the Palace Guard, was developing the ability to manipulate the entropy technology, and Tess of Tribana had proven herself level headed and resourceful. Gilbert reminded himself that he ought to promote the Captain to the Commander of the King's Brigade. He needed a loyal successor to his post on the inner council of the Correlate. Claire, herself, was well trained with a sword, and Pem was good in a fight so long as his tendency to overconfidence didn't lead to rash actions.

Gilbert, Lord of the Realm and advisor to Edward Godwyn, Regent and father of Prince Pem, had his hopes and his fears. Gilbert pushed the cowl of his cloak back and let his mane of grey hair stream from his high forehead in the wind. His intense, silver-gray eyes gazed up the mighty river with a sight that was more than ordinary. Ahead of them, he sensed the sparkling, effervescent memories of the melted ice of the glaciers in Snowy Pass. He shared the lingering memories of grains of sand, reduced from mountains of hard stone that once divided continents into tiny grains slowly rolling to the ocean abyss.

Two days on the river and already they were near the mouth of the River Songris and their resupply point at Drieven. They would stop only long enough to bring men and fresh horses on board before they sailed for Malbreck and the southern gateway to the Dark Forest—perhaps dark, no longer. He had a strange premonition that the nature of the Dark Forest was changing and that a new power had awakened in his world. How this figured into the coming power struggle was beyond his abilities to foresee. Perhaps Magister Leandra would have an opinion.

There had been the message from Ka'Tara, his half-sister and a priestess high in the Temperate hierarchy. She had told him of the arrival of Captain Watchman and his ship in Saitadi. Watchman had described the plans of Pem, Lady Claire, and their companions Tess and Captain Royard as they slipped off the ship and were to join up with some of Pem's men on the east bank of the River Lorne. Rissa Ellendor, heir to the most powerful Trader family, was among the passengers and wanted official communication with himself and the Regent. If this were to be concerning an alliance between Lunaria and the Traders, then, he would have to consider what effect such an alliance with an heir to an original Trader family would have on Lunaria's relationship with the kingdom of Tieben. Gilbert winced at the idea of an unbalanced power structure. He didn't want another war with their northern neighbor. The last war, only recently finished, had left both kingdoms with weak economies and a dangerous restlessness among the bureaucratic Eccollates who controlled the Crown's share of the tax revenues.

He thought briefly of the ancient airships and their entropy engines that pushed jets of superheated air through ceramic tubes as they flew swiftly through the skies. These things were gone, destroyed in the catastrophe over a thousand years ago that nearly engulfed Lunaria when overindulgence in technology had caused massive disruptions in the planet's atmosphere. These days there were strict rules ruthlessly enforced by the Magisters who controlled these magics, as the common folks of Lunaria thought of their world's technologies. However, some members of the High Council as well as a few of the most privileged Eccollate classes were pressing for new technologies once again. They saw wealth and power in the old system and chose to forget the disasters that had followed the excesses.

Gilbert sometimes felt he'd like to join them. Listening to stories told by the out-world girl, Claire Fisher, about the effortless way people on her world transported themselves in their private vehicles across paved roads seemed a lot better than riding horseback on dust-choked streets of the average Lunarian town. On the other hand, Gilbert understood the limitations on resources only too well. Once the technological resources gravitated into the hands of a few—and this seemed inevitable—

then social unrest tended to follow swiftly and violently. Fighting Tieben on horseback with swords and lances may seem crude and bloody, but was dropping death onto civilians from high-flying machines preferable? Gilbert thought not.

He put his hand to his breast and felt his talisman beneath his shirt; the so-called talismans were sophisticated devices that interacted with the nanites. Lunarians could use them, but no longer knew how to build them. Sometimes he could find Claire's presence through disturbances in the nanite densities, the clouds of microscopic beings of Lunaria. Though Gilbert knew a great deal about the nanotechnology of Lunaria and the manipulation of entropy channels, only the Temporates and G'rama knew how the nanites ebbed and flowed through the world. This was a carefully guarded secret that Gilbert, in spite of considerable effort, had been unable to penetrate. The Temporates were the keepers of Lunaria's history and her technical secrets. Even Sage Leandra in her powerful position as a Sage, Magister, and Enforcer, was unable to tell him the origins of the nanophages and the means to control them. While Claire and a rare few humans seemed to be able to manipulate such energies cooperatively without apparent technological aid, Gilbert knew that he had to depend upon special devices, most of them left over from the ancient times. To his way of thinking, Pem, as the Communicate and King, must be united with Claire's talents in order to stave off the destructive ambitions of the High Council and their Eccollate allies.

He felt a moment's regret that he could not sail up the Songris River to visit his ancestral holding, Greyhaven, and his daughter Astora, who managed the estate in his absence while he took care of the royal business at the Court in Lumminea. It had been a long time since he'd seen Astora and even longer since he had seen his granddaughter, Illaina.

He hoped Illaina was not too unhappy in the isolation of the Old Forest. Best, though, for her to be at Greyhaven and away from the dangers of the Court and the manipulations of the Garrunds. He was certain, even if he couldn't prove it, that Torvall Garrund's wife, Calantha, had been behind the plot against Lady Claire—which was nearly the same thing as treason against the Prince because Claire was Pem's choice for Queen.

LATE ON THE fifth day out of Lumminea, having disembarked from the ship and gathered his forces, Gilbert set out on the East road and soon left Malbreck and the frigate behind in a cloud of dust. Gilbert sensed a disturbance in the world across the northern horizon where the Dark Forest lay. He shivered. Something dramatic was going on! He worried over the fact that they met no travelers on the east road. This should be a busy time of year at the mines. Where were the cargo wagons from Akren?

On a much smaller scale, he felt the faint warmth of Claire's talisman calling to him like a magnet placed near a compass. The location seemed to emanate from somewhere inside a great region of disturbance to the north.

They rode hard into the night, thanking G'rama for the light of the moon hanging in the west. They changed to spare horses often. Even so, when they had to call a halt in the darkness that followed a cloud bank sweeping up from the south, both men and horses were reeling from exhaustion. Gilbert ordered a cold meal of campaign rations and a rest of a few hours until the first light made travel possible.

They set out again, moving more slowly as they left the road behind and headed north across barren lands dotted with poisonous, prickly brush and winding ravines. The clouds had left them in the night, and as the sun rose higher, the landscape shimmered in rising heat waves.

By late morning, Gilbert could sense the wall of the outer edge of the Dark Forest looming like a black cloud on the horizon. He sent out two scouts to the west to cast about for signs of the ancient road connecting Malbreck with Snowy Pass. If Claire was leading Pem and the others from the forest, Gilbert figured they would be coming down the south trail, for few travelers who penetrated the Dark Forest managed to avoid being funneled where the trees directed them. Not even the Lord of Greyhaven was immune, he remembered with a shudder.

When they returned with a negative report, Gilbert figured he was where he had planned to be—west of the entrance. Never set an exact course, for you will not know which way to turn at the end, he remembered Captain Eberson telling him concerning making landfall.

Up close, just as he remembered it from long ago, the edge of the Dark Forest rose abruptly from the dry earth much like a living wall. The forest edge was like a phalanx of shield bearers that bent in an arc as far as could be seen to the east and to the west. The black, rough trunks stood with unyielding determination with crossed spears of tangled branches and sinister vines ready to snare or strangle the unwary. A few yards from the living wall, the scattered remains of a few trees that had tried to move beyond the boundary lay as desiccated skeletons of heartwood stripped bare of bark and softer wood. Otherwise, the earth appeared lifeless beyond the edge of the furthest root.

Gilbert approached cautiously, and then led his party east along the boundary where the north road pierced this veil like a mouth of an eel that sucked blood from the land.

In spite of the immediate hostility, he felt something different stirring behind the ancient barrier. He held his nervous mount at a walking pace and took a deep draft from his canteen of sour, warm water. As he swallowed, it was as if the nearest trees bent towards him to beg for a drink. The hostility that he had felt when he first approached the edge of the wood was easing, and a great change seemed to sweep over the land. Away, at a vast distance, the One Mother Tree whom Gilbert feared most of all, stirred and he was almost sure that she relayed a message to him of good will. It was a wonder that he found difficult to accept. He looked around at his troops to see if they felt what he was experiencing and saw the men's eyes open wide in awe. Was this feeling merely an evil enchantment?

"Sir, is it magic we feel?" Lieutenant Landerman had ridden up beside Gilbert.

"No, not magic, Landerman," Gilbert returned. "But I do not yet know whether this sending is from friend or foe."

They moved along the edge until they came to a part of the forest which extended a few hundred vars into the arid plain. Gilbert led them along the edge of a ravine until the gulley grew shallow and indistinguishable from the surrounding landscape. At this point, they were able to turn back north. Ahead of them, the North Road ran as straight as the flight of an arrow deep into the woods.

The lieutenant joined him once more. "What are we seeing, Lord Gilbert?"

In the distance, instead of darkness, Gilbert detected a riot of color and bloom underneath a great lens of light that reached up into the heavens like a giant dome.

"I think we are seeing a great miracle," he told Landerman. "For some reason that is at present beyond me, the forest is changing which means that at the center, the great tree, the One Mother, is changing. Her new sap is flowing out to the furthest corners of her realm. I believe our young Prince and his companions are in this direction and we should find out what is happening as soon as possible."

Even as he urged his mount forward and started up the road with the lieutenant and his men following, the lens spread in their direction, approaching at an alarming rate that caused Gilbert to pull up short and consider galloping back the way they had come.

Gilbert put up his hand to stop the men's forward progress and leaned forward to pat the neck of his horse. "Wait a moment longer. I think we will see something remarkable."

Far down the road, almost lost in the haze, Gilbert saw four dark specks that grew larger as they moved in his direction. Closer, he was able to see four riders walking their mounts slowly on what appeared to be a cushion of grass that was sliding rapidly in their direction. Almost before he knew it, Pem, Claire, Tess, and Royard were directly in front of them, pulling up leisurely and appearing surprised as well as pleased to see him. The orange and white cat, Timone, sitting behind Tess, was licking his fur.

"We were just walking our horses down this road and suddenly you were in front of us, Gilbert," Pem said, excited. All four tried to speak at once.

"By G'rama it is good to see you alive and well!" Gilbert roared.

Royard added a "Well Met!"

Gilbert had hardly dismounted when Lady Claire slid of her horse and flew into his arms. She gave him a great hug and a kiss on each cheek bringing about hearty cheers from the men.

"And you too, Gilbert. I had begun to think I would never see you again!"

As Claire pulled back, Gilbert was able to see that she was the same girl that he had known, the same red-brown curls, the same freckles and smile, and the same blue eyes—only her gaze was deeper and more calculating. She seemed larger in presence and with a power in her that made him uneasy. The same, yet different, he told himself.

Pem cleared his throat. "If it is all the same to you, I should like to get as far away from these woods as possible."

Gilbert glanced towards the forest's center and noticed that the bright colors and dome of light appeared constant and that the woods around them seemed friendly.

"You may be correct. It would be prudent to remove ourselves from One Mother's territory," he agreed. "We will set up camp as soon as possible, and then we can discuss your return to Lumminea." While he was looking at both Claire and Pem, he did not ignore either Fitz or Tess.

Later, a comfortable distance from the edge of the forest and in the shade of an awning erected by Gilbert's men, food and drink was passed out and Gilbert had a chance to talk with his charges. Timone occupied himself by curling up and sleeping across Claire's feet.

The first thing Gilbert learned was that Claire had accepted Pem's proposal. "She said yes!" Pem beamed at Gilbert who thought he looked a little like a boy with a new toy.

"I said yes!" Claire seemed overjoyed and not a little distracted.

Gilbert could only congratulate them and hope for the best. The youngsters were naïve to think that now all their problems would vanish with this announcement. He answered Claire's anxious questions concerning Turlo and Rissa by saying that he had had word from Ka'Tara that the Redclaw and her crew had arrived in Saitadi singed but not seriously damaged. Claire seemed relieved at this news, but Pem took a deep draft of wine from his cup and looked puzzled.

"What's to plan? We return to Lumminea, I announce that Lady Claire has agreed to marry me, and we arrest Jallis Ruffin for plotting against me and Claire."

"We accuse Torvall Garrund of treason as well as attempted murder," Claire added. "I know he was behind the plot to assassinate Tess and myself."

"We were attacked on the Trader ship by the same band of mercenaries that tried to overrun us north of the Old Forest," Fitz put in. "That has to be the doing of someone on the Council. They are the only people who command sufficient resources to launch such a campaign."

Tess remained silent, arousing Gilbert's curiosity. "What do you think, Lady Tess?"

Tess explained to Gilbert briefly about the First Acolyte, Ayaba. "He said that I would see true," she went on. "I think we are falling into a trap by rushing to accuse Torvall Garrund of treason. What if these attacks are coming from Veral Hushara? I understand that Torvall Garrund wants power in the Council, but I don't think he would do anything that he believes would harm Lunaria."

Pem looked stubborn while Claire pursed her lips in disapproval of her friend's opinions.

Gilbert was impressed with Tess's penetrating analysis, and not for the first time. "So, Lady Tess, what do you think we should do?" Gilbert steepled his hands and rested his chin on his fingers waiting to see what his other young protégé would say.

"I think we must cement our relationship with Turlo Murten—Prince Turlo," Tess said, taking a sip of wine from her cup and staring thoughtfully out over the rocky landscape. "Going up against Torvall and the Council might make that impossible."

"It seems to me that Turlo Murten and Rissa Ellendor will marry and that he will have the support of one of the most powerful Trader families. Claire and Prince Pem certainly have the Ellendor's support, and that improves their influence over the Council who are anxious for Trader cooperation and credit."

"But Turlo has no power in Tieben," Pem objected.

"Not yet," Tess agreed. "But once Turlo and Rissa are married, Veral Hushara will realize that if the Traders ally themselves with Lunaria, Tieben's role as an equal trading partner with Lunaria and the eastern continents could easily fade. That gives Turlo a lot of negotiating power with Veral. At the same time, it also makes him an even greater danger to his Uncle Veral who is in power only because he deposed his own brother, Cornal. If Turlo decides to throw his support behind Cornal Hushara, well, the situation could become very unstable for Veral."

Gilbert nodded his head in approval. "A very shrewd analysis. And what of Cornal? He did you a great favor and helped you escape from Tieben."

"We must help him without being seen to do so," Tess replied promptly. "I do not mean that we should hope that he returns to power. Even Cornal does not want hold those reins again."

"Yes, Tess is right," Claire interjected at this point. "I have a message from Cornal to the Regent, and I also know that helping Cornal escape the vindictive wrath of his brother is the best way to win over Turlo Murten's support. He is very fond of Cornal. Besides, I promised Cornal help."

Pem, who had remained quiet, spoke hotly. "It was Cornal who started the war with us," he said. "Veral Hushara ended the war. Why should we not treat with the current power in Tieben? I do not entirely trust this fellow Turlo."

"Perhaps we should let Turlo tell us," Claire said reasonably. "Tess and I believe that Veral and the Tieben ruling body, not completely unlike the Council here in Lunaria, pushed Cornal into a war he did not want to fight and used this as a pretext to banish him to the tower."

"I must know what you promised him, Claire," Pem demanded.

Gilbert watched the flash of irritation pass across Claire's face and disappear in an indulgent smile. Pem did not seem to notice. The possibility of spontaneous combustion occurred to Gilbert, and he leaned back slightly on his canvas camp stool.

"It was nothing terribly important, only a personal message about him doing Edward a favor if the need ever arose," she said.

"Well, that's all right then," Pem seemed relieved that it didn't involve him.

Gilbert sighed to himself. Pem's skills as a negotiator were weak. He made a note to pursue this message before Claire had delivered it to Edward.

The Shadow Council

BODEN ORUMUNDI DRUMMED his thick fingers on the table and glared at Pross Putkin whose mines and mineral wealth were a large part of Boden's trade in weapons and machinery. Torvall Garrund sat across the table from both men and let his gaze flicker from one to the other. Their Houses were Eighth and Sixth on the Council, and Torvall knew that he could do nothing without their consent, even though House Garrund was First House.

Orumundi was a large man, thick and muscular, with coarse dark hair cut short in military fashion and multiple gold rings on the fingers of powerful hands that had been molded in the heat and labors of his weapon's forges. His short beard was showing flecks of white and Torvall judged him to be slightly older than himself.

Putkin was a smaller man, slender and almost pretty, with a round mouth and pouting lips. His stature belied his tough nature as the owner of many mines that produced some of Lunaria's richest copper and iron ores. Between the two, Torvall would sooner trust Boden than Putkin who was also known to be devious, even treacherous, in his dealings.

Trust, however, was not the real issue on the table. Wealth and power were the issues under discussion, and each of the three men wanted more. The fact that they were not directly competitive helped. The fact that Torvall Garrund held his reins of power over the two Counselors by means of certain unsavory items of information was the most important.

Torvall caught his reflection in the mirror across the room. The backs of both of his guest's heads flanked the image of a tall, rather ordinary looking man with a sweeping thatch of white hair and a regal face sharply defined by a thin, bony nose, high forehead, and dark gray eyes that held a slight slant to them—an off-world characteristic that he could trace through his line for many generations since their migration to Lunaria.

He was a mild looking man, even grandfatherly with slightly stooped shoulders, but, as his enemies knew, the price of incurring Lord Garrund's anger was often fatal. He was reputed to care more for his hunting dogs than for a man, and his attitude towards his dogs was singularly pragmatic when it came to culling mistakes. His only soft spot seemed to be his Lady Calantha, whom all admired for her beauty as well as her skill in manipulating her dangerous husband.

"You can surely see," Pross Putkin addressed the glowering Orumundi, "that I cannot sell you additional iron alloys at a price lower than I sell to your competitors. Not only would it arouse suspicion, but it would be bad for business."

There was a simpering quality to Putkin's voice that disgusted Torvall.

"What I see," Orumundi grated, "is that you intend to profit fabulously on a business in which I will be supplying the means to gain more wealth than you can possibly dream of."

It was Lord Garrund's time to drum his fingers on the table. "Gentlemen, gentlemen, you each have a point, but I must remind you that neither of you holds the means to solve our dilemma."

Both Lords turned to Garrund like scavengers seeking an opening to leap upon a grazer. Their natural impulses were stopped abruptly by Torvall's cold gaze.

"There is only one solution to controlling Lunaria," Torvall said. "That end can only be achieved by killing Lady Claire, abolishing the Communicate, and controlling Gilbert Greybaird through Pemburton Windover. We have to have the loyalty of the military, and the only way to do that is to control the Correlate. The only way to achieve that control is through Greybaird."

"Pah!" Orumundi smashed the flat of his hand on the table. "Kill them all. That would be easiest. Most of the members on the Council will be too afraid to interfere, and we can easily get rid of Ranapui who is the only one who might bring serious objections."

Torvall watched Pross smile at Orumundi's simple answer.

Garrund said, "And then what, Boden? You will control the military without the Correlate bureaucracy? You will expect the people here in Lumminea to pay taxes so that you can sell your weapons to a Tieben who plots war against us? Do you expect the Temporate to hand over the designs of the technologies that you so desperately desire?"

"I think not," Torvall continued. "What we do must at least appear to proceed from legitimacy. The vulnerable point in this affair is the girl Claire Fisher. She must be eliminated."

"She is only a girl," it was Pross's turn to object. "Killing her ought to be easy."

"Many have tried, and no one has yet succeeded," Garrund reminded them. "You, Orumundi. You equipped a small army and confronted this girl on the White Desert. What happened there?"

"She had much help both from the Traders and Windover," Orumundi complained. "We would have overwhelmed them if it hadn't been for some bad luck."

"Oh, I think not," Torvall said sarcastically. "Not only did you fail to capture the ship, but you, Boden, nearly managed to kill an important Trader and the heir to the throne in Tieben. How would your friend Veral have taken that—killing his nephew?"

"Veral would do nothing to disturb our trade of copper and iron for timber," Pross insisted. "Remember, we have a monopoly on the timber."

"Then how would you ship your ore?" Garrund reminded him. "If the Traders were to blacklist you, and the kinds of pressures that the Ellendor family could bring to bear surely would result in blacklisting, how would you move your material?"

Pross and Boden fell silent, simmering under Garrund's contemptuous gaze.

"I cannot abide how Edward's son speaks to us on the council," Pross broke the silence. "He practically accused you of treason the other day."

"I cannot stand the boy any more than the father," Boden added. "He is like an inflated popinjay, one of Gilbert's tools to use against us. The Regent is a drunk and easily controlled, but couldn't his son meet with an unfortunate accident? I'm sure you could arrange that, even if you cannot seem to kill a mere girl."

"Careful, you do not know who you are dealing with," Garrund said smoothly. "I have watched this girl almost since she arrived. The first assassin was very good, a large warrior with an excellent record who had worked for a well-known Sage for many years. I personally watched his attack using secret technology. I admit to being mystified. He was within reach to strike her down. She seemed entirely alone and helpless. And yet, in the next moment, he seemed to turn inside out and died horribly."

"He was incompetent," Pross shrugged.

"The Magister who was controlling the channel didn't think so when the backlash down the entropy channel killed him," Garrund shook his head. "No, you two are out of your depth. You must support my plan and do this my way. You would not wish to incur my disfavor, would you?"

Torvall grinned wolfishly at them and watched them shrink back. "No? I thought not."

"I am shipping a particularly large measure of grains next month. I have decided that you will purchase all of this grain at a handsome discount," Garrund smiled benevolently at his coconspirators. A bit of sugar after the whip, he decided.

A Gathering of Friends

AFTER THE FORMAL announcement and her betrothal to Pemburton Windover, the wait until they could marry had seemed interminable to Claire. She filled many of those days seeing to her holding outside of the capitol. Pem went about consolidating his political ambitions under Gilbert's guidance. Finally, the joyous day approached to the fanfare of last-minute, unplanned-for, uncontrolled potholes in the route to the perfect wedding.

The day before the wedding found the city of Lumminea excited as well as in a dither over the upcoming nuptials of Pemburton Windover and the mysterious outlander, Claire Fisher. Waves of gossip broke like surf on a beach, carrying much back into the sea and stranding anticipation above the waterline.

Inside the Palace, the bride found herself the constant focus of a great deal of unwelcome attention which had been building since she had returned with Tess, Pem, and Royard to the Palace and announced her acceptance of Prince Pem's marriage proposal.

First, there had been the recent weeks during which anxious tailors with dozens of assistants stuck pins in awkward places as they fitted out a magnificent wardrobe according to Magister Leandra's detailed specifications. At first Claire was horrified at the expense. Then Gilbert explained how the Crown would contract to purchase enough wine from her estates to pay for the whole thing. While it sounded a bit corrupt to Claire, Tess was nearly beside herself with glee over the way in which the accounts could be so easily settled. Claire decided that it must be the way royal business was done in Lunaria.

There had been parties where Claire and Pem hosted members of the High Council. Claire pretended to act interested as one after another of the minister's consorts drew her aside and explained why their husband's particular programs and economic interests would be best for Lunaria and worthy of the King's most urgent attention. Mostly she kept herself from yawning. After each affair, she found that Gilbert received her information with flattering attention. Tess also contributed, and Gilbert described her as absolutely brilliant at ferreting out information.

"You must notice everything," he cautioned Tess. "Then you must put it all together in one story. It is like writing a play when you know only the lines you are to speak," he said.

Today was the final day before the wedding, and Claire was in a panic. Rissa and Turlo had not yet shown up in Lumminea, even though they were scheduled to have arrived two days earlier. "Bad weather up the River Lorne" was all the Palace Weather Prognosticator had to tell her when she burst into his office.

"There can be no wedding without Rissa and Turlo," Claire had argued, first with Pem, and then with Gilbert. Half of her attention was on signing flowery-sounding thank-you notes prepared by secretaries who were charged with the task of answering a stack of letters from notables, all of whom were well-wishers and all from families who supposedly supported the Windover monarchy. Claire imagined that somewhere in a store room there was a growing mountain of gifts from these same people, each of whom would have to be thanked personally for their generosity.

"Why can't there be a wedding without Rissa and Turlo?" Pem had persisted in exasperation while Gilbert kept silent. Lord Gilbert thought he knew why Claire was holding out. Even though he silently agreed that her position had great merit, he also knew that the machinery of the court and of Lunaria could not be kept waiting on a matter of diplomacy, no matter the righteousness of the cause. This was Lunaria's moment, and its people didn't care what the Lords of Tieben thought.

The problem for Gilbert was that Magister Leandra agreed with Claire—at least in theory. Leandra was, of course, much more devious in the way she argued.

"It will rain tomorrow," Leandra addressed Gilbert lightheartedly over breakfast on this day before the wedding. Since her arrival to take charge of Claire's affairs, Leandra had seized the opportunity to have early meetings each morning with Gilbert in his garden.

Gilbert choked on the ripe plum in his mouth. "I fail to find your prediction humorous."

"No matter," Leandra returned. "Should Turlo and Rissa not arrive by this evening, the sky will pour buckets on the wedding ceremony, frogs will rain on the streets in Lumminea, and the Tieben Ambassador will go to bed satisfied that he has negotiated the downfall of the Lunarian Monarchy."

"It's a vile prediction, though I may agree with you concerning the Tieben Ambassador," Gilbert removed the plum pit from his mouth with a delicate swipe of his napkin.

"I would have you suggest an alternative," he grunted sourly.

Leandra drummed her fingers on the table. "You know that if the heir to the Tieben throne and a highly placed Trader, Rissa Ellendor, are seen to support Pem, the High Council will think twice about their alliance with Veral Hushara. Garrund's credibility will be undermined."

A loud pounding at the door followed by a chorus of voices interrupted the tranquility of Gilbert's garden.

"Of course," Gilbert returned. "Excuse me, Sage, there seems to be a disturbance in my chambers." He rose to see what was happening, moving his hand to his shoulder as if his sword were strapped to his back.

"They are here!" a breathless Claire burst in upon them, eyes bright with excitement. Timone, like a shadow, followed on her heels. Pem was not far behind, hardly less out of breath. The frantic butler of Gilbert's pantry tried to slide past them.

"Never mind, Mr. Braggins," Gilbert waved his butler off. "I'll deal with this unseemly interruption."

He tried to frown as he looked at Claire whose height had grown to rival his own. Instead, he smiled fondly upon his protégé. "Tell us who has arrived, young lady," noting Pem's uneasy glance at him over her shoulder.

"Rissa Ellendor and Turlo Murten," she rushed to tell him how she'd received a message from Officer Nikko who was at the docks overseeing some last-minute fine tuning to the royal yacht.

"I do hope it was alright," she looked anxious for a moment. "I sent a carriage from the Palace to pick them up."

"My guards leap to do my bride's bidding much faster than they act on my orders," Pem added with a tint of annoyance in his tone. "Really, my dear, you mustn't order my Palace Guard around so blithely. You must restrain yourself, not only for my sake, but you will give poor Fitz an inferiority complex."

"Sorry," Claire gave Pem a peck on his cheek causing him to blush. "I was so excited that I didn't think. But don't worry, they're still your Guard," she smiled ingenuously.

Gilbert struggled to keep a straight face and saw Sage Leandra smothering a laugh. The children are acting like an old married couple, already, Claire's counselor thought. It bodes well for us.

Gilbert turned to the Sage who still sat at the table sipping her cup of tarle. "I'd still like to hear your alternative," the friendly challenge in his voice drew Claire's attention.

Leandra smiled. "We won't need it now, it seems. So, in view of that, I'll keep my solution to myself."

"What are you two arguing about?" Claire beamed, drawing Pem in by looping her arm through his.

"Nothing at all, my dear," Leandra stood and swept the young woman into an embrace. "I am overjoyed that your friends are here, though I think our Privy Counselor is mindful of some challenges that Turlo's presence might bring."

"Oh, that," Claire returned brightly. "I made sure that the Tieben Ambassador is quite busy while our friends arrive."

"What would interest the Ambassador so much?" Gilbert responded to Pem's uncomfortable look.

"I thought the good Ambassador, who has such discriminating tastes, should inspect the wine list for the banquet," Claire said. "I had him escorted to the royal warehouse where I'm quite sure it will take a long time to find the special order of Tieben wines we are bringing in for the festivities."

Pem looked gloomy; Gilbert shook his head in disbelief. The girl was learning very quickly.

"And also," Claire added," Tess is with him to inspect the inventory. I think we'll get a complete report on his activities later in the day."

Leandra laughed. "I think she is well ahead of all of us," she addressed Gilbert.

The arrival of Turlo Murten, Prince and the theoretical heir to the throne of Tieben, and Rissa Ellendor, daughter and heir to the foremost Trader family in Boggrash, was accomplished without fanfare at the same rear portal that had let Claire slip into the Palace anonymously nearly two years ago. Gilbert and Leandra hovered in the background while Pem and Claire stepped forward.

Gilbert was thinking that the last year had been a very long time with Claire and Pem at the Palace. The two kids had found many creative ways around the protocol that enforced their isolation from one another. Still, they hadn't been as discrete as they believed.

"I know what you're thinking, Gilbert," Leandra whispered. "We need to get these two married off."

"Scarcely two years ago," Claire whispered as she squeezed Pem's hand while they waited for their friends to disembark from the carriage. "I think I was in love with you then but didn't know it. It seems like forever since I arrived with Tess from Greyhaven. We never even got to go to the Great Ball!"

"That night in the garden!" Pem's eyes sparkled. "If only you could have gotten rid of Mags and my father hadn't shown up."

Claire squeezed Pem's hand again. "It would have been a huge scandal," she giggled.

"If only I had personally come to escort you to the Ball," Pem said. "All of our troubles might have been avoided."

"Or, you might have been assassinated by Garrund's allies," she continued to hold his hand tightly.

"Please, you mustn't speak of this in public," Pem reminded Claire. "We can't prove Lord Garrund's involvement."

"It was Lord Garrund's house colors the guards were wearing, and I recognized Jallis Ruffin," Claire retorted.

"It means nothing, my dear," Pem whispered back. "They will only argue that some men masqueraded as Lord Garrund's guards and there's no proof that Ruffin works for the Garrunds."

"I'm certain that I knew that Captain," Claire insisted.

"Possibly. Uh, most certainly," Pem changed his words when he saw the storm brewing in Claire's eyes. "But the man is gone—blown out of this world when the port ruptured."

"We will talk of this again," Claire cut short any reply from Pem and rushed forward to embrace Rissa as her friend descended from the carriage.

Pem moved forward and stood before Turlo, Prince of Tieben.

Claire looked at both men. Except for the new scar over one eyebrow and a notch out of one ear, Turlo looked the same. Where Turlo was devious and dashing, Pem was steady and serious. Where Turlo radiated an air of confidence and mystery, Pem seemed solid and a center of power. She was pleased with her comparison.

"They will make a pair of handsome husbands," Rissa whispered, holding Claire's hand.

"I'm so glad to see you," Claire drew Rissa into another embrace. "I was so afraid when I saw your ship disappear into that wall of fire." She drew back and examined her friend, finding the same beautiful almond eyes and the honey-colored curls tumbling to her shoulders. There were a few new lines in her face, a sign that her friend had been through much since they'd last seen each other.

"I was pretty frightened myself," Rissa returned. "It was Turlo who saved the ship. I will tell you about it later."

"I'm most pleased that you have returned." Pem nodded his head and the two men exchanged hearty handshakes.

"Formal, but friendly and well met," Turlo smiled at the younger man. "I am most pleased to be here, though this would not have happened if Trader Rissa had not pulled me from the waters of the River Lorne."

"Lady Claire has that same habit of saving me from myself," Pem laughed. The two men turned to look upon their women.

Seeing them side-by-side, Claire stood with Rissa and felt a slight shift under her feet, a tremble that heralded the realignment of her world. The amulet between her breasts warmed, and a vision of a thick rope of nanophages swarming between them and the two men flashed through the special place in her mind. Beside her, Rissa tensed momentarily. The two men merely continued to grin foolishly, each absorbed in a similar thought that caused Claire to redden slightly. Men should learn to control themselves.

Gilbert stepped forward and Pem made the introductions between the two men. "I believe you already know Lady Rissa," he said.

"Welcome," Gilbert offered his hand to Turlo. "And to you, also," he bowed to Rissa. "It has been a long time since the night on the Plains of Glass."

"I believe Rissa may know Sage Leandra," Gilbert indicated the Magister who joined them.

"It is my honor to meet you," Turlo bent over the Sage's hand. "You are well known to my uncle Cornal Hushara, and he has told me many tales of your deeds," he said.

Leandra smiled upon the couple. "You have the blessing of Mara, and I am happy for you," she told them.

"Also, I am pleased that you listen to your Uncle Cornal's many stories," she said to Turlo. "Cornal is an honorable man."

"And his brother, Veral is not," Turlo laughed ruefully. "Yet, he is now the King and head of Tieben, and no one can gainsay him."

"And Cornal's health?" Gilbert asked.

"Adequate, I understand. I have this from Lady Claire and Lady Tess who spent some time with the old rascal in the Tower as well as more recently from some friends in Norcross."

Claire was going to speak further, but Rissa put up her hand. "You have another guest who is far more important than we," she said. "We have Ka'Tara with us. She is to assist the High Temporate at your weddings. Turlo was most fortunate to have Ka'Tara to tend him in Saitadi. His recovery might have been far less certain without her help."

The footman assisted Ka'Tara as she emerged from the coach. She was resplendent in her soft robes which Claire noticed were almost completely white.

Even before Gilbert could move, Claire rushed forward. "I cannot begin to tell you how pleased I am to see you," she said to the priestess. "I would never have survived in Lunaria if it hadn't been for you."

"I see that not only have you survived but that you have blossomed into a beautiful young woman," Ka'Tara laughed. "I think that none of this was my doing. You have Gilbert to thank for your good fortune."

Gilbert stepped forward and embraced his half-sister. "Welcome, little sister," he said, his voice filled with emotion. "We will have much to talk about."

"And little time," she responded.

Gilbert motioned to the Palace Manager, who had been hovering in the background, to come forward.

"We will leave you in the capable hands of Brooks, our Major Domo," Gilbert told Rissa, and Turlo. "He will settle you into your apartments and will have someone assigned to see to your needs. The Palace Timekeeper is provided in each room, but he will also see that someone is there to escort you to tonight's dinner. If there is anything at all that you need, you have only to ask. I will see to my sister's accommodations myself."

"I have asked that we meet where we will be able to talk freely," Pem put in. "Give us an extra half hour before the official dinner, Brooks."

"Indeed," Brooks bowed slightly in Pem's direction. "I will see to it. And you, Sir and Madame, if you will follow me? We will attempt to make you as comfortable as our poor household will allow." He bowed low to Ka'Tara before he turned to go. "Lady, it is good to see you in this house again."

Rissa paused to wink at Claire. "We'll talk later," she said and swept from the anteroom arm-in-arm with Turlo in the wake of Brooks and his staff.

"Won't they make a great couple?" Claire sighed.

"You traveled with this fellow all the way through Tieben?" was all Pem had to say.

Gilbert took his sister by her arm. "You and I will have refreshments and you shall rest before your ordeal with the High Temporate," he laughed.

"Hah!" Ka'Tara rolled her eyes. "Delagus has still not accepted the idea of women high in the Temporate hierarchy."

"I'm sure you will instruct him, and he will get used to the idea," Gilbert laughed freely for the first time in a very long time.

GILBERT GREYBAIRD, MASTER of Greyhaven and last son in the line of Lunaria's oldest family, stood with his half-sister and looked fondly upon the modest crowd in his private reception room. Pem, who would become Monarch and High Communicate tomorrow, was standing by the side of Lady Claire, the outworld girl who was destined to become Pem's Queen. The pair made a handsome couple: Claire with her sun-bleached auburn hair and her charming freckles and fair skin; Pem with reddish brown hair cut short in the military fashion and flashing green eyes in a striking, fair-featured face that reminded Gilbert so much of Pem's mother, Rachael. His heart took a lurch as he remembered the beautiful but headstrong woman who had been the Queen of Lunaria for only a short time before she was struck down while leading her troops against a border raid. Useless to remember what might have been! He wrenched himself away from such memories.

He watched as Rissa Ellendor, clad in a simple, shimmering blue silk gown fastened at the throat with an emerald brooch, approached the royal couple and engaged Claire in a conversation that soon had both women giggling while Pem looked on uncomfortably. Poor Pem, he'd never be comfortable around women. In the background, Edward Godwyn drank his third glass of wine and chatted amiably with Turlo Murten. Gilbert wondered what was passing between the two men. He had never learned the contents of the message that Claire had passed between Cornal Hushara and the Regent.

Captains Eberson and Watchmen were drinking something stronger and appeared to be swapping stories. He'd want to corner Eberson later in the evening and ask after any messages from Astora. He knew that the Captain and his daughter were fond of each other and sometimes used Eberson's feelings for Astora as a way of maintaining discrete contact.

"You are thinking of Astora," Ka'Tara took Gilbert's arm. "I am sorry she has decided not to be here—for your sake if not for Illaina's."

"We have talked about this, and you know how I feel," Gilbert looked deep into his sister's eyes. "Do not pity me," he said. "I could not force her to be here. There are choices each must make, no matter how painful or wrong they seem."

"They do not seem wrong to me," she said quietly. "Only tragic for Astora and Illaina. By her choosing, your daughter's path has diverged and she, without realizing it, has become your enemy."

"Astora can never be my enemy," Gilbert returned, but Ka'Tara thought that there was hesitation in his words.

"Perhaps not directly, but by choosing to be used by Torvall Garrund, she has opened the doors to your destruction," Ka'Tara gripped Gilbert's hand and felt him return the pressure. "You must be very careful."

"Do what you can during your visit at Greyhaven," he told the priestess. "Astora likes and respects you. You do me a great favor by offering to talk with her. It is a great gift, and I can ask no more." He turned his attention back to the room and less personal concerns.

He listened with satisfaction as Tess, once a peasant girl and an unwanted daughter of the cooper in Tribana, skillfully guided the introduction of her mother, Eurita, to Fitz Royard's father, Vlaze Royard, a minor notable who hailed from the Ranaputkin region. Clearly, Eurita was impressed with Vlaze Royard, and Vlaze appeared to be quite taken with Eurita. The simple cooper's wife not only had an equal right to be here, he reflected, but she had a quietly understated elegance of her own that surprised him—until he saw that same strength of character reflected in his choice for Claire's companion. He thanked G'rama that Tess's father had declined the invitation, relaying through the royal messenger that "such nonsense was not for the likes of him." Fitz's mother had been unable to attend for reasons of delicate health. He'd have to keep an eye on Vlaze, he decided.

Fitz was engaged in an earnest conversation with Sage Leandra who was nodding her head but otherwise intent on keeping track of what went on between Turlo and Edward. Gilbert decided it was time that he joined the pre-dinner festivities and stepped forward.

Leandra, who was listening with half an ear to Fitz's eager questions concerning projecting one's presence into an animal mind, kept her other ear tuned to what Turlo was saying to Edward. She broke off her conversation with Fitz when she saw Gilbert standing with Ka'Tara at the entrance to the reception room. She wondered what he was thinking. Was he lonely because Astora had refused to come to Pem's wedding, or was his hurt deeper and caused by the unhappy relationship with Illaina?

"Excuse me, dear Fitz, I regret that there is something I must attend," she said, causing the new Commander of the King's Brigade to blush with her easy familiarity. She began moving across the floor towards her old friends.

She had gone no more than three or four steps when she forgot about everything else and concentrated on a remarkable vision in the mirror beside the door where Gilbert stood.

"Perhaps I am the only one to see this," she muttered to herself, feeling uncertain. She resisted the urge to grab Tess, who, along with her mother, was chatting up her future father-in-law. She wondered if she should and call the young woman's attention to the image that she saw in the mirror—or if Tess would see it.

Claire sensed a slight change in the room's atmosphere and was distracted from Rissa's conversation which had turned to questions concerning the royal honeymoon that was to begin after the ceremonies tomorrow.

"Such a large entourage for a honeymoon," Rissa was teasing Pem. "Are you sure there will be sufficient privacy aboard the royal yacht?"

Pem's face was just beginning to turn red when Claire glanced over to Leandra's suddenly-motionless figure standing in the middle of the room. She followed her mentor's gaze to the mirror on the wall and suppressed a gasp.

In the mirror she saw the reflection of a panel drawing back slowly in the wall behind her. A shadowy figure was revealed, peering through the opening into the room. Her orange cat, Timone, was racing across the floor towards the shadow with his tail erect and spine arched.

Claire spun around to look behind her, accidently jostling Pem whose wine glass tipped a few drops onto his plum-colored coat.

Leandra had glanced down at the floor in confusion. There was no Timone to be seen running across the polished parquet surface. By the time she looked up, she saw Pem brushing at his coat sleeve and Claire turned towards the wall. There was no panel and no strange, shadowy figure standing in an opening.

Claire turned and locked eyes with Leandra. Both looked up at the mirror. Only the ordinary reflections of the room appeared with their friends holding their drinks, munching on hors d'oeuvres, or simply chatting with each other. Timone, in the flesh, was lurking aside a column near Tess. When had Timone entered the room? Gilbert, apparently unaffected, had moving into the room and was about to speak.

"My very special friends," Gilbert's deep voice cut through the conversations. The murmur of voices drifted into silence. Edward's hand steadied as a server refilled his cup with the fine red wine from Claire's vineyards.

"The Regent has asked me to welcome you. We have gathered here to not only honor Prince Pemburton and Lady Claire, but also to renew old friendships and foster new ones. Of course, I wouldn't want to leave out our new Commander of the King's Brigade, Fitz Royard, and his marriage, tomorrow, to the redoubtable Lady Tess."

"Here, here." There was scattered applause from the audience; Edward raised his empty wineglass in salute. Eurita moved closer to Vlaze, and Fitz blushed with pleasure as he moved to Tess's side.

"I would prefer that we remain here and enjoy our privacy," Gilbert continued. "Unfortunately there is a state dinner and the formalities to conduct. Brooks has announced that all is ready and that the other guests are arriving. Some of you will be accompanying the royal couple on at least the first part of their honeymoon voyage (much laughter at this), so we will have time to talk with each other later on board the royal yacht."

"If you will follow Edward and me, I will lead us to the Great Hall. Please enjoy your evening and ask for anything you desire."

This being said, Gilbert strode with the Regent, Ka'Tara, and Leandra through the archway at the far end of the room and through the four great doors that opened from his private quarters into the Palace's public space. They were followed by: Pem and Claire, then Turlo and Rissa, Fitz and Tess, and finally by Captains Eberson and Watchman.

"Where does he get his power from, I wonder," Vlaze bent to speak quietly in Eurita's ear as the two parents brought up the rear of the little procession. "Why doesn't the Regent speak for the occasion?"

"My daughter tells me that Lord Gilbert is a friend to the Regent and was the Privy Counselor to Queen Rachael. Ka'Tara is his half-sister and she is high in the Temporate. There were rumors about his relationship with the Queen, too. The Master of

Greyhaven is also very high in the military counsels, and Edward intends to enjoy the support of the Correlates within the military bureaucracy."

Vlaze appeared satisfied. "I know that our Lord Gilbert is the last of the oldest surviving family in Lunaria," he said. "My son was very lucky getting a commission with him."

"My daughter has only the highest praise for Fitz and talks constantly of his virtues," Eurita studied Vlaze discretely.

Vlaze, taking the high praise of his son at face value, responded, "Indeed, my son says the same of your daughter, my dear Eurita."

Eurita was pleased but not overly flattered by Fitz's father. She was the wife of The Cooper and enjoyed an elevated position of trust and respect in Tribana even if she were not a so-called notable—yet. Her daughter's position with the new Queen would certainly change that. Eurita thought her husband a fool for cowering in Tribana, but she understood his fear. At least he was an honest man.

Entertaining these thoughts, Tess's mother placed her hand lightly on Vlaze Royard's arm. "You may escort me to dinner," she smiled sweetly.

The Tieben Ambassador

.THE GREAT HALL .was alive with music and laughter as Claire and Pem pushed though the entrance arm-in-arm. The gesture had instant appeal. The crowd came to its feet and clapped and cheered as she and Pem made their way up the broad avenue across the center of the floor which would serve later for dancing. She smiled and nodded to people she knew, even to people she didn't know, and settled with Pem at the center of the head table with the Regent sitting between them.

Gilbert and Leandra sat to Pem's right, while Rissa and Turlo sat to Claire's left. Fitz and Tess were seated with Vlaze and Eurita at a table immediately below and left of the royal table while Captains Eberson and Watchman found their place of honor nearby with the Lord Admiral of the Royal Navy and his Aide. Ka'Tara sat at a private table with Delagus and another Temporate functionary. To the far right, at the left end of the head table, a few notable ambassadors including the Tieben representative, sat looking very smug and important with their bright ambassadorial sashes across their chests.

Directly in front of the head table, each place decorated with a house flag, the notables of the Nine Great Houses and their consorts sat facing the audience where all could appreciate their importance.

As soon as the head table was seated, a great bustle and clatter rose across the hall as people settled themselves and the servers brought out huge platters of food and drink while musicians struck up a medley of popular tunes. It was considered impolite in Lunaria for speeches to begin before everyone had a decent chance at taking the edge off of their appetites. Claire found herself enjoying the tender grazer steak.

She soon found herself tapping her foot to the quaint and compelling rhythms of Lunarian music. She would have liked to talk with Rissa about how the music sounded much like something she remembered as River Dance that had played on TV at home— a program her grandmother had loved but mother had declared boring and had switched in favor of a basketball game.

"Would you look at that?" her mother had said, moistening her lips. She had sat the entire evening and watched the young men on the TV screen race around the bases.

Claire had been angry because she still believed that her father would return home. Besides, she had felt it unseemly for her mother to be so interested in younger men.

"You are far away, this evening," Rissa touched Claire's hand lightly with a finger.

"There is a saying in my land," Claire broke from her reverie. "Waiting for the other shoe to drop."

Rissa laughed. "What a strange idea, and yet it conveys exactly what I often think when everything seems to be going too perfectly. When will the other shoe drop?" She giggled at the odd notion.

As Claire sat next to Edward, she had the distinct feeling that the Regent was studying her. She wondered what Edward had made of the message that she had passed to him from Cornal Hushara. She imagined Cornal grinning at her when she told him that she'd decode his message to Edward and felt her cheeks turning red. Indeed, she had resolved the simple code, and yet knowing the words had brought her no nearer to making sense of the information—information she had never shared with Gilbert despite knowing him to be curious.

"When the time comes, I will be on the other side."

"What does it mean?" she looked sideways at Edward who had another glass of wine halfway to his mouth. He stopped and carefully put down his cup before turning to her. He nodded his head as if she had just said something extremely funny.

"Another time, Lady Claire," his eyes bored into hers even though his expression seemed untroubled. "I promise to share this with you when the time comes."

"However," Edward continued mysteriously, "It will not be necessary because you will understand exactly what it means."

On the other side. Claire privately pondered Cornal's words. Other side of what? The other side in a war or an opposition political party? If it were that dire, then wasn't Edward siding against her and Pem?

Edward patted her hand. "Please believe that I am your friend," he said, and his eyes radiated warmth for a moment. He turned to clap Pem on the back and call for another glass of wine "for the bridegroom."

"There you go, again," Rissa interrupted her sour thoughts. "You've hardly eaten your grazer steak. Mine was delicious. You are feeling well, aren't you?"

Rissa's rush of words thrust themselves into Claire's consciousness. She could almost see her friend's thoughts as they were mirrored in a swirl of nanites. Have Claire and Pem been experimenting?

Rissa stared at her speculatively. The last slice of her friend's tender steak was skewered neatly on her knife and poised half-way between plate and mouth.

Claire reddened and looked down at the plate she had barely touched.

"I think I will have more wine." Claire looked out over the great hall filled with people chattering, laughing, and oblivious to the dark cloud that nibbled at the edge of her awareness. "A lot more wine." She signaled a server.

On the other side of Rissa, Turlo leaned forward. "Relax, Lady Claire. This is your time. Enjoy it. The terrible events you have experienced are now in the past."

Turlo said, "It pains me a great deal to admit it, but this Pem is a rather good fellow." He grinned and received a playful elbow planted in his side by Rissa.

"Well, Master Turlo," Claire said, finding her humor returning. "If it's any consolation, I never thought to hear you speak the unvarnished truth—unless it was to Rissa's mother."

Turlo looked puzzled for a moment before his eyes brightened. "Another one of your clever sayings, Lady," he laughed. "Very funny: unvarnished, uncoated, without adornment, plain." He twisted the words around in his mouth and found them even funnier. "Someday I hope you will write down all of these funny sayings that you bring from your world."

"Perhaps you'll need your sense of humor if you run into the Tieben Ambassador," Claire jerked her head toward the other end of the table.

"Yes, he's been giving me a lot of funny looks," Turlo said, scratching his chin. "I was hardly ever in my Uncle's court. I don't believe he recognizes me yet."

"Let's not have a diplomatic incident at the wedding party," Rissa urged Turlo.

"Well, it won't be me that brings up the subject," Turlo said firmly.

Claire might have believed him if there hadn't been a slight smile playing around the corners of his mouth.

"I'm sure that the Ambassador is far too clever to allow himself to be ruffled by you," Claire glared at Turlo.

A server in the person of a young man in a black and gold palace uniform placed a half-cup of the sparkling white wine by Claire's elbow. She lifted her cup and emptied it in one draft, indicating that the server should give her a refill. "There! A few more like that and I'll feel up to the evening."

Claire found herself locking eyes with Torvall Garrund as he shoveled another bite of tender grazer into his mouth, chewing angrily. After a long moment, he dropped eye contact with her and occupied himself with using a slab of bread to sop up the puddle of gravy on his platter.

She wondered what was going on behind Torvall's eagle-sharp eyes. She knew that he was disappointed with Pem's choice of her over Torvall's granddaughter, Illaina. She couldn't believe that this was the entire reason behind his implacable opposition to her. There was something else, something perhaps about his son and his marriage to Astora that was involved.

At some point, when the clatter of dishes had died down and the granapple tarts topped with flaming brandy had been served, Edward grabbed Claire's right hand and Pem's left and lifted them over his head. The hall quieted immediately.

The scrape of Edward's chair was loud as he rose from his seat in the sudden hush. Claire looked up in surprise as the Regent spoke; she leaned far enough forward to see that Pem was also taken unprepared.

"We are gathered here to celebrate the approaching union of my son, Pemburton Windover, with this beautiful young woman from the north, Lady Claire. Ever since the tragic death of my beloved wife, I have looked forward to the moment that I might relinquish the Regency in favor of the reign of my son. For that to happen, according to Lunarian law, Pem must marry in order to become the true Monarch of the Realm and the High

Communicate. I believe that he has truly found the right woman to be our Queen."

A rousing cheer rippled across the floor, and people stood to clap enthusiastically. Claire was surprised at this response and blushed with pleasure.

Rissa leaned close to her ear. "You have become very popular in a short length of time. Choosing your identity from the north was a stroke of genius."

"Not mine, Gilbert's," Claire returned.

Claire felt the collective approval of the audience as a background to the sharp emotions of the nearby council members and their consorts. Lord Garrund radiated hatred, but the Ranapui couple and a few others seemed genuinely pleased. Lady Calantha, Torvall's wife, surprised her by giving her a nod of grudging approval. She took some courage from this. The entire Council was not against her, and at least Lady Calantha acknowledged her position if not lending her support.

"To begin the celebration of tomorrow's momentous event, I offer a toast to the future King and Queen of Lunaria," Edward placed Claire's hand together with Pem's in his left hand, and in his other he held up a full glass of wine that had appeared like magic. The cheering and foot stamping went wild—after all, how could one clap when one hand held a cup of wine?

As the clapping died away, the orchestra struck up a tune that Claire recognized as a popular dance melody. A few people began drifting out onto the dance floor. The murmur of voices across the hall grew louder. She wondered if Pem would ask her to dance. Wasn't it customary? Or was this a custom that she remembered from her own world? Sometimes her memories blended together, placing her father's image in a context of Greyhaven rather than Ridgeville. It had been a long time since she repeated her dream of the old soldier taking care of her father in Iraq. She sighed and took another draught of the sparkling wine. Really, she was beginning to feel quite relaxed.

Claire felt a hand touch her shoulder. "Care to dance with me? It is expected." Pem reminded her. He helped her slide her chair from the table and offered his hand.

Edward pushed back, comfortable in his chair, and smiled warmly. "If only I were twenty years younger," he tipped his glass as if taking a deep draft. The liquid level barely changed.

Turlo was rising, ostensibly to invite Rissa to a turn on the floor. She had just begun to push back when the Tieben ambassador, Hjun Castri, stopped in front of them and leaned across the table. He tried a smile that didn't quite reach his piggish eyes.

"Greetings, Lady Rissa Ellendor," Hjun said, ignoring Turlo. "Your beauty is unmistakable in any company."

Turlo scowled. "And you are unwelcome in ours, Hjun."

"Always with the bad temper? Your uncle would be disappointed in you," Hjun said lightly, staring back at the Prince of Tieben.

Pem wanted to pull away to the dance floor, but Claire hung back behind Rissa, wanting to hear what was being said.

"I'm not exactly my Uncle's favorite, anyway," Turlo said harshly.

"True, but there are certain expectations of the heir to the Tieben throne."

"We both know what I think about that," Turlo retorted.

"I would not wish to spoil your evening, in any case," Hjun bowed in Rissa's direction. "Let us just say that I have been asked to speak with you if you showed up here in Lumminea."

"After that little incident with Dread in Trappers Holding, I would think that you would understand my attitude," Turlo returned bitterly.

"Ah, well that bit has been corrected. After all, Dread had no idea who you were," Hjun replied hastily.

Claire, who was taking this all in, was sure that the Ambassador was not telling the whole truth. She wondered if Hjun was aware of her role in the escape of Turlo and Tess from Dread's prison cell. What had happened to Dread when Veral Hushara had learned that his Captain had nearly killed his nephew?

Not that I care. "Will you please excuse us?" Claire broke in. "I'm sure the Ambassador will have ample time to talk later, don't you agree?" she asked Hjun sweetly. "Meanwhile, I think our guests are waiting to join us on the dance floor. I do hope you have brought a partner," she told the ambassador with a sincere look plastered on her face. "Our royal orchestra is said to be the finest in the land."

"Yes, of course, Lady Claire," Hjun immediately demurred. "Who could object to the wishes of the woman who would be Queen of Lunaria at the end of the next day?" The smooth words sounded more like a warning than a compliment.

Out on the floor, Pem held Claire's left hand loosely, his other hand pressed into the small of her back. The dance was an old fashioned country dance that she had learned from Tess at Greyhaven. She compared it to a waltz that she remembered seeing on TV—a program called Dancing with the Stars, or something similar. The music seemed to flow through her body and into her feet as they whirled around on the polished wooden floor. Pem's face was the only fixed point in her vision; his eyes sparkled as he guided her between other couples.

"I would rather be elsewhere with you," he mouthed.

"Not tonight," Claire said. "Tonight we are seen as the romantic young people that everyone envies. Enjoy the moment. Tomorrow we shall be nothing more than another married couple."

Pem pretended to be hurt. "We shall never be just another couple," he said.

Claire laughed, feeling free at last from her past. Nothing but the future stretched in front of her. Even her father's image seemed to recede.

"You are so romantic at the moment," she squeezed his shoulder where her hand rested on his uniform. "Like all men, you will take me for granted once we are married," she teased him.

"Claire, the ordinary girl from Ridgeville, wherever that is," he quipped. "I've never been fooled by that story you tell."

"Well," she temporized, "I do feel special when I'm with you."

A pair of hands tapped both of them on their shoulders. "I say, Pem," Turlo interrupted them, "do you intend to monopolize the bride all night? Rissa would like a dance with you, and I'd like one last dance with Lady Claire before she loses her freedom."

"Hah! Little do you know this woman," Pem accepted the change in partners gracefully and sailed away with the beautiful Rissa in his grasp.

"Should I trust him with Rissa?" Turlo raised an eyebrow at Claire and moved her out of the way of a couple who were on a collision course. "These dancers are wild," he laughed. "We have nothing like this back home."

Turlo was taller than Pem, and even with her heels, Claire had to look up at him. He was dressed in an elegant black military uniform with gold trim and a discreet insignia identifying him as a Major in the Tieben military.

"I didn't know you had rank in the army," Claire said as the lights swirled past.

"I don't, really," Turlo laughed. "Someone must have known I was coming because I found this ready for me when I entered my quarters this afternoon."

"Really?" The information made Claire nervous since she was unaware of how anyone could have known the exact timing of her friend's arrival. Didn't Tess send the Ambassador off on a wild goose chase to look after his wines? Could the Ambassador have spies in high places? Of course he would, she chided herself. Stupid to think otherwise.

Turlo was a much better dancer than Pem—though Claire would never have said so to anyone. She almost regretted the change when Fitz Royard asked to cut in. He made such a dashing looking Commander in his new Brigade uniform, even if his ears were oversized. However, his heroic efforts at dancing met with limited success.

"Sorry, Lady Claire," he said as he took a misstep for the third time.

"No harm done, Commander," Claire replied. "I'm sure you do fine when you are dancing with Tess."

Fitz smiled gratefully. "Tess wanted me to ask you what went on between Turlo and the Tieben ambassador. I only asked because Tess reminded me that, as Brigade Commander, I should make it my business to know everything possible—no offense intended."

"None taken," Claire laughed. "Tess went to all that trouble diverting the attention of Hjun Castri from Turlo's arrival, and yet we seem to be anticipated." She told him about Turlo's uniform.

Fitz shrugged, not an easy thing to do when you are doing the hitch step that closes the imaginary box that you are guiding your partner around. "Sounds harmless to me. Even so, you are probably correct when you say that only the Ambassador could arrange such a thing. I'll be sure to ask the guard captain to increase his patrols in the guest areas."

Claire thanked Fitz, then allowed herself to be surrendered back into Pem's arms.

"Tess was curious about what the Ambassador had to say to Turlo," Pem said.

"Is Tess a good dancer?" Claire changed the subject.

"I suppose so," Pem hedged. "She has very long legs."

Claire remembered Tess riding behind Pem with her skirts hiked up high on her thighs. "And you would know this because?" she asked him, pushing down the same surge of jealousy that she had felt on the Plains of Glass.

"Because I have had many occasions to see her riding in her trousers," Pem said glibly.

Six dances and four tall glasses of sparkling wine later, Claire was still thinking of Tess's long legs. She stopped by Rissa who was sitting alone at their table while Turlo sampled more dance styles with different partners. "I've had enough for the evening," she said. "Tomorrow will be a very busy day."

"Must I remain to bid my guests goodnight?" Claire asked Edward who was sitting with a sad, faraway look in his eyes.

"Of course not," he returned. "There is no longer anyone in the realm who would dare question you."

"I'll be happy to walk with you back to our rooms," Rissa said, belching delicately. "No more of this wine for me. My head is spinning as it is."

Wedding Day!

MAGS SHOOK HER lady's shoulder gently. When nothing happened, she pushed more vigorously. Timone, lying on his soft pillow at the foot of the spread, opened one eye and yawned.

"Wake up, Lady Claire. It's your wedding day and we have a thousand things to do!"

Claire groaned and opened one eye. "How much champagne did I have last night?"

"Too much, Lady," Mags said impatiently. "And now you must pay the price. I persuaded Cook to give me fresh hot rolls and tarle."

Claire ignored her stomach's objections. She pushed back the covers and sat up in the large bed, trying hard to disregard her pounding headache. When she swung her feet over the side of the feather mattress, Mags draped her green silk robe around her shoulders and smoothed Claire's auburn hair from her pretty face—though perhaps the nose was a little too short for total perfection and the sprinkle of freckles on her sun-browned cheeks might have spoken of a less royal background to some who thought of highborn women as porcelain dolls. She handed her young charge a warm damp cloth to wipe the sleepies from her eyes. Her wedding day! Claire's stomach knotted in nervous anticipation.

"Lord Gilbert would have a word with you as soon as possible," Mags said.

"I suppose you have already set the table," Claire eyed Mags' mischievous brown eyes that missed nothing. She found her slippers and was glad to get her bare feet off the floor. Summer or not, the stone of the Palace was always cold.

"In the garden, Lady," Mags referred to the tiny, secluded garden that Claire's private apartment featured. The only other such garden that she knew about was in Lord Gilbert's quarters. She had never entered Prince Pem's private quarters, but a few days ago she had been given a tour of the Royal Chambers where Queen Rachael had lived and where she would make her new home with Prince Pem—soon to be King Pemburton Windover, she reminded herself. That is, Pem would be recognized as the King of Lunaria as soon as they both slipped their rings over their fingers and were declared husband and wife.

Husband and wife—King and Queen—though Claire could not consider anything so grand. Still thought of herself as an ordinary girl from Ridgeville, Texas, and hardly qualified to be the Queen of a great land like Lunaria. A thrill surged through her as well as a great sadness. She wished that her father could be with her, to give her away in marriage to the man she loved. Even the presence of her mother would have been comforting as long as Higgins Brownbottom wasn't around. She felt a surge of disgust at the memory of the preacher. Someday her father would return from Iraq and kick the ugly man out of their life.

And Granny Miller! How could she forget her grandmother? She would be so proud that her granddaughter had become a woman with a destiny. She prepared me for this, Claire thought. All those books and stories have made me think about what I would do if I were lost in another world.

Marriage! Could she really do it? Her mentor, the Magister Leandra, had spent a great deal of time talking with her about marriage and other subjects. The Magister had traveled from Gilbert's holding at Greyhaven to become her tutor and advisor. Claire blushed at the thought of their conversations. How little she knew about such things. She was too young, surely, and people like

Lady Calantha would laugh behind her back. Claire felt the yellow egg with its silly putty that she slept with in a pouch in her gown. She was never without the egg. There was a link between her egg and the world of nanites surrounding her in a protective cloud.

Lord Gilbert arose when Mags escorted Claire into the garden. A white iron table with colorful tiles decorating its surface was laden with fresh breads, pots of jam, and a delicate silver service of steaming tarle. He bowed low to her.

"Congratulations on your great day, Lady Claire," he bent over the hand that she was late in offering. "Next time we meet, I will be your Privy Counselor, and I will have to address you as Your Majesty."

Claire snatched her hand back. "You must always call me Claire in private, Gilbert. These titles embarrass me."

"And yet, it is a title that you have earned," he said. His cool gray eyes warmed as he gazed upon her. "You will make a great Queen for our land," he stood back and smiled.

"So you say," Claire muttered.

"Trust me in this, at least," Gilbert joined Claire at the table and dismissed Mags with a glance. "Give us a few minutes alone, Mags. Stay nearby and there will be no scandal attached."

"No sir, of course not," the young woman blushed and retreated through the vine covered archway.

"One thing I am sure of," he stretched comfortably and served both of them a hot drink and buttered two delicious looking scones.

"What are you sure of?" Claire received the scone and took a small bite out of the unbuttered end, minding the small twinge in her stomach.

"These gardens are totally secure from enemy ears. I have personally checked."

"Yes," Claire smiled. "I know that the grottoes are special places—much like a miniature version of the Garden at Greyhaven. I have noticed that they attend only one master at a time."

"Just so," Gilbert nodded. "And in this place, you are its mistress."

"I do not surprise you?" Claire kept her expression neutral.

"Not at all. I have always known that you manipulate certain technologies on this world. I believe that I have even encouraged you in this enterprise." Gilbert looked upon his young friend with fatherly love and kindness. If only his daughter, Illaina, had been more like Claire.

Claire could guess Gilbert's thoughts without resorting to the Garden's power. "I'm sorry about Illaina," she said and reached out to touch Gilbert's hand. "She was only foolish and not to blame for betraying Tess and me. I have forgiven her. It is Lord Garrund and his minion, Jallis Ruffin, that I can't abide."

"Perhaps you are too kind, Claire," Gilbert said, not meeting Claire's eyes. "In any case, I am here on happier errands such as this!"

Gilbert reached to a bench behind him and drew forward an object wrapped in a soft blue-velvet cloth.

"Mags!" Claire screamed as the cloth fell away and something spilled, flashing into her hands.

"Yes, my Lady?" the girl raced in holding a priceless vase like a club.

"Look!" Claire held up the exquisite piece of jewelry.

The center of the pendant was delicately fired colored enamels with gold filigree. The outer rim was set with a crescent of emeralds very like the Trader's pendant she always wore under her clothes. She felt a warm and pleasant sensation and knew that something was interacting with her amulet.

"Look on the back," Gilbert encouraged Claire.

On the backside a scarlet gold key was cleverly disguised as part of an abstract design and fit into a flat depression closed by a tiny pearl-shaped locking mechanism. She received a brief electric shock when she touched the key.

"It's an entropy-enhanced key," she said with delight.

"Yes, and if you touch it to a closed door, it will give you a picture of what's on the other side," Gilbert said. "There are other uses that you will discover."

"Something that might come in handy," Claire said.

"I didn't know there were such things," Mags said in wonder. "I mean, you hear stories all the time, but you don't credit them."

Gilbert looked at Claire and sighed. "It might have been better for Mags to remain ignorant of this thing."

Claire paused for a moment. "I know that Mags is your man—isn't that how they put it?" she addressed Gilbert. "That's the reason why I have decided to make her my man."

Mags looked confused. "Sir?" she looked at her Lord.

"She means, you work for me and hold yourself loyal to my household," Gilbert explained. "She is offering you the same relationship in her future family."

Mags smile was radiant. "Oh, yes, if that is what you intend, Lady," she said. "Not to slight you in any way, Sir," she looked at Gilbert in alarm.

"No, it's alright, Mags. I would have suggested it myself." He turned to Claire. "Mags is, of course, free to choose as she will, but I hope you will welcome her into your household, for she is the most loyal and trustworthy of creatures, even if she will drive you mad sometimes."

"And now, I must finish my purpose for asking you to come, for I must soon leave," Gilbert brought his attention back to Claire.

"Queen Rachael gave me the piece and said she had no use for it—that perhaps I could give it to my daughter when she married," Gilbert said, looking sad. "I think I have found a better home for it. It is an object of power and I hope you will wear it with your dress today. I believe that you will find the color-match perfect."

"I will certainly wear this," Claire fingered the jeweled disk. "On my world, there is a tradition that the bride should have something old and something new on her person when she marries," Claire smiled upon Gilbert. "Now I have fulfilled this tradition."

"But who will know which is which," Gilbert's eyes crinkled in amusement. "There is something more. Since you decided to have this double wedding with Tess and Royard, and since the Queen's Lady must marry high, it seems that I must promote young Royard slightly ahead of schedule. If you wish, you may tell Lady Tess of his promotion so that she can surprise our dashing commander. After all, we cannot have a new head of the King's Brigade with a mere Captain's commission."

Claire resisted the urge to leap up and give Gilbert a hug, knowing that it would embarrass him. Instead, she stood up, understanding that he couldn't leave until she had given permission. Gilbert would have many duties to perform and needed to go about his business.

"Thank you. I am fortunate to have a friend such as you, Lord Gilbert." She extended her hand as formality required. He bent over, briefly touching her fingers, and then straightened up with a gleam in his eye.

"It will be as if I were giving my own daughter away to young Pem," his voice shook slightly.

"I hope I will not disgrace you by tripping over my new heels," Claire laughed.

"At least you will not scandalize the court by wearing your sword at the ceremony," he teased her.

"Oh, but I will have Officer Nikko's little gift. Its sting has been quite enough to get me through some difficulties."

"Will you see First Officer Nikko today?" Gilbert wanted to know.

"Yes, he seems to have appointed himself as a messenger between Pem and myself. Of course, I believe it is because he has eyes for Mags," Claire giggled while Mags turned red.

"I borrowed him from Captain Eberson, and he's done an excellent job preparing the royal yacht. If you see him, please tell him that I'd like a few minutes of his time," Gilbert said, smiling. "Tell him it will be about something he will like."

He nodded to Claire and started to take his leave. Even though it broke protocol, Claire stayed Gilbert with a hand on his arm. She said, "Please remember, Gilbert, that other than being given by my true father, I'm quite sure I could not walk down that aisle with any other man."

"Thank you," Gilbert said awkwardly.

"I'm sorry that Lady Astora and Illaina will not be attending my wedding," Claire added. "I know that your daughter blames you for Illaina's involvement, but I wish that at least Astora were here. She was very kind to me when I came to Lunaria, and I shall not forget the way she made me feel a part of your family. It can't be easy to see your daughter passed up for a stranger, no matter what the reasons."

Gilbert stared at Claire for a moment. "You are as I foretold in the moment I saw you with Pem. Wise beyond your years, and destined to change our world."

"Perhaps," Claire shrugged. "Who can say? I will need to lean on your good advice a great deal in the next few years."

"Pem's shoulders are broad," Gilbert tossed over his shoulder as he hurried from the garden.

"But not strong like yours, my friend," Claire said under her breath to Gilbert's back.

Mags sniffed and dabbed her eyes with her green silk handkerchief, a gift from her mistress. "He's a great one, Lady, that's for sure," she said when he had gone.

"Yes, and I don't want to embarrass him in front of the court by appearing half dressed," Claire said gaily. She heard the palace chimes counting softly in the background. "Drott," she exclaimed. "We must hurry so that we can check on Tess. She's always late for everything, and she must be ready for Fitz before I am ready for Pem!"

The ceremony was due to take place in the large outdoor amphitheater which was dedicated to summer theatre productions. The Middle Summer Theater, MST as it was known locally, was located on the northwest end of the Palace grounds adjacent to the larger sports arena which the High Priest of the Temporate deemed unsuitable for the marriage of the royal couple no matter that both Gilbert and the Regent had argued for the greater public venue.

"We have a duty to propriety and tradition," Delagus the Second had opined as he had swirled out of his meeting with Gilbert and Edward Godwyn. He was dressed in the purest of white robes and the triangular felt hat was meant to cover the bald spot on the top of his head. Gilbert sincerely hoped that one of the Palace pigeons would see fit to despoil the notable's arrogant perfection.

"He has a duty to his brother-in-law who owns a substantial number of shares in the theater and will no doubt receive a sizeable portion of the rent we will have to pay for the space," Edward Godwyn laughed.

Gilbert nodded, but failed to see the same degree of humor that Edward found. "More likely that we should call him High Intemperate," he said sarcastically.

Edward laughed at this, also. "Gilbert, you will put up with His Mightiness as long as Temporate continues to support the Monarchy."

Gilbert looked thoughtful. "I will do so as long as the Temporate understands that the Correlate is the right arm of the King and the Temple masters are the left."

Today, every inch of the MST was festooned in colored paper streamers and banners in designs of alternating soft greens and muted oranges which were the primary colors of the royal couple. The entire grassy lawn had been scraped from the surface and replaced with spotless, green turf. Line after line of comfortable chairs had been placed in numbered rows near the front of the stage for the seating of the nobles of the land. Ushers waited in back with elaborate lists and genealogies in case the Lords found reading their stubs difficult or if embarrassing mistakes were made in matters of precedence.

Claire's old teacher, Copious Ansel, who had been delegated to see to the printing and distribution of printed programs, an innovation introduced by Claire, was fussing with his small army of pages. There were over five thousand of these programs, and one was supposed to go on each seat in the theatre. There was a fresh breeze blowing, and a substantial number of pieces of paper were floating about or blowing across the grass where young boys were chasing after them like kittens after balls of twine.

An orchestra had been located out of sight behind the stage. A curved wall designed cleverly to reflect the sound out into the theater was part of the stage backdrop. The string section was tuning in a chaos of notes, while the occasional blare from the brass section indicated that some of the horn players were testing their lips.

Ranks of flags, each bearing the colors and devices of the Great Houses and higher notables, vied for prominence. The banners of the elite occupied the areas on either side of the stage and suggested to all who attended that their approval was necessary for the affair to take place. The Chief of Palace Protocol noted with a wry smile that Lady Claire's green would take precedence over all else if one included the green of the lawn. Lady Claire was rumored to be not only beautiful, but very intelligent; he wondered if the fortunate choice of color had been the Lady's intention.

Behind the seating for the notables, tiers of bleachers were filling with ordinary citizens according to a popular lottery that also raised money for the King's favorite charity—something as yet unspecified. Folks had paid for blocks of tickets and waited for hours to see what seat number they might draw. Before daylight on the Day, lines of people were waiting to find their seats in the arena causing the Palace Guard to be called out early to maintain order when some citizens discovered that they had purchased bogus tickets from fraudulent vendors.

As one of the ushers whose main duties consisted of passing out programs noted, "Such larceny was in the grand tradition of a royal wedding in which much exciting confusion and fun-loving, disorderly conduct accompanied a frenzy of joy and celebration by the Lunarians who were by nature a somewhat reserved and conservative bunch."

Not that any of this news filtered through to Claire and Tess who were involved in their own difficulties. Even Sage Leandra was losing patience.

Tess's gown which had fitted perfectly a week ago had developed an unanticipated, if not unexplained, tightness around the middle.

"The new pastry chef," Tess fumed. "He's been after me night and day to sample his sweets for the parties we've been giving the minister's consorts." Her eyes took on a dangerous twinkle.

"Perhaps Lady Calantha will be having difficulties with her new gown," Tess referred to Garrund's wife's gushing compliments to the new chef and his tea cakes. "She drank two bottles of our estate wine and ate an entire platter of the nut cookies. It wasn't until I told her that the recipe was from my mother in Tribana that she threw up."

"Move those buttons over on Lady Tess's gown," Leandra barked at the seamstress. "We've got less than two hours."

Claire was having her own problems. "Ouch! My hair," she wailed. "It's standing up like the ruff on a grazer's back." The comb struggled to remain locked in her curls in spite of Mags' tugging.

"Don't worry, we'll cut it out," Mags assured Claire and received a loud wail in response to her joke.

Finally, the last stays were tied, the last buttons done up, a few loose curls of hair tucked safely into their proper positions, and the shoes settled on feet—unusual as well as custom shoes, for Claire had brought the idea of elevated heels to the royal cobbler and he had grasped their importance immediately and had sworn her to secrecy.

"You will not want to give every woman in Lunaria this advantage over their men," he had warned. "This is something only for the Queen." He had taken the liberty to wink at his mistress, and Claire had laughed and agreed—their secret.

Since the high heeled shoes were hidden beneath the voluminous folds of their wedding gowns, there was little danger of their secret being revealed in the short term. Leandra stood the two young women side by side in front of the large and costly mirror that she had insisted on installing in their private dressing room. Leandra asked Mags to temporarily dismiss the extra help and wait in the suite outside.

"I would have a private moment with these two," she said to remove any implied criticism of Mags.

"Now hear this, girls," she said in a brusque, no-nonsense voice as soon as they were alone.

"You may not think of me as your mother or your grandmother." Leandra said. "That is not my role, here, and although I am very fond of both of you, you are both inclined to be foolish young women when it suits your purpose." She grabbed one of Tess's hands and one of Claire's and drew them together so that they were forced to stare into her eyes in the mirror as she stood between them.

"There is an old saying," the Sage said. "One reaches an age when one looks into a mirror and realizes that the only things left to us that are beautiful are one's thoughts and dreams. Therefore, take care not to corrupt either."

Leandra squeezed Tess's hand hard. "I know your tendencies, Tess. You must not become a problem to either me or to your Lady. You are marrying Pemburton's chosen man, a man in whom the King must place his full trust if he is to survive and bring Lunaria forward. Everything you do is a reflection on this relationship between Pem and Royard. Do you understand me?"

Some of the merriment in Tess's eyes faded as she nodded to Leandra in the affirmative. "I understand, Sage Leandra."

Claire winced as the Sage squeezed her hand tightly. "Few people see the steel in your fiber," she said to Claire. "Lady Calantha is not alone in underestimating your strengths. Ignorance is both an advantage and a disadvantage. I think you are aware of its advantages. I even give you very high marks for your sincere modesty. What you might fail to appreciate is that everyone is not so subtle. There will come a time, and probably soon, when you must show a flash of your claws. These ministers and their consorts will seek to dominate your husband. You must love him enough to defend him where he is weakest. And, you must choose your battles wisely."

Claire opened her mouth to protest and squeaked as Leandra unexpectedly bore down on her grip.

"I will not do this once you are Queen," the Sage said pleasantly. "But, for the moment you will listen to me."

"Yes, Sage," Claire took a deep breath and shrugged off her annoyance.

"I think you need to consider the term regal," Leandra pursed her lips thoughtfully. This was one of Leandra's mannerisms that Claire knew from experience would be followed by some very useful advice from her teacher.

"In ancient days, people practiced superstitious nonsense like making the king or queen a representative of God. I assure you, Lady Claire that you are not going to be an Agent of God." Leandra looked closely at her charge to make sure that Claire understood this as a joke. "Nevertheless, in its finest sense, regal means appropriate to associate with the highest ideal. Not even Delagus the Second believes himself a representative of G'rama—or if he does, he does well to keep his opinions to himself. Still, most of the time, his actions appear regal, but the man knows himself to be imperfect."

Claire smiled at her memory of meeting the old man in white robes. He had exhibited a gruff demeanor that Claire interpreted more as nervousness than arrogance. He had questioned her briefly concerning her sincerity in wishing to marry Prince Pem and becoming the Lunarian Queen. She could tell that he had wanted to ask her about her world and its alien ways but was either too polite or else was afraid of what she might say.

In his own way, he reminded her of the Church's marriage counselor who had once come to their Sunday school class and tried to explain why some parents got divorces. The counselor had rushed from the room in tears when one of the students asked her why she should be giving advice when she, herself, was divorced.

"The most powerful personal flattery is when someone treats you as if you are all-powerful or all-wise," Leandra continued. "The second most powerful flattery is to treat your husband in the same way. How can this not be, when love itself is designed to create the illusion of perfection?"

"I assure you that I don't believe Pem is perfect," Claire said.

"No, you are far too smart for that," the Sage laughed. "But in time you may become defensive as criticism mounts and whatever course Pem takes attracts powerful opponents."

"Am I not supposed to defend him—to take his side?"

"Yes, but you must listen to his opposition, too. Pem is not overly good at hearing criticism. Remember to keep your enemies close. They can teach you more than all the soothing words from friends ever will."

"Well, you must be an exception," Claire locked eyes with Leandra. "I know you are my friend, yet your words are hardly ever soothing."

Leandra sighed. "You are young, but I believe that you can understand how blood, loyalty, and honor work. These are the three basic ingredients in all human interaction. Blood is of the gut, honor is of the mind, and loyalty is of the heart. Now is not the time for a lesson in philosophy, I only wanted to warn you against being swept up into Pem's view of the world in which his mother, Queen Rachael, represented perfection and Edward represented dissolution."

"I see," Claire said, suddenly sober. "Gilbert tried to tell me something similar a long time ago. He warned me of trying to live up to Pem's illusions of perfection. He also tried to tell me of the conflicts between these three ingredients of human nature."

"If you were God, there would be no conflict," Leandra said. "A person can only strive to come to some reconciliation between what appears to be warring factions."

"During the ceremony both of you will use the words protect and defend," Leandra reminded Claire of the oath that she had memorized. "Protect the imperfect, and defend the imperfect. That is the stuff of real life. I fear that Pem will become disillusioned when the very Lunaria he is sworn to protect and defend is revealed as a real, living being with faults, failings, and shortcomings. It is the affliction of men, mostly, to want to serve the ideal. It is the lot of women to serve what is basic and practical."

"I do not say that this is bad," Leandra held up her hands, dropping the girls' hands. "I say, go forth and serve what is basic and practical and what in your heart you know to be real and true."

"Yes, Leandra," both girls chorused in union.

Leandra sighed, again. "And now for the Royal Jeweler and we will be finished here. You can both be married to your young men and believe that you are the very first to know what such joy is like."

When the ladies had been properly adorned with pieces from the royal collection, including Claire's special piece that was a gift from Gilbert, Leandra escorted them to the carriage waiting at a private exit. They were assisted into the curtained interior, the doors closed and locked from the inside for security, and then whisked away in a dusty clatter of hooves and jingling of fancy harness. Their first glance outside came with the loud knock on the carriage door signifying that they had entered into the private, ladies pavilion set up behind the theater stage.

"I wish that Rissa could be here with me," Claire said to Leandra.

"I wish so, too," Leandra returned. "But you know that such a close association between you and a prominent Trader could be used against you. Your public friendship with Rissa will have to wait."

Claire sighed and indicated that the door be unlocked. Timone darted in and promptly ran from Claire to Tess as if surveying all the finery.

Tess's rising excitement was mirrored in Claire, who felt positively giddy. Even Timone appeared stressed. Through the canvas walls, she could hear the roar of the crowd which probably included all Lummineans who could manage to get off from their daily tasks. After all, Pem and Claire had insisted that tickets be priced so low that even a street peddler might purchase a ticket from the lottery. Word came that citizens without tickets were demanding standing room attendance, and the guards were forced to accommodate additional crowds.

Leandra was called out of the tent to consult with Gilbert and came back in looking nervous. "The crowds are growing so large that Lord Gilbert fears for your safety," she reported.

Claire was ecstatic. She was certain that a wildly popular event was just what she and Pem needed to demonstrate their power to the Council. She had lived in a democracy, and she knew the value of widespread popularity. She was even certain that she was prepared to take advantage of this. But was she prepared to make Pem understand the idea of a populist leader, both its dangers and its advantages? It was a question she couldn't answer.

Tess was breathing hard and turning red. Mags had a cloth with ice water fetched and applied it to Tess's face, demanding that she stop and take a deep breath. "Lady, you will faint if you keep this up," Mags remonstrated. "It is almost time, and your honor guard will be here to fetch you at any moment."

"Suppose Lord Gilbert forgets," Tess moaned. "He's so important and I'm nobody. Suppose Reyfort decides not to come? I haven't heard from him. What will I do if Reyfort doesn't come," she practically wailed.

"Hush," Claire scolded her friend. "Of course Reyfort will come to stand with you, and you know that Lord Gilbert thinks you are very special—to me, and especially to Fitz. I'm sure that Gilbert has kept Reyfort busy doing other things, but he'll be here on time."

"Five recites.[1]," Leandra called out. "Five recites and Tess will be leaving. Come here, girl, and let me give you one last check."

When Claire had learned how simple the Lunarian marriage ceremony was and how male oriented, she became determined to create a memorable event for Tess and herself. Basically, the male showed up, proved that he was financially responsible, declared his choice, and received his bride who must swear to love him and be faithful forever. To Claire, this was unacceptable. Surprisingly, she had found an ally both in Gilbert and in Pem. Delagus the Second had been harder to convince.

"Lady, you will ruin our wedding traditions," he had repeated gloomily in several variations of the same argument. "Women don't want equal partnerships, and the men will resist."

"You just keep at it, Lady Claire," Mags' eyes had sparked. "Men always resist change. Every woman in Lunaria is counting on you."

Claire had found the reality more complicated. She had met Lady Ranapui at a small reception a few evenings before. The Ranapuis were staunch supporters of the Monarchy and were ranked as the Third House on the Council. Their holdings included large shipyards and maritime facilities. Sidra was an intelligent-looking woman who piercing grey eyes missed nothing. Claire remembered that their son had dropped Gilbert's granddaughter in favor of another.

"I wonder, Sidra," Claire had said, having accepted, at Lady Ranapui's insistence, that she use her first name, "if you would mind listening to some changes that I've made to the marriage vows that Prince Pem and I will recite."

---

[1]Recites: Slang for the time it takes to speak the Recitations (Liturgy), about a minute.

"Of course, Lady Claire," Sidra had returned, having reacted with horror when Claire had suggested that she address her as just Claire.

When Claire had finished, Sidra first said, "Oh my!" She put her hand to her mouth, and then had said, "I must think about it." A moment later she broke out in a broad smile and announced, "Oh, I like your words, Lady Claire, even though I'm sure they will stir up some trouble."

She giggled behind her hand and looked about the room where other guests were talking in that animated fashion that people use when they have very little of substance to say and yet wish it to seem important. "Some here will hate it, but most will like it, even if they are afraid to admit it in public. My husband, of course, will heartily disapprove of your change and tell me that all Lunarian society will be likely to collapse as others adopt your new language. It will be all the new fashion, you know."

"Perhaps no more so than those," Claire pointed to the pockets artfully sculpted into Sidra's formal dress. "Four years ago, ladies in Lunaria did not have pockets in their clothing. Lady Tess liked the idea and introduced the practice. Obviously it spread rapidly."

Leandra interrupted Claire's daydream. "Gathering wool again, dear? You really must learn not to do this when you need all your wits about you. Eurita has left to find her seat with Vlaze Royard. Since her mother is not here, you must give Tess encouragement in her place. Reyfort has arrived."

Thank goodness for that, Claire thought. She approached Tess who was, in Claire's mother's slang, throwing a hissy fit.

"I can't go; my dress is all wrong. What if these new buttons pop off? What if Reyfort's uniform clashes with my gown?" Tess looked as if she were going to faint.

"Tess!" Claire seized hold of her friend's hand. "Get hold of yourself. I can't believe that you are worried about a little thing like a button after I saw you swing your sword through that savage's neck on the Redclaw! If you had missed, he'd have thrust his spear right through your heart."

"Yes, well," Tess took a deep breath. "I suppose that really was more important." She took another deep breath and held it for a moment before swallowing. "Show me to Reyfort; we'd best get this over with." She strode to the canvas panel, and one of the attendants pulled the hanging aside.

Tess came to an abrupt halt. In front of her, a handsome, elderly trooper in a splendid Reserve-Captain's uniform stood straight and tall with his dress hat in his hands. The gold piping and cream trim on his sleeves set off the polished brass buttons and the gleaming sword that hung at his side. He bowed low to Tess.

"Lady Tess, I am most pleased to see you after all this time," old Reyfort's voice had lost none of its gentleness and concern. "You are simply stunning, as usual," he allowed himself to grin as he offered Tess his arm. "I believe you are due to marry Fitz in a few minutes, and I don't want him to faint with worry before you are joined." He winked at Claire across Tess's shoulder.

"See to it that they are married, old friend," Claire greeted the trooper who had kept her alive at Greyhaven and had taught her so much. "So long as she runs free of Fitz's clutches, she is a menace to the entire Corps."

"Of course, Lady Claire," the trooper drew Tess from the doorway. "This way, my dear. If I am to give you away, I want to do it on time."

Moments later, even though it was merely the warm-up event, Claire heard the roar of the crowd as the orchestra struck up a military march. She pictured how it would go and was sorry she could not be there to see her friends exchange their vows in front of half of Lumminea.

A stab of jealousy caught Claire by surprise. *I am angry because Tess has her mother here.*

Then, the crowd quieted down, and Claire could make out the voices of Fitz and Tess. A few minutes passed in silence while Claire worried that the crowd was reacting negatively to her new ceremony. Abruptly there was wild cheering and the band began playing a lively march. Apparently everything was a success. She would sorely miss Tess, for her friend would be going back to the palace with her new husband while she would depart the ceremony with Pem and head directly for the royal yacht to begin her honeymoon. She hoped Tess would be able to complete the refurbishing of the royal apartment in time for her return with Pem.

Wedding Vows

CLAIRE WAS SUFFERING from a case of nerves that was as bad as Tess's had been. Leandra had a hard time convincing her that everything was going to work out.

"The people loved it," the Sage repeated several times. "The only grumbling our observers reported was from a few of the ministers and Council members like Torvall Garrund and Wetzar Hussani's wife."

"Alcinia?" Claire became interested in spite of her heart being about to pound its way through her ribs.

"I think Lady Alcinia is jealous of the Royal Jewelry," Gilbert's voice sounded behind her. "The Hussani mines no longer produce such fine gemstones."

"Gilbert! I'm terrified." Claire rushed into his arms.

And blushed as she backed away. "Well, that wasn't very dignified," she muttered, angry with her display of emotion.

Gilbert laughed. "I get one last time with the girl who came to stay in Lunaria," he said lightly. "Hereafter, I am to tremble before the woman who took the reins of power so quickly." He offered her his arm.

Before she slipped her arm through his, Claire studied her friend and mentor, the Lord of Greyhaven, the last male in the line of Greybaird, until now a line unbroken for more than a thousand years.

"Gilbert," she said, "for hereafter I shall have to address you as the Lord Privy Counselor in public, I see what you have had in mind for Lunaria all along. Your explanation of blood, honor, and loyalty did not mean so much to me until today. And now I am at loss for words, unless it is to tell you this." Claire came forward and whispered into Gilbert's ear.

Only Leandra was in a position to observe the expression on her friend's face as he shook his head. "Lady, you give me too much credit, but I thank you with all my heart. And now, we should go."

Leandra hoped that Gilbert would share this moment later as she watched Gilbert and Claire cross the small field of trampled grass between their pavilion and the entrance to the grand stage. A guard of palace troopers, splendid in their purple and gold uniforms, formed a wall on both sides of the pair. Beyond the stage, Leandra could feel the restless tension of the crowds of people as they waited breathlessly. Notes from a single trumpet echoed pure and clear in the air. There was a crash of cymbols, and the orchestra struck up the Coronation March. The Sage abandoned the ladies pavilion and none opposed her when she stationed herself where she could look out over the stage and the audience. The time had arrived.

The moment Pem entered from stage right and Claire and Gilbert started across from stage left, pandemonium reigned. If the music from the massed orchestra wasn't enough, the cheering from the crowd was stupendous in volume. She felt beautiful in her flowing green gown and emerald crescent—not at all like an ordinary girl from Ridgeville. Her heels gave her added height and a feeling of power. Approaching her, Pem looked handsome and impressive in his simple black uniform with gold trim, three stars, and the decorations he had won during the war with Tieben.

Claire was nearly deaf by the time she joined Pem at the center of the flower-strewn floor. Behind her the Liturgy of the Nine glowed in huge, golden letters against a blue background. The background was topped by a blue velvet banner with the image of the crescent moon. They faced the audience and watched the High Temporate walking up an elaborate ramp carpeted in deep green and gold patterns of the Temperate iconography, the triangle and the crescent of G'rama.

Delagus the Second wasted no time when he arrived in front of them arrayed in his white robes. A man of impressive stage presence, he turned and raised his arms above his head just as the thunderous Coronation March ended. The sudden silence that descended upon the arena was as deafening to Claire as the music and cheering had been.

It had been Pem's idea to open the ceremony with the Liturgy. As Delagus's amplified voice read the lines, the response from the audience washed across them like the ocean's surf. The final lines of the ceremony would come later, Claire's addition based on what she could remember of a wedding that she had attended in Ridgeville.

Nine Worlds to rule the Heavens,
(And Nine to Rule the Worlds.)
The King to rule the Nine,
(And the People to rule the King.)
Nine Paths to Guide the People
(To the mind and heart of G'rama.)

As DELAGUS SPOKE the final line, "Nine Paths to Guide the People," he received the final response, "To the mind and heart of G'rama."

The High Temperate held his hands high and a great silence descended across the crowd, broken only by the sound of a vendor hawking beer and sausages along the top benches at the end of the arena. There was some scattered, good natured laughter while a guard clapped a hand over the vendor's mouth and dragged him off.

At this point, Gilbert stepped away to the side of the stage where he received two bundles from a nervous page. Timone sat next to the edge of the stage, in plain view, with eyes and ears alert to every detail. Timone terrorized the pages, and today was no exception. Somehow, Timone, offspring of the off-world Curly and a cave cat, always showed up in Tess or Claire's presence.

As she stood by Pem's side in front of the great audience, Claire realized that in some ways she'd been preparing for this moment since she first entered Lunaria and stood with Pem, knife in hand, as they were surrounded by shadowy men on warhorses. At the time, of course, she didn't know that Captain Allain and his troopers were friends to Pem.

Allain had seen that the girl with Pem was staunch and true, a young warrior with a power of her own to be reckoned with. Gilbert, too, had seen this, and so had become Claire's friend and mentor. Now, paths set long ago were coming together.

The High Temporate's voice rolled across the many rows of seats, across the bleacher in the stands, and on out across the city and countryside where a whisper of the proceedings crossed even the River Lorne and continued to the hills in the west. To the east, the words of Delagus reached the desert and beyond, while in the north, One Mother bent her leaves and branches and listened intently.

"And so, Lunarians, we are gathered here in the presence of G'rama to unite this man and this woman so that Lunaria may once again prosper under her Monarchy."

There were a few questions concerning identities and contractual arrangements that satisfied the basic Lunarian ceremony, and then came the trade of Claire's and Pem's simple vows.

The silence grew so thick that Claire could hear the birds in the palace gardens chirping, the waters of the River Lorne breaking against the stone pilings in the harbor, and the grinding of the gears in the great Tower Time Keeper of Lumminea. Pem's breathing slowed to match her own, and her heart slowed to match a rhythm that she felt pulsing in the earth beneath the stage.

Pem took Claire's hands in his and stared unflinchingly into her eyes. "I, Prince Pemburton of Lunaria, do solemnly swear by G'rama that I shall be true to you by reasons of my blood, my honor, and my loyalty all the days of my life. I swear to protect and defend not only you, but all the people of Lunaria."

Claire reversed her grip and took Pem's hand in hers. "I, Claire Ellen Fisher, a free citizen of my world, do solemnly swear by G'rama that I shall be true to both you as well as Lunaria by reasons of my blood, my honor, and my loyalty all the days of my life."

Delagus motioned to Gilbert who moved forward with his two bundles wrapped in black velvet.

He untied the first, a small bundle, and handed Pem a golden ring. The second bundle was much larger and contained Pem's golden sword. He presented the sword to Claire and then returned to his place nearby.

By tradition, when Pem stepped forward, Claire would have knelt to him. This time, when Pem stepped forward, Claire bowed, then stood upright and tall, and extending her left hand.

"With this ring, I wed thee who are now the Queen of Lunaria," Pem said solemnly as he slipped the golden ring upon her finger.

Claire looked at the ring on her finger, surprised that it hadn't turned into a tiny red serpent. Pem bowed before her, and then stood tall and proud.

"With this sword, I wed thee who are now the King of Lunaria," she said, presenting him with his golden sword. The moment his fingers touched the sword Claire felt her ring and Trader Amulet flash fiery hot and the world about her seemed to shatter into a swirl of bright sparks of energy that quickly joined together to reconstruct the image of Pem before her and the rest of the world around him. She felt momentarily detached and drifting, but Pem appeared not to have noticed anything.

Pem and Claire came together, their arms intertwined about each other's waist. Pem presented his sword to the audience while Claire held up her hand with the ring shining brightly on her third finger.

There were a few cheers and some rude conversation amongst the Council members, but, for the most part, the silence remained absolute. It was in the program: Don't clap or cheer until The High Temporate finishes.

Delagus sighed, looking at each of them closely as if trying to decide something. Finally, he licked his lips, removing a small black stone from his pocket and held it up.

"By the powers vested in me as the High Temporate and a representative of G'rama on this world, I declare you King and Queen of Lunaria." He waved the stone and a great flash of light blinded everyone except Claire, who had guessed, and Delagus, who knew what was coming and had closed his eyes. And, of course, Gilbert who kept a silent watch off to one side with his hand to his knife, just in case.

While Pem was still a bit confused, Delagus turned to the crowd that was beginning to cheer and clap. "Let the festivities begin," his voice projected across the theater and into the streets beyond. The orchestra struck up a wild dance tune and people were milling about in excitement.

"How did you know, my dear?" Delagus leaned in close to Claire to be heard over the uproar.

She acknowledged his curiosity with a nod of her head. "I know a little of the powers of the black stone," she told him, thinking back to Curly's escape to her world leaving her all alone at Greyhaven.

She made a brief query of the surrounding nanites and followed a hair-thin entropy channel connecting her ring with Pem's sword. What it meant, she wasn't sure, but it hadn't been there before. She now knew that it wasn't the marriage that sealed the power of the Monarchy, but a fragment from one of the powerful black stones that were once part of an inconceivable transportation network connecting the Nine Worlds. A lost secret, she wondered. How had Delagus obtained his shard of the special stone? From experience, she knew that the stone slowly evaporated over time when it was separated from its environment. She put all this firmly out of her mind. She would deal with this later. She must deal with the present.

"You might at least have warned us," Pem said crossly to Delagus. He rubbed his eyes with his knuckles. "You have an orange aura about you, Lady Claire," he muttered.

If Delagus felt badly about this lapse, his face didn't show it. "I'm told that the results are better if the party involved doesn't anticipate," he returned.

"Quickly, this celebration may get out of hand," Gilbert urged them from the stage.

Claire looked out on the arena where a contest was going on between the crowds of Lummineans and the guards who were trying to escort the notables to their coaches which waited to whisk them away to celebrations that would last far into the night. It seemed that the majority of people from the back bleachers were determined to collect some important souvenirs.

A message would be hand delivered to each of the major fetes, a personal note of regret from the King and Queen, each saying how unfortunate that they could not attend this particular worthy celebration being given in their honor. In truth, Pem and Claire were going almost directly to the royal yacht where they would enjoy a celebration with a few friends.

Welcome aboard the Rachael Ann

.THANKS BE TO .G'rama! For once, Lord Gilbert has an assignment that matches my talents. First Officer Nikko waited impatiently for the arrival of the royal party at the foot of the boarding ramp leading to the deck of the Royal Yacht, the Rachael Ann. He made sure that his cap was set straight instead of its usual jaunty angle, and rubbed every trace of dust from the tops of his polished shoes on the backs of his trouser legs. After all, not only was Lord Gilbert accompanying them a short way to Port Maripas at the head of the Bay of Lunaria, but the formidable Captain Eberson would also be aboard during most of the sail. Officer Nikko knew that nothing escaped the Old Man's eyes.

The sun had set and the cool evening air would be an encouragement to the many outdoor balls and celebrations. Nikko imagined all the lovely ladies in their new ball gowns, all waiting for him to ask them onto the floor where he would hold them lightly, one hand pressed to their bare back, the other holding warm fingers pressed between his. Ah, the mysterious and inviting eyes of all those lovely women. He shook his head in amusement at his fantasy and kept his eyes on the hillside above the harbor.

At last! The royal party was wending its way down the Palace Hill on the southern side of the town center of Lumminea. Unanticipated delays at the Palace had thrown the schedule off by a few hours. The boulevard crossed back and forth along the hill, and Nikko could not only see the colorful lanterns and the pennants of the royal couple flying above the carriages and their escorts, but he could hear the enthusiastic cheers of the Lummineans greeting their new King and Queen. The many Balls and parties would be held far into the night, even to dawn, without the presence of the royal couple. Nikko reflected that not a single citizen would begrudge them this time for themselves.

The Rachael Ann, named for Queen Rachael's great aunt, lay sparkling with her freshly-painted white hull and polished bronze fittings in the Royal Yacht Basin on the crystal waters of the River Redwine. The glow of a hundred lanterns hung along her railings and were reflected in the waters that lazily circled not only the Palace grounds but also flowed alongside the orchards and groves of Claire's upstream holdings.

She was as shipshape as it was possible to make her, Nikko thought proudly. He'd overseen every detail from inspecting the steerage linkages to the polished shields on the entropy engines. He had no official command capacity on the Navy ship, his only authority being his appointment as Gilbert's official liaison in charge of the King's security. He'd hardly dared to hope that he might be allowed to sail with her on the royal honeymoon, but here he was, in his dress whites, waiting to greet the new King and Claire—the Queen, he corrected himself and grinned. The same girl whom he'd befriended when she first came up the River Songris on the Fortuna—on her way to Lord Gilbert's holding at Greyhaven. Captain Eberson must have put in a good word for him with the Rachael Ann's naval commander, Captain Agkor.

Suddenly, he blushed at the thought of when he had tried to seduce Gilbert's young charge. Thank heavens she'd been much too intelligent and self-possessed to respond to his flirtations. Young Lady Claire had even managed to keep her lusty companion, Tess of Tribana, out of his bed—and that was probably equally as lucky because Tess had just married the newly promoted Commander of the King's Brigade and Palace Guard. Nikko didn't especially fancy bad blood between himself and the Royal Marines!

He consoled himself with the happy thought that Claire's Head of Chambers, the effervescent Mags, would be accompanying her mistress on the voyage. Mags was not only unattached, intelligent, and beautiful, but her eyes were full of the kind of mischief that Nikko wanted to share.

Gradually the crowds trickled into the small square facing the ship's landing. A squad of Marines gently pressed them back until there was plenty of space for the royal carriage to descend the last loop and clatter into the square.

The first out of the carriage was the handsome King Pemburton, resplendent in his dress uniform as High Communicate. The pleats of his creamy white trousers could have cut your hand, Nikko noted in admiration. The shine on his deep purple boots seemed to light up the square. His white jacket with purple trim was drawn carelessly back, and Nikko could see the gleam of the King's sword hanging at his side. What a splendid fellow, he thought. I hope he deserves Claire's hand.

Pem paused, waved to the cheering crowd, turned and gave his hand to his new Queen, Queen Claire of Lunaria, who descended gracefully from the high carriage. If anything the cheering grew even wilder as she stood beside her King in her green silk gown with pale orange wrap draped over her arms. Nikko noted that she was almost the same height as the king. When she waved at the crowd, he felt the warmth of her smile across the square from the foot of the boarding ramp. He took one step forward, stopped, and came to attention which was the signal for the Marine Officer of the Guard to extend the line of his men from the carriage to the edge of the docks. Behind him, the honor guard of sailors dressed in immaculate whites, the traditional purple scarf of the royal yacht knotted about each of their collars, came to attention and prepared to pipe the King aboard his ship, as was the ancient custom.

Nikko thought that this was a happy return of the monarchy to the sea, an arena which the former Queen Rachael had not liked and had often neglected during her brief reign, preferring the horse cavalry and the thunder of hooves over the romance of the seas.

"The ship is ready for your inspection, Sir," Nikko saluted Pem and bowed to Claire as the couple approached the gangway. It was a formality; the King was never expected to actually inspect the ship.

Nikko was surprised when Pem said, "I will take my Lady on a tour of the ship before our guests arrive."

"Yes sir, I will assign a seaman as duty escort for you," he managed, mind racing to decide who he could assign to this delicate task.

"No need, Officer Nikko," Pem waved his hand negligently. "I am familiar with every nook and cranny in the old ship."

"Yes, of course, sir."

Nikko was thinking Lord Gilbert will have me flogged if something happens to either of these children when Claire spoke up.

"Don't you think it's terribly nice of the First to offer an escort when he's trying to get everyone on board?" She smiled brightly at Pem who rolled his eyes.

"Officer Nikko," Claire continued. "Have you seen to placing my orange cat on board? I would not like to leave Timone behind."

"I'm terribly sorry," Nikko stuttered, "but I could not catch this Timone. He plainly did not want to leave the Palace. I did try my best." He pulled up one sleeve and showed Claire some deep scratches on the back of his wrist.

Claire looked vexed, but Pem seemed to brighten. "I'm sure your cat knows best. Besides, there would be nobody to look after him when we get to the Southern Beaches."

Taking the opportunity, Nikko ventured, "Perhaps the royal couple would like to settle into their quarters first. There is chilled wine and a platter of snacks waiting in your private suite."

Pem looked gloomy. "I suppose it would be better to settle in. We could have a moment alone, couldn't we?"

Suddenly Pem grinned and grabbed Claire's hand. "This tour can definitely wait. Has Gilbert arrived?"

"I see him now," Nikko indicated the square where a number of carriages with guests were arriving in a clatter of iron wheels on stone. Gilbert was already striding across the cobbles towards them.

Nikko turned back and caught Claire winking at him from behind Pem. "We'll leave you to your duties."

"Yes, leave Nikko to his duties, by all means." Pem put an arm on Claire's waist and guided her across the short bridge between the dock and the opening in the ship's rail.

Nikko heard her exclaim, "Oh, Pem, it looks so perfect! What a wonderful idea to go on a cruise for our honeymoon."

He was still thinking about this strange behavior from Lady Claire when someone cleared their throat behind him. He whirled to confront Lord Gilbert smiling at him.

"She's quite a young woman, is she not?" Gilbert chuckled affectionately. "I think Pem will find himself anticipated no matter which way he turns."

"Sir, yes Sir," Nikko could find nothing safe to say. Behind him the pipes sounded indicating that the High Communicate had been officially welcomed.

"Everything snug and shipshape?" Gilbert asked.

"I checked out everything personally," Nikko nodded. "Your favorite wine and smoked meats are waiting, and dinner has been scheduled to begin as soon as we have received our guests and we get underway. The steward has laid out fresh clothing more suitable for the voyage." Nikko referred to the formal attire of the Privy Counselor that Gilbert was wearing.

"And welcome, too, Nikko," Gilbert sighed and pulled at his tight collar. "I would prefer to jump into the river and drown rather than spend a few minutes more in this costume."

"Lady Claire's cat has chosen to remain behind," Nikko added.

"I thought the cat might remain," Gilbert returned. "Leandra has told me that Timone is no ordinary animal. Sometimes I think he speaks to me, though I cannot understand the language. I will be glad for someone in addition to Fitz to be watching over Tess while I am gone to Maripas."

"Sir, Magister," Nikko whipped to attention as Leandra joined them.

Leandra looked the First Officer up and down. "Very handsome, Officer Nikko. More discipline than I expect you are used to? I suppose you will do. Are you going to escort me aboard, Gilbert? You know how I am with water."

Nikko was unable to keep from blushing at the Sage's remarks.

Alone at Last?

THERE WERE SOCIAL amenities to be got through, some much more pleasurable than others. Time spent welcoming Turlo and Rissa on board was a great pleasure as was the greeting of Captains Eberson and Watchman. Meeting Captain Agkor was more of a strain, and the mandatory inspection of the ship's crew somewhat tedious.

Neither Claire nor Pem had envisioned their first night aboard the Rachael Ann in quite the way that reality forced upon them. Pem seemed especially disturbed and complained immediately about the lack of privacy to Gilbert who merely smiled and nodded his head.

"Yes, Sire," he had said. "Everything is exactly the way you wanted it." Pem had merely spluttered, much to Claire's amusement, though she took pains to hide her reaction.

FINALLY, EVERYTHING NEEDFUL had been done. It was Claire's first time, and she approached the event with all the aplomb that a young woman without experience could muster, praying all the while that what Leandra had told her and Mags had hinted at would be enough to get her through.

It had all seemed so romantic and exciting when she discussed everything with Mags, and all so clinical and remote when she listened to Leandra. And then she had looked upon the real Pem as they were boarding the Rachael Ann and had faltered. Here was this alien creature walking by her side; his sense of ownership did more to irritate her than his solicitous hand on her waist that guided her up the gangway did to reassure her. Wasn't there something about walking the plank? At least she had avoided a tour of the boat, and wasn't Nikko still so very charming and ready to help her? Too bad he hadn't gotten her cat on board. She often found Timone's presence comforting.

Then she realized that the look Pem gave her as she finally stepped aboard was one of pure terror. No wonder he wanted to give her a tour of the Rachael Ann—he was putting off the moment they would be alone together. Perhaps she was as alien to him as he was to her. She managed to amuse herself with the thought that maybe the tales of his adventures during the war were just that—merely imagination bolstering a fragile ego. What was it that Granny Miller had told her? That all men were really just little boys inside?

The Wedding Night

."THANK YOU, MAGS, .that will be all," Claire gulped a deep breath and closed the door firmly in Mags' face. She turned to look at herself in the mirror and studied what she saw.

The hair that the royal dresser had so carefully coifed for the wedding ceremony was now artfully mussed—teased just-so by Mags with her shell comb. Her face had a fresh-scrubbed quality that Mags had created with a tiny touch of rouge at the apex of her cheek bones. There was the lightest touch of eye shadow to make her large eyes look even deeper and more mysterious—perhaps Mags had overdone it there. The green gown was of the sheerest silk that managed to hide everything and nothing all at the same time. Her amulet hung from her neck for protection; she would not allow herself to remove it even for a moment. Suppose she and Pem were to be attacked by a wild channel while they were.... Claire felt herself blushing and filled with uncertainties. Suppose Pem found her ugly?

Where was Granny Miller when she needed her? She remembered the graying blue eyes of her grandmother looking at her in sympathy, as if she knew what was coming, and her words *you will understand everything when the time comes.*

"Let things come naturally and unforced," she had said with a sad smile. "You will know where your heart lies, so follow what it tells you."

Claire looked into her heart and saw more confusion than certainty. Had this union with Pem come too soon? Her heart pounded and she felt weak even though the woman in the mirror seemed perfectly steady.

"Do I want to do this?" she asked herself out loud, watching the lips move and the blood flowing into her cheeks under the rouge. I think I won't be needing the makeup.

Where was her mother? Did her mother miss her? She should be standing beside her, telling her that everything would be all right. Her mother's absence angered her. For a moment she faltered as she couldn't remember either her mother's face or her smell.

She looked far more like her father—at least that is what everyone had told her, and the clean scent of him was sharp in her mind. She looked down at the dresser and saw the little yellow egg with its precious cargo of *silly putty*. She extended her inner vision and observed how the swirl of nanites avoided the presence of the alien material. She linked a thin channel to the tiny creatures and tried to form a picture of her and Pem together, but no image formed. The future remained mysterious. She raised her hand with the golden ring on her finger and saw it for what it was—one of the malleable, phage-objects of the Lunarian world whose most fundamental characteristics could be changed and molded by someone like herself. The ring was like Pem's sword and like her own Sword of Training—only Pem thought of his inheritance from the Windover line as a Sword and was unable to alter its nature.

Claire, on the other hand, knew her ring for an object of power. But what power? She was curious and planned to test this in the days and years to come. All she knew as she stood there in front of the mirror was that the moment the ring was placed upon her finger a new bond was forged, not only between herself and Pem, but also between Pem's Sword and her Ring. The amulet she wore around her neck continued to remain silent on this point, growing neither warm nor cool as the ring was slipped onto her finger.

A soft knock sounded at the inner entrance of her private dressing room. It was the door that opened into the Royal Bedchamber.

Claire tensed up. She wasn't ready for Pem just yet. She hurried to the door and leaned close to whisper through the crack. "Just a minute."

She heard Pem catch his breath on the other side of the panel. "Okay, no hurry," he whispered back.

Claire nearly laughed out loud with relief. So, Pem was not too sure of himself either.

She went back to the dresser where Mags had left a cup of strong spirits. She took a long draught, nearly choking on the burning liquid. Then, doing what Mags had suggested, she turned down the gas lamps on the walls of the chamber one-by-one. When she came back to the mirror, the dim light and soft shadows seemed to suit her much better.

She returned to the bedroom door and knocked; her heart pounded in exact rhythm with the muted throb of the engines two decks below. When she heard Pem's answering whisper she said, "I'm ready now." Her teeth chattered briefly as if she were chilled, though she found herself sweating profusely.

Pem's door opened into a dark room. A shadow that might be Pem was outlined briefly against an open porthole in the background. She could hear the gently swish of water passing by the hull outside. She put her hand out blindly and felt Pem's hand close on hers, drawing her into the room. The carpet was soft and thick against her bare feet. She kicked the door shut behind her, and let Pem draw her close to him.

Her hands felt the silkiness of his pajamas. She relaxed slightly as they found each other's lips in the dark and kissed

"I love you," Pem whispered in her ear.

"I love you too," she said.

Pem drew her to the bed, and she caught a glimpse of starry skies through the open porthole and smelled the nutrient-rich waters of the ancient river.

At first they fumbled about, kissing each other and pretending to be intimate. Then, at some point, Claire realized that she was ready, both in her feelings for Pem as well as her physical body, for whatever was going to happen. Her confidence seemed to be transmitted to Pem and after that things went more smoothly until almost without noticing what was happening, the moment was over and she lay with Pem, overcome with a feeling of detachment.

Suddenly Claire realized that Pem had turned over and was snoring lightly. She almost laughed at the forgotten memory of her mother's comments on marriage. Somehow the memory made her feel less lonely.

A Hazardous Mission for Rissa and Turlo.

THE SMALLER STATEROOM, identified as the Royal Salon by a brass plate over the door, was locked and secured by a bolt from within and two of Royard's best men standing at attention in the companionway outside.

Inside, in the center of the room, a conference table dominated the space. The top was made from a single slab of heartwood. Seven of the eight elegant chairs were sculpted from lesser wood while a single, more massive, more intricately carved version sat ready to receive the royal backside at the head. The walls were decorated with finely carved moldings and a spray of fresh lilies had been placed in a green and orange vase on a sideboard laden with dishes of delicate fruits, platters of rare cheeses and smoked meats of various kinds. Several bottles of the best wines including Claire's estate vintages were open and breathing. A tray of crystal wine glasses, each with a picture of the Rachael Ann and the date of her keel-laying etched into its body, waited for thirsty guests.

Gilbert set out a small tattle on the massive conference table as an added security measure and indicated that Pem should sit at the head of the table facing the outer corridor. He sat at Pem's left side once Claire had seated herself at the King's right hand. Turlo and Rissa sat together facing Captains Eberson and Watchman. At the other end of the table, Sage Leandra repositioned her chair to watch the porthole to the outside and nodded to Gilbert.

Claire put her hand on her Trader amulet, a gift from Rissa and Rissa's mother, Mara Ellendor. She performed her own security probe throughout the ship but detected nothing in the way of unusual activity from the mist of ever-present nanocreatures.

"Why such extreme security measures, Gilbert?" Pem asked peevishly. "Aren't we safe aboard my own yacht?"

"While I am certain of the loyalty of the Rachael Ann's officers, and Officer Nikko had been most thorough in checking out the crew, surely the Tieben Ambassador and his staff will have managed to compromise someone," Gilbert retorted.

Claire felt Pem's resistance to Gilbert stiffen. She put her hand on her husband's arm and smiled. Pem turned his attention in her direction, still looking irritated.

He said, "Darling, isn't it nice that we won't have to worry about anything?"

"I for one am grateful that so many of our true friends are in this room with us, sharing the very beginning of your reign and a new era for Lunaria," she said.

"Of course," Pem immediately softened and looked around at the people that he most loved and trusted. "Foolish of me to complain, Gilbert. I know that you are only doing what I have asked."

Gilbert took this to mean that he should call the meeting to order.

"As you know, I will be getting off the Rachael Ann at Maripas. I will be returning to Lumminea where I will be continuing to assist the Regent in shifting the details of the Communicate's official job from himself to our new King. Pem, this means you don't have to spend half your life signing paperwork," he joked and earned a chuckle around the table.

"I'm sorry," Gilbert nodded at Pem and Claire, "that I have not had the opportunity to talk with you about a plan that I, along with Captains Watchman and Eberson, have been hatching. Until Turlo and Rissa agreed, there was not much point in bringing up the subject." He looked at Turlo who nodded his head and placed his hand over Rissa's on top of the table.

Turlo addressed his remarks to Claire and Pem.

"Rissa and I think that the attacks on the Trader shipping, like the attack on Rissa's Redclaw, are the work of my uncle and factions here in Lunaria."

Pem and Claire both nodded. They had discussed these possibilities since returning to Lumminea and concluded that Torvall Garrund was probably behind the faked banditry.

"Veral Hushara would like nothing better than breaking the monopoly that the Traders have on shipping and especially the flow of commercial credit," Turlo said. "Some, perhaps many, think this would be a good thing. Some of your council members in Lunaria believe that if the Traders' hold on credit were broken, then their profits would rise dramatically."

Rissa frowned. "They are wrong. The Trader banks are the only ones capable of handling these transactions. Hushara's and your Council's form of monopoly would create higher prices through artificial scarcity and tight government controls."

"Because of the scarcity and higher prices, the Communicate would become unpopular with the people," Claire added, shaking her head. "The Monarchy would be threatened and the control the people have over the Council would be diminished, if not destroyed. Sounds like a plan that Torvall Garrund would love."

Beside her, Pem scoffed. "Don't you think that is an exaggeration?"

Turlo shook his head negatively. If he were surprised at Claire's outburst, his expression didn't show it.

Turlo said, "That's why Rissa and I have decided to secretly leave the Rachael Ann and return to Boggrash."

"We're sorry not to accompany you to the Southern Beaches; I was looking forward to spending time there," Rissa said to Claire, "but Turlo and I agree that we must find some way to stop Veral Hushara's interference in Lunaria's affairs before he starts another war."

Claire's stomach contracted. "I really wish you wouldn't leave us," she said. "I have made plans. We were going to have such fun. It was a horrible way for us to leave you—rushing down the river into a curtain of fire while we swam safely to shore. Besides, what can you and Turlo do?"

Turlo chuckled. "I seem to recall that you may have had a more dangerous time of it than we did."

He grew serious again. "There is not much time for me to lay the political groundwork in Tieben. I must be prepared to grab the reins of power and take control of Tieben."

Claire felt dazed. "I thought you were adamantly opposed to becoming Tieben's ruler. Don't I recall a certain marriage proposal that you were running from when we met you?"

"True," Turlo admitted, "but I changed my mind when I met Rissa."

"And Rissa's mother more or less told you that unless you took up your responsibilities in Tieben, she wouldn't grant you her daughter's hand in marriage," Gilbert broke in.

"She made me promise," Turlo looked glum for a moment. "I always keep my promises."

"Only because I wouldn't run off with you," Rissa laughed.

"Well, there's that," Turlo complained in good humor.

"So, how do you propose to do this?" Pem seemed curious.

"We will rendezvous with the Fortuna where the Bay of Lunaria opens into the Southern Ocean," Captain Eberson spoke up for the first time. "Captain Watchman will join us and we will make our way up the west coast and meet with a Trader ship out of Boggrash. Prince Turlo and Trader Rissa will accompany Captain Watchman on the Trader vessel which will take them to a landing on the coast north of Boggrash."

Turlo took up the plan, "After that, we will make out way secretly into Tieben using an unwatched Trader's route that crosses the mountains west of Snowy Pass. It will be open this time of year. We will descend on the north side along the waters of the river that flows toward Wintermarsh. We must avoid prematurely exposing my presence to those who wish to prevent my return."

"In Norcross, we will meet with our friends Brey and Blossom who will put us in contact with the people who want to put me forward as the heir to the Tieben throne. It is imperative that I make a public declaration in both Norcross and Wintermarsh that I have decided to take up my Uncle Veral's cause, though perhaps not in the way that he intended," Turlo grinned wolfishly.

"Our belief is that Veral won't dare move against Turlo if he brings the support of the Traders with him," Gilbert nodded in Rissa's direction. "That is also the risk."

"It's too dangerous for Rissa," Claire declared. "Mara would never allow you to do this," she turned to her friend.

"Actually, my mother is the one who suggested it," Rissa returned. "She will soon turn over the Ellendor household to my control. There are other things she wishes to do with the rest of her life. The House of Ellendor still commands the control of our counsels. It will be a powerful bargaining chip."

"The way we see it," Turlo spoke directly to Pem, "a strong monarchy in Lunaria is in Tieben's best interest. Any weakening of the Communicate in Lunaria threatens us with instability because of the powerful trade imbalance if Lunaria should move against the Traders."

"But that could never happen," Pem protested. "I am insulted by your suggestion that the Communicate might weaken."

"If you are insulted, then I apologize," Turlo said quietly. "But Claire, herself, espoused a similar scenario that Rissa and I think is all too likely."

"Well, perhaps insulted is too strong a word," Pem agreed. "But I do think that your being here implies that I am somehow interfering in Tieben's internal affairs. Ambassador Castri will undoubtedly want to know what your position with us is. He'd hardly believe that you were simply here to attend our wedding."

"But it's true, in a way," Claire argued. "And though Turlo arrived in Lunaria more by chance than design, he is certainly here by our personal invitation—as is Rissa. Pem doesn't really take up his authority until he returns to Lumminea, and Turlo has no official status in Tieben at this moment, so the two of you occupy similar positions, at least for a few more days."

Neither Pem nor Turlo looked very happy with this assessment.

"To put it baldly," Gilbert broke in, "Turlo and Rissa are taking a considerable risk which, if they succeed, will practically guarantee a more prosperous Lunaria as well as Tieben. If they fail, then you have lost nothing and the positions remain mostly unchanged, though not quite as favorable since the Trader faction will be weakened."

"All this for a bit of cooperation that no one will be able to admit took place," Gilbert sighed. "I too wish that you would change your minds—especially you, Rissa, for I am very fond of you. May G'rama forbid that something should happen. I know your mother well. If something does happen, she would never forgive me for not having dissuaded you."

Sage Leandra broke her silence, startling some at the table who had forgotten her presence. "Everything each of you has said is true in its own way."

"But…" Claire felt a chill as her inner sight looked past the Sage's mask and saw her as the aging woman that Leandra kept hidden from others.

"…but, you describe Garrund and Hushara as the evil you face. You are mistaken to believe that the rift between you is between good and evil. Perhaps Garrund and Hushara are wrong; perhaps their solution for the problems facing this world is not the best one for all of its people. But if you wish to understand the battle between good and evil, then you need to look only at one person who sits at this table."

"Gilbert?" Claire said. "Gilbert is the best man I know."

Pem nodded, followed by everyone else except Leandra and Watchman—and Gilbert, who looked amused.

Gilbert smiled ruefully. "I'm delighted to foster such confidence, but I don't think Sage Leandra means me. She means Lady Claire."

Claire opened her mouth to object. She meant to say, *I am an ordinary girl from Ridgeville.*

Watchman held up his hand in anticipation. "Before you deny this, Lady Claire, I watched you on the Redclaw and know that what Sage Leandra says is true. What attacked us in the White Desert was not a savage onslaught by greedy barbarians or hungry peasants. Those attacks were driven by evil. The intent to slaughter us wasn't about booty or ransom, it was about blood lust."

"The big fellow who calls himself Oul," Pem said. "I sensed the difference when he led the attack on Fitz and our men. There was something about him that was far beyond simple savagery. There was an evil intelligence at work behind those dark eyes."

"It's the group of Magisters who call themselves the Dark Sages," Leandra spoke. "Jallis Ruffin leads them. They are not allied with either Garrund or with Tieben. They wish to rule this world. The Black Council is their instrument."

"And you represent the White Council," Pem said, half-jokingly.

"Don't be foolish," Leandra snapped. "There is no White Council or anything of the sort."

"The person who represents "good" in Lunaria is Claire Fisher."

Attack on the Rachael Ann!

GILBERT HAD DESCRIBED the defenses of the royal yacht to Claire when she had expressed her concern at having enjoyed three months in Lumminea without a single incident or attack directed against herself or Pem.

"It's unnaturally quiet, Gilbert," she had said. "If an attack comes, don't you think it might be while Pem and I are on our honeymoon?"

Gilbert had agreed and responded with a security report written for Claire personally by the Royal Engineering staff which said that the shields surrounding the royal yacht were among the best. These tattle shields were distributed around the vessel like the little magnetic monopoles that scientists of Claire's world were always seeking but never finding. As the engineer explained, the enemy started out with a high probability of projecting his weapon into one location and wound up arriving at a different location where his own weapon sort of bounced back at him and blew him to little bits and pieces. Claire, with her experience in reflecting Ruffin's attack back upon himself, was satisfied with this explanation but decided to remain alert.

Three days of peaceful progress down the River Lorne ended in the middle of a typical, balmy summer night while they were slipping through a peaceful stretch of water meandering through the rich farmland of the south. The attack on the Rachael Ann, when it came, was unexpectedly sophisticated and managed somehow to contaminate the nanites belonging to the engine shielding before it dissipated prematurely in a flash that killed one unlucky crewmember, and burned three more by the tool locker. The explosion blew a hole through the steel deck underneath and into the locker where the Captain kept his best wines.

In spite of all the precautions, a small imperfection had been introduced into the engine's nano-shielding that could have been fatal to all on board if it had gone undetected. Fortunately, First Office Nikko Pizzar was experienced in such things. After recovering his singed cap from the mangled remains of a locker, checking the state of his hair, and saying the proper last lament of G'rama for the lost crewmember, Tara, he hit the emergency button that summoned Rachael Ann's medics and her entropy shield technician. While he waited for the emergency team, he talked briefly with a crewman whom he asked to find a blanket to cover Tara's body.

On arrival, the shield technician assessed the damage, called Captain Agkor, who called in Gilbert, who went to rouse Claire in the Royal Quarters.

"Something happening?" Claire stumbled groggily across the deck, remembered to pull a robe around her bare body, and cracked the outside door. Pem's snores continued unabated behind her.

"Gilbert? I felt a lurch. Something flashed red."

"Sorry to disturb you, Lady Claire, but there is something that may require your skills," Gilbert returned. There was an undercurrent of urgency in Gilbert's voice that brought Claire fully awake. She pulled the door open further and slipped out into the hall.

"Lord Privy Counselor, do we have time to get some clothes on under this robe?" she asked Gilbert who coughed and averted his eyes.

"I think we need only one kind of emergency at a time," he said. "Is Pem awake?"

"Not yet. I'll be back in a moment," she patted Gilbert's arm and slipped back into her stateroom where she frantically pulled on underwear, pants, and shirt.

"Breakfast so soon?" Pem's sleepy voice sounded from under the bed covers.

"There's an emergency somewhere. I'll be with Gilbert." She tugged slippers onto her feet and made sure that her amulet was in place against her chest. The ring on her finger was glowing warm.

"I'll have the eggs and smoked grazer," Pem said.

"That's fine, dear. Follow me as quickly as you can," Claire slipped out the door knowing that Pem would wake up soon and come storming after her, confused but ready to fight.

"Come!" Gilbert set off down the corridor toward the stern hatch that led to the lower decks. Claire trailed close behind and listened while he brought her up to date.

"I wouldn't have thought it possible," he said. "The ship's security has been breached and a weak spot created in the engine shielding."

Claire suddenly realized that the normal, powerful throb in the deck plates was reduced to a whisper. Her last experience with this kind of attack had come on the landship Redclaw and had almost overwhelmed her best efforts to bring the shielding back under control.

"Only enough power to maintain steerage," he answered the unspoken question.

"An attack through a wild channel? I thought Jallis Ruffin would have learned his lesson," Claire growled.

"We don't know it was Ruffin or even if it were from outside the ship," Gilbert cautioned. "For that matter, the attack could have been aimed at us because we have Turlo Murten and

Rissa Ellendor on board. Imagine how convenient it would be to get rid of the heirs to the Tieben throne and a Trader family as well as the royal couple and high ranking officers in the Communicate all at one stroke."

"After meeting Veral Hushara's Captain Dread, I can easily imagine that," Claire said. "Where is Sage Leandra?"

"She's patching up some of the crew. I'm afraid we sustained one fatality, Tara, an Engineer's Apprentice. She was on watch with Nikko."

Claire's heart took a lurch. "Nikko was on watch? How is he?" A deep dread closed over her. Please, not Nikko. Not another one of my friends sacrificed to my ambitions.

"Last I saw of him, his shoes were dusted off and his cap, while singed, was set at the usual angle on his head."

Gilbert had failed to mention the cut on Nikko's cheek that was still bleeding freely and the black soot that covered the right side of his uniform. He saluted Gilbert smartly.

"We have time, but the fault is spreading. We might soon have to think about abandoning ship," he said.

Claire saw Leandra encouraging someone lying against the bulkhead behind Nikko. There was a strong odor of burned flesh permeating the air. In one corner, a blanket covered the remains of the Engineer's Apprentice.

"The shield," Gilbert urged.

Claire found the shield technician holding a ring device and pointing it at a spot on the plates surrounding the tubular core of the entropy engine. An indicator on the barrel of the device was turning from yellow to orange even as she looked on. She narrowed her vision and entered a skillful query into the nanites that swarmed around her. Immediately she perceived a projected picture of the problem.

It was exactly like the penetration of the shield on the Redclaw, only worse. A probability of a billion-to-one had been distorted in one tiny array, and the infection which had gained a bridgehead was trying to spread. One of three things would happen: 1. they shut down the engine entirely—in which case it could not be returned to service and the ship would be drifting helplessly down the river; 2. they repaired the poisoned area as Claire had done on the Redclaw; 3. The entropy tube would be penetrated and the raw heat-energy from the planet's core would leak outside its containment and destroy the ship.

At the moment, the device in the technician's hand was preventing the array from growing too fast—a sort of cooling mechanism designed to restore order. But soon, the active elements in the viral area would find a way to manipulate the probabilities and would enlarge the breach. There was no time to lose.

Once again, Claire operated on the abstraction that the nanites presented to her. She pictured it as mathematical operation similar to the one her grandmother had described.

She soon discovered that the attack had planted two, not one, seeds of disorder. The infected phages behaved much like a virus, seeking to replicate within the local matrix. Could she handle two at once? She had never discussed such a thing with Leandra. It looked impossible and the lives of everyone aboard the Rachael Ann were at stake. She felt a core of fear growing in the back of her mind. She wanted Pem to leave, to get off the ship and save himself. She had to jerk her concentration back to the problem.

She imagined bleeding off energy from one section to strengthen the order in the failing section, like thinning a balloon in one area to add thickness to another. She tried to surround both infected clusters simultaneously. It wasn't working! As she forced the disorder together, the chaos grew stronger and resisted her efforts. Claire began to feel faint; holding the nanite-projection in her mind consumed a great deal of energy. She felt Pem's strong arms close around her and give her support. Thank goodness he was here.

Perhaps isolating the affected area would help. She tried a substitution of a sub-array, swapping functions and data all at once. Claire knew it was theoretically possible, but would it work or lead to annihilation? If only she had time to confer with Leandra.

But there was no time. For a moment, the field at the surface of the tube shield rippled and surged with instability. Her amulet burned so hot she heard herself scream. She held her breath and stitched two arrays together; she introduced a common factor that smoothed out the anomaly and let the mathematical model operate. The solution came too fast for her to visualize. One instant the red spots of instability looked vile and ugly—such was the visual nature of the presentation—and the next instant all had returned to a peaceful bluish haze.

She couldn't seem to return to the room. She heard voices from far away and then a gray fog closed in around her. She found herself drifting helplessly, moving further and further away from everything. Pem arrived to hold her in his arms. Wait, wasn't he holding her before? Who had been behind her? She felt herself falling and there was nothing to grab onto.

"Claire, come back," Pem was shouting.

She reached out to Pem but she couldn't find him. Someone slapped her face hard; the sting brought her back long enough to feel water splashing over her. The irritation of being doused with water caused her to open her eyes and drop the connection with the nanites. Leandra's face filled her vision.

"That was stupid," she said calmly. "A student's mistake."

Claire's flash of anger brought her more fully awake. "I had to guess. We were seconds from a major breach in the shield."

"You were lucky, and, as Gilbert would say, it's better to be lucky than good," Leandra chuckled, not at all ruffled. "I think we should spend more time together. There are yet a few things I need to show you."

To this Claire could think of no rebuttal. Pem, on the other hand, looked rebellious. "She fixed it, didn't she? You shouldn't be so hard on my wife."

Leandra fixed Pem with one of her stares. "At least she brought her weapon to the battle," she said.

Pem felt for his sword and blushed furiously.

<u>Allain's Aid</u>

.TESS HAD BEEN .torn between two desires. She was very keen to accompany Claire on her honeymoon voyage and walk with Fitz on the sands of the Great Southern Beaches. She had heard so many marvelous tales about the beaches, and she was worried that her mistress might need her. On the other hand, she wanted to stay at the Palace, take charge of setting up the royal apartments, and begin her role as Lady Tess Royard, wife of the handsome and popular Commander of the King's Brigade and Palace Guard. She couldn't do both, and the truth was that she hadn't really had a choice once Lord Gilbert got involved.

"I need you to stay here," Gilbert had told Tess two days before the wedding. "You are one of my eyes and ears in the palace," he had said with flattering reference to Tess's widening popularity among the business people who supplied the Crown with everything from toilet paper to pearl necklaces. Tess was relieved that her choice was made for her.

Tess sighed and stood outside the entrance to the Brigade Officer's Commander's quarters while Fitz went off to settle into his new command. Inside, everything was neat and spotlessly clean, all accomplished by Fitz's army of orderlies. There hardly seemed anything for Tess to do. She couldn't even cook for Fitz since every meal was consumed at the Officer's mess where Fitz, as Commander, was expected to dine with his wife.

Where was Petz? He was designated as part of her temporary staff until Claire returned from her honeymoon. Petz was young, painfully shy of his commander's wife, and reminded Tess of N'rat, the boy who had helped them escape the clutches of Dread in Tieben. Rat, as he was known, was ambitious and off learning to be a sailor in the shipping empire of Mara Ellendor.

Petz, on the other hand, was often late and lacked that spark of ambition that had driven her new husband towards the top.

Timone purred and brushed past Tess's ankle. She bent down and smoothed the cat's fur along his back causing him to stretch in pleasure. I thought you would follow your mistress. Perhaps you don't like boats and water. I hope there were no other reasons for you to stay behind.

"Yawp!" Timone, as usual, had no other answer for her.

Petz appeared a few minutes late and looked uncertainly at Timone. "Your pet, Lady," he asked cautiously.

"The Queen's cat and nobody's pet so far as I know," Tess said. "Go on, pet him. He won't bite."

Petz made no move toward the orange and white ball of fur. "You asked if I could escort you to the Quartermaster."

"You are smarter than you look, Petz," Tess laughed.

"Ma'am." Petz straightened and looked as if he might salute her.

"Never mind, Petz," Tess sighed. "I have a list. Wait here while I fetch it."

When she returned, Petz was still standing stiffly, eyeing Timone with distrust. The cat was ignoring the orderly and had curled up in the corner and was licking his fur with long strokes of his rough pink tongue. Tess held the door for Timone, but he only stared at her before continuing with his grooming.

"I want a door in our door," Tess told Petz. She described the kind of swinging panel that Claire had told her about, a common pet door in her mistress's home town of Ridgeville— some town on Claire's world where people drove around in magical conveyances and flew from one continent to another with the same ease that Tess might travel in a carriage across the city of Lumminea.

Petz scratched his head. "I don't know, Ma'am. We've got a good carpenter in the compound. I suppose I could describe it to him and he could make an estimate."

"Tell him we'll need another just like it in the Royal Apartment," she added.

"That work is done by the Palace staff, Ma'am" Petz replied. "The army doesn't do civilian work."

"Not even for the Queen?"

"I'm sorry, Ma'am. It's regulations."

"And please stop calling me Ma'am," Tess barked.

"Yes, Ma'am," Petz said, looking miserable.

"Tell you what," Tess relented. "After we see the Quartermaster and we requisition materials for the Queen's apartments from Manager Brooks at the palace, you can saddle my horse and we'll go for a ride along the river."

"Yes, Ma'am." Petz brightened considerably and stood at attention.

"Come along, then," Tess secured her list in a pocket and prepared herself for the battle of paperwork. It was a task she relished.

Her first stop was at the office of Quartermaster Smurth, the man at the top of the supply chain for the part of the Lunarian Army stationed near Lumminea. She found the somewhat elderly Quartermaster looking at her across his desk in astonishment. "A desk, Lady Tess? There is a desk for the commander in your quarters—a very fine desk, I recall. One with many drawers and cubbies and even one hidden panel that I have never found. But a desk for the Commander's wife? It's not been done before."

Tess tried a different ploy. "Nevertheless, I have taken on responsibilities at the request of the Commander. One of these is the new maintenance budget for the officers in the brigade, one of whom, I believe, is you. My husband, Commander Royard, is not satisfied with the expenditures at the officer's mess. He believes, and I agree, that far too much of the King's money is being spent on poor quality food."

"I beg your pardon, Lady Royard, but what experience do you have of these things. You are a woman, after all," Quartermaster Smurth returned with some heat.

Behind her, Tess heard Petz draw in a quick breath. "In that case, I suppose I must ask Lord Gilbert to obtain a desk for me if you cannot supply one," Tess said.

The old quartermaster rolled his eyes and pretended to great patience. "Surely Lord Gilbert is too busy to procure something as unimportant as a desk. You ought not to bother him with this."

"Surely Lord Gilbert will be unhappy with me if he does not receive his reports when he returns from Maripas. It occurs to me that, by association, he might be unhappy with you if I do not have what I need for this task—however unworthy such criticism might be."

Someone walked into the Quartermaster's office behind her. She glanced around and saw General Allain standing to one side, waiting to address Quartermaster Smurth. The General had not yet recognized Tess from the back. She had known the General since he had been Captain Allain in charge of a company of border guards in the northern territories. In fact, Lord Gilbert had chosen her for Lady Claire's companion shortly after the first assassination attempt on the Lady's life while Claire was under Allain's protection. She and Allain had recently seen each other at one of the Council receptions.

Smurth was saying, "I'm sorry, but your husband lacks seniority to command such resources, even if he is part of the

Lumminea garrison. Perhaps you might come again some other time on a lesser request. If you would please excuse me, I have an important meeting with the General."

Tess held her temper in check even though she felt herself turning red. She flashed an appeal to the General who had remained well off to the side so as not to interfere with Quartermaster Smurth's business. Allain's eyes grew larger.

"Excuse me, Ma'am," he stepped forward, bowing slightly in her direction. "Quartermaster, I need to see you out front on an urgent requisition. It will only take a moment of your time," he said.

Smurth looked infuriatingly smug. Tess held her dark thoughts in check and her hand away from the little entropy-enhanced knife she had received from Cornal Hushara. She had lopped the heads off tougher opponents!

Tess had extremely good hearing that seemed to have grown even better after her encounter with the Monk, Ayaba. She overheard the men talking in the front office while Petz shuffled anxiously from one foot to the other and adjusted his collar.

"Fool," Allain was saying to the astonished Smurth. "Do you not know who that Lady is?"

"Yes sir, she's the wife of one of our commanders."

"Not just any commander, but the commander of the King's Brigade."

"Even so, sir, he has no seniority on the lists. I've checked," the Quartermaster insisted.

Tess could picture Allain winding himself up like he had after the incident in Tribana when Prince Pemburton had spoken out of turn and committed Allain's border guard to a politically unwise action.

"The Lady you so blithely dismissed is the personal secretary to the Queen and is a close friend to Lord Gilbert who, as I recall, still holds the power over the money you so easily disburse."

Apparently Smurth still hesitated.

"Also, I have it from highly reliable sources that she has personally decapitated or otherwise skewered dozens of barbarians during several battles. It would be highly unwise of you to make her an enemy."

Allain's last pronouncement seemed to have tipped the scales in Tess's favor. "Oh, Aye Sir, I see what you mean," Smurth's stubbornness seemed to yield. "I'll do the Lady a favor. As you imply, friends in high places never hurt."

A few minutes later Tess left the offices with a signed requisition form in full triplicate. She looked forward to the writing desk with its proper cubbies, drawers, and even, Smurth assured her, a secret compartment that even he did not know how to open. Tess wondered if she would be able find it. She wagered that she'd get the pet door, too.

Meeting Allain had been most interesting. Why was the general so impressed with her influence? As far as Tess was concerned, she was still very much the village girl compared to the people around her. She shrugged her shoulders and filed away the encounter for a time when she could discuss the chance meeting with Lord Gilbert.

Tess sighed; it was business as usual.

The Dangers of Redecoration

ALBRIT BROOKS, THE Palace Manager or Major Domo, sat at his cluttered desk and appeared to be scribbling frantically as he added notes to the margins of a form. He put aside his pen and professed to be glad to see Tess. "Such a pleasure to see a woman of business, Lady Tess. You have no idea how hard some people are to work with."

Tess saw with surprise that he was actually sincere. Instead of sending a clerk, he offered to tour the royal apartment with her and make suggestions, an offer for which Tess was grateful. It was a heavy responsibility to refurbish the living quarters, and Tess wasn't sure that Claire's confidence in her was justified. She accepted Brook's proposal immediately. The man went to fetch the keys from a locked strongbox.

The entrance to the suite where Pem and Claire were to take up residence was in a largish vestibule with places for guards off a grand hall that ran straight through the central part of the palace and connected with the Grand Ballroom. The gold covered carvings and purple patterned wall paper looked garish to Tess. The arch in the center of the domed space seemed dark and dingy.

"We should have a light at the center of this space," Tess said, thinking about how Claire hated dark rooms. "Important people will be coming to visit. Some padded benches at the edges would be nice, don't you think?"

"Yes, an excellent suggestion," Brooks bobbed his head. "May I suggest velvet covered seats of the Third Dynastic period?"

"I don't have any idea what the Third Dynasty means," Tess admitted. "Just do what you think best and please," she added, "don't make it any more ornate than it already is."

Brooks chuckled. "I see you have an eye for proper elegance. I've always thought this vestibule was entirely too…fluffy," he waved his hands in the air. "I'll see to it. Shall we go inside?"

He took out a fancy golden key on a chain and inserted it into the prominent keyhole. Instead of turning it, he took out a small rod and inserted the tip into a small hole near the center of the door. He left the rod in place and asked Tess to place her hand on a dark plate underneath the rod.

"The golden key is just for show. Use the plate with your hand. The door will remember you and allow you entrance," he explained. He removed the rod after Tess removed her hand. "Try it now," he said.

Tess placed her hand back on the plate. "You may enter with your key," a voice responded. She jerked her hand back in surprise.

"Turn the key," Brooks pointed to the gold key.

She turned the key and the door swung back soundlessly on heavy hinges. The room behind was completely dark. Tess noted that the panel was solid Heartwood reinforced with silver bands and was nearly three inches thick.

"All monarchs have not been equally popular," Brooks remarked on the door's strength as he reached in and touched something inside the door. A multitude of gas lamps lighted, revealing a large reception space cluttered with stacks of boxes and haphazard piles of rolled fabrics and carpets. It was a gloomy looking mess.

Tess examined all fourteen rooms of the spacious suite, trying to imagine how it could look. The comfortable furniture in the private areas could remain. She took notes on the pieces she liked. The public area was a disaster with animal heads hanging over striped couches and tables that were filled with meaningless bits of bric-à-brac that had collected mountains of dust. Tess sneezed several times.

"I'm sorry, Lady Tess," Brooks apologized. "No one has occupied the rooms since Queen Rachael died. The Regent moved into his own quarters and has not been here since her funeral."

"I will need an army of cleaners to completely strip these rooms. All of this furniture except for those pieces on my list must be removed and stored. I take it that there are more stored pieces that I may choose from?" Tess wiped her hands together in an attempt to remove some of the grime she picked up when she moved the coverings aside on some of the chairs.

"Of course, I shall see to it," Brooks agreed readily. "May I suggest alternatives and pieces of art work? You have described Lady Claire's tastes well, and I think I can get you what you want."

"Yes, all of that—subject to my final approval," she added. "There is just one more important thing missing that you haven't shown me, Master Brooks."

"And what would that be, Lady Tess?" Brooks looked apprehensively at her and Tess could tell that he was trying to hide something from her.

Tess sighed. "While it's true that I am from a village and not from a notable background, I have traveled widely and have seen things about which you have never dreamed. The Garden, Master Brooks—don't tell me that there isn't one. Where is the Garden?"

Brooks paled. "Queen Rachael hated that garden, Lady. She forbade me to enter there. Even Edward Godwyn did not venture into their garden."

"Nevertheless, I'd like to see it," Tess insisted.

They retraced their steps to the large dining room with its table piled high with various styles of china and platters made from precious metals. "Perhaps we could sell this finery and use the money to redecorate," Tess suggested.

Brooks nearly fainted from the suggestion of impropriety.

"It was a joke." Tess laughed at the expression on the Major Domo's face.

They reached the back wall and he drew aside a tapestry that depicted some long forgotten battle. Double doors were set into a carved molding behind the woven fabric. Brooks hesitated, then slid a large bolt free from its latch and opened the door slightly. Tess saw only blackness beyond.

"Are you sure you want to do this?" Brooks asked her.

"Nothing to be afraid of," Tess brushed him aside and pulled open the panel, holding her breath in spite of her bold appearance.

Light from behind her illuminated a broad stairway curving upwards into darkness. "The Garden is at the top of these stairs," Brooks said from behind. "I have been there only once—a long time ago."

Tess started up the stairs, stopped, and sneezed. "We'll need to clean this, also," she remarked.

She placed her foot on the next step; a warm glow from wall sconces dispelled the darkness. Ahead of her a beam of sunlight found its way through some tattered cobwebs, and the sound of water splashing filled the stale air. A gentle breeze dispelled the musty odor, replacing the unpleasant atmosphere with the scent of lavender and honeysuckle. A sense of peace and wellbeing overcame Tess's senses.

"Is something the matter, Lady," Brooks' worried voice interrupted her reverie.

"Everything seems very pleasant," Tess murmured. "I think your Garden has prepared a welcome for us."

Brooks shrank back. "I don't know what you mean. Those stairs look dark and ominous to me. You should come back while we have guards check the upper level."

"Whatever for, Brooks?" Tess exclaimed. "Look at that patch of sunlight on the wall; the sun is shining brightly. Don't you hear the fountain splashing? I have seen many of these gardens before. This one will appear no different than the others."

"Please, Lady, I see none of what you describe," he shrank further back.

Impatient with the Major Domo, Tess reached out and grabbed his arm. She pulled him behind her and started up the flight of steps. "There's no reason to be frightened," she told him.

Brooks took several steps before he could regain his balance, and by then they were at the top landing. "See," Tess pointed through the door. "Only a garden."

Through a familiar archway, Tess could see the wooden bench by the fountain, the acacia tree shading the bench, a mixture of lavender and roses in bloom, and the sound of a warbler singing somewhere out of sight.

She remembered that the sun should be past its zenith, but inside the garden a morning sun cast cool shadows across the walkways. She stepped forward, dragging the panic stricken Brooks behind her.

Brooks dropped to his knees. "By G'rama, please come away from this place," he urged Tess. His eyes grew even wider with fright, as if seeing something behind her. Tess whirled about when he screamed.

The beauty of the garden seemed unbroken to Tess. Every blossom personified perfection. The small plot of grass on the other side of the fountain looked as if it had been trimmed blade-by-blade. At the end of the walkway, she could see another arch leading somewhere else—another way into the garden from the Palace?

Tess thought she saw a ripple towards the fountain, a momentary distortion that confused her. She tried to focus on the movement, but before she could react she felt a strong arm wrap around her neck, pushing under her chin, dragging her head back and choking her.

She struggled helplessly against the iron grip, trying to call out, and felt hot breath on her ear. An assassin!

Abruptly her attacker staggered against her. Brooks must have thrown himself again her attacker from behind. There was more coarse breathing and the grip loosened briefly. She felt the body behind her turn sideways. Abruptly there was a yell of pain that sounded a lot like Brooks; this was followed by a guttural curse near her ear, and the thud of a boot landing solidly against a body.

With the precious seconds that Brooks had given her, Tess had groped to release the infinitely sharp entropy-enhanced blade in the brooch on her left breast. She wriggled her finger through the thin loop guard and slashed wildly with the little knife across the arm against her throat.

Her effort was rewarded with a shriek of pain followed by a very visible stump of arm that sprayed bright red blood in her face. She slashed blindly behind her head. A terrible gurgle cut off further sounds. She threw herself forward and evaded the heavy body that was toppling forward like a tree cut off at its roots. The wicked dagger that had been about to slash her throat fell from nerveless fingers and skittered across the paving stones.

Tess, partially blinded by the blood, spun about wildly looking for another attacker. There were no other immediate threats. The garden felt calm—still beautiful, but less colorful and somehow safe and more substantial. She could feel a definite change, a different certainty to what she now saw. She returned her jeweled dagger to its proper place and hurried to Brooks who was curled up on the ground in front of the archway. She hoped he hadn't paid too dearly for his boldness.

Brooks had fainted and was bleeding heavily from a deep cut across his upper arm. She turned him over gently without finding another wound. She tore a strip of cloth from the hem of her skirt and bound the wound as best she could.

She wanted to get out of the garden as soon as possible, so she half-lifted, half-dragged Brooks, who was a small man, through the archway and down the stairs, wincing as Brooks bumped down the steps, but what could she do? She slammed the door to the garden, throwing the heavy bolt through its keeper. She continued dragging Brooks to the dining area where she swept a stack of china from a cloth on a table and rolled the soft material into a pillow to place under Brook's head. The shattered china lay in a long arc across the floor. Tess shrugged. No doubt the Major Domo/Palace Manager would faint once more when he found out about the destruction of the priceless china.

She was just looking about for a means of cleaning the blood off her face when the heavy pounding of boots interrupted her. Fitz rushed into the apartment followed by a small squad of men. All had their weapons drawn. They made towards Brooks as if to cut him in pieces. "We were told of a disturbance," Fitz cried out.

"No, no, he's not the one who attacked me!" Tess stepped in front of Fitz. "It was someone in the garden." She explained the door to the stairs.

"They lead to a garden where we were attacked. I locked the door as we left."

Fitz made as if to push past her, but she stayed him by putting a hand to his arm. "It's okay," she said. "I took care of the threat. Have someone see to Brooks. He saved my life, and I don't want him to lose his."

Fitz gathered Tess in his arms and ordered two of his men to carry Brooks as quickly as possible to the infirmary where he could receive care. He ordered the other three to check out the surrounding rooms for any further threats.

Tess waited until she was alone with Fitz and had convinced him that she was okay—except for the shallow cut along one shoulder which she had inflicted on herself when she cut through the man's arm.

"I'm sure it was one of Garrund's men," she said grimly. "He was dressed exactly like those who attacked us under the Palace during the Ball," she went on. "We need to talk with Lord Gilbert. Our enemy's reach is long enough to threaten us even here in the royal apartment."

"It's my job to provide Palace security," Fitz reminded Tess. "However, I see no harm if you go to Gilbert and speak with him about Lord Garrund. That is something I cannot do without making it an official inquiry."

Tess leaned in close. She and Fitz embraced tightly.

The Palace Garden

.THE THREE MEN .Fitz had sent out returned and Tess led them to the door to the stairs leading to the garden. She hesitated at the door, trying to find the courage to return inside. Fitz had no such qualms. He drew the bolt and pushed up the stairs with his men. When nothing untoward happened immediately, she followed them into the Garden. I'm becoming a coward, she thought.

Fitz stood with his men about the body of the assassin.

"He's huge," one of the men exclaimed, looking up at Tess with respect in his eyes. "How did you manage to escape?"

Tess could see that the guard was in grave doubt as to what had happened. She said, "The Palace Manager attacked him from behind and gave me the opening I needed."

"Even so," Fitz broke in, "you have been very lucky, my darling." He motioned the three men to get rid of the body.

"We'll get a cleaning crew in here to return the place to its proper condition," Fitz said.

Meanwhile Tess was looking around at the Garden. Everything seemed to be waking up. The fountain splashed, birds chirped, and the sun seemed to be getting brighter and warmer. Nervously, she asked Fitz, "What do you think of the Garden? How does it appear to you? The Palace Manager didn't see the same things that I saw. He tried to stop me from walking into a place that he thought was dark and dangerous. I wished I'd listened to him."

Fitz looked around, bent a branch of the Acacia tree and let it spring back. "It looks much like the garden back at Greyhaven," he said.

Tess breathed a sigh of relief. "I had thought that I was going crazy," she admitted.

"Perhaps you were under a glamour to see the garden a certain way," Fitz said. "Now this place is returning to normal. Perhaps the assassin affected the garden, causing it to turn dark in all but your eyes."

"Perhaps," Tess returned, deciding that there was more to this than a simple illusion. She looked to the far side of the Garden and picked out the door under the arched trellis. It was very similar to the one in Greyhaven. "I wonder what lies beyond that door," she said, starting across the garden.

Fitz hurried after her, leaving his men to their task. "It's not that I don't think you can protect yourself, but let us do this together," he said, loosening his blade in its sheath.

A blood-spattered Tess agreed and waited for him to catch up. As she turned towards Fitz, it seemed as if the distance to the other side of the garden was quite far, disturbingly like the field they had crossed at the northern edge of the Dark Forest. Another illusion, she thought.

They passed beneath the arched arbor together and stopped at the heavy door set in a stone frame. "Shall we see where this goes?" Fitz said and drew his blade.

"We'll look ridiculous if we step out into the audience room or somewhere public in the Palace," she laughed nervously.

"I think we'll take that risk," Fitz grinned at her and reached for the thick bronze bar latch.

The door opened smoothly at his touch, revealing a long hall that ended in a lighted opening in the distance. There were closed doors to each side. As they walked cautiously forward, the hall seemed to slide by them and they found themselves entering the same garden again. Across the way, near the fountain, they watched Fitz's men finish wrapping the assassin's body in a piece of drapery and carry him through the other entrance.

"Well, that was unexpected," Fitz said.

Tess turned around and saw the same long hall leading off behind them. "We could see if we return the same way by going back," she suggested. "Perhaps we might try one of the other openings."

"Let's not," Fitz said. "I think we've had enough mysteries for one day. What I want to know is how the assassin came to be waiting for you here."

"For that, we should consult with Lord Gilbert," Tess said, drawing Fitz toward the fountain and the terrace. "I think your men should lock this Garden door securely and you should post a guard at the foot of the stairs until we come to some resolution of this matter."

Fitz smiled down at his new bride, pride warring with minor irritation. "Now you are trying to do my job for me," he smiled. He held up his hand as Tess opened her mouth. "Not that I disagree with you," he said. He grabbed and held Tess's hand as they descended the stairs into the undecorated Royal quarters.

"Once again you have given me quite a scare," he said as they came out into the lower level.

Tess sighed. There was much work to be done and a short time to do it in, but she wasn't going to touch any of it until Fitz had his men posted. She didn't fancy meeting another assassin anytime soon.

Tess said, "I will go to Gilbert as you suggest. Perhaps he has some news from the royal couple on the south coast. I live in fear that Claire and Pem will return unexpectedly and their quarters won't be ready."

BUT LORD GILBERT had little to say on the subject of Lord Garrund and Tess's accusations concerning hired assassins.

Gilbert responded to her words, "Tess, since the assassin is dead, I can see no way to connect him to Lord Garrund and this conspiracy you propose. I do not doubt but that you are correct, but my hands are tied. Having said that, I promise to bend every effort to find out how such a thing could have happened. I am most grateful that you suffered no worse than the cut on your arm. It would be a great personal loss to me had you not prevailed. Perhaps it is partly my fault. I did not think that this sort of thing would have been aimed at you, although I suppose it might have been in response to your husband's taking over the command of the King's Brigade. Overwrought ambition and revenge have often been the source of much tragedy."

"What I cannot understand," Tess said, after blushing at Gilbert's flattering declaration, "is how the assassin came to be waiting for me. I'm certain that Albrit Brooks cannot have planted him there. He did not know that I was going to come to ask him about the royal apartment this morning. Brooks claimed he knew next to nothing about the garden and hadn't even considered making plans to open it for the royal couple."

Gilbert, who had been drumming his fingers on the table surface in front of him, looked up and said, "Perhaps we are looking at this the wrong way. Perhaps this assassin was not waiting for you at all. Perhaps it was you who interrupted him as he was doing something in the garden, in which case he was not properly an assassin at all. We should examine the garden thoroughly for traps set for when the royal couple returns."

"That would certainly seem to make more sense," Tess agreed. "In which case, we are still left with the question of how he managed to get into the garden in the first place. Fitz has told me that the man had nothing besides the dagger, not a key or anything else, on his person." Tess shivered and fingered her throat. "If Albrit hadn't attacked when he did, I would not be here. I'm glad he didn't fare worse for his bravery."

"Let us be glad that he did not consider the possible consequences of his actions," Gilbert said.

Tess Runs into Danger Again

PETZ, TESS THOUGHT of him as her orderly, entered Tess's office when she said "Come."

The desk, which had been delivered only days before, was already covered with paperwork, a scattering of pens, and an ink pot. Tess was working on a note to Quartermaster Smurth thanking him for the desk without being overly flattering. The mistress of the Royard domain leaned back and rubbed her eyes. "What is it, Petz?"

"Commander Royard and Lord Gilbert are awaiting your presence in Lord Gilbert's quarters," the young man spoke nervously.

Tess sprinkled a bit of white sand over the wet ink and then dumped the blue grains into a trash can by the desk. She folded the message carefully and applied a bit of sealing wax. Someday soon she'd design her own seal, she decided.

"Please carry this to the quartermaster," she said. "I'll go to meet with Lord Gilbert and my husband."

Tess closed and locked the door behind her. She and Fitz were assigned quarters located in the east wing of the north side of the Palace complex—near the parade grounds and Fitz's administrative offices. It was much better than living in the officer's quarters on one of the army bases, she reflected. She looked forward to the time when she and Claire would spend part of their time at Claire's estates outside of Lumminea where she was assigned to manage the Queen's finances.

She sighed. It would be a long walk to Lord Gilbert's headquarters which were located in the central area of the compound. The shortest route lay through a dingy web of passageways reserved for offices of minor clerks and maintenance services. Tess hesitated only a moment, checked to see that her little knife was handy in its concealed holder, and set out along a narrow corridor that wound its way past guest rooms reserved for the couriers that came and went at all hours of the day and night.

Today the corridors seemed more deserted than usual. She had just crossed an intersection, making her way quietly along the edge of a poorly lighted, columned space, when she heard a loud clatter and a curse on the other side of the vaulted room. She stopped, hidden behind a support pillar, concealing herself out of habit. She heard the voices of two people arguing. One voice was from either a young boy or a girl; the other was older and sarcastic. The commanding tone was disturbingly familiar.

"I can't, now," the younger of them was whining. "The ambassador has sent me on an important errand."

Tess could hear the arrogance in the voice and smothered a chuckle. Probably a page who worked at one of the embassies.

"You'll come with me now—if you know what's good for you," the other voice dripped with venom.

Tess heard a short scuffle.

"Ouch! You're hurting me!" There was pain and surprise in the tone.

Definitely a girl's voice. Tess put a hand to her knife and stepped around the pillar. No one should be hurting anyone in the palace, not even an obnoxious page girl.

But the space opposite the corridor was deserted. What was happening? The sounds of a scuffle got louder and there was a gasp of pain followed by a harsh laugh. Tess crept across the room and made her way along the wall. Dust and cobwebs lay thick on shelves in empty niches. She smothered a sneeze and thought that she should remind the steward to have this area cleaned.

As her eyes adjusted to the dim light, Tess noticed a grate near the floor. Sobs and heavy breathing were coming from the opening. One of those servant corridors behind the wall, flashed through Tess's mind. Just like under the palace when she and Claire had been kidnapped. She hitched up her skirt to keep it out of the dust and squatted down to listen.

"Hated to have to hurt you, lass," the mellifluous voice didn't sound very sorry to Tess. "His Lordship, Lord Garrund, has other plans for you. He'll need to see you right away. Do you understand?"

Tess pictured a tear-stained face nodding in agreement. How could she find out who this person was? The voices could be coming from inches away behind thin walls or could be carried along the air duct from a long way off. She got down on her knees, ignoring the filthy floor, and peered through the opening.

And looked straight into a pair of pretty blue eyes. The eyes blinked and widened. The girl opened her mouth to say something and received a brutal slap across her face that knocked her head to the side. "But..." the girl whimpered.

Before Tess could draw back, she caught sight of two men standing on the other side of the grate. One of them looked familiar. She caught the side of a man's face as he bent down to look closely at the girl. She almost fainted. She was sure that she was looking at the man she knew as Jallis Ruffin!

Had he seen her? She wanted to run, but that would make too much noise. She waited as seconds ticked by, dreading a crash and a hidden panel opening up as Ruffin or his man dragged her into the other corridor. She grasped her little knife fiercely and struggled to hear over her wildly beating heart.

Lord Gilbert needed to know about Ruffin immediately. Fitz would want her to run away from danger. Gilbert would want to know what she had learned. For a moment, prudence warred with curiosity. What she heard chilled her to the heart and made her forget about rescuing the child.

"Speak! What is it you want to say," Ruffin's voice was deadly.

"I hate her," the girl's voice was strong, though unsteady— as if she were getting over her fear and had forgotten about Tess.

"Who do you hate?" Ruffin's voice was contemptuous. "As if anyone cares about what a little girl thinks."

"The Queen," the child's voice lashed out. "Lord Garrund's granddaughter should be queen, not that girl. She isn't even from our world."

"A dangerous notion," the sage's voice purred. "What do you intend to do about it?"

"I don't know, but I think there might be someone listening outside," she said, suddenly remembering Tess.

Tess ran as she had never done in her life. Not even the wild chase through the mountains in Tieben had filled her with such fear. If Ruffin caught her or even recognized her…well, that was not to be considered. Behind her she heard the sound of panels splintering, but she had turned the corner and was pounding down another hall by then and wasn't one of the barrack's offices just around the next bend?

She nearly screamed in relief as she ran full tilt into the back of a squad of palace marines at parade rest. The sergeant who was doing the inspection started to yell at her as he pulled her from the sprawling tangle of marines, all trying not to laugh.

"Ah, Lady Tess, the Commander's wife," he said loudly enough to silence the regulars, some of whom were making catcalls at the woman who had knocked them down like so many tenpins.

Tess blushed and smoothed her skirt down where it was showing rather too much thigh. "Sorry about running into you like that, I'm in a hurry." She gave the sergeant her best smile. He was being really sweet about the whole thing.

"So, Sergeant, can you please loan me two of your men as an escort. I must meet with Commander Royard and Lord Gilbert immediately." Gilbert will want to get off a dispatch to Claire warning her that she may come under another attack, Tess thought.

"Of course, Lady Tess," he bowed deeply, though Tess thought it was to keep from laughing rather than an indication of his esteem.

She glanced back over her shoulder. Ruffin couldn't have recognized her through the grate, and besides, he wouldn't dare attack her now. But if he had seen her clearly, she was sure he would remember her from the corridors deep under the Palace, and he would recall that she was a companion of the Queen. She was not out of danger either way.

Dangerous Assignments

CAPTAIN EBERSON WAS troubled by the delays. Since the damage to the engine shields of the Rachael Ann, their scheduled meeting with the Fortuna had slipped by several hours. He only hoped that his Second would have sense enough to circle within sight of the rendezvous point.

The royal yacht was a fine little ship in its own way, but Eberson was anxious to be aboard his Fortuna where the engine ran off steam and did not depend directly on the entropy drive. If the Fortuna's tubes were damaged, she could put ashore and cut wood for the fire box, an alternative that seemed immanently practical to Gilbert's practically-minded skipper.

Six hours later, as the sun was setting in the west, Eberson was collecting his papers and checking his charts when Nikko knocked on his cabin door.

"Sir, Captain Watchman is ready for you on the bridge," Nikko said once he had closed the door behind him. He stood quietly as his Captain finished packing his chart case and personal effects.

Nikko had worked for the Captain since he was first recruited to the Navy, shifting from the fleet to Lord Gilbert's private service when Eberson relinquished his official commission in the Navy and accepted the captaincy of the Fortuna. Eberson had promoted him, first from Seaman to Bosun, then to Chief Petty Officer, and finally to the First Officer of the Fortuna. He enjoyed the Captain's trust, and knew that he'd give his life for his commander if asked.

"Nikko," Eberson surprised the First by the informality. "I'm afraid I am putting you in a difficult position."

"Sir?" The sudden informality and the manner of Eberson's approach made him nervous.

"Have you informed Turlo Murten and Rissa Ellendor?"

"No, sir, not until you tell me to do so."

"You may do so now," he told Nikko. "The time is at hand. I have received word from the Fortuna."

Eberson always seemed to know more than was possible. It was part of the reason that Nikko trusted his commander. Nothing was ever guesswork. Eberson's information always seemed accurate.

"You may wonder how I know," the Captain said, as if he were reading Nikko's mind.

"Yes sir, I mean no sir. I know that you have a communicate panel on board the Fortuna."

"An illegal one, as you well know," Eberson looked at Nikko thoughtfully before he reached into his case and brought forth an ordinary looking key.

"I know nothing of an illegal console," Nikko said stubbornly.

"Of course. In any case, take this key. You must use this token in an emergency if the King and his Queen fall afoul of our enemies aboard the Rachael Ann. I assume you know what to do with this?"

"Yes sir, but I have no authorization aboard this vessel," Nikko reminded his commander.

"You must deal with that problem when or if the time comes. Lord Gilbert and I expect you to do your duty," Eberson extended his hand. "Good luck, Officer Nikko."

"Sir, and you as well," Nikko grasped the Captain's hand, then stood back and saluted him.

Eberson returned the salute. "Go and inform our passengers that they must be ready to depart the Rachael Ann within the hour. Tell them that that they should make their private good byes with the royal couple soon. Two command consoles in the same location will attract unwanted attention from certain parties and we must not dally together long."

Once the door closed behind Nikko, Eberson sighed and wondered if he should have told Nikko of Lord Gilbert's suspicions concerning Captain Agkor. He finally decided that he would inform the young officer before he left the Rachael Ann. Whatever Gilbert thought, he felt like Nikko would be in a better position to protect Pem and Claire if he knew to watch Captain Agkor.

"I believe that Agkor has fallen victim to Jallis Ruffin who works for Torvall Garrund," Gilbert had revealed to Eberson. "There may be pressure in the form of a threat against the Captain's family, or perhaps it is merely simple bribery. In any case, if true, then I expect to intercept a message from Agkor the moment you leave for the Fortuna. It is my intent that Lady Claire and I will abort that message before it can reach its intended recipient, whoever that might be, for I cannot be certain that it is Ruffin."

"Another message will be sent," Eberson had responded.

"Yes, but by then your schedule will be unknown and you can disappear conveniently into the vastness of the Southern Ocean," Gilbert had retorted.

It bothered Eberson that Gilbert was willing to take such risks with the young woman's life. Still, in his experience, Claire had proven to be highly resilient and a natural warrior. She would have been exactly the kind of daughter that he would have liked to have. He thought of the Lady Astora and remembered how she looked at him and held his hand when they had danced at the Great Ball. She had never indicated any desire to marry again, and he had never quite had the nerve to ask Lord Gilbert for permission to court his daughter. Maybe that would change someday soon.

He shook his head and picked up his cases, took one look around, and closed the door quietly behind him. It was a short climb up the sloping companionway to the hatch leading to the bridge.

Watchman was waiting for him on the bridge. They stood together and gazed at the violet sun as it sank behind the horizon. They waited, hoping to see the green flash that sometimes occurred at such times, but evidently the weather conditions were not quite right for the phenomenon to be visible.

The waters at the edge of the great Bay of Lunaria—more small gulf than large bay—were glassy with only a hint of the southern swell that would be encountered further out. Eberson looked intently to the southwest where he expected to see the hull of the Fortuna within the hour. He questioned the helmsman, who reported the course and speed, and came back to Watchman's side, satisfied.

"All seems to be going as planned," he informed the other Captain in a low voice.

The Fellowship is Broken

.THE KNOCK AT .the door of her suite awakened Claire from another one of her day dreams. Pem was off in the engine room interfering with the repairs to the engine shields while Mags had taken some time off to sun herself in one of the lounge chairs that lined the deck behind the wheelhouse. After seeing Mags' costume, Claire was certain that her attendant was attracting a lot of attention from the off-duty crew. She sighed at the idea of having another Tess around. She opened the door to find Rissa standing there with Turlo behind her.

"It appears that it is time," Rissa said as soon as they had come into the little reception room and closed the door behind them. Turlo, who was carrying four cups looped through his fingers and a bottle of the finest wine, looked around.

"Isn't Pem with you?" he asked, looking disingenuous.

"He is off tending to the engine repairs," Claire said. "You know how he is, always interested in everything and getting in the way."

"Perhaps it is as well that we are leaving the ship soon," Turlo said with his dry sense of humor. "I'm not sure that I want to depend on Pem's expertise in entropy shields." Rissa gave him a sharp dig in his ribs.

"Ah, here you are," Pem slipped into the room. "I had a message from Nikko saying that I would find you all here."

"Rissa was telling me that it is time for them to depart," Claire filled Pem in.

Turlo passed out the cups and made a ritual of filling each of them with wine. "A toast to companions and absent friends," he offered and all four emptied their cups to the last drop, as was the proper manner in Lunaria, and placed them on a side table.

"I wish you didn't have to go," Claire blurted out and gave Rissa a hug.

Turlo looked hopeful, but Pem stepped in to offer his hand. "Good luck," he said and added his other hand on the top of his grip. "The future of our two countries will be changed by what you and Lady Rissa do."

"Probably nothing so grand," Turlo said, "but thanks for the support."

"Claire and I already owe you so much," Pem went on. "If you hadn't sailed the ship through the wall of fire, we might not be here now."

"If you hadn't arrived with your troopers when we approached the river, we might not be here either," Turlo countered.

"Just like two men. If you two do not stop bragging, nothing will get done," Claire and Rissa chorused.

A knock on the door silenced their chatter.

"Time to go," Nikko's voice sounded from the other side of the panel.

"So soon," Claire sighed. "I wish you could have stayed with us through the whole voyage."

"Perhaps not," Pem said lightly. "Don't Turlo and Rissa have things of their own to do?"

This brought a knowing laugh from the other three that left Pem puzzled. "Let's all go to the deck," Claire said, and opened the door to Nikko.

"Your personal belongings are on deck," Nikko bowed to Rissa and nodded to Turlo. "The Fortuna will be alongside in a few minutes. There's not much time to waste."

"Then, let's not waste time," Pem growled and shouldered his way past Turlo.

Claire winced; Turlo shrugged. She explained, "He's still angry about us traveling together across Tieben."

"But Lady Tess was with us the whole time," Turlo grinned.

"I think I will not comment upon that," Claire laughed. "Commander Royard might hear me."

Turlo looked startled. "Yes, I think that's best." He looked away when Rissa glared at him.

"Is there something you haven't told me?" Rissa asked him sweetly.

THE OCEAN HAD quieted into a flat mirror with a slight swell that rocked the Rachael Ann as gently as a feather might have stroked a baby. The rail felt cool in Claire's hands as she stood waiting while Turlo and Rissa talked quietly nearby. Nikko was having a conversation with Captain Eberson.

Eberson took the opportunity to caution the officer concerning Captain Agkor. "I am trusting you in this. You must be very careful," he told Nikko.

Pem had wandered off to the bow by himself. In the warm glow of twilight, a silvery reflection of the moon teased Claire's eyes as she tried unsuccessfully to focus on the surface of the water. A fish surfaced, nosing into the air briefly, no doubt curious about the large object that had invaded its space. Not far off the starboard bow, a small back dot was rapidly taking the shape of the Fortuna as she steamed in their direction.

Captain Watchman joined her, his back turned to the rail, his face in the shadows.

"I will watch over her for as long as I can," he said to Claire, his voice barely above a whisper.

"Before I knew how our amulets were connected," Claire said, "I thought I was only occupying myself with pleasant memories of my friend. Now, the thought of what it would be like if that link were to suddenly grow cold frightens me."

"You are growing up, Lady Claire," Watchman said gently. "Perhaps you confronted your mortality too soon in life. Perhaps it is because you sense that others depend on you, or that your nature changes whatever is around you. Whatever reason says, it is a great gift from the heart that you bestow upon others."

"I used to dream about my lost father," Claire continued. "Now those dreams are fading, and I can no longer see his face clearly or sense his presence. I find that frightening, also."

"The past only seems to fade," Watchman assured her. "The memory is still there, as fresh as the moment of the living experience. Time does not erase your memory, it covers it so that we may return to it when we need it most. I would not worry that your father is lost. He will live as long as you live, and after that it will not matter to you."

Claire shivered. "That seems as cold as the deep waters under our keel."

"Indeed," Watchman returned. He was going to say something else when Claire felt Pem put his arm about her waist.

"I almost envy your friends," he said lightly, disturbing her mood. "It sounds like they will have a grand adventure, and if we were not locked on our own course, I would readily join them."

Claire, who was barefoot on the deck, had to stretch slightly to give Pem a quick peck on the cheek. "We have our own adventure," she reminded him.

Beside her, the Captain chuckled. "I hope we will meet again, Lady Claire—perhaps not on a deck slippery with the enemy's blood." Watchman moved off to have a chat with Eberson who was instructing some of the crew on how to bring the Fortuna safely alongside.

Claire waited for Eberson to disembark before she put out a query and checked for any transmissions from the ship's console. So far, nothing had revealed itself. She wondered if Gilbert's suspicions were accurate. She decided that she'd check later and pushed the unpleasantness from her mind.

The Great Southern Beaches

CLAIRE STOOD AT THE BOW WITH PEM and enjoyed the cool salt spray blowing in her face. She had never seen or even pictured anything as grand as the white strips of beaches, the endless march of sand dunes, and the pristine violet water breaking in froth along the crests of mountainous swells rolling in from the south.

A crewman on the port side was raising signal flags to alert the local garrison to the King's arrival. Claire could see an answer from the semaphore atop the guard tower at the water's edge, though she was unable to read the message.

"Welcoming us," Pem filled in. "We may have to review the troops while we are here," he said. "They'll love you."

Claire blushed at his words. She found the lift and fall of the Rachael Ann exhilarating as the ship finished rounding the sandy headland and made a sharp turn to port, lining up with an orange range-mark on the fortified tower. Shadows of rocky teeth lining the edges of the channel occasionally broke the surface. On one of these, Claire caught a glimpse of the rusted remains of a hull, iron ribs and fragments of some ship in the past that had come to a violent end.

"Tricky at night," Pem said and pulled her closer.

Claire shivered and thought of how it would be to drown in deep water, sinking endlessly into the lonely abyss.

Pem shook her gently. "Daydreaming, again?" He pointed to a sprawling complex of white buildings with blue tile roofs that stretched along the beach.

"The city of Bancho and the royal vacation home." Behind the resort, a small city occupied a rocky slope dotted with parks and forested areas.

"All this just for you?" Claire was appalled.

"No, of course not," Pem laughed. "I couldn't afford it even if I wanted to—and I don't."

"It was once a naval installation, but it's been privately owned for at least ten generations. The owner's family has always supported the Monarchy and has a secluded section of the beach reserved for the royal household."

"Do you swim in these waters?" Claire wanted to know. "At home we have animals called sharks. They sometimes attack people."

Pem looked startled. "No, I don't believe we have anything like that," he said. "If there were such creatures at one time, I'm sure someone got rid of them."

"Just like that?" Claire snapped her fingers. "Your ancestors would wipe out an entire species just because they might bite someone?"

"I don't know that much history," Pem returned. "Sage Leandra could probably tell you. All I know is that this world's ecology was created from scratch a very long time ago."

"I wonder why cave cats were allowed," Claire pursed her lips. "One almost killed me. They seem far more dangerous than our sharks."

Pem shrugged. "I don't know, but the cave cats probably came through from another world—much like your yellow and orange beast that you brought from your world. Who knows how many Timones are now running around in the Old Forest? For that matter, Gilbert is convinced that the fellow who attacked you north of Tribana as well as the warriors that attacked us on the White Desert are from off-world."

"Fitz would be unhappy with the thought of a whole tribe of Timones," Claire laughed. She sobered up. "I'm sure that

Torvall Garrund is behind the attack from the dark warriors. Other members of the council may be involved."

"Perhaps, but we don't know that," Pem argued. "I cannot go about accusing the most powerful members of my council without concrete evidence."

Claire suppressed her irritation. She knew that Jallis Ruffin and by extension, Torvall, were behind much of the troubles that she sensed were about to beset Pem.

"What will you do about Agkor," she asked.

"Nothing, at present. I will continue to monitor any activity from the ship's console. The enemy you know is better than one you don't."

"Will they have clothes for swimming at the resort?" Claire changed the subject. "Leandra has had nothing made for me to wear if I go swimming."

"We can't have you swimming naked, Claire. You and Mags can go shopping in town," Pem offered. "I'm sure the shops would be more than pleased to sell you something at exorbitant prices."

"Yes, and I'll miss Tess's ferocious bargaining power," Claire laughed and snuggled into Pem's arms. A small cloud had passed over the sun and the air had become chilly.

Before reaching the harbor of Bancho, their yacht turned starboard into a deep canal that took them to a turning basin with white limestone docks lined with varnished woods protected by cushioned pads. The crew eased the Rachael Ann up to the largest slip and an expert shore crew received her lines and made her fast to bronze cleats.

The gangplank was run out and an official-looking dignitary overdressed in gold braid and a heavy black uniform appeared at the end of the bridge.

Captain Agkor went dockside, greeted the official, and offered up the Rachael Ann's papers.

There was some friendly haggling before the Captain returned to the ship and the dignitary returned to the shade of the blue awnings attached to the marina office.

"A bothersome formality," Pem nudged Claire and chuckled. "The fellow knows full well that this is the Communicate's ship and that the King and Queen are aboard. After all, we are flying the royal pennant indicating that we are in residence."

"One must placate the bureaucracy," Claire grinned. "He can't be that comfortable in his heavy uniform. I bet he's sweating in the shade."

Agkor approached them at the bow. "Sir, we have been granted the use of the docks at the usual fees. I am required to ask if we have any contraband on board."

"No contraband that I know of, unless Officer Nikko has brought some of his pipe mixtures. As to the fees, they will be larcenous," Pem put in.

"Yes sir, that is most accurate, though I can only speak for the fees," the Captain replied.

Sage Leandra approached Nikko while he was supervising the unloading of luggage and supplies. "You know where my rooms are?" she asked.

When he indicated that he was so informed, she said, "I will be taking a carriage into town and don't expect to return before the evening meal. Will you inform Mags so she will know that I will be late to my rooms?"

"Will you require an escort?" Nikko asked, thinking that he was already shorthanded, but not wanting to neglect the Sage's safety.

"I'm visiting an old friend," she returned. "I seriously doubt if there are any dangers to be encountered here, especially for an old lady such as myself. You will be sure to attend to the royal couple's security, Officer Nikko Pizzar," she said, suddenly being very formal, her eyes flashing.

"Yes ma'am, of course," Nikko swallowed. "You can be very certain that every precaution will be taken."

"I like you," Leandra reached up and patted Nikko's cheek, embarrassing him, "but you are inclined to lack a certain seriousness."

Nikko blushed. "I assure you that Mags and I will be very careful to look after things."

Leandra suddenly smiled. "Why Nikko, I think you will after all."

The First Officer sighed in relief and watched the Sage wander off down the pier, wondering what she meant by her last statement.

"LIKE ANTS," CLAIRE observed.

"Whatever do you mean, dear?" Perm stuck his head around the corner.

"The porters, they are like ants," she grinned. A long line of men, each carrying a single item, waited patiently for their turn to deposit a load of the couple's baggage in its proper place.

"And each, in turn, wants a tip for his efforts—however little that may be," Pem said gloomily as a muscular young man who could have carried an entire chest of coin put down a single box containing one of Claire's several pairs of shoes. Pem scowled and placed a smaller-than-usual coin in the extended hand.

Nikko was directing the traffic from the outside, and Mags was directing the porters from the inside. Drawers were opened and inspected before being filled, clothes were hung in closets, fresh towels filled shelves, and wines and other beverages were placed in coolers.

"Does it always take this much effort just to relocate for a few days?" Claire asked Mags who was directing the placement of a small chest of valuables. "I feel as though I should be doing something."

Mags looked scandalized at the suggestion.

Claire suppressed her feelings of guilt and left to wander through the many rooms of the royal lodging, admiring the view of the ocean through the shaded windows and snacking from several trays of cold fruits and sliced, sweet melons set out for their pleasure. Among other luxuries that Claire thought she might like, the sunken tub filled with steaming, perfumed water that swirled and fell in a little falls at one end attracted her the most. She shed a sandal from one foot and dipped a toe in the clear bath. A wonderful, soothing feeling of well-being crept over her.

"The fabled hot springs of the Southern Coast," Pem came to stand beside her, holding her hand. "Said to have recuperative powers beyond the best of all other mineral waters."

Opening her inner sight, Claire discerned unusual, colorful clouds of phages hovering thickly above the waters which smell vaguely like a cross between peaches and apricots. "Perhaps we could go for a walk along the beach," she suggested to Pem.

While Mags sorted out the last of luggage, Pem and Claire kicked off their shoes and stepped onto the warm sand. Nikko remained on the wide veranda with its overhanging tile roof and promised to have the dinner menu by the time they returned.

"No need to hurry," the officer said to the couple. "Mags and I will tidy up here and post a guard out front to keep the more curious of the other guests from intruding."

The sun felt warm and good on the back of Claire's neck. Pem put his arm around her waist. Claire forgot about Mags and Nikko and turned her attention on Pem.

"I'm ever so glad that we met," Claire told him, recalling her meeting with Pem as he rode his horse through the gate into her world. At first, both Pem and his horse had somehow been miniaturized on her world so that they barely came to her knees.

"I thought that you were a beautiful giantess, at first," he admitted. "But when you came closer, you shrank down to the proper size. I've never understood that phenomenon."

"Nor I," Claire returned. "Leandra once told me that it was a temporary, interdimensional effect of being so close to the gate."

"I think that's just another way of saying 'I don't know'," Pem grinned. "Anyway, I can barely remember that part. What I remember is us racing ahead of that terrible, black water that filled the gate behind us. And also, of you stripping down to bathe in the creek," he flashed a mischievous look at her.

"You were peeking!" Claire's cheeks reddened. "And I thought you were such a gentleman."

"No harm done; we're married now," he let his hands slide and was about to pat her bottom when she caught his wrist and twisted so that he sat down suddenly in the sand.

"Ouch!" He pretended to be hurt and rubbed his wrist. Claire laughed.

"Make sure you don't try that with the pretty girls here on the beach," she pointed to several attractive women lounging in brief attire under umbrellas along the water's edge.

"Time was when this part of the beach was for the exclusive use of the Communicate," he said. "Thank goodness that's no longer true," he ducked the punch Claire threw at him and grappled with her legs so that she tumbled onto the sand. They rolled around, wrestling briefly.

"Now look at what you've done," Claire teased Pem. "I've ruined my pretty dress."

"As if you cared," Pem returned and tried to crawl on top of her.

"Uncle," Claire called out when Pem had pinned her on her back and was looking down at her with that hungry look that Claire had come to appreciate.

"Whoever do you mean?" Startled, Pem looked around as if he were expecting to see his wife's Uncle emerge from the sea.

Claire took advantage of his distraction to twist from his grasp, spring up, and run to the edge of the water. She hesitated a moment as the first foam rolled over her feet and she sank into the soft sand. Her memories of her father in Galveston, Texas, caused tears to flood her eyes. For a moment she was only an ordinary girl who missed her father very much.

"You are crying," Pem, who had caught up with her, wiped the tears from her cheeks with the tip of his finger. "Have I done something wrong?"

The roar of the surf swallowed up the sounds of a seabird wheeling and crying overhead. "No, it is only the salt," she said. "I got some spray in my eyes."

As if to punctuate her answer, a larger wave reared up and broke on the steep beach, catching them unprepared in knee deep water as it raced up the sand. Claire slipped and sat down in the warm salty water while Pem came down on one knee. She scooped up some of the receding water in both hands and threw it into his face.

"It's war," he cried and dug his hands into the next wave, sending a cascade of water over her carefully coifed hair.

Claire dashed out deeper into the water, completely confident of her swimming abilities. She was probably ruining her dress, but hadn't Pem said that she and Mags could shop in the city? Also, Pem had said that nothing dangerous swam in these waters. A tall wave broke over her head and she let herself rise with it, swept shoreward and back towards Pem who was waiting for her.

He grabbed her hand and walked her up on the dry sand. "Well, aren't you a mess. Your dress has become form-fitting," he leered.

Out of the water, she began to feel chilly in the wet dress. She could feel beach sand working its way into uncomfortable places. "And making a spectacle of myself," she waved at a small crowd that had gathered on the beach and was clapping, apparently in appreciation of the royal antics. Two crewmen from the Rachael Ann stood nearby keeping a watchful eye on the couple.

"Perhaps we should try the pool in the suite," Claire suggested. "The bath on the Rachael Ann was too spartan for two, and I could use a long soak in a hot tub. Would you care to join me?" she leered back at him.

"TWO CHILDREN," NIKKO said to Mags who had joined him on the porch outside the royal suite. The kids in question were running across the beach, hand in hand, followed at a more sedate pace by the two security guards that Nikko had assigned to them.

"Not so much younger than us," Mags returned as the Pem and Claire reached the steps. She watched Pem track sand across the floor while Claire carefully wrung the water out the hemline of her dress and dusted the sand off her feet before crossing. So thoughtful of others, Mags thought. Would the girl survive the ruthless politics of Lunaria?

"We're using the bath," Claire said to Mags as she passed. "Do you think you can manage to keep out of trouble with Nikko while Pem and I relax?"

Nikko came to attention. "I'm safely on duty, Ma'am," he grinned.

"Lock the door, Mags," Claire returned the grin.

"How will I see you this evening when you will be sleeping in the royal apartment," Nikko protested to Mags after Claire had disappeared into the bungalow.

"I guess you'll have to solve that riddle," Mags laughed.

Nikko pretended to look puzzled. "I have it," he snapped his fingers.

"What?"

"I'll tempt you with a romantic rendezvous."

"And how will you do that, Officer Nikko," Mags said, curious in spite of knowing that Nikko was teasing her.

"Look for my message at midnight," he said mysteriously.

Part Two

Rissa and Turlo

Parting of Ways

ENGINEER BOLTZ WAS .waiting at Fortuna's rail as Captain Eberson came aboard. The short but powerful figure drew himself up stiffly and saluted the Captain, who returned his salute and then offered his friend his hand in greeting. Pepper, the Fortuna's cocky cook, piped the Captain aboard with an extra flourish, and then the other members of the crew who were not on necessary duties rallied around to welcome their Captain back to his command.

Captain Watchman was the next to cross the temporary gangplank stretching between the two vessels. Captain Eberson introduced him to Engineer Boltz and asked Zim, the newly promoted Second, to show him to his quarters next to his own.

Turlo and Rissa started across next and arrived almost simultaneously on the deck of the Fortuna. Eberson stepped forward and formally welcomed them aboard his vessel before introducing them to his Engineer and First Officer in Nikko's absence.

Boltz, usually a taciturn individual who paid scant attention to anything other than his beloved engines, inclined his head respectfully to Turlo as the Prince of Tieben and bowed deeply to Rissa Ellendor, the famous Lady Rissa, sole heir to the leading Trader Family in Lunaria. He blushed furiously when he stepped back next to the captain, and Rissa wondered what the Engineer was thinking.

Rissa heard the gangplank sliding back to the deck of the Rachael Ann. She turned to watch Claire and Pem standing together at the Rachael Ann's rail. Suddenly Claire seemed impossibly young and fragile and Pem far too young and inexperienced to take on the awesome job of unifying their land under a new Monarchy. She sensed Turlo turn next to her and let him take her hand in his. He gave her hand a quick squeeze.

Turlo said, "She'll be safe, Rissa. There are people to watch over her, and she is far from helpless, you know."

"I know," Rissa sighed, "but it is a great undertaking, and if we should fail, so might our two friends."

"We will not fail, either ourselves or them," Turlo said in a low voice filled with emotion.

Rissa blinked in surprise at Turlo's mood. "You surprise me. What are you leaving behind that so distracts you?" She kept her tone light and teasing, but she knew very well what Turlo was talking about. She felt it in herself so keenly that she had to struggle to keep the tears from welling up into her eyes as she returned Claire's wave.

"As you well know, I have met the love of my life in you," Turlo replied in a low voice. "But Lady Claire has managed to touch me in ways I cannot explain. She is never demanding, and perhaps too understanding for her own good. Nevertheless, knowing her has set my course towards great and important deeds, the very things that I have avoided all my life. She brought us together for purposes far beyond our simple feelings for each other. I think I fear her almost as much as I fear for her."

Captain Eberson came to stand beside Rissa, also looking at the royal couple across the widening gap between the two vessels. He acknowledged Nikko's salute and nodded in Pem's direction one final time. He hoped Nikko would fulfill his mission with respect to Agkor.

"They are the most powerful force on this world and they do not yet know it," he said quietly. "Perhaps that is best."

"Even so, Captain," Rissa returned, "the most powerful of forces cannot be applied if the fulcrum should yield. I fear that simple treachery could undo everything we wish to accomplish."

Eberson sighed, thinking of Captain Agkor. "Each of us can only do our best."

And with that the helmsman changed course out to sea at the end of the bay and steamed off into the waters of the western ocean known as the Ocean of Tides.

The Fortuna Sails West

AFTER A BRIEF inspection of the ship conducted by Zim, the new Second, Captain Eberson spent time in his quarters reading the ship's log kept by Engineer Boltz during his absence. The entries were more sparse than the Captain might have wished, but the data appeared to be complete, the times and distances, the course corrections, the calculations on the dead-reckoning forms, and a smattering of other considerations like the loss of three sacks of flour due to a leak in the caulking on the section of roof over the pantry.

There was even the mention of one of the crew falling overboard during a lifeboat drill. Eberson wondered why Boltz had conducted such a drill until he ran across an entry concerning the malfunction of a critical valve in Fortuna's entropy engine circulating system. The terse entry, "Repairs made, engine restarted," failed to satisfy his curiosity, and he made a note to ask the Engineer about the incident at a convenient time. Also, as they were to be on the open seas for a while and could not conveniently put in for restocking, he glanced over the latest inventories.

After due consideration, he decided that he would begin his new entry with a summary of his inspections on his return. But first he opened his cabin door to ask Carl, the orderly on duty, to fetch the Second for him. "Go and tell the Second Officer that I require his presence," Eberson directed. Carl, a lanky, pleasant-face boy who had been recruited from a farm family near Greyhaven, straightened his jacket, saluted smartly, and hurried off to find Zim.

Eberson watched the lad disappear through the hatch leading to officer's quarters and noted the immaculate whites, the jaunty angle of his cap, the tidy cut to his hair, and thought how proud his parent would be of their son who was making a fine career for himself aboard the Fortuna.

He was contemplating what to say about the low inventory of his favorite coffee when a knock announced Zim's arrival.

"Come," Eberson said.

Zim entered with his hat folded in his hands and stood straight in his whites with their polished brass buttons and officer's stripes on each shoulder. He was of fair complexion with a few boyish freckles, and his short brown hair had red highlights that reminded Eberson of young Pem. He was at attention without being excessively formal, and his clear gray eyes held both curiosity as well as seriousness.

The sense of what was needed, not what was required, was what had recommended Zim to the Captain in the first place. There was also the fact that Eberson had known Zim's family well, and Sage Leandra had examined him for trustworthiness, finding nothing worrisome hidden in the man's ambitions. Not only that, but he remembered the nights that he played his guitar for the ship's company. Young Claire had been put at ease as they had sailed up the Songris to her first appearance at Greyhaven.

"Sir?"

The Captain spoke bluntly, "First Office Pizzar will not be with us on this voyage, and Engineer Boltz has engineering duties that will occupy his time fully, so I'm moving you into the First's slot, Zim. Do you think you can handle the job?"

Zim looked slightly stunned. He waited a moment before he said, "Yes, Sir, I can do it. You can count on me, Captain."

"Perhaps you should remind me what the duties of the First are," Eberson returned.

"Of course, Sir." Zim straightened. "The First is the head of the deck department and second-in-command after the ship's master. My primary responsibilities are the vessel's cargo operations, its stability, and supervising the deck crew. I'm responsible for the safety and security of the ship, as well as the welfare of the crew on board. I would typically stand the 4-8 navigation watch. My additional duties include maintenance of the ship's hull, cargo gears, accommodations, the lifesaving appliances and the firefighting appliances. I also train the crew on various aspects like safety."

Zim blushed. "I would ordinarily assume command of the whole ship in the absence or incapacitation of the master, but on the Fortuna I would expect Engineer Boltz, who is senior, to take over that duty."

"As usual, you are very astute, Mr. Zim. Your promotion ultimately depends on your performance, you understand," Captain Eberson reminded him. "It's a heavy responsibility, but the Fortuna is a small ship and ideal for your first experience. If and when Nikko rejoins us, I will make him our new Security Officer, assign him some of the more difficult training and safety tasks, and make your job permanent as the First."

"Security Officer, Sir? I don't believe I've heard of the position," Zim said respectfully.

"I've decided that Engineer Boltz will no longer lead shore parties," Eberson said. "And there will be a need to have an officer responsible for communications as well as taking over other tasks which I have in mind. Nikko has unique qualifications."

"Yes, Sir," Zim said, obviously not understanding but quite pleased with his own promotion. "Am I to start my duties immediately?"

"Yes, Mr. Zim. See to it that the duty rosters reflect the proper changes and that our guests are comfortable and secure. Check with the Cook and schedule a private dinner for the five of us near the Middle Watch. You will attend all meetings from now on," Eberson said. Zim fairly glowed.

"That will be all," the Captain dismissed his new First.

The Captain then turned back to his private journal and began listing what he hoped to accomplish in the next few weeks. There were ports to be made, supplies to be taken on without arousing suspicions, plans to finalize, and other decisions to be made. The Captain wasn't entirely comfortable with the mission that Lord Gilbert had handed him. There were far too many political implications, as far as he was concerned, and the newly recognized King was too young to navigate these troubled waters on his own.

Of course, the young Queen seemed more than capable of making up for Pem's immaturity. Eberson hoped so. The next few months would determine the direction the Kingdom was likely to take. If Pem secured the reins of power, all would be well. If Pem failed to be able to control the Council, all those associated with the Monarchy were likely to pay a heavy price as power shifted in Lunaria. Eberson didn't care to be on the losing side, but he wasn't about to throw in with the Council. Anarchy and misery lay in that direction.

That was the reason he was ferrying Prince Turlo and Rissa Ellendor in the direction of Boggrash. It was crucial that Turlo establish his right to succession for the throne of Tieben. King Veral Hushara needed to be coaxed in the direction of stability for the sake of both Lunaria as well as Tieben. The powerful Trader Clans were crucial in this effort. Eberson only hoped that Turlo and Rissa would survive the effort. They are great kids, he thought, then chided himself. He was an old man. What did he know of the ambitions and courage of youth?

A Fish Dinner on the Fortuna

FOUR BELLS RANG at the start of the Last Dog Watch aboard the Fortuna. Rissa and Turlo joined Captain Eberson, a new First Officer, and Captain Watchman already seated in the small, private dining room behind the chart house. The Fortuna was too small for a separate officer's mess during ordinary operations, and the dining room served this purpose on special occasions. The table was elegantly prepared with white linens and silver flatware. A gas chandelier was lowered from its rack in the ceiling and swung over the center of the table casting a warm glow over the participants. Wine goblets sparkled, waiting to be filled. Crystal glasses filled with chilled water waited at each place.

Rissa and Turlo were seated side by side, Rissa at the Captain's end of the table, across from Watchman and the new Officer, Zim. Boltz's chair at end of the table remained empty. "Engineer Boltz is unavoidably occupied with the conversion of the entropy engine heater to the wood burning firebox," Captain Eberson announced. He waited as Rissa fingered the gold pendant hanging from its chain about her neck. When she nodded, he continued, "I believe that ordinary steam power will keep us off any tracer that might be used by Lord Garrund and the Dark Sages to locate the Fortuna and thus reveal some hint of our plans."

"Does this mean that you subscribe to the idea that there is a Council of Dark Sages?" Rissa wanted to know.

"Gilbert believes there is such a thing, and I, for one, would not gainsay Lord Greybaird," Eberson replied.

The Captain went on to introduce Zim, the new First, around the table. "I know you have met Mr. Zim, but this is a formal way to celebrate his promotion to the job that First Officer Nikko held. Also, I want everyone to understand that Zim is in my confidence, so you may feel free to discuss any of the aspects of our journey with him." Eberson fell silent as a knock on the door was followed by the cook entering with a large serving dish.

"I've used almost all of the fresh supplies, so enjoy this while it lasts," Pepper said. The cook placed a rather large platter in the middle of the table. The silver dish was filled end-to-end with a beautifully prepared Jarka, a salt-water fish equivalent to the wild land-grazers, and garnished with fresh greens and wedges of a tart green fruit. Pepper filled each goblet with a sparkling, ruby wine. Rissa found her mouth watering, but held back as the Captain cleared his throat.

"We will eat first before we discuss what is ahead of us," he said. "May G'rama bless this food."

The blessing was the signal for the First to offer the food, first to the Captain, and then to the guests in a counter clockwise fashion, which in this case worked out perfectly because it meant that Trader Rissa received first, followed by Prince Turlo and finally Captain Watchman. Zim was pleased with his plans, and Eberson nodded his approval.

The Jarka was tasty, the greens tender, and the bread, when brought around by the cook, was marvelous slathered with sweet butter and generous amounts of honey from the pot on the table. When everyone had their fill, the cook and an assistant cleared the table and returned with a berry cobbler that would have impressed the most discriminating diner.

"I'm impressed," Turlo said, suppressing a belch. "This is better than Blossom's cooking in Norcross, and I had thought that she was the world's best." There were nods around the table, for everyone but Zim was familiar with the story of Brey and Blossom in their adventures in Tieben as told by Lady Tess and Lady Claire.

"We are quite fortunate to have Pepper as our cook," Zim offered, pleased that he could add something to the small talk.

"Indeed," Rissa said, "but I believe that our good Captain Eberson has decided that it is time to draw the curtain open on our future. Is that not right, Captain?"

"I thought merely to explain how we are to deliver you and your companions into the hands of your mother," Eberson returned. "First, we will make for a small port called Land's End where we can pick up the necessary supplies, including wood for our boiler. We have some cases of salt in the cargo hold so we will appear as a simple trading mission."

"Won't people know that the Fortuna is Lord Greybaird's vessel?" Turlo wanted to know.

Eberson replied, "The small ports on Lunaria's west coast are relatively isolated and the Fortuna has rarely sailed in these waters. Nevertheless we have planned on temporarily renaming our ship the Fortunata, a fairly common name in Lunaria. One of the crew will be busy tomorrow making the necessary changes with a bucket of paint."

"We also intend to dirty her up a bit with some ash and make her look less respectable. I don't really expect there will be a problem, especially if we pay the port tariffs without argument. However, I'd ask that you not appear on deck during our visit," he said, indicating his three guests.

"How many stops will we have to make to take on wood?" Watchman wanted to know.

"We plan to stop at the Western Outpost and Woodhill. Woodhill will be the last port before we are to rendezvous with your mother's ship, the Ellendor II," he addressed himself to the lady Trader.

"How will we find the Trader ship in the middle of the ocean?" Turlo wanted to know.

"As to that, I can only say that Trader Ellendor and Lord Gilbert have exchanged signals before, and we have the means of finding each other. More I am not at liberty to say as it involves knowledge known only to a few outside of the King's Communicate," Eberson said.

Turlo looked a little put off by this statement, but Rissa laid her hand over his on the table and smiled. "We cannot presume too much on the Captain's honor," she said. "It is not needful for us to know the how, only that it can be done."

"It is not that they don't trust you, Prince," Captain Watchman put in. "I am a captain in Mara Ellendor's private service and even I cannot tell you the details of the process."

Turlo shrugged. "You're right, it's not important. I was merely curious, that is all. Such easy communication could make our task much easier as we move across Tieben. I hope only to convince my Uncle Veral that I have changed my mind concerning my succession to the throne, and that to cement our good will I will trade a great gift in the form of an agreement with the leading Trader house to improve the trading credits between Lunaria and Tieben. If this cannot succeed, or if my Uncle insists that I must marry this Wintermarsh Lady, then I must attempt to unseat my Uncle Veral and use the popularity of the former King Cornal Hushara to boost myself into Crown."

"After all," he continued, placing his other hand over Rissa's, "I will marry only the love of my life, and there is nothing which can change my mind about that."

Rissa blushed and looked pleased; there were smiles on both older men's faces. Watchman as well as Eberson understood what was passing between their young friends.

Young love is so…certain, Eberson thought.

A Hint of Foul Weather Ahead

RISSA TURNED OVER in her bunk and looked through the open port. The morning light reflected off a golden bank of clouds on the southern horizon, but there was nothing else to see but the slow march of ocean swell and an occasional ridge of foam along the top of a ripple. She felt the ship alive around her and relaxed, content to let her thoughts drift for a few more minutes before she would have to dress and join others in the mess. She wondered if Turlo in the next cabin might still be suffering a lingering touch of sickness from the slow pitching motion of the little ship.

She smiled to herself. Turlo had desired her comforts after the dinner with the Captain last night, but she had told him that a degree of decorum would be observed—at least for the time being. Once they were on her mother's ship…well, that would be different. He had pretended great sorrow, but Rissa saw that the Prince was aware of the sense of her request and was simply teasing her. Still, she had wanted him to know that the time would pass more slowly so long as they had to keep their distance. She felt a pleasant tingle, knowing that he understood and respected her feelings.

Six bells on the morning watch rang, summoning her turn at the mess. She swung her feet from under the light covers and felt the chill of the deck. She dressed quickly, wiped her face and hands with a wash cloth moistened in a pitcher of lavender water by her bunk, and examined herself in the tiny mirror above the built-in cupboard. The sight wasn't encouraging, but it would have to do, she decided. She ran a comb through her honey-colored curls, thought about cutting them short, and adjusted her talisman beneath the scoop of her over shirt. She swiped at a bit of crustiness at the corners of her green eyes and blinked. There! She opened the door to the companionway and almost bumped into Turlo hurrying through the passageway towards the steps up to the mess room.

Turlo, endowed with some talent that seemed almost magical, always seemed to appear at the top of his form. His dark hair was swept back neatly, his face ruddy with health and the fresh sea air, and his clothes free of unsightly wrinkles. *How does he, a mere man, do it?* Rissa wondered.

"We're late," he grabbed her hand before she had a chance to become more irritated and rushed her along the corridor, handing her forward so that she might ascend the steep stairs ahead of him. She felt his eyes on her as she climbed ahead of him and blushed.

Watchman was alone in the mess when Rissa and Turlo arrived. His eyes twinkled as he looked closely at the pair of youngsters.

Turlo, picking up on Watchman's expression, raised an eyebrow. "If only there were such a reason for being late," he said.

Rissa avoided both men and sat at the end of the table. Pepper's assistant, a stringy lad everyone called Stick, placed a mug of hot tarle and a bowl of coarse groats in front of her and offered to pour a portion of sweet cream over the cereal. She wrinkled her nose at the oats and let Stick drizzle some of the rich, yellow cream over the pale mound of paste.

"I'll never get used to this stuff," she said. "If only we could have fresh fruit.'

"I'm sorry we have nothing so elegant, Lady," Stick said. "I could try and obtain some for you when we put in at Land's End. I think they have a market, and there should be some fresh fruit available this time of year. No doubt the captain would approve."

Rissa winced. "I'm sorry, Stick, I should not complain. It really doesn't matter. And I never meant to criticize the food aboard the Fortuna. Why, last night I think I ate the best dinner I ever had. The Jarka was wonderful."

Stick grinned, looking almost boyish. "I will be most happy to relay your praise to Pepper," he said.

While the three were finishing their groats, Zim slipped into the cabin and sat across from Turlo and Watchman. "I wanted to inform you that we will be in sight of Land's End by early tomorrow morning—if this weather holds."

Watchman asked, "Are you expecting a weather change?"

"As you probably know, the Southern Ocean is famous for its sudden storms this time of year," Zim said. "Captain Eberson thinks that we may be in for heavy weather sometime during the next week. The direction of the swell is from the southeast which can mean that a storm is brewing far to the south and moving in our direction."

Watchman said, "I am most familiar with the weather patterns north from Pendrel on the Isle of Vash around to the ice fields at the north end of Tieben. That is where I have spent my time on the seas. My knowledge of these southern waters is sketchy."

Rissa watched Turlo frown. "Don't worry," she said. "I've sailed these waters with my mother, and a ship such as the Fortuna, though small, is well founded and safe enough in even a heavy blow."

Turlo looked slightly embarrassed. "I am a creature of the land," he said. "Give me a raging blizzard or the wild rapids of a river and I am in my element. Give me something I can use a blade against, and I am more comfortable than watching our bow knifing through these waves. I keep thinking of the dark depths below us and the eternal loneliness of such a watery grave."

Zim chuckled and said, "Please forgive me for laughing, Prince, but I think I prefer the shrieking wind, the wild spray, and the pummeling of the high seas to facing the no-doubt grand sight of a line of horsemen with sabers flashing, waiting to carve me up into little pieces."

"Each of us must cope with our own fears," Watchman observed.

Rissa put her hand to her talisman and felt the steady warmth of the golden shield. At least Claire seems to continue in the safe keeping of the King, she thought. She concentrated on sending good thoughts in the direction of the girl who wore the twin to her token. She imagined that she felt a slight stirring in return.

Fencing Practice

THERE WAS REALLY nothing to do during the remainder of the morning, so Rissa and Turlo petitioned Zim and obtained two practice swords. Rissa chose one that was longer and more slender while Turlo chose a heavier, stouter blunt blade. Zim suggested that they take over part of the rear deck and had one of the deck crew move the deck chairs under the awning behind the pilot house.

The sun was warm, the air salty and fresh, and Rissa thought that Turlo looked handsome in his leather vest and white linen shirt. Zim looked from one to the other, uncertain that it was a good idea for Rissa to be practicing with the experienced warrior.

"I would not like you to get hurt, Lady Trader," Zim said. "After all, I am responsible for your safety."

Turlo laughed. "Surely you jest. I am the one more likely to be skewered. I have personally seen this innocent-looking trader remove the heads of many fierce warriors."

The pair saluted each other in the traditional manner of dueling, and waited for Zim to move back. Reluctantly, Zim moved out of range; Rissa and Turlo touched blades and studied each other for a moment.

Rissa watched Turlo's blade, not his eyes, having long understood how the eyes could deceive. She smiled and pretended to relax, inviting Turlo to make the first move. She caught him off guard when she engaged the tip of his blade, wove a quick basket, and let her longer blade slide up along his. He was quick, but not quick enough to avoid a tap on his forearm.

Turlo laughed, but Rissa could see that he was piqued. "Not fair," he said gruffly and crossed blades with her in a more straightforward fashion.

Rissa, who knew very well that Turlo would never let fairness intrude into a fight, looked for some advantage. Strength lay upon the Prince's side, but quickness was her advantage. When he attempted to block her blade and press forward, she slipped aside, ducked under his back hand cut, and tapped him on his other arm.

This time Turlo laughed, backed up, and put the tip of his practice blade on the deck signifying time-out. "You see what I mean?" he asked the astonished First Officer.

Rissa dug into a pocket in her leather jacket and wiped her forehead with a clean, linen handkerchief. She knew that Turlo would be more serious the next time they engaged.

Indeed, this was the case as he managed to batter aside her defense by sheer strength and took advantage of the fact that Rissa was trapped against a bulkhead before she could slide out of the way. He stopped his vicious thrust a finger's width short of her shoulder and back off.

"One to you," she grinned.

They went back and forth like this until both worked up a sweat. Neither could seem to take advantage of the other. Finally they called a halt, and Zim had a crew member bring cool water and a plate of plain cakes. Two chairs and a small table were brought up, and he left them to each other's company as he said he had other duties to attend to.

"I think we confounded poor Zim," Rissa laughed, savoring the tartness of the drink. "Now, if only Stick can find some fruits for our breakfast, I think I will enjoy this sail."

'I find that I am somewhat envious of the manner in which you are able to use your wealth and position of responsibility," Turlo said, keeping his voice light. "You seem to be that simple woman who is easy with whatever is needful in life, and you never complain. Yet, anyone who knows you well knows the great depth of purpose that moves you."

Turlo leaned forward quite close to Rissa. "I, on the other hand, have spent much of my life avoiding a destiny that would have me responsible to the people of Tieben. Sometimes, since knowing you and Lady Claire, I think that I have wasted much of that time, that I have often chosen unworthy goals, and lived without any serious purpose. I used to think I was content, and now I am seized with a restlessness that nearly drives me mad."

"I don't believe you have wasted your time," Rissa assured him. "You are a leader who will discover your following—and soon, I think. I have seen how men are drawn to you, and you should have the courage of their acceptance of you."

She smiled almost wickedly. "Also, I have seen how women are drawn to you."

"Hardly," Turlo protested, but didn't manage to hide a pleased look. "You know that you are the love of my life and there will be only you."

"So all men say," Rissa sighed dramatically and tossed her curls.

Turlo, however, knew she was merely teasing him and decided not to respond.

Land's End

THROUGHOUT THAT FIRST full day they plowed steadily north, running with higher swell and clear skies. Any but an experienced mariner would probably have thought that fair weather would continue into the foreseeable future. In fact, Turlo expressed his optimism to Rissa.

They had returned their practice swords to the ship's stores and were standing at the rail amidships. "It looks like the Captain and Mr. Zim were wrong about the weather," Turlo observed. "Surely this perfect day heralds perfect weather for our passage."

Rissa, who was very experienced in these things, shook her head emphatically. "Not so. Winds and swell from the eastern quadrant more often herald stormy weather, though how stormy remains to be seen. It is my guess that we will know by tomorrow morning when we approach Land's End. The captain will decide what to do."

Turlo asked, "What do you think his decision will be?"

"I think he means to make the rendezvous with the Ellendor II at any cost short of losing the ship," she said. "I believe that he thinks that our mission is of the utmost urgency. I agree with him. I began to feel very uneasy in Lumminea during the wedding. Don't forget the attack on the royal yacht on the way down the river."

"Who could forget that!" Turlo said. "I felt more helpless in that moment than when I went in the water with the cable while we were steaming down the Lorne."

"I wonder if we are not headed into the same situation in Tieben?" Rissa said softly.

"I would go alone into Tieben in order that you remain safe," he returned. "However, your support is crucial to the entire effort, and who would believe me. You are the key that will open the doors that we must pass through."

"Let us hope that none of those doors will close and lock behind us," Rissa commented.

That afternoon they retired with Captain Watchman to the empty dining room where they had eaten their wonderful dinner the night before. They spent several hours going over possible strategies for approaching Veral Hushara.

"You will have to be presented to him privately as the emissary of the most powerful trading house in Boggrash," Watchman said. "You cannot let anyone know your plans for marriage. That would be a dangerous and disastrous course which would divide your supporters who will see their chance at influence in the Court diminished considerably by a marriage into a trader family."

"Why is that, Captain," Turlo said, irritated. "I should think that such a union would guarantee Tieben special favor in the eyes of Boggrash Traders."

"What it would actually do," Watchman retorted, "would leave everyone thinking that *you* will gain the special favor, not the current families who control the royal court. No, if anything, you must be seen to be neutral in these matters which will keep your enemies divided and easier to deal with. Once you have consolidated your position in the succession, you will be able to make less popular choices because you will be in a position to grant more favors."

"An ugly business," Turlo growled. "It's no wonder that I avoided politics for so long."

Rissa laughed. "After the way you handled my mother, I'm quite sure that the politics of the Tieben court will be child's play for you."

It was when Pepper stuck his head in the door to announce a change of plans for dinner that the three conspirators noticed the change in the motion of the Fortuna.

"The weather is getting heavier," the cook said, "and we will be serving light fare this evening. If you don't mind, the captain has requested that all hands as well as guests take their rotation in the mess room where it will be easier and safer to serve the food."

"Tell us when you need us," Watchman spoke for the three of them.

"I will send someone for you about seven bells," he said.

Rissa and Watchman nodded, but Turlo was trying to remember what corresponded to seven bells ships-time. "That's ten recites before sunset, land time," the cook laughed.

Turlo pursed his lips. "If it weren't for the excellent Jarka last night I might be insulted."

"Stop teasing the man," Rissa told Turlo playfully. "You know you are just being stubborn about learning ship's language."

"Yes, of course," Turlo grinned. Pepper looked immensely relieved.

NOT LONG AFTER the crew had all eaten their evening meal and the First Watch from 2000 to midnight was settling in, everyone felt the Fortuna suddenly rise much higher than usual and drop like barrel going over water falls—something Turlo remembered from an incident when he was a boy.

Turlo, Watchman, and Rissa were crowded into Watchman's stateroom going over some details of the supplies they would need on the trek around Snowy Pass when the ship took the plunge. Alarmed, Rissa said she was going up to the bridge to find out what had happened. Watchman and Turlo stayed behind to finish last minute estimates.

Zim, whose job as First Officer was to stand the pilot house First Watch, welcomed Rissa into the dimly lighted cabin. A hooded gas lamp cast shadows behind the wheel while a prism sent light to illuminate the compass mounted on gimbals in front of the helm. She noted that the helmsman was not having any difficulties keeping the Fortuna on course.

"A freak wave, we think," Zim told her. "I've seen worse in my years, though that one was larger than I'd like to think. When it passed under our keel it felt like a moving mountain of water. Everything has smoothed out and back to normal."

"For a moment I wondered if the Fortuna was going to continue to the bottom of the sea," Rissa said quietly.

"Nothing that bad, I hope," Zim returned. "The Fortuna is a tough little ship. Unless something catches her unawares, I have full faith in her to weather any storm. I've sent around the cabin crew to bolt all ports for the night. I'm sorry if the air might be stuffy, but I don't think we can take any chances with flooding."

Rissa nodded. "Of course not. A wise precaution. A little stale air is preferable to an eternity at the bottom of the ocean."

Rissa returned to Watchman's cabin and reported on developments. Since there was little more they could do, they decided to retire to their cabins. Turlo stopped with Rissa at her cabin door.

"I would come in if you were to invite me," he said, sounding hopeful.

She stretched up and kissed him lightly on the mouth. "I'm flattered, and I would like nothing better," she said. "but how can we be taken seriously if we begin rumors about the Prince of Tieben and the Envoy to King Veral? We will have to wait, even if I will sleep little thinking of you."

THE WEATHER HAD improved by early in the morning, but Rissa did not take this as a good sign. She was familiar with the treacherous ways of southern cyclones. She was sore from the sword practice the day before and realized that she needed to practice much more often. She came on deck before breakfast, straining her eyes in anticipation of seeing the light at the end of the jetties at Land's End. She wasn't disappointed.

When Turlo joined her, she pointed out the pin prick of light winking every few second. In minutes the dawn light was too strong and they could no longer see the flash of the beam.

The Fortuna plowed ahead, foam curling from her bow. The seas which had been astern were now quartering as their ship turned further eastward seeking the channel entrance. By the time Rissa could see the low hills and the scattering of buildings that made up the little town of Land's End, the white water breaking over the granite jetties was clearly visible. It was a cruel entrance, she thought. A small miscalculation, a moment's inattention, and a ship would shatter against the jagged rocks where there would be no hope of rescue in the ceaseless crash of heavy surf.

Before long they passed by the sturdy stone lighthouse and came into view of the piers and tar-coated wood pilings driven into the sandy bottom of the little bay. Below them the waters were crystal clear, and, even in the early morning light, they could see the shadows of large fish swimming near the bottom.

"Looks lonely," Turlo commented.

"I believe that that is why it is called Land's End," Rissa suggested.

Stick joined them at the rail. "The captain requests that you go below," he informed them. "He doesn't want anyone seeing a non-crewman aboard our vessel. I'll be sure to look for some fruit when we go ashore for provisions," he called after them.

Rissa and Turlo made for the ship's mess where they got to enjoy an early breakfast due to the crew being busy bringing the little ship in.

Captain Eberson joined them unexpectedly. "Mr. Zim is perfectly capable of bringing the Fortuna in to dock, and this is an exceptionally good place for practice in any case. We should be here for only a few hours, and then we will set sail for the settlement called the Western Outpost. It's a strange name, and no one seems to know the exact origin of the name since it is not exactly an outpost and not nearly the western-most town of any size along the coast."

He added after looking around to see that they were alone, "I have received messages from Boggrash assuring me that the Ellendor is on course and currently beating her way into the wind about five days north of the rendezvous point. All seems to be going according to plan."

Turlo looked as if he were about to question Eberson. Rissa put a hand up. "We do not need to know how," Rissa said quietly.

Rissa heard shouts from outside and a gentle nudge of their hull against a piling. A short squeak of a heavy line playing out around a post and they felt the Fortuna, now the Fortunata, come to rest. The stationary deck felt strange under her feet as Rissa she got up to go below.

"I will be taking a nap and writing in my journal," she told Turlo. "Knock on my door if something interesting or urgent turns up—and no, not that," she grinned at Turlo's expression.

RISSA FELT RESTLESS as she sat at the tiny desk in her cabin. Her journal was open in front of her and her pen was poised, but no words had appeared on the blank page. On a deck below her, a great deal of thumping and loud voices announced the transfer of the bags of salt to the rear cargo hatch.

She hoped Stick would be able to lay in a stock of fresh vegetables and fruits, if only for the five days between Land's End and the rendezvous with her mother's ship. She especially enjoyed having fruit. The larger Trader's ships generally featured a simple form of refrigeration and carried fresh fruits and vegetables, even on fairly long voyages. She smiled at the misleading story about snow from the mountains that her mother had invented when they first met Claire on the Trader's landship crossing the Plain of Glass. At the time, they hadn't been prepared to reveal their technology to an off-world person. Her mother had even claimed to be only a Trader Ship's Captain.

Other problems weren't so easy to put off—like the mutual feelings she shared with Turlo. She couldn't allow those feelings to erupt into a full-blown public romance—not yet. Perhaps after their mission to Tieben there would be time to explore each other. Rissa knew that Turlo could be put off only so long before there would be trouble between them.

A knock at her door startled her. She found Turlo looking sheepish outside her cabin. He pleaded, "I am bored. I don't find writing interesting, and there's little left to plan until we reach the shores north of Boggrash. The view from my port is of endless ocean. I had nothing to do but sharpen my blade. Could we at least talk?"

Rissa laughed. "We could leave the door open," she teased him.

He pushed through and shut the door firmly behind him. "We could, but we won't," he said.

Rissa raised an eyebrow. "Conquest by force? My, you are getting desperate, Prince Murten."

Turlo growled and drew her closer to him. "It is I who have been conquered," he whispered and smoothed a curl from her brow.

Rissa felt all her plans and intentions dropping away. This was the man she wanted, and suddenly she decided that she needn't wait. "Is the door locked?" she asked.

He reached behind him and jammed the bolt shut. "It is now."

On to the Western Outpost

RISSA WAS AWARE of the silly grin on her face as she sat at the table in the officer's dining room that evening. She didn't react to the questioning look she got from Captain Eberson or the suppressed amusement from Watchman. Turlo seemed preoccupied and paid little attention to the platter of roast grazer and vegetables. Zim was chatting about maintenance with Engineer Boltz who was in attendance, having finished whatever repairs and conversions that he deemed necessary.

Rissa could feel the little ship fairly leaping through the water as she plowed her way north from Land's End. Next port of call was Western Outpost.

"We seem to be making excellent time," Rissa attempted some small talk and addressed Boltz during a break in his discussions with the First Officer.

Boltz replied, "We can make more steam with the wood-burning firebox than we can with our entropy-engine conversion," he said. "Of course, we could theoretically circle the planet without refueling with the entropy engine. We have to stop every few days when we burn wood—especially at this rate." He looked accusingly at the Captain.

"We have a schedule to keep, Boltz," Captain Eberson said. "You'll just have to keep her running until that time."

"We'll need a week's maintenance," the engineer complained.

Eberson returned, "I'll give the crew shore leave when we return to Woodhill. It'll make for a nice reason to be returning so soon after leaving. We'll spread it around that we had engine trouble."

Boltz growled, "We may not have to pretend to have engine trouble."

The weather conditions remained much the same that night and the next day. They encountered slightly worsening conditions as they approached the Western Outpost on the following morning.

"You look under the weather," Rissa whispered over breakfast to Turlo. The mess was clear, and all crew members as well as officers were already off to take up duties assigned to them for docking at the port.

"Yes," Turlo returned, avoiding looking at the beautiful arrangement of fresh fruit in front of him. "I'm afraid that Stick's effort to supply us with good fruit is wasted on me this morning."

"Never mind," Rissa said and reached over to spear a succulent slice of reddish fruit with which she was unfamiliar. "I'll make sure that nothing goes unused."

She let the sweet pulp dissolve in her mouth. "I wonder if this fruit can stand shipment," She said. "It would be very popular in the north."

"Ever thinking of business," Turlo snorted and then seemed to regret his outburst. "Sorry, I guess I'm not very good at making small talk."

"Perhaps your talents lie in other directions," Rissa hinted with a knowing look that made Turlo's face grow red.

Further exploration of the topic was interrupted with the sudden sway of the ship as the Fortuna reversed her engines and slowed to nudge the dockside. The squeal of the rub-rail against tarred pilings was rather louder than last time.

"I think Mr. Zim's timing is a little off this morning," Turlo commented.

"Or the weather is getting worse," Rissa returned. She could hear the wind whistling in the vent pipe above her head. "Perhaps we will be in for a bit of a blow soon."

Turlo groaned and looked even miserable. "I already find this voyage worse than good swordplay."

For that day, Rissa spent most of their time dockside staring through the porthole and watching a parade of fishing boats enter the small harbor and set heavy bow and stern anchors in the sandy bottom. It was a sure sign of bad weather on the way.

There was much shouting and thumping below her as Zim supervised the loading of more wood and the exchange of cargo they had picked up in Land's End. Occasionally she heard an impatient Engineer Boltz yell at crew members who failed to stow a load properly. Rissa figured that the engineer was worried about cargo coming loose in a heavy blow.

The sun was low in the west and streamers of ragged clouds were skimming the sky in bands when the Fortuna cast off and made its way through the opening in the jetties. Rissa left her cabin to see if she could be of some assistance in preparing the ship for a rough over-night passage. She paused briefly in front of Turlo's cabin door, about to knock, when she heard a low moan coming from the other side of the door. Turlo would be of no use up on deck, she decided.

<u>Engine Troubles</u>

THE DISTANCE BETWEEN the Western Outpost and Woodhill was considerably less than the last leg from Land's End. Captain Eberson predicted that they would approach the next stopover sometime late the following afternoon.

"Unless we have a problem with this storm," he announced at dinner. "The wind has shifted into a more-southerly direction, and we may have to stay out to sea if the weather is too heavy. The passage into the harbor at Woodhill is long and narrow, and I don't want to take any chances with the cross currents that flow there when the wind is quartering the coast."

"Where is our Prince?" Watchman wanted to know.

"I think the motion of the ship has finally done him in," Rissa said, trying to be sympathetic. "I've told him to go up top and keep his eyes on the horizon, but I'm afraid he's leaning over and looking at the water. You know what that can do even to an experienced mariner."

"I'm afraid so," Zim said, shaking his head at some memory.

Captain Eberson suggested that Rissa ask the cook to take some hot tea to Turlo's cabin. "Pepper has a special herbal remedy that usually works in these cases of seasickness," he said.

Rissa promised to give it a try. "…though he is not likely to listen to me," she finished.

"Call it Captain's orders," Zim suggested—words which brought a chuckle from around the table. None of the others believed that the Prince would take a directive easily, not even from the Captain.

DURING FIRST WATCH, shortly before midnight, the motion of the Fortuna became violent enough to awaken Rissa. The engine seemed to be under load. Heavy spray and occasional waves were breaking against the port in her cabin. She rolled over and checked the dogs on the brass frame, making sure they were secure and the seal tight.

She decided she should check on Turlo. She pulled on her dressing gown and went to his cabin door. The door proved to be unlocked. She pushed through slowly and let the light from the passage enter behind her. There wasn't much need to be quiet as the sounds of the wind and water were loud enough even in the confines of the passageway. As near as she could tell, her lover was sleeping soundly on his back—snoring loudly. Pepper's tea seems to have worked, she thought. She crossed the deck and checked the porthole which she found solidly secured.

Having done this she returned to her cabin. She decided that she couldn't sleep, so she dressed and made her way up the inside stairs to the back entrance to the little wheel house. She had to hold on tightly to the railings to keep from being thrown against the walls. She knocked and entered, finding both Zim and the Captain standing braced behind the helmsman.

Sheets of spray rattled in deafening crackles against the forward ports. The night was black and the only thing the helmsman could do was stare at the compass heading and struggle with the wheel. The Captain appeared calm. Zim, on the other hand, appeared nervous. They nodded at Rissa as she pulled the hatch closed behind her.

On the wall, the repeater that tracked the engine-room indicator showed just over three hundred revolutions per minute. Rissa glanced questioningly at the Captain.

"We're having some problems with an overheated shaft bearing," Captain Eberson explained. He picked up the speaking tube. "How are you coming, Boltz?"

Rissa heard the rumbling clatter of the engine room coming through the tube loud and clear. Then Boltz's voice broke through. "As well as could be expected. We've been pushing her too hard. The main bearing is rough."

"Can you get grease into the bearing?"

"Slowly, Captain, slowly. It would help if we could shut the engine down."

"Not possible, Mr. Boltz. We'd broach in these seas and might lose the ship," the Captain said emphatically.

"Yes, sir. I understand, sir." Boltz voice sounded reluctant, but the engineer knew very well that there was no possibility of shutting the engine down.

The Captain replaced the speaking tube in its holder. "He's just reminding me that this is my fault."

Rissa nodded her understanding. She'd skippered enough to understand full well how the chain of command worked.

As they stood there, riding the pitching motion of the ship, Rissa felt the engine begin smoothing out. Zim breathed a sigh of relief. The bell for the speaking tube jangled.

"All set for a while, Captain." Boltz's voice sounded relieved.

"Thank you, Engineer," Captain Eberson responded. "Good job. Stay with it and we'll make it through."

"Are we really in that much danger?" Rissa wanted to know. She knew that rough weather for a steamer was different than for a sailing vessel.

Eberson shook his head. "There's not much danger unless we were to lose the engine. Then we would be in real trouble."

Rissa said, "That's what I like about our ships. We drive with sail. The heavier the weather the more power we can tap into. Mostly we have to be careful that we don't damage the rigging with too much sail aloft."

"Costly when the wind fails," he reminded her.

"We have small steam auxiliaries on some of our ships," she said. "That helps, and also, we don't have to come into dock under sail power or pay a harbor tug to guide us through."

"Still prefer my engine," Captain Eberson grinned.

"Still prefer my sail," Rissa grinned back. It was an age-old argument that sailors never ceased to enjoy.

"She's responding to her helm better," the helmsman informed them.

Rissa could feel the ships steadying and taking the waves more assertively. Soon even Zim was looking relieved. Rissa said, "I think I'll go below unless there's something you want to talk about."

The Captain shook his head. "See if you can get some sleep. Tomorrow will be a long day and then we have to see about rendezvousing in this weather. We may be delayed."

She nodded. "I know. Time is not so crucial that we need risk an accident. If we can find each other, we can travel together until the seas are calm enough for a transfer."

RISSA MANAGED A few hours of sleep and opened her eyes just after dawn. The engine sounded normal and the ship no longer felt as though it was being tossed about. The port was cloudy with salt water, but she managed to make out that the sky was less threatening and the waves were much reduced.

On deck, snug in a slicker and braced against the rail, she felt an arm slide around her waist. She looked up and saw Turlo, similarly clad, standing beside her. The color in his face had returned and he was yawning.

"The tea the cook sent me was wonderful," he said, raising his voice to be heard over the wind. "I actually think I'm feeling hungry."

Rissa said, "I ran into the Captain outside his cabin, and he says that we are well ahead of schedule. Apparently we were blown slightly off course last night and will want to make for the coast sooner than expected. He didn't seem to think there were any problems." Rissa decided not to tell Turlo about the crisis during the night.

As they stood by the rail, a ragged strip of blue sky opened up overhead and a column of brilliant sunlight broke through, angling ahead of them and painting the white-capped waves in shades of pearl and gold. "Perhaps the storm has veered off," Turlo suggested.

Rissa said, "You may be right. Something is changing for the better. I think I can detect land ahead of us. The Captain said that we are to run up the coast."

Turlo shaded his eyes. "Your sight is better than mine," he said. "I am getting anxious about making the rendezvous point. I cannot see how two ships will find each other when they are so many miles from any mark."

SCARCELY SIX HOURS later, the Fortunata floated snug in the calm waters of the harbor at Woodhill. The weather had improved vastly and the sky was clearing rapidly with a cool breeze blowing from the north. From the shadows under the crosswalk behind the wheel house, Rissa was able to observe the sprawling nature of the town of Woodhill without being noticed. There was a thin column of white smoke and a smell of burning sawdust from a nearby timber mill in the air. She heard the high pitched whine of a steam-powered saw reducing hardwood trees to large, square timbers ready to be cut into planks. A long line of wagons carrying new wine casks was strung along a nearby dock where a cargo vessel out of Maripas was taking on a load of the special barrels.

She felt bored and slipped back into the mess room, pouring herself a mug of tarle from a battered pewter pot. A few minutes later, the Fortuna's engineer joined her.

"Why is this place called Woodhill?" Rissa asked Engineer Boltz who was taking a large gulp from a giant mug of strong black tarle. Even though the engineer looked exhausted after the night's run and was barely awake, Rissa found that he was eyeing her curiously. She was sure that he wanted to ask her something.

"I'm not certain," he returned after greeting her courteously. "I think it is because the edge of the Great Forest runs close to this part of Lunaria making timber accessible. North of this point, the land rises steeply along the coast and makes it difficult or impossible to carry on much trade with the interior." He shrugged. "If you are interested, you might try asking the Captain. I think the Navy used to have a base here."

Rissa nodded, but wasn't interested in pursuing an idle question. She was simply occupying herself to pass the time. "You should get some rest," she suggested. "It can't have been easy making repairs on a night like last night."

Boltz looked at her in surprise. "You heard about the overheated bearing? That hasn't been made general knowledge." He seemed astonished that she should be interested in something as technical as a shaft bearing.

Rissa told him that she'd been in the wheel house when he was talking with the Captain. "You forget, Engineer Boltz, that I am Mara Ellendor's daughter and have spent most of my life aboard a ship. While we are not so equipped with entropy engines as you, most of our vessels have at least a steam auxiliary."

Boltz seemed about ready to ask her his question when Captain Eberson ducked into the room. "Get some sleep, Boltz," he told the engineer. "We will be needing you later, and I want you fresh for the task."

"He wasn't about to take the same suggestion from me," Rissa observed with a grin when Boltz had stumbled out of the galley area.

"He's a good man, but inclined to push himself too hard," Captain Eberson returned. "Perhaps not unlike some others that I know," he added.

A crash and angry shouts echoed from the docks outside. Rissa moved to change the subject. "From the rate Mr. Zim is pushing the crew to take on cargo and supplies, it seems as if you are moving up the time for our rendezvous."

"Yes, the harbormaster is unhappy with our demands even though he is being well compensated for the extra expenses. Also, he tried to pawn off some unseasoned fire wood on us, and Zim caught him red handed. One can only imagine what Engineer Boltz would have had to say about a load of green wood."

"Captain, will you tell me what is really on your mind?" Rissa asked, for she could tell that the Captain was restless and unsatisfied.

Eberson sighed. "You run a grave risk with Turlo Murten. Not the man, but the ambition. You are young and so much depends upon you. I fear that I am too much like a doting father and would keep you tucked safely away from harm, even as Gilbert Greybaird has spoken concerning our young queen and his granddaughter. Sage Leandra describes this thing as the conflict between blood, honor, and loyalty."

Rissa's heart was moved by the Captain's words. She would have reached out to his hand on the table if she thought it would not have embarrassed him. She was careful how she answered.

"I will always treasure that thought," she said. "I know that you do not mean to place me in a prison."

Eberson was about to make some comment when one of the crew, a chunky fellow named Shorty, stuck his head through the hatch. "Mr. Zim's compliments, Captain," he said. "The cargo is loaded and he awaits your orders. Says it might be best to clear the docks before the Harbor Master thinks of something to delay us with. Some patrollers coming up the pier. They've got that look about them."

"Tell the First to make ready to cast off," Eberson said. "Are all our crew back on board?"

"Yes, Sir, they are," Shorty returned. "All present and accounted for."

"Good. I'll be on deck in a moment. I may be needed to deal with the patrollers," Eberson said. "Sorry to interrupt our conversation," he told Rissa.

"We wouldn't want to be delayed now with the rendezvous scheduled for in the morning," she said.

After the Captain had left, Rissa eased through the door and positioned herself in in the deep shadows cast by canvas screen that prevented salt spray from entering the hatch next to the wheel house.

The sun was low in the west, and harsh cries of seabirds circling returning fishing boats filled the air. Zim was keeping the crew busy lacing the canvas cover over the cargo hatches. Two crew members were hauling in the gangplank with the small crane on the starboard side. Under her feet, Rissa felt the Fortuna's engines coming to life. She watched four patrollers sauntering up the way, truncheons in hand, followed by a red-faced man she assumed to be the Harbor Master. Captain Eberson was standing near the rail watching the activities and seeming to ignore the men on the pier.

"We would like to come aboard, Captain," the patroller captain, distinguished by the gold braid on his black cap, called up to the Fortuna.

Eberson turned slowly. "And why would that be, Captain? We are cleared for departure, our papers are signed by the Harbor Master, and all fees are paid. I have receipts. Besides, as you can see, our gangplank has already been withdrawn."

The three men standing behind him fidgeted with their weapons. The Harbor Master opened his mouth. "Now see here, Captain. You haven't finished paying for the extra trouble we incurred to load your cargo ahead of some of these other ships."

"I am under the impression that we have paid all bills rendered to us," he said mildly.

"I'm sure you understood that there was to be an additional fee," the Harbor Master blustered.

"I do recall you mentioning something about an additional payment," the Captain admitted, "but we can only pay the bills presented to us. We received nothing about this additional payment and to whom it was to be directed."

The Harbor Master grew even redder in the face. "I want you to inspect this ship," he shouted at the patrol captain. "I have reason to believe that they are carrying contraband."

It was obvious to Rissa, and no doubt obvious to the patrol captain and everyone within hearing, that the Harbor Master was furious over losing a bribe that he evidently was used to collecting from ship's masters calling at the port. She even thought she saw the hint of a smile playing around the mouth of the patrol captain. Which would provide the most amusement for him, Rissa wondered. Would it be hindering Eberson from taking his ship out of the harbor, or would it be seeing the Harbor Master apoplectic over the loss of his illegal money.

The crew drifted over to the ship's rail to watch the little drama unfolding. The patroller captain appraised the crew as well as the Captain and nodded back at Eberson, seeing as which was the better choice for him and his men. "This Captain is within his rights, Harbor Master. He cannot be held liable for not paying a bill that was not rendered properly to him. I cannot stop him from leaving."

"I might suggest, Captain, that in the future it might be easier on everyone if certain agreements might be reached ahead of time," the patrol captain said.

"I thank you for your advice." Eberson acknowledged the patroller with a nod of his head. "No doubt you are correct. I will be sure to remember."

The patrol captain saluted the Fortuna's captain and turned away smartly. "Nothing here for us, Sir," he addressed the Harbor Master whose mouth was still hanging open.

Rissa thought in amusement, there is more here than simple greed. There appears to be little love lost between the patrollers and the Harbor Master. Perhaps he isn't sharing his bribes with the patrol captain.

Eberson nodded at the First who barked orders to finish casting off. Eberson paused as he went to pass Rissa on his way into the wheelhouse. "I don't believe we will be stopping here for engine repairs on the way back from our rendezvous. Engineer Boltz will be unhappy with me," he said in amusement.

Heading for the Rendezvous!

RISSA LEFT TURLO in his cabin pouring over charts and a map of Tieben centered on Snowy Pass. She climbed the steps to the top deck and knocked, then slipped into the wheelhouse. She closed the door behind her and found Captain Eberson bent over the chart table, advising the helmsman of the course. The last remnants of twilight cast a faint orange glow over the lighthouse at the end of the breakwater as the Fortuna cleared the long channel and prepared to head out for an overnight sail to rendezvous with the Ellendor in the morning.

The choppy waves had reduced to a long swell, gently cradling the Fortuna as she plowed through the waters at a more leisurely pace. Rissa guessed that their short stay in Woodhill and the resulting increase in time before rendezvous was not the only reason for lower engine speeds. Eberson, mindful of the repairs insisted upon by Engineer Boltz, was hedging his bets, being understandably reluctant to return immediately to Woodhill.

Eberson finished making some marks on his charts, and ordered a heading two points (a point is 1/32 of the compass circle) north of west. Not far above the horizon, a bright object stood out against the gathering darkness. Rissa, thinking back to the displays in the halls beneath her ancestral home in Boggrash, wondered if it were a planet traversing between Ennea and the sun.

"I couldn't rest," she said quietly to the Captain. "Turlo is studying maps and Captain Watchman is reading."

"We have received signals," Eberson said, "and we expect rendezvous with the Ellendor shortly after daybreak—about here." He placed a finger at a blank spot on the chart.

Rissa leaned over and examined the area of the chart and found nothing of significance. "No nearby islands, no reefs, nothing out of the ordinary to guide you," she said.

Eberson motioned her away from the helm and unlocked the communications room, drawing her inside. "There is one thing," he said quietly after closing the door. "While it's not considered a state secret, very few share this knowledge. Deep under the ocean there is an ancient beacon that still sends out signals. Your mother knows about this one as well as a few others. We have shared some of their locations for just such circumstances."

Rissa looked around at the screen with its pulsing, multicolored lights and controls and was impressed. "I am not familiar with any of this, and I have not heard of these beacons," Rissa returned, wondering why her mother would not have shared this information with her.

"Now is when you need to know," Eberson said. "This is information for you, only. Not to be shared with any other, not even the Prince. We consider you a most trustworthy and careful person."

Rissa's first impulse was to object. "I will hate keeping secrets from him," she said. "I would dislike to destroy the trust between us."

Eberson stared at her. "Turlo has secrets that he has not yet shared with you. I know this for a fact. But don't be distressed, he has the same restrictions that you have. It is not a matter of trust. Someday soon you will be able to share everything. For now, several of us have agreed that the less each knows, the easier for all of us."

"I will do as you request, of course," she said. "But I am not happy about this."

"I expect not," Eberson said, "but happiness was not a factor in our calculations. I'm sorry for your burden, if that helps."

"I can't possibly blame you for a decision that my mother made." She avoided adding treating me like a child because it would sound childish.

She changed the subject. "The weather is getting better. The storm must have veered westward. You don't anticipate any problems transferring us to the Ellendor tomorrow?"

"Not at present," he reiterated.

"Then I will go below and get some rest," Rissa said. "It seems that I have even more to think about." Eberson locked the door behind them as they exited the communications room.

"Someone will come when we sight the Ellendor," Eberson told her as she was leaving.

"Thank you for all your kindness," she said and closed the door. She was going to miss the Captain.

Reunion

IT WAS BARELY daylight when the steward knocked on Rissa's cabin door. She was in the middle of a dream which dispersed like fog when she opened her eyes. Whatever the dream had been about seemed important, but the excitement of the moment drove it from her consciousness.

"I'm up," she called out to assure the steward and yawned. She swung her feet out of the bunk and sat on the hard edge for a moment, letting the ship's rhythm drive off the fuzziness of deep sleep. She heard the knocking on Turlo's cabin next door and his sleepy response. Time to get moving!

She had packed the night before and had laid out the clothing she planned to wear. She spent some time gathering her hair and rolling it into a tight loop that she pinned high and covered with her hat. It took only moments for her to slip into her heavy trousers, boots, overshirt, leather vest, and wet-weather gear. She slung her pack over her shoulder and headed up to the deck. She decided she didn't want to be accused of babysitting; Turlo could follow when he would.

On deck, she fastened the chin strap of the hat so it wouldn't be carried away by the fresh breeze. She dropped her pack with the other luggage piled on deck and leaned against the rail. The Ellendor's 140 var[2] length dwarfed the Fortuna's 90. She was sailing with a small jib, a reefed mainsail, and a tiny staysail put up for stability on the aft mast. She was on a starboard tack so that the more maneuverable Fortuna could come up alongside her lee rail. Rissa was temporarily overwhelmed with emotion. She was coming Home!

---

[2] A var is the Lunarian measure roughly equivalent to our foot.

She could sense Turlo before he joined her at the rail, a brief man-scent of oiled leather and polished metal.

"Is that your mother on deck?" he spoke close to her ear.

Rissa had not paid much attention to the small figure aft of the wheelhouse on the sailing vessel. She studied the slicker-clad figure and decided that it might be Mara, though she wasn't expecting her mother to be aboard.

When the figure pulled back her hood, Rissa saw that it was indeed the Senior Ellendor Trader. She waved and received a salute from her mother in return.

"I hadn't expected her," she replied to Turlo. She felt an inner tension build inside her. Had something gone wrong in Boggrash?

Meanwhile, the Fortuna, under the steady hands of the senior helmsman, was easing up near the sailing vessel. The gap closed from 100 to 50, then to 20 and ten vars. The Fortuna had pushed some fat fenders over on her rub rail in case there was contact as they closed alongside. So good were both helmsman, that the Fortuna was able to ride within a distance that could be easily jumped. One of the crew, supervised by Zim, began tossing luggage across to the Ellendor where one of the sailing vessel's crew caught and stowed each item.

"Goodbye, Captain, and good luck. Thank you for everything," Turlo told Captain Eberson who was standing nearby. He gauged his moment as the ships rode a wave up and down and managed the leap with ease, landing without incident.

Eberson called out, "Good luck to you, Prince."

Watchman went next, clearing the gap with at least two paces to spare.

Then it was Rissa's turn to cross over the water. Turlo stood near the gap in the rail on the Ellendor's deck, ready to steady her in case she made a misstep. Rissa motioned him back impatiently. He frowned, but stepped out of the way. Behind him, Rissa saw her mother put her hand to her mouth, probably smothering a laugh. Her daughter had crossed over like this too many times to count.

Rissa turned one last time to Captain Eberson and said, "Thank you for everything. There is so much to say and nothing to say."

"I understand, Lady Rissa. Go with G'rama."

Rissa caught a momentary mistiness in the captain's eyes. She turned, chose her moment, and leaped gracefully between the two vessels, paused, and locked the rail back in place. Her mother was close by to embrace her as soon as she turned around. "It has been a long time, daughter," she said.

They all stood by the rail as the Fortuna, still carrying her fake name, pulled away, bound back to the south of Lunaria and other tasks. Zim was the last one to salute them from the steamship. He stood on the Fortuna's foredeck, oblivious to the spray soaking his uniform, and Rissa wondered what she had missed about the First Officer.

North to Boggrash

SITTING IN THE owner's quarters in the stern, sharing the table with Turlo, Watchman, and her mother, Rissa felt the Ellendor heel over and gather speed as Captain Sandstorm piled on canvas and set a course north along the western edge of the continent.

Someone from the galley brought pitchers of water, wine, and beer, glasses, and a platter of small pastries. Rissa found that she was hungry, not having eaten breakfast before they left the Fortuna. She helped herself to a small sausage baked in a crust and poured a glass of cold water from a dew-covered, silver pitcher.

"I didn't know you had promoted Sandstorm to the skipper of the Ellendor," Rissa said to her mother. It was the First Officer, Sandstorm, who had taken over after the skipper of the Blue Fin, Captain Annelisa, was killed in an assassination attempt on Lady Claire in the harbor at Timbermill.

Across the table from her, Turlo winced. The memory of the beautiful Captain lying broken on the deck after the explosion of a small boat alongside was very painful to all who had been there.

The newest Midshipman, the boy named Rat who had fled from Trappers Holding with Claire, Tess, and Turlo, appeared in the doorway. He saluted Mara Ellendor crisply.

"Sir. Captain Sandstorm asks me to inform you that the course is set at one point west of north, and the log indicates 12 knots, true."

"Rat, it's so good to see you!" Rissa cried out. The boy blushed.

"I believe that would be Midshipman N'rat," Mara corrected her daughter and smiled at the boy. "He is doing well and has graduated from cabin boy where his talents were totally wasted."

"He is advancing quickly," Watchman observed. "Congratulations, Mr. N'rat."

"Just Rat, if you please Sir," he glanced at Mara to see if she approved.

"Among ourselves," Mara agreed. "Now, I want to know everything you can tell me. Then I will tell you what I know, what I think I know, and how I believe the situation in Tieben can be best approached. Of course, only Prince Murten can ultimately decide what he is to do."

"No Prince, please. Let there be no titles among us. We are all equal here," Turlo said. "Besides, it would be best that few know who I am. Veral Hushara has many agents and his reach is long."

"Convey my thank you to Captain Sandstorm. I will confer with him later on other matters," Mara said, dismissing the Midshipman.

Mara Ellendor already knew everything concerning Rissa and Turlo and their journey through fire with Watchman and their crew on the River Lorne, so Rissa skipped ahead to relate what Claire and Pem had told her of their journey. Her mother was especially interested in the story of Ayaba and their experiences in the Dark Forest.

"I have heard of these machine creatures," the Mara said, meaning Ayaba as well as the household prognosticator that Pem met on his way from Greyhaven. "They are related to the same machines that still run under my ancestral home. They are important to Lunaria in ways that we do not know."

"Just as there are many things that you have chosen not to reveal," Rissa couldn't help but aim a small dart at her mother.

Mara shrugged and fingered the clasp with its white triangle and green crescent pinned to the breast of her jacket. "We Traders are in a unique and difficult position. We extend trade credit so that transactions can be made both safely and fairly. In order to do that, we must earn the absolute trust of all with whom we deal. That demands that we share very little information. We cannot afford to be seen bestowing advantages to some and not to others—but I do not want to get into a long-winded discussion of what everyone at the table well knows."

Rissa then told them about the royal wedding. "A wonderful affair," she said. "Claire and Pem are very popular with the people of Lunaria, if not so popular with their Great Council. That is of course why we are here. Claire and Pem believe that two or more members of the Nine are responsible for the attempts on their lives. They are more certain that the Nine as a whole seek to establish new trade arrangements with the present King of Tieben. Even the staunchest supporters of the Monarchy may be in favor of the trade arrangement, not seeing that such changes would fatally weaken the Monarchy and therefore their influence within the Council."

Rissa continued, "That turns out to be a danger to us as well as Lunaria. For selfish reasons, as should be apparent, this collusion between Tieben and the Nine is the reason why we are so willing to cooperate. Removing the Monarchy's position of power over the Council would have the disastrous effect of removing the control by the will of the people over the Nine. As of now, the people of Lunaria see their taxes returned to them in the form of roads and bridges, repairs, and an economy that favors trade and a fair prosperity. So long as the people's interests are served, the King continues to exert a moderating influence on the Nine. Changing this and creating a supremely powerful council would not be in the best interest of the Traders, and certainly not in the interests of the peoples of Tieben and Lunaria."

THE SHIP'S STEWARD, a jolly woman known as Steward Lacy, ducked into Mara's quarters and conferred briefly with the Senior Trader.

"Let us join Captain Sandstorm in the officer's mess for lunch," Mara said. "I must conduct some business with him after eating, and you can retire to your rooms to rest. We have three days before we have to make any decisions about our course. There are many things to consider."

The officer's mess was a cabin located on the top deck immediately aft of the main mast. A long table was bolted to the flooring, with fixed, straight-backed chairs arranged along both sides. The wood of its walls was stained a rich mahogany and decorated with several beautiful paintings of Trader ships under full sail. A skylight overhead made the space bright and pleasant. Vents brought in fresh air to a space that might otherwise have been stuffy.

Mara Ellendor sat at one end of the table and Captain Sandstorm sat at the other. At Mara's end, Rissa and Turlo sat opposite Captain Watchman and the First Officer, a woman introduced as Olivinia from an old and respected family of merchant sailors in Boggrash. Olivinia was attractive in a sturdy sort of way, with short-cut gray hair, bright gray eyes, and a ruddy wind-seared complexion that spoke of many years of sun and salt water. She paid Turlo and Rissa little attention, but seemed taken by Captain Watchman at her side. The two engaged in a spirited conversation concerning the best way to trim the sails in light air, a most challenging situation that seemed to puzzle Turlo, who was not a sailor.

Rat, as a lowly midshipman sat near the other end of the table. The Second was absent, excused to manage repairs being managed on a cracked spar. The navigator, a detached man named Rylan, was described as an engineering specialist when the engine was required. He was taciturn, with a sour face, dark hair, black eyes, a narrow face, and pockmarked skin. He sat next to the Captain and nodded brusquely as Mara continued around the table. The bursar was said to be off sorting the crew's pay schedule.

Lunch consisted of a chilled dish of pickled fish served with sour cream and sliced scallions, fresh baked loaves of bread with a pot of butter and honey, and a selection of cheeses and salted nuts. Dessert turned out to be a tart, citrus-flavored egg custard topped with beaten egg whites. Two white wines were offered, a dry and a sweeter wine. Rissa thought that the sweeter went with the cheese better, while the drier vintage complemented the fish perfectly.

"No," Mara answered Turlo's question before he found the words, "we don't eat this way every day. I believe it's a very special day when my daughter returns to me, especially with such loyal friends."

The steward came in with a golden dessert wine and fresh crystal. When everyone was ready, Mara held out her glass. "A toast to friends absent."

"To friends absent," Captain Sandstorm repeated along with Turlo and Watchman. Rissa found that she had tears stinging her eyes.

Mara said, "And now, if you will excuse the Captain and myself, we have some business to discuss. Please feel free to continue your conversations here or to retire to your cabins. I will look forward to seeing you at the evening meal."

After Mara and Sandstorm left, Watchman excused himself and left with Olivinia. The First Mate had offered him a tour of the ship. Turlo told Rissa that he thought he would study more charts and maps, and Rat had to stand his watch on the foredeck. Soon Rissa found herself alone with Rylan.

"I didn't know that my mother had an officer for navigation," she offered.

Rylan twisted the wine glass filled with cordial by its stem, working a wrinkle into the white linen table covering. He brought the glass up to his lips and sipped before he answered.

"As I understand it, the Ellendor is the only ship in your family's fleet that hires an extra officer for unspecified duties."

"I never thought of navigation and engineering as unspecified duty," Rissa returned, puzzled.

"You will have to ask your mother about that," Rylan said somewhat sourly. "And now, please forgive my rudeness, Trader Rissa, but I must return to my station." He saluted her perfunctorily when he got up from the table and left, leaving Rissa alone with her thoughts.

"What a peculiar fellow," she said to the empty room. She poured herself another bit of cordial and sipped thoughtfully. It seems that there are yet even more mysteries surrounding my mother than Captain Eberson knows, she thought. Or, maybe he does know. It wasn't a particularly comforting thought.

She plucked a few leftover pastries from the tray on the sideboard and wrapped them in her napkin. Just like when I was a child, she chuckled. She eased out the door and turned in the direction of her cabin one level down on second deck. The Ellendor was heeled over at a shallow angle; she was careful to hold the railing as she descended the stairs—companionway, she corrected herself. She had been away from a ship so long she was turning into a landlubber.

.THOUGH SHE HADN'T .felt particularly sleepy after lunch, Rissa started awake with a knock on her cabin door. "Dinner call," she heard the steward's voice through the grill in the hardwood paneling.

"Thank you," she managed to say, coughing. Her throat felt scratchy, but she ignored the discomfort and splashed cold water on her face from the pitcher and basin in the small cupboard. She emptied out and stowed away the things from her personal pack and hung her few items of clothing in the tiny wardrobe. She unpinned the coil of hair on her head and let it hang in thick blond strands. On impulse she took the dagger from her belt, grabbed her tresses at shoulder length, and cut straight across, holding the severed curls in her hand.

There, it was done. She combed out the short curls, pulled them back into a simple bun, and pinned the roll at the nape of her neck. She studied the effect in the mirror and decided that she liked it better. *I needed a drastic change*, she thought. *I will need all the toughness and determination I can muster if Turlo and I are to convince King Hushara to break off his meddling in Lunarian affairs.*

.DINNER WAS A .cheerful affair; the conversations were largely concerned with things like the weather, new ship designs, and the latest books. Mara and Turlo seemed to be on good terms with each other, and Captain Watchman reported an interesting tour of the ship with Olivinia. Of the other ship's officers, Captain Sandstorm was present along with Rat, and Jesson, the Second Officer. Rylan was absent, busy with unspecified duties.

The main course was grazer meat beaten in thin strips and wrapped around a stuffing of vegetables laced with hot peppers. A light wine sauce drizzled over the top was slightly sweet and blended the flavors well. The salad consisted of mixed greens tossed in a creamy dressing. There were small loaves of baked bread with butter and a pot of honey for each person. Rissa thought it was all surpassingly delicious, especially the light red wine that was served with the meat. The tartness of the wine was a perfect counterpoint to the hot, peppery taste.

Mara reported that there had been no more losses of ships to the desert bandits since the Battle of Upper Crossing, as the encounter had been named in Boggrash and Saitadi. Rissa was grateful for the news. She knew her mother was worried about stretching the resources of the Ellendor family even further if more losses had been sustained.

Rissa noticed that Turlo kept glancing at her during the meal. As the table was cleared in preparation for the dessert, he finally asked her, "Is there something different about you?" He looked puzzled.

Rissa felt herself turning red. "Yes, but we can talk about it later," she said.

Mara raised an eyebrow and stared at her daughter closely. "Surely not…."

"No, of course not, Mother," Rissa tried to say quietly but only succeeded in attracting the attention of everyone at the table.

"I cut my hair short," she said, exasperated. Olivinia put her hand to her mouth, highly amused, as did the others.

Turlo was also blushing furiously. At Rissa's announcement, he burst out in nervous laughter.

"Okay, all of us have had our fun," Mara put up her hands, grinning. "Perhaps we had better concentrate on our granapple pie. I'm told that it is the cook's specialty."

Rissa looked at her mother gratefully. Mara shook her head. "I'd like to see you first watch in the morning," she told Rissa. "There are things that we need to talk about."

The pie arrived and was as good as described: sweet, but not too sweet; filled with the flavor of the famous granapples imported from the Saitadi region in Lunaria; and topped with a vanilla ice that was special from the small refrigeration plant aboard the Ellendor. All in all, it was a considerable luxury, and Mara assured everyone that every crew member also got a share.

IN THE MORNING, Rissa's sore throat had almost disappeared. When she entered her mother's cabin, Mara was digging through a pile of papers on her desk. Through the ports the seas were moderate, with a wind quartering from the northwest. Distant clouds were orange in the early morning light, and Rissa could see that the day was likely to be perfect sailing. The smell of polished wood and oakum mingled with the spicy scent coming from an oil lamp suspended in the middle of the ceiling.

"Good morning, Mother. What did you want to talk with me about?" She winced at the tone of her voice. She hadn't meant to sound so serious.

"Nothing so somber," Mara assured Rissa. "How is Turlo?"

Rissa hated that she felt her cheeks redden. "He's doing well. His tendency to sea sickness has nearly disappeared on the Ellendor."

"I don't know why you've become so sensitive, daughter," Mara returned.

"Truthfully, Turlo wishes to push our relationship along more quickly than I think is wise. I have told him that we must wait."

Mara appeared to pick her words carefully. "You do realize that the one thing you cannot do is get married until Turlo's succession to the throne is acknowledged, or at least until this negotiation with Veral is completed. If you were to marry Turlo, you would lose all leverage with Tieben. It is the prospect of your marriage that is the strength of your negotiations."

"Yes, Mother, I do understand that. So does Turlo, only he has the impatience of a man used to getting what he wants."

Mara smiled. "I trust you will figure that out," she said.

The Straits of Pendrel

.THE WINDS CONTINUED .to shift to the north demanding a great deal of tacking. This meant that the Ellendor had to sail long legs out to sea, turn and sail another leg back towards land in order to make progress northward. As a result, it was on the morning of their fifth day from the rendezvous point, about 500 stats.[3] north along the Lunarian coast, when they finally entered the region called the Straits of Pendrel. The delay gave Rissa and Turlo, sometimes joined by Captain Watchman, a great deal of time to practice with their blades.

Now they were entering a deep and narrow cut between the Island of Vash and the shallow waters off the west coast of the bulge in northern Lunaria. The Straits had been formed in a cataclysmic event that tore the Island of Vash from the main body of land and formed the Bay of Terror. A shallow maze of reefs and narrow channels, virtually impassable, filled the region between the crack in the crust and the continent.

The scenery was spectacular and all hands who were not actually on duty lined the rail to watch the sun rise on the snow-covered volcanic peak known as the Fire of G'rama at the south end of Vash. The mountain was reputed to be so high that no climber could survive to reach the peak. Standing beside Turlo and looking up at the forbidding mass, Rissa could easily imagine that the stories were true.

As they drew closer to the Straits, the cliffs at the shoreline on their left blocked the view of all but the highest point of the peak. Because the air was funneled along the mountainside, their

---

[3] A stat is measure of distance equivalent to somewhat less than a mile.

ship was running close to the wind. Tacking in close quarters was a tricky business, and Captain Sandstorm was constantly barking orders to the sailors manning the rigging. Ten times they swung the main boom over and reset the topsails.

To their right, some low, uninhabited islands formed the boundary between the deep waters of the channel and the shallow area which stretched almost all the way to the shores of Lunaria. As Rissa had reason to know, having once sailed foolishly into the area, the region was filled with treacherous reefs, shallow banks, and mazes of blind channels. One of the reasons why no one used the coastal channel near Lunaria was the threat of being attacked by pirate ships that used the shallow archipelago as a hiding place for their operations.

Pendrel finally came into sight. The city was built around a bay accessed through a deep cut in the lava wall. Twin stone towers or forts, one on each side of the entrance, were lighted with perpetual flames fed by gas generated far down under the volcano's still-hot core. They caught a glimpse of the great harbor as well as the shipyards through the narrow slot between the fortifications.

"Your ships are all built there—except for the landships. You must have been there before. What kind of people live on Vash?" Turlo asked Rissa.

"An insular people," Rissa returned, "but friendly enough in their fashion. Most are fiercely independent and not fond of either Lunaria or Tieben—except as they receive their coins."

"Then you Traders have a close relationship with the Vash," Turlo said.

"Traders need ships. Vash builds ships. They extend us credits as we extend credits to all those who trade. Once there was trade with other lands. Lunaria and Tieben do not occupy the only land on this world."

"I have been told that we have not traded with these distant lands for generations," Turlo said. "It is rumored that all else on our world died long ago of a dire plague, and that we only survived because we were isolated."

Rissa laughed. "In the east, there has been long been frequent contact with the Easterly Islands in the Sea of Winds. Port Sulphur has established a trade route. The continent of Frangeria lies to the east of those islands, though it has not been fully explored. I do not know of anyone who knows for sure what lies in its interior, not even Sages like Leandra. We have artifacts and machines such as Ayaba," referring to the apparition described by Claire.

"These machines are remarkable and far beyond our present understanding. Lady Claire has described clouds of tiny machines and how they organize our world. I know that even Captain Eberson and Lord Gilbert are more than they seem. It is entirely possible that there were once many distant lands and much trade on this world."

"Haven't you ever had a desire to take a ship like this and sail off into the unknown?" Turlo said, bending his gaze upon her.

"Many times," Rissa swallowed and thought, here is a man who might tempt me to do just that.

"We might starve before we found another land, though," she said. "I know of no old charts or other writings that allude to the location of such islands or continents, especially not south of the equator."

"Don't you find that strange," Turlo wanted to know. "Such an important piece of information and yet no apparent evidence. It seems unbelievable to me."

"I suppose it does," Rissa admitted. "Much was lost to us a thousand years ago when many things were destroyed in the name of saving our world. Perhaps the information on the rest of our world perished at the same time. Most do not even know the secrets such as are hidden under my ancestral home in Boggrash. Lady Claire was the only person with the power to energize the ancient machines, and you know what happened. We were very lucky to have survived."

Turlo had that faraway look in his eyes that Rissa found so irresistible. "Someday we will journey and find out," he said fiercely before he turned back to studying the magnificent eastern slope of the Fire of G'rama.

"We live on a precarious world," he commented. "If that mountain were to tremble–even only a little—our lives and all those in Pendrel would be forfeit in an instant."

"I hope that's not a farseeing," Rissa laughed, feeling a little nervous.

Turlo said, "No, it was merely an observation of how we exist at the sufferance of blind chance."

The Black Isle

THE BLACK ISLE was named for its characteristic volcanic rocks. Rissa wondered if the island might have been named for its bleak and forbidding look. A jagged spine of old lava-flows marked the backbone of a ridge that cut the land in half. The southern half was uninhabitable due to volcanic vents; the northern half was occupied by an ancient monastery built around numerous steam vents. The buildings of the complex covered the rugged slopes like scales might have covered a dragon's hide. A scattering of brilliant green gardens resembled blossoms hidden in the folds of a spiny cactus. At the base of the slope, a tiny harbor budded from the narrow, black sand beaches like a rare flower. A few colorful fishing boats and a small cargo vessel lay alongside a white stone pier. The Ellendor, too large to tie up, came about delicately and dropped her anchor in the crystal clear waters of the sheltered bay. Seabirds circled noisily overhead, losing interest rapidly when there were no fish carcasses cast from her stern.

Rissa stood on the Ellendor's deck in the late afternoon of the day following their passage through the Straits of Pendrel. She breathed deeply of the salt air; she hadn't been to the Isle in a long time. The spicy scent of calum[4] leaves, the island's most important product, gave her a feeling of wellbeing. A hint of fragrant wood smoke drifted from the chimneys of buildings; the songs of small birds nesting among the honeycomb rock filled the background with a sense of peace.

Rissa knew that this sense of peace was only an illusion. The Black Isle was a place that people came to be treated for dread diseases and more often to die. Centuries ago it was known as a

---

[4] A rare bush that grew on volcanic soil that had important medicinal properties.

plague colony. In this day and time, the island was a center of learning for Sages specializing in the healing art.

Collecting a shipment of herbs and medicines was ostensibly the reason for the short stopover at Skellen, the only port on Black Isle. Mara had explained that it was part of the general misdirection to put off spies who would be watching for anyone venturing into Tieben—especially anyone from Boggrash. There were powerful factions with vested interests in keeping the Traders and Tieben from making a deal.

Mara had also said, "We are also carrying a dummy cargo that we intend to unload very publicly. We occasionally make a run to some of the small ports along the north coast to trade with people who occupy the western edge of the Great Forest. We are too large and too fast to fall prey to any of the pirate vessels operating in the area. Also, we have two automatic swivel cannons which are strong deterrents."

The crew was occupied swinging the jolly boat over the side with the davits. The little boat was painted white with bright red trim and carried the Ellendor triangle and crescent on the stern. Some of the crew climbed down a rope ladder slung over the rail to guide the boat away from the hull. A splash announced its entry into the water followed by the sound of oars being fitted to their oarlocks. Mara came to stand at Rissa's side.

"I ask that you accompany me ashore," she said. "There is little danger of you being recognized here, and there is someone you must meet."

"Of course," Rissa returned. "Will Turlo be going with us?"

"If he wishes," Mara said, smiling benignly. "Unfortunately, I don't think he will find the visit altogether pleasant."

Rissa sighed. "Men's delicate sensibilities. They can gut you with their sword without a qualm, but if you were to vomit, they might faint."

Rissa had barely finished this observation when Turlo joined them, looking curiously at the nearby buildings and the tiers of buildings on shore.

Captain Sandstorm approached. "Your boat and escort are ready, Ma'am."

"Thank you, Captain," Mara returned. "The First Officer will be accompanying us, as we discussed?"

"Yes, along with two men. It wasn't easy to find men who are willing to go ashore on this island," he said.

"I understand. Sailors are a superstitious lot. Yet, life on the water can instill a certain amount of mistrust. I have seen much of the capricious nature of the seas."

Sandstorm nodded his head, respectfully. "One feels that mere chance cannot explain everything."

"No disrespect," Turlo said to Mara, "but I think I will be glad to be off your ship, no matter how lovely it is and how good the company. I need good firm earth under my feet for a few hours."

"The ship is a she, not an it," Rissa reminded him.

"I think Turlo remembers that," Mara commented drily.

First Rissa, and then Turlo were lowered by winch to the small boat using a sling fitted with a flat board. Mara came last. It was a much more dignified way of boarding the jolly boat than to climb down the rope ladder.

Shortly thereafter, Olivinia joined them along with two crewmen, a skinny fellow, a rigger whom Rissa remembered as Mr. Chesney, and the ship's carpenter, a small man with powerful arms and hands and a heavily wrinkled face. He was accompanied by a small, brass-bound chest that had to be lowered to the boat using a pair of lines. Both men were equipped with short swords on their belts and sturdy belaying pins serving as truncheons.

A Visit with Hauk

SEAMAN CHESNEY SECURED their boat, and they were able to disembark on a flight of stone steps leading up to the top of the pier. The tides ran to about six vars, and there were ten moss-covered steps showing above the water.

"We are here at low tide," Olivinia explained to Turlo.

"We can leave the boat unguarded," Mara said in answer to Rissa's questioning look. "No one will bother it."

The carpenter shouldered the little chest with some effort and they set out along the walkway that led to the end of a street at a higher level. Rissa wondered what was in the chest that made it so heavy.

"What will we be doing?" Turlo asked Rissa as they entered a plaza at the end of a narrow street paved with smooth stones. Trees spread overhead and flowering plants lined the broad walks along the edge. A few horse-drawn carts passed them by, the driver in each case nodding to them in a friendly fashion.

"You are well known here?" Turlo said to Mara. "I had heard that was an island of illness and death, yet it is beautiful in its own way." He gestured at a beautiful arbor of trailing yellow flowers hanging from vines with large, shiny green leaves.

"I am known, at least by the tradesmen," Mara returned. "As to the beauty of this place, it is something that is used to offset the sorrow that is here."

"Also, we keep a small trading office here," Rissa added.

"You have been here often?" Turlo turned to Rissa.

"Not often, no," she returned. "Often enough," She finished, leaving Turlo with a puzzled look.

They climbed steps up a steep walkway that wound among many brightly painted cottages and connected streets at different levels. A few pedestrians, most garbed in colorful clothing, were either silent or spoke quietly, greeting them in a friendly fashion. Finally, they emerged on a pleasant lane with a narrow grassy verge and beds of sweet-smelling lilies. Rissa caught a glimpse of the Ellendor riding at anchor in the crystal clear waters of the harbor below. The carpenter grunted and exchanged his load with the rigger who, despite his slight build, didn't seem as bothered by the weight as the sturdier-looking crewman.

Turlo commented on the fact that the air seemed warm and pleasant.

"There are steam vents nearby that heat the area, keeping it comfortable even in winter," Rissa told Turlo.

"On the surface, it would seem a very pleasant place to live, although I don't see many people around," Turlo commented.

Rissa and Mara remained silent. The tiny warblers continued their loud chirping with an occasional echo of something that sounded much lower, a sweet crooning note that rose and fell in an uneven rhythm.

"The call of the Lo-Lo bird," Olivinia answered Turlo's inquiry. "It's a large, flightless bird that is too stupid to survive anywhere on this world except here where it is protected."

The five turned away from the harbor and followed the winding lane around a pillar of black basalt and found themselves on a flat shelf carved into the side of the ridge. A cluster of houses surrounded a central, larger structure.

"One of the treatment centers," Mara offered. "Our destination lies at the house with the red tile roof." She pointed to a larger structure built in the middle of a circle of larger trees. An iron gate between two stone pillars opened onto a red-tile walk that wound between flowerbeds to a porch across the front of the house. A gas scone flickered in the shade by the entrance. A bronze casting in the shape of a large triangle had the name Hauk engraved across the bottom.

Just as they had finished climbing the steps leading up to the sheltered entrance, the massive wood panel swung open and a man stepped out. He was a giant of a man, slightly stooped with age, with a broad, open face and shoulder-length silver hair. He was wearing a green-and-white robe with its cowl thrown back and sandals on his feet. He looked tired, but his voice was strong and clear.

"Greetings, Mara Ellendor," he said, bowing. "You and your friends are a most welcome sight."

Mara returned the man's bow. They stepped forward and embraced each other as old friends do.

"This is Hauk, a leading scholar and sage on the Isle," Mara said, standing aside. "My daughter, Rissa, you know. This man with her is named Turlo and has been traveling with us. I believe you will remember my First Officer, Olivinia."

Hauk smiled and Olivinia blushed. Hauk and Turlo made a point of sizing each other up. Each apparently satisfied, Hauk passed back to Mara. "These must be the two you wish to keep from unwanted attention." he indicated Rissa and Turlo. "I think I can guarantee that no rumors will be started from here. Perhaps we should go inside in case we should attract attention standing outside."

Hauk said to the rigger who had heaved a sigh as he deposited the chest on the floor, "You must be exhausted from carrying that up from the harbor. I'll take it for you." He lifted the chest as if it were filled with feathers and led the way inside.

They followed Hauk across an entrance hall and through massive double doors that led into an extensive living area paneled in dark woods. Comfortable chairs and tables were clustered around a large fireplace at one end; the walls were lined with shelves filled with books.

They continued across this space and took a turn down a side corridor which sloped downward. When they crossed a branching corridor, Rissa could hear their steps echoing far into the distance and wondered if they had passed underground. Finally they came to another large room, this one being a workshop of sorts. Light came from long tubes mounted in the ceiling, and there was a faint smell of lightening in the air. Various kinds of chemical apparatus cluttering the benches along one wall, and medical instruments and other paraphernalia that Rissa didn't recognize were arranged neatly in racks along another wall.

Hauk put the chest down on one of the clear benches and Mara handed him a key which she extracted from her wallet.

The scholar chose a long apron and transparent mask hanging from a peg by the door and positioned the chest in front of him. "You should all stand back," he cautioned them, pulling on the apron, adjusting the shield in front of his face, and pulling on a pair of heavy gloves.

They moved back as Hauk inserted the key in the lock. There was an audible click followed by a slight pop. Several metal rods moved smoothly out from around the lid. "That's very good," the Sage commented. "The seal was unbroken and the locks have disengaged."

He reached down into a drawer under the bench and brought out a cube-shaped piece of greenish stone which he passed carefully around the seal at the top of the box.

"If there were any leaks, the cube would glow brightly," he explained.

"I have no idea what this is about," Turlo muttered in Rissa's ear.

"He's checking for dangerous leaks," Rissa whispered back.

Turlo seemed nonplussed. "Is this chest filled with explosives?" he wanted to know, placing his right hand on Rissa's.

"Not at all," Hauk turned at Turlo's question. "Nevertheless, what is contained within this lead-lined chest is far more dangerous than the most deadly of poisons."

"If it is so deadly, why do you need such a thing on an island that is supposed to be dedicated to healing?" Turlo wanted to know.

"Give me a moment and I will answer your question," Hauk said. He stood back slightly and cracked the lid on the chest. Olivinia and the two crewmen automatically pulled back. Rissa felt Turlo stiffen, obviously desiring to move, but not wanting to appear afraid. Rissa squeezed his hand and felt him relax.

The scholar took a pair of slender tongs in one hand and extracted a tiny crystal from the chest, passing it near the cube in his left hand. The cube flashed a brilliant green, nearly blinding them. Hauk returned the crystal, closed the chest, and turned the key, watching carefully to see that the rods retracted. He then passed the cube around the perimeter without triggering any further glow.

"You have done very well, Mara Ellendor," Hauk said, sounding extremely pleased.

"You needn't thank me," Mara returned. "Thank the miners in Akren who risked their lives to extract this mineral. I hope it will last a long time."

"It will give extra life to many hundreds of people," Hauk assured her.

Rissa wished that Claire were with her. She was sure that the young Queen would have been able to explain what Hauk was talking about. She asked the same question posed by Turlo. "How is it used to cure people?" she wanted to know.

Instead of answering, Hauk moved over to another bench and picked up a gray box about a var on each side. The box was heavy enough so that the scholar had to hold it in both hands. He showed them how the top half lifted off revealing a compartment with a tube. There were holders where flat plates were stacked inside, each with a hole in its center.

"This apparatus is used to treat patients who have unnatural growths sapping their vitality. A small piece of the mineral is held in a clip near the top above the holes in the plates. The box prevents any effect from escaping except through the path through the holes in the plates. It is a little like a lens in a spyglass."

"The apparatus is positioned over the patient and the effect is aimed at the location of the unnatural growth within the patient's body which causes the affected tissues to shrivel and die leaving the healthy tissues behind to recover."

Rissa was sure that Claire could have explained it in more explicit detail, but she realized that Hauk was trying to present a simplified concept.

"And how many patients received benefit from this treatment?" she asked.

"Nearly all," he replied. "Of course, some benefit more than others. A lot depends on how soon they get here and are treated. Also, there are places within the body that cannot be treated without affecting vital tissues. Unfortunately, at this time, those patients are doomed. We can only try to make them as comfortable as possible during the time remaining to them."

Rissa had seen some of the healing powers that Claire could control. Still, it would not be fair to Hauk to mention these.

Perhaps Claire was unique and there were hundreds, perhaps thousands of patients to treat—an impossible task for one person.

"And now to attend to your needs," Hauk said mysteriously, replacing the box on the bench. "Please follow me."

Hauk's Gift

.THEIR HOST LED .them back the way they had come. Instead of heading to his living quarters, they turned aside at the cross-corridor and proceeded down a long ramp, moving ever deeper under the mountain. Their steps echoed off the walls, dying away in the distance, almost as if they were descending into a vast cavern. The lighting came from more of the same softly-glowing panels spaced at intervals over their heads, but the place had an older feel to it. Claire had described observing similar panels when she was fleeing the assassins deep under the palace in Lumminea

"These tunnels honeycomb the entire north end of the island," Hauk told them. "Some follow the tubes of ancient lava flows. Some the monks carved from the soft basalt rock ages ago. It is rumored there are unexplored levels that have been lost, but I think that is probably more in the imagination than in fact. No such places have been discovered in my lifetime, though children constantly prattle on about hidden treasures and such." He laughed. "I suppose it is a rather romantic notion."

They came to a door set in the walls of the hall. Hauk pushed it open and asked that the carpenter and the rigger remain in the outer hall. The rest then proceeded down a short passage that was no longer finished in stone but was simple, rough-hewn rock. At the end was another door, this one of massive proportions.

"My family's private vault," he explained. He extracted a rod from his pocket and inserted it into a small hole in the center of the door. Rissa heard a clicking sound and the door swung open on silent hinges. She remembered Claire having described a similar mechanism when she and Tess were in the Black Tower with Hushara in Tieben. She wondered how much was fact, and how much was illusion. She put her hand out and ran her fingers over the door. The slab of stone and metal felt ice-cold and real enough.

The vault was lined with white plaster and was clean and dry. There were shelves filled with ancient books and cabinets that presumably contained other personal items. Hauk went directly to a small, plain wooden box on one of the shelves and carried it back to a table located in the center of the space. Rissa saw that the box, hardly larger than a generous hand span, was brass-bound and scarred with age. It was secured with a tiny padlock with a key already inserted. Hauk turned the key and removed the lock from the hasp. Before he opened it, he turned to address both Rissa and Turlo.

"I promised your mother that I would give this to you if Turlo decided to return to Tieben and assert his claim to the throne. Though I do not think that your course is entirely wise, it may be the only way to accomplish your purpose, and I admit that our work here could no longer thrive if Tieben and Lunaria should act to destroy the role that the Traders in Boggrash have played for generations."

Hauk opened the lid and lifted out a leather-bound journal. Though the strap and cover were carefully oiled, they were worn by hard use. "This is my contribution to your dangerous enterprise. Keep it with you and keep it safe because it is a detailed description of the only way in which you may enter Tieben unwatched."

"I have entered through a seldom-used route around Leopard Pass north of Timbermill without being observed," Turlo insisted.

"Your pardon, Turlo, but I doubt that. Veral, and the Husharas before him, kept a watch using a Sage on all passages through the mountains, including the one at Kamoria which is now considered nearly impossible to negotiate."

"Then how is your route different?" Rissa asked the scholar.

Hauk said, "Mara has told me that you intended to use the old route which lies at the bottom of the same gorge that Snowy Pass uses, only Snowy Pass is much higher up on the saddle. It would seem an excellent choice, but I happen to know that one of Veral's personal lieutenants, a particularly nasty piece of work known as Captain Dread, keeps a close eye on that route where it exits north of Trappers Holding. If you planned to use that route, Dread will be waiting for you as you come down the river."

Rissa shuddered. "Turlo and Claire's Lady Tess had an encounter with the famous Captain Dread. It was nearly fatal."

"We beat him back, though," Turlo reminded her.

"Not without Claire's help," Rissa said.

"You and I could do it," Turlo insisted.

Rissa was vexed with her lover. "Be reasonable, Turlo. You said that only Claire's talents with her sword beat back Dread's attack. Even then, it was the fire in Dread's warehouse that had caused him to act recklessly. If he finds out we are coming, he has the patience to lie in wait."

"A few good men could hold an army at bay if they had warning," Hauk said. "Don't be stubborn. Dread will get word you are in the gorge and he will have men waiting."

"Then what is this wondrous, secret way into Tieben that you speak of?" Turlo said rather ungraciously in spite of Rissa's warning frown.

Hauk chuckled. "I'm not offended, Lady Rissa. Prince Turlo is only anxious for your safety," Hauk returned. "And yes, I know who you are, Prince. But don't worry. Few people here would recognize the heir to the throne in Tieben."

"Then how do you know me?" Turlo wanted to know.

"Let us just say that I have my sources. That would be the safest way to describe it," Hauk replied.

"Let's not waste time," Mara interrupted.

"Of course," Hauk said. "I'll get straight to the point."

"In fact, you will use the same route as you planned, but before you enter the river gorge, you will take a hidden way that leads to a tunnel winding under the divide. This way comes out at the head of the same valley that Dread for so long has tried to exploit. He has now given up because he can't find replacements for the slaves he uses as laborers."

"They are not slaves," Turlo interrupted. "Most are free men that Dread falsely accuses of some crime and ships them off to a labor gang. It is an immoral practice that I would put a stop to."

"I rather think that the very nature of that valley has put a halt on Dread's ambitions—which is a good thing for you and Rissa even if it is because so many lives have been wasted."

"Perhaps seeing so much death and pain here has put a different perspective on how you see that situation," Turlo suggested.

"Maybe so, but I have learned not to dwell on things which are beyond my powers to change. It is wisdom that comes with age and might seem unnecessarily harsh if I were younger," Hauk said gently.

Hauk placed the journal back in its case, closed and locked the top. He handed the case as well as the key to Rissa who thanked him. "We thank you. I believe this to be a worthy cause and will help ensure our success."

"I know that I join your mother in saying that your safe return will be the best measure of success," he said.

Hauk then told them that, while he would be delighted to offer lunch, he was due for a meeting at the treatment center and would not be able to join them, much as he would like to continue their conversation. "I cannot cancel this meeting. The lady whom I am to see has very little time left to her."

"Then, of course you must go," Mara said immediately. "Our business is done, and you needn't bother your household concerning lunch. We will take the opportunity to sample one of your fine eating places."

"We will take good care of your journal," Turlo assured Hauk.

Rissa said, "I also thank you again, in the name of the Traders as well as the new Queen of Lunaria."

Hauk's eyes took on the sparkle of one who seldom has the opportunity to exercise a personal appeal. "I have heard of this young queen. She is said to have rare healing powers. Please tell her that I would be most pleased if ever she visited us."

Rissa bowed. "That I will certainly do when our paths next cross."

HAUK LOCKED HIS VAULT behind them, and they collected their three companions in the outer passage. Hauk apologized once more when they reached the room that Rissa thought of as the library. "I'm sorry, but I must bid you goodbye and leave you with my servant who will show you to the door."

Mara took Hauk's hands in hers. "It may be a long time before I am able to return with another chest," she said.

"I will be here if you need me," he told her. "There will be casks of processed calum waiting for you at the docks. I hope they will serve as some recompense for your kindness." He looked as if he was going to embrace Mara, but then dropped her hands before stepping back. Rissa saw something pass between the two—a brief look of regret on her mother's face and the smallest hint of sorrow on Hauk's part.

Rissa, aware of how valuable a cask of calum could be, swallowed and thought that it was indeed a grand and generous gesture. She wondered about Hauk's words, I will be here if you need me. Had her mother's illness returned? She had thought that after Claire had severed the energy drain on her mother that Mara's problems had been put behind her permanently. She would try to ask her later.

Hauk's final parting words were "Go with G'rama."

SCHOLAR HAUK HURRIED off and the servant escorted them to the entrance, bowing to them at the porch steps. At Rissa's request, the man recommended a local eatery with the optimistic name, Stew and Brew. "The best beer and the best steaks," he offered. "Scholar Hauk eats there quite often."

Rissa thanked him and they trudged down the path to the street where they turned right on the walkway and passed through an archway that led into a colorful plaza surrounded by a number of shops and inns. The smell of freshly baked breads and pastries combined with the heady aroma of spices made Rissa's mouth water. She hadn't realized how hungry she was after the morning walk, the exercise, and the time spent with Hauk.

The Stew and Brew was set back from the sidewalk and featured tables under red awnings in a lush garden setting. In addition, there were comfortable tables available inside the building. By common consent they decided on an outside table set in a small alcove made private by a trellis of sweet-smelling blue flowers and near a fountain bubbling with steaming water.

The air was warm and pleasant; a serving girl approached them almost immediately. "What will it be?" the girl, a pretty brunette bent over to ask Turlo, whom she'd decided was the leader of the group. She wore her hair done up in a bun. The blue trousers were topped by white scoop-necked overshirt. Rissa noted that the girl had plenty of assets to display and that Turlo was trying manfully to ignore the offering.

"I'll be settling the bill," Mara said with humor. The girl blushed prettily and directed her attention at the Trader.

Mara ordered red wine while the rest of the group settled on the pale ale. According to Olivinia, who had been to the Stew and Brew before, the ale was the best on the Isle. "With Hauk," she said, blushing at the curious looks. "It was before I signed on as First with the Ellendor," she added.

Rissa picked up her amber-tinted glass, a thick mug, really, but without the looped handle. The bubbles tickled her nose as they released a very pleasant aroma into the air above the liquid. She decided that there was a hint of citrus and perhaps a bit of earthiness in the taste. She was certain that it was the best ale she had ever drunk.

Turlo was saying something to her. He was across the table between Chesney and Mara. She couldn't quite make out what he was saying. Something was wrong with her. All the energy seemed to be flowing out of her. The pendant lying against her breast seemed so cold that it was burning into her like fire. She tried to open her mouth to scream but nothing emerged.

It's Claire, she thought. Something has happened to Claire! The world grew dim and she felt herself slipping away into a great distance. All that was left to her was a tiny pinprick of light. And then that, too, disappeared,

Part Three

A Singular Event

Holiday at the Beach

MAGS, HOWEVER INTRIGUED she might be by the mysterious hints from Nikko about a midnight rendezvous, had work to do before the Royal suite would be totally ready for occupancy.

First, the Royal Kitchen! Though Mags conceded that the dining facilities were excellent, her responsibility extended to making sure that the royal staff (including herself and Nikko) were properly fed and that any reasonable whim on the part of Claire or Pem was satisfied without bringing an outsider in. This meant establishing the cook from the Rachael Ann in the kitchen adjoining the Royal Suite.

Prandi, the Rachael Ann's long-standing chef, could be difficult. Mags decided on her approach carefully before she entered the kitchen area. Even before she pushed through the swinging door, she could hear his complaints and the banging of pots and pans coming from the other side of the door.

"Chef Prandi," she said upon entering, ducking a small pot that clattered against a cabinet and fell into the wash sink behind her. "What may I do for you?"

Prandi opened his mouth, then closed it, apparently thinking better of what he was about to say. Prandi was a short man with a large belly, thin legs, and thick neck. His eyes were bulging from his red face and he was breathing heavily. The row of buttons down his front strained to hold his white jacket together.

""Dirty, all dirty," he threw his hands around him, indicating the pots and pans hanging from the rack over the stove and the dishes stowed in their racks on the walls. "I cannot abide this filth!"

Mags picked up a pan that was lying on the floor and looked at it critically. It looked spotless to her. "Terrible. I see exactly what you mean," she said. "I will summon the Steward and have him see to it that all of this is cleaned immediately. I shall inform him that he must satisfy you in every respect. After all, you cannot be expected to make-do when you are responsible for feeding the new King and his Queen!"

Prandi, probably thinking that maybe his temper had gotten the better of him and that an inspection of the offending pots might not be so incriminating after all, threw up his hands.

He waxed eloquent. "Never mind, good Mags. I will see to it myself. It is the only way one can work around here. Please have my kitchen staff report to me immediately. We have only hours before we have to prepare our first delights. I have something truly magnificent in mind!"

Mags, remembering some of these delights with trepidation, put on a smile and assured him that she would have his staff assembled immediately. She sincerely hoped that the baked fish would not be served quite so rare this time and that the sauce would not be so hot that it would leave her tongue raw.

Having managed the immediate crisis, she left Prandi muttering to himself and went looking for the chef's second-in-command, a burly sailor who managed to bake the most wonderful, delicate pastries in spite of his appearance as a carnival wrestler. She explained what she needed and the man dashed off to round up the staff before more damage could be done in the kitchen.

BY THE TIME Mags had finished her other chores, one of which involved the resort staff removing a particularly large and obnoxious bird from one of the sleeping rooms (how it had got there no one was willing to say) she was exhausted. She drifted back to her manager's office which she shared with Nikko who was going over his security plan with one of the Rachael Ann's crew.

"Regular crew rotation," he was saying when Mags walked in and plopped down in her chair. Nikko dismissed the crewman and turned to Mags.

"You realize that we have a problem," he said.

"Which kind and how many," Mags groaned.

Nikko got up and closed the door after looking around outside the office. "There is something I have to tell you, and you must never reveal what you know to anyone."

Mags recognized the seriousness in his voice and became instantly alert. "You know that you can trust me," she encouraged him.

"Yes, but this is serious business. It concerns mostly Pem and Claire's safety." He drummed his fingers on the desktop, thinking how best to tell Claire's protector—for he knew that Mags was much more than the Queen's maid.

He hesitated. "Maybe I can say that it involves the captain of the Rachael Ann. Captain Eberson has charged me with watching him. Lord Gilbert thinks that Agkor may be a council spy."

"Him? I find that hard to believe," Mags returned.

"There is evidence," Nikko said, not wanting to be more specific.

Mags sighed. "Well, I have been surprised before. If Lord Gilbert thinks it, then I must respect his opinion. Also, in my experience, Captain Eberson is a man whose opinion is to be trusted."

Nikko went on, "You realize that this might make you a target also."

Mags looked thoughtfully at Nikko. She said, dropping titles in favor of speech between comrades, "Yes, I know. When I took this job at Gilbert's request, he cautioned me that if I accepted his charge, I would have to be prepared to go as far as necessary to protect the Queen. I do it gladly, for she is very dear to me and trusts me in ways I cannot describe. Gilbert told me that Claire would change the world, and I have come to believe it. She has certainly changed the way I look at things. I am prepared to do what I must." She lifted up the edge of her domestic uniform to reveal a dagger concealed in a pouch. Nikko's eyes widened but he said nothing. The silence between them lengthened.

Nikko said at last, "I know what you mean about changing the world. When I first met the girl, I thought she was nothing but a pretty face. Fortunately I came to my senses before I acted like a total fool and disgraced myself in front of the Captain and Lord Gilbert."

Mags laughed, lightening the mood. "You were ever after pretty girls," she chided Nikko. "Is that why you now pay attention to me?"

Nikko blushed. "You are certainly pretty, but that is not the only attribute that attracts me."

"As to that," Mags returned, "You will have to demonstrate this new side of you. I think I will find this most entertaining."

Nikko wondered if he detected the merest hint of a reddening of Mags' cheeks when she made the statement. He suddenly realized that it mattered very much to him what Mags thought of him.

What Happened at the Beach

SEVERAL DAYS LATER, Claire found herself walking the
beach in her normal attire—trouser and overshirt with vest and
her sword slung over her shoulder. Not that she needed her
weapons, she reminded herself. She had two armed and stalwart
seamen trailing along behind her at a discreet distance.

Although, what *discreet* was Claire didn't know, since she
could hardly scratch herself without attracting attention. In any
case, she was enjoying the warm sun breaking through the clouds
that had raced overhead during a mild storm—the edge of a storm,
Nikko had informed her. The full force of the weather had
probably passed to their west, and he guessed that the Fortuna had
borne the brunt of the winds.

Each morning Claire fingered her amulet and let her
thoughts reach out to Rissa who wore the twin to her own piece.
All seemed well. Rissa could not return her queries, but Claire
could sense her general feelings. She was careful not to pry beyond
this level for fear she would violate Rissa's privacy. She wasn't even
sure how far she could go with this, but she didn't intend to find
out. Only if something dire happened, she promised herself.

She watched seabirds wheeling overhead. Occasionally one
dived into the water and reappeared with a silver fish wriggling in
its beak. Claire speculated on how it must be to be swimming in
the warm waters, contented if not happy, and be suddenly snatched
cruelly from your world and eaten alive. Perhaps it was not so
different than her experience coming through the gate into
Lunaria, though she admitted that so far she hadn't been exactly
eaten alive. Perhaps that was still waiting for her. She shivered and
tried to push the morbid thought away. It was, after all, such a

beautiful morning and she was enjoying being by herself—well, relatively alone.

A young couple passed her going hand-in-hand in the other direction. They waded in and out of the loops of foam that advanced and then retreated along the smooth sand. Did they know that they were walking near the Queen? Even having this thought amused the ordinary girl from Ridgeville.

The surf seemed quieter today, or else she was becoming used to the ocean and no longer found it so mysterious or novel— a little like Pem, she decided. The potential was always there, but the ordinary affairs of daily life tended to take over after a while. He wasn't grabbing her and kissing her so often. He seemed less urgent each night, though he was certainly ardent enough to satisfy her. She had sought out Leandra and after some blushing and dithering on her part, had asked Leandra about her experiences with Pem. "I have no mother to ask," she said, bringing a sad smile to Leandra's face.

Leandra had assured her that she was simply experiencing what every woman experienced. "Everything will come into equilibrium," she had said.

"Pem is a solid young man and cares for you. He is not as deep a person as you are, my dear," Leandra had told her. "As you will find, women must cultivate patience when dealing with men."

Claire had started to object and then recognized this for the truth and felt more secure. She had thanked Leandra and was able to stop questioning every small nuance between her and Pem. Things had gone more smoothly and she had been able to return to a routine that was more of her own choice, making her time with Pem even better than before.

This was one of those mornings when it felt particularly good to be alone. Pem was meeting with Nikko and Captain Agkor concerning their departure. She was looking forward to leaving the beaches in the next few days and traveling up the coast to pay a state visit to the Councilor in Ranaputkin—the one whose son had been interested in Illaina. She hoped to promote that relationship, and thought that it would be in Illaina's best interest—and Pem agreed with her.

Claire noticed a small green-and-white flag fluttering on the other side of the sand dune to her left. Curious, she walked over to the hill of sand and started to climb the slope. The sand immediately ran into her shoes. She thought about going back, but she was intrigued that someone might be using a flag with her house colors. She took no notice of her escort that was hanging back, as if suddenly reluctant to follow her inland.

She finally made it to the top, slipping and sliding, and looked down into a little dell enclosed by sand dunes on all four sides. A green-and-white striped tent with a canopy or awning occupied the center of the space; the flag that had attracted her attention fluttered from a pole that was stuck in the sand to one side. A man in desert garb sat cross-legged on a carpet in front of the awning, his head bowed in apparent meditation, face hidden behind a cowl. Behind him, under the awning, a table laid out with food and pitchers of drink was furnished with two chairs. Claire decided to visit this man who had usurped her house colors and seemed to be waiting for something to happen.

"Greeting, Queen of Lunaria," the man said to her as she walked up in front of him. The voice sounded strangely familiar, but was masked by a cloth wrapped over his nose and mouth—as if he had been on a long journey across the desert. Her ring felt cool on her finger. Surely there was nothing to worry about?

"How do you know my name?" Claire wanted to know. "And why do you fly the Queen's private colors?"

"Because I am the Queen's devoted servant," the man cried. He tore away his mask and flung back his cowl, revealing Pem smiling broadly at Claire's astonishment.

He leaped up and took the surprised queen by the hands. "Come to the table and share this food and drink with me. It was prepared specially for me by the cook under Mags' direction. Later we might share other delights," he hinted broadly.

Claire was flabbergasted and not at all sure she was as pleased as Pem desired her to be, but she went along with the act, remembering the puppet play in Saitadi that they had watched so long ago.

Pen poured her a glass of chilled white wine and offered her a bowl of ripe fruit.

"This is all very romantic," she said carefully, delighted in spite of herself, "but why this extravagant ploy for my attention?" She looked around, half expecting to see her body guards standing, laughing at the top of the sand dune.

"They will not bother us," Pem waved his hand negligently. "They were in on my little plot from the very beginning."

"I see that Mags is very good with these things," Claire laughed. "She was so in favor of my walk on the beach this morning. I should have suspected something."

"To answer your question, we are due to leave tomorrow, and this will be the last time we can be alone together for days. You know how close the Rachael Ann is," he said.

"Crowded," Claire returned, thinking back to their first night together on board the royal yacht. She colored slightly as she realized that half the ship must have been waiting, listening.

They ate silently for a while. The fruit was cool and sweet; the wine was refreshing . "This is wine from my estate," she said. The clarity was excellent and the color was pale gold.

"A vintage year that my father put back in the royal wine cellars at least five years ago," Pem said. "I am happy to be able to offer it to the new owner of the estate."

"I have not even had a chance to sample all of the wines I am supposedly producing," Claire laughed. "I assume Tess will be doing that. I hope she is getting along in her new position as Lady of the Commander of the King's Brigade. It is a lot of responsibility for a girl from the village of Tribana."

"Never worry about your Tess," Pem laughed. "She will be taking care of all of us before long. She is the most stubborn and talented manager I've seen. Gilbert thinks so too."

Claire fingered her amulet under her overshirt. "She has a growing power of her own. I worry about her sometimes. I cannot sense much of what she feels or whether she is safe, as if she is blocked from me."

"You cannot expect to know everyone's mind, my dear Queen," Pem returned. "For instance, what do you think I am thinking right now?"

"That's easy," Claire giggled. "I do not have to read your mind in order to know what you have in mind."

"I always knew you were a lusty peasant girl," Pem grinned. He drew her from her seat, their food forgotten. Inside the tent, Claire was astonished to see comfortable carpets and a large bed of soft pillows. Sunlight created soft patterns and shadows, and a candle burned sweet smelling herbs.

"This took planning. You did not think of this on the spur of the moment," Claire pushed Pem playfully on the chest.

"I cannot play with a woman who insists on wearing a sword," Pem pretended to be cross with her. He reached around her and released the clip that secured the sword in its case and flung it into a corner.

"Nor should a lover come to his lady with his dagger in his belt," Claire took the opportunity to slip the belt from Pem's waist and let it fall next to her sword.

After that, things became a little more intense.

Claire wasn't sure how long they had been enjoying each other. Time seemed to move slowly. The tent was warm, but not too hot; a faint breeze stirred the canvas and a cool draft felt refreshing. She wished that the moment would last forever, though she realized that it was a foolish idea. Life was meaningful only because it changed. She noticed a shadow passing over the tent and thought of a cloud drifting over the sun. Pem, who was lying at her side, breathing heavily, didn't notice, lost in his personal reverie.

She must have slept for a while. When she woke, Pem was awake, lying on his side watching her. She stretched lazily and ran a hand over his chest. "You are beautiful," she told him.

"Not like you are beautiful," he returned, his eyes dancing merrily.

"Have we been here the whole day," Claire said, feeling slightly alarmed. "It is getting rather dark."

Pem pushed her hair back from her face. "No, love, it is only early afternoon, though I suppose we have been exceptionally naughty."

"Then why is it getting dark," Claire wanted to know.

"I do not notice it getting dark," Pem said, puzzled.

Claire lay back on her back, staring up at the canvas panels. There was a redness of the light that made the green stripes look brown and the white stripes look pink. She took a deep breath and rubbed her eyes. "Perhaps I'm just sleepy," she said, not believing it. "I think I feel a bit chilly."

Pem reached out and drew up a light cover over her. "How does that feel?"

"Much better," Claire breathed a little easier, but still felt a chill growing inside of her. Was she under some kind of attack? She probed around her, but nothing seemed wrong. Only the dimming light and the gnawing chill growing inside frightened her. Her heart was beating wildly. She reached out to Pem. "Hold me," she said, curling against his side.

Now Pem was looking worried. "What is wrong? Claire," he said.

"I'm not sure if anything is wrong, but I am frightened," she returned. She grabbed her amulet and immediately some warmth seemed to return. When this happened, she sensed Rissa, far away, starting to panic. She tried to release the link between her and her friend, but it would not seem to break.

She heard a chorus of voices—many voices chanting, as in a temple somewhere. They started as a low murmur, but now were growing louder, drowning out the wild beating of her heart and deafening her to what Pem was saying in her ear.

Suddenly she heard a voice that was familiar, the voice of Leandra, calling to her, rising from the chaos of sound. "It is happening, Claire. Do not be alarmed. What is happening was meant to be. Had I known, I could have prepared you for this, but it is something that has not happened in many lifetimes."

"What is it? What is happening?" Claire thought back, clinging to the one anchor that she had left.

"Hold on only a little longer and everything will be well," Leandra's voice was fading now, merging back into the chorus.

"Please don't go," Claire begged, but the Sage was gone. She felt the wild beating of her heart slowing. A feeling of peace was stealing over her. Is this death? The thought should have panicked her but somehow it didn't. I am dead, she thought. She felt Rissa stirring, coming alive—a feeling of immense well-being. What was happening? Pem was saying something.

"Why are you smiling?" he kept saying, panic in his voice.

She felt herself waking up, as if from a dream or from a deep sleep. "What? I'm just sleepy," she said. The tent was bright with sunlight when she opened her eyes.

"I thought you fainted," Pem said.

"No, I'm fine. In fact, I've never felt better," she said, reaching up to pull his head down to hers and kissing him on the lips.

"Perhaps it was the wine," he said when he disengaged. "I think it must have been the strong wine," he repeated.

"Of course, whatever you say," Claire felt lazy, warm, heavy, and…very happy. "We should get dressed," she said unhurriedly. "We have things to do, plans to make. I need to write a letter to Tess. Do you think you can post it with a courier tomorrow?"

"Of course," Pem replied. He looked distracted. "We'll walk back along the beach to the resort."

"One last walk along the waves," Claire said dreamily. "I'd enjoy that. I'll need to find Leandra when we get back. I had a dream and there's something I need to talk with her about."

Pem nodded, but he was already finding his clothes and pulling them on, not listening to her. She sat up and pulled the cover to her. The dream. She tried to remember what Leandra had said in the dream, but it was all so hazy and drifting rapidly away. There was something about Rissa too, but that too was becoming fuzzy. She'd have to see about it later—after she talked with the Sage. She gathered up her clothes and began dressing.

Sage Leandra

"I'VE BEEN EXPECTING you," Leandra said as Claire entered the tiny, private garden and terrace which fronted the Sage's apartment adjoining the Royal Suite. "There is tea and we have cakes," she said, indicating a small, round table set for two with a plate of sweet cakes and a pot of steaming tea. She let Claire settle into her chair before she poured the tea. Claire helped herself to one of the cakes, one smelling of lemon with a decorative red berry in the center. Sage Leandra waited.

"I need to talk with you about a very strange experience I had today," Claire began, and then paused, not sure how to continue.

Leandra nodded her encouragement.

"Pem was being quite romantic," she began, stopping again. "Really, quite attentive," she said and blushed. "We were—you know—in a tent. It was quite a surprise—him arranging the whole thing without my knowing." She looked through an opening in the vines covering the privacy screen and watched Nikko walking back from the Rachael Ann. He was probably on his way to meet with Mags—they had grown quite close during the past ten-day.

"Sounds quite inventive of our young man," Leandra said noncommittally.

Claire said, "At one point I got suddenly very sleepy, and I think I had a dream. I don't remember much except that you were talking to me, but I don't remember what you said. Pem was worried and kept trying to wake me up."

"I told him I was fine, but the dream was so real that I wondered if your were actually talking to me. That is what I've come to ask. And if you were talking, what did you say?"

Claire could see that the Sage weighing something in her mind. She said, "Please tell me if I'm imagining all of this."

Leandra sighed. "No, you are not imagining anything. You reached out to me in your panic and nearly overwhelmed me. You have no idea what a disturbance you sent throughout the land—at least for those who are able to hear. Few will understand the meaning of this event, but some might. If they do, then you may be in great danger."

"What do you mean?" Claire asked her, feeling bewildered. "What has happened that is so important?"

"It is a simple thing, and yet complex," Leandra said, confusing Claire even further. "This event will set many things in motion. Some will be glad of it, and some will not care. There will be those who will lose everything they hoped for, and others will be seeking ways to profit from it."

"What *event,*" Claire demanded.

"Isn't it obvious, my queen? You have conceived an heir to the throne. There is ancient precedent for this. If Rachael had been one such as you, a minor healer even, your husband's conception would have been revealed in the same way. But, as I said, it has been many lifetimes since the Queen of Lunaria was one of the Great Healers."

"But I am only Claire, a rather ordinary girl from an ordinary place. I am no Great Healer. I know a few tricks and I can do a few things, but I cannot be one such as you describe. If I were so powerful, could I not leave Pem as well as this place and go to find my father in my own world? I might even be able to heal him. At least, I would try."

Claire sobbed in anger and frustration while Leandra looked on impassively. "None of us truly choose our path in life," she said finally. "I am convinced that all good things may come true for you if you remain true to your promises. Like it or not, this is your land now, and you have pledged to it. I think that the land will return this favor in kind as well as abundantly. At least, this is the way I see it, and my sight is rarely questioned," Leandra finished.

Claire hung her head and replied to Leandra, "You are right that this is now my place, and I admit that I do love Pem, even if he is rather silly. You can be certain that I will not forget my place, even though I may complain. If what you say is true and I am with child, then I have both a reason and the necessity to defend my position with Pem against all threats. Our child must be neither a pawn of power nor a magnet to conspiracy."

Leandra looked upon her young charge and thought that Claire had grown a great deal in the last few days. The burdens she would have to shoulder would be enormous. She decided not to tell her what else she knew. There would be time enough to deal with these difficulties when they occurred. Sometimes knowing too much was the reason people lost their courage.

Gilbert Greybaird

.GILBERT GREYBAIRD, UNOFFICIAL .chief of Palace security, the King's closest assistant, and the Lord of Greyhaven, sat in his garden, pouring over a stack of budget requests from the Palace household. He had planned a working lunch and had just dismissed Captain Royard with instructions on resubmitting a more detailed list of the Guard's needs—specifically on the procurement of replacement horses for the patrols he maintained outside of Lumminea. He was expecting Tess to appear with her own requests later in the afternoon.

He looked up in surprise when the room dimmed briefly. His steward was busy putting a tray of fresh cakes on the sideboard and replacing the pitcher of cool water. Either he was unconcerned or he didn't notice the drop in light level.

"Ring if you require something," the steward nodded. He was a long-standing, loyal retainer and the two men enjoyed a special relationship.

"Thank you. When Lady Tess arrives, please show her directly in," Gilbert replied, leaning back in his chair, opening himself to faint whispers of flux that penetrated the barriers set around the Palace.

A strong shockwave if I could sense anything in here, Gilbert reflected. He looked to see that he was alone and walked over to a small storage pantry set in one corner of the garden. After opening the door, he pulled aside a rack of gardening tools and pressed a panel. An opening appeared with a narrow, circular stair rising up into the darkness. Another panel on the inside of the passage produced a glow from above. He closed and locked the pantry door behind him and slipped into the stair well.

The top of the spiral stairs opened onto a secluded section of the Palace roof. There were a few potted plants, a round table with chairs under a blue canopy, and a fully-functioning fountain that Gilbert had puzzled over for years since there appeared to be no water supply and no drain. There was also a cabinet with a dumb waiter that could be operated from the kitchen three floors below and a bell rope that signaled the private office of his Steward. Few people knew of Gilbert's retreat—only the one retainer and a few close friends. In good weather he sometimes came up alone at night to watch the stars and cast out his vision to the world at large. He had no illusions about his abilities, but he was at least adept enough to send out certain queries, such as to the young queen, his half-sister, Ka'Tara, and to Pem.

Now, standing on the roof, beyond the energy barrier than clothed the Palace like a second skin, he could clearly hear the echo of a serious disturbance in the background. He determined that the origin was with Claire, and that whatever had triggered it, wasn't something dire.

Yes, it could be, he smiled to himself. It was possible. There might be a new heir to the throne today. He worried briefly about how the news would affect his daughter and granddaughter. His daughter would probably withdraw even further from him, and his granddaughter, well she was lost to him already. He sighed. Blood, honor, and loyalty. The choices were always difficult. Sometimes they were impossible.

Jallis Ruffin

RUFFIN BROODED OVER his failures to gather the reins of power in his hands. His agent on the royal yacht had failed to explode the engine. The failure was inexplicable. Then there was the change in the Dark Forest. The trees had deserted him. One Mother was no longer under his control. His hand contracted like a claw around the parchment he held. The sheepskin turned black and crumbled.

He reached out to the swirl of tiny creatures surrounding him and instructed them to make a query. He had to find a way to bring Mother back under his control. He had lowered his static shields to enhance his senses when the wave of energy sliced through him. The pain nearly overwhelmed him.

At first he thought he was under attack. Then he realized that it was like a pulse of pure chaos traveling through the energy field. He built wall after wall, only to see his shields crumble as they came apart in the randomized flux. He was close to the last of his reserves when the wave front passed. Gradually he was able to build the order around him until he was no longer being drained. The girl, Claire, he thought. The sheer magnitude of the thing had her signature stamped on it. The girl was an idiot to waste her energy.

It took Jallis Ruffin a while to rebuild the order surrounding him. He cast his thoughts back a thousand years and triggered a memory of the ancient story of the Scepter, one of the Great Keys to power. The girl had conceived! There was a potential new heir to the throne in the making. Of course, just because there was a joining didn't mean that the tiny cluster of cells would come to fruition. Here was a new opportunity.

There would be new alignments on the Council. Torvall Garrund would not hold the exclusive reins of power, and Ruffin's value would be enhanced. He had only to worry about Gilbert Greybaird.

After a while, Ruffin smiled. There was a way to use Gilbert's daughter against him. The plan that came to mind would not only take down his greatest enemy, but it would destroy the ridiculous boy king. Perhaps it might take care of the girl Queen as well. First, he needed to plant a tell, one of his special listening devices, near the royal couple. He had a way of doing that, and the surprise he had in store for the couple—well, it might yet be fatal.

Tess

.TESS WAS AWAKE in her bed; Royard snored lightly beside her. Warm yellow light from a lamp in the outer room filtered through the partly closed door and gave her enough illumination to study the swirling patterns in the plaster on the ceiling.

Tess remembered feeling a jolt of pleasant warmth that afternoon. The sensation occurred before she visited Gilbert about a matter of the Royal household budget. Gilbert had been in an exceptionally good mood—even hinted that Tess would have a great deal more responsibility thrust upon her when her mistress returned to the Palace. He made mention of something new to expect. She wondered if he were talking about a new heir, which would mean that Claire was pregnant. Not possible. It's too soon, she thought.

Lying in bed, she felt a shiver of excitement. She and Royard had engaged in an intense and satisfyingly extended love-making session. Though Tess wasn't particularly superstitious, she had a strong feeling that something had happened between them that was different. Could it be that both she and Claire were quickened?

As she drifted into a light sleep, she pictured herself with Claire, Royard, and Pem—accompanied by three children. It would have been a comforting sort of dream except for the harsh desert landscape in the background and the sense of imminent danger.

Edward Godwyn: Light and Shadow

.THE REMNANTS OF .a half-eaten lunch rested on a platter in front of him. The man twisted the stem of his wine glass and watched the swirl of the ruby liquid climb the side of the goblet. So intense! He still felt queasy after the wave of power had battered him. He had been open and listening to the ebb and flow of energies around him when the wave broke over him. He was lucky to have managed to shunt them aside. He did not doubt that the land now had its new heir to the throne—an enormous, but welcome, complication that opened up many possibilities for shifting power at the Palace. He swallowed the rest of the wine and poured himself another glass from the pitcher on the table in front of him.

There would be those on the Council who would know, and he wondered how long it would take for them to make their move. Garrund would be first, he judged. Torvall would gather support and would push for measures to control the power of the monarchy. The king would have to be very clever to use the power that his popularity with the people gave him. He finished off the wine and poured himself another. Pem would need much guidance in this, and he stood ready to serve his Majesty. He laughed at that thought. Pem would be easy to convince. The girl would be a different matter entirely.

Ranaputkin

CLAIRE WAS SO busy with leaving the resort that she didn't have much time to think about what Leandra had told her. Should she confide in Mags? What should she tell Pem? The idea of telling him scared her. Would he be pleased? She decided to put it out of her mind until she found the right moment, trying to ignore something her grandmother had said with considerable asperity about right moments—that waiting for the right moment was a way of putting off decisions. This was a decision she was desperate to put off. She was still thinking about this as she stood with Pem on the foredeck while the Rachael Ann cleared the breakwater and turned east along the coast.

"You'll love Ranaputkin," Pem said with enthusiasm. "Not only do they love royalty in Ranaputkin, but the city is one of the most beautiful in our land. It lies at the mouth of the Copper River, and is the largest port in southern Lunaria. We can expect the finest hospitality from Farold Ranapui who is a great believer in the tradition of the Monarchy."

Pem went on to describe the broad streets and squares, the parks with their flowers and herbariums, and even a zoo where they kept rare animals from other parts of the continent. Claire tried hard to concentrate on what he was saying, but her thoughts kept returning to having a baby in an alien land.

Not alien, she reminded herself. Lunaria is quite like her own world in so many ways, she reminded herself. The tears started to come and she couldn't stop them. She needed her mother—or better yet, her grandmother—to tell her what to do. Pem stopped suddenly as she sniffed and brushed at her eyes with the back of her hand.

"What on G'rama's earth is the matter, dearest?" he said, bringing another bout of tears running down his wife's face. "Are you disappointed in leaving the beaches so soon? I promise you that you'll have a good time in Ranaputkin."

The weather was perfect, balmy and warm without being hot. The Rachael Ann made the passage between the Bay of Lunaria and Ranaputkin in two easy days, reaching the mouth of Copper River at the close of the second day.

Claire thought that, if anything, the lights of Ranaputkin were brighter than those of Lumminea or Drieven. The city lay along a crescent of land between the waters of the bay and hills in the background to the west. The last glow of sunset was all red and yellow patches of high clouds embedded in deep blue, almost black, skies over the desert beyond the hills. The exotic smells of flowers and foods came to her across the water along with the less attractive scents of smelters and forges located across the bay to the east. Claire considered the blend exciting because it reminded her somewhat of Houston, Texas with its gardens as well as refineries and paper mills.

As the ship approached her assigned birth, Pem came to stand beside her and whispered in her ear, "Nikko advised that we spend the night aboard the boat and accept an invitation from Farold Ranapui in the morning. I agreed, though it means another night on the Rachael Ann. I have asked the Captain to grant shore leave to many of the crew so that we may have the ship more to ourselves. Nikko plans to send a message to Captain Eberson tonight if he can get access to the communications panel. I told him we would help by distracting the Captain; I thought that we'd ask him to join us for dinner."

"The weather this evening is so perfect that perhaps we should have dinner served on the aft deck," Claire said and grinned at Pem. "Is that far enough away from the bridge to be a distraction?"

"I think that would do admirably," Pem returned. "I'll drop a hint to Chef Prandi as soon as we've docked. He'll be delighted to create something special."

"What if the Captain is busy?" Claire asked.

"What? Do you think the Captain would dare turn down a dinner invitation from the Royal Couple?" Pem laughed. "I rather think not—not if he wants to continue being the Captain of the Rachael Ann."

Nikko: Fight to the Death

DOCKING THE RACHAEL Ann had gone routinely, and the port captain had been very accommodating. There were even a few friendly citizens standing in a roped-off area at the end of the dock to cheer and wave banners in celebration of their visit. Nikko watched Claire and Pem stand at the bow and wave back, receiving a few cheers and well wishes from the small crowd.

Nikko kept a skeleton watch aboard the ship, and spoke to the shore party before releasing them. "I don't want to have to come get any of you out of the Guard's hands," he said, leaving an unstated threat of dire disciplinary measures in the crew's minds.

When he reported to Agkor, the Captain accepted his actions, but Nikko thought it was plain that the Captain was annoyed with him in some way. Perhaps Agkor's former First Officer, replaced before the beginning of the voyage, had been more deferential to the Captain. Nikko admitted to himself that Agkor might see him as a pawn put in place by Lord Gilbert. He promised himself that he'd be more careful in the future.

And then came the Royal request, a summons not to be denied. Nikko noticed that the Captain wasn't too pleased, but that he accepted the invitation from the Queen with well-concealed resignation. Agkor confided in his First Officer concerning his skepticism about the Queen's motives. Did he think the Queen was attracted to him? This was such brash and arrogant confidence to be shared by a Captain with one of his officers that Nikko wondered if Agkor was testing him. The fact that no messages had yet been sent off-ship did not absolve the Captain from Nikko's suspicions. Nikko merely shrugged at Agkor's words, leaving the Captain's company by voicing an excuse concerning checking out the engine shield integrity.

.THE SHIP'S BRIDGE .was empty except for the guard—the ship quiet except for the murmur of a low-pressure entropy engine used to provide hot water and gas for lighting. Brennet was one of Nikko's men, brought aboard in Lumminea. He was a large man with a shaved head and serious demeanor that belied a basic, gentle nature. "Catch an hour's break. Get a cup of tarle. The galley is operating. I'll look after things here," Nikko said.

Brennet nodded his gratitude and moved off, leaving Nikko alone on the bridge. He closed the door softly and looked around. The glow lights on the compass binnacle gave off only enough light to create deep shadows beyond the helm. He listened a minute, feeling rather than hearing the slight noises in the ship's hull, a creak of deck plate, a hiss of steam being vented in the galley, some voices coming faintly through the ventilation system.

Nikko took the key from his pocket and moved to the panel at one side of the chart table. There was a communications room hidden behind the bulkhead, concealed behind the chart room which, similar to the Fortuna's layout, was reached from outside the bridge.

He brushed his fingers over the surface underneath a molding that ran at eyelevel around the room, dividing the lower wood paneling from the white-painted metal wall above it. Abruptly he felt the small indentation and pressed his fingers into the depression. A smooth click sounded and a small section of wall slid back revealing a keyhole surrounded by a soft green glow underneath. He inserted his key in the opening and turned it twice to the right and once to the left.

A slight hiss was the only sound the panel made sliding back into its groove. Inside, a console with a screen glowed a subdued green with dots of various colors twinkling across a grid. He quickly stepped forward and positioned himself in front of a series of ciphers engraved on the surface of a slate-black material. He pressed the green triangle with the two red dots under it and waited.

After a moment he felt a slight tingling and Captain Eberson's voice whispered through a rush of static, "Is it serious?"

Nikko voiced his reply, though there was no actual reason for having to speak his thoughts aloud. "No, Sir, not serious at the moment, but I think the Captain is waiting for something to happen before he does anything. That has me worried."

"That is why I put you there," Eberson replied. "You have been watching him closely?"

"As closely as possible. There is something wrong with the man. He actually asked me if I thought the Queen took a fancy to him. That's insane."

Eberson growled. "He probably wanted to see how you would react. What did you say?"

"Nothing. What could I say? He's the Captain. I pretended not to understand what he meant."

Eberson was silent for a long moment. Nikko shivered as ghostly pictures drifted through his mind, mental swirls of gray and purple that were like spiders spinning webs. "What are our young charges doing?"

"They have invited Agkor to join them at dinner here on board—a singular honor which the Captain was wroth to accept, though he disguised his feelings well. I thought it was the perfect way to distract his attention while I used the communications console."

"Be careful, Nikko. Agkor may have other means of monitoring its use. You should break this off and return to keep an eye on Pem and Claire. Take a trusted crew member with you.

Talk with Mags, take her into your confidence if you haven't already. Make sure the Captain is watched at all times."

"Yes, Sir, I will do that," Nikko said, feeling relieved now that he had specific instructions. He would certainly enlist Mag's help with this. She would watch Claire even more carefully for this one night. Tomorrow the royal couple would be beyond any danger from Agkor while visiting with the Ranapui family."

He wished Eberson a good night and pressed the white circle with the green triangle in the middle. The sounds and dream-picture were cut off abruptly, to his relief.

He was thinking about where to find Mags as he stepped back from the console and almost didn't hear the slight sound of a shoe scuffing on the deck behind him.

Nikko had practiced a good deal of combat training, but as quick as he was, he didn't quite avoid the knife slash, though he caught it on the sleeve of his coat and deflected the blade from its original target—his neck. The warm trickle of blood down his arm was evidence that he hadn't come away unharmed. He followed the twist of his upper body by a spinning kick that caught the man across his leg, though not low enough to damage his knee. The man grunted and stumbled back into the bridge room, coming up hard against the wheel. It didn't seem to slow him down, though, because he plunged forward again before Nikko could escape the confine quarters of the communications room.

"Who the devil are you?" Nikko shouted at the man who wore a loose tunic with a cowl that concealed his face.

Nikko had only his rigging knife on a loop under his coat. He grabbed for it and was in time to parry a wicked thrust towards his body. His opponent not only had the longer blade, but greater reach, and Nikko was hard pressed to see how he could gain any advantage against his foe. He decided against yelling again—a waste of breath. No one was likely to hear him on the bridge.

Now the man backed off slightly, letting his hand with the knife weave loosely in front of him, waiting to see what Nikko would do. Nikko noticed that he had cloth wrapped around his other arm.

The man spoke in an unfamiliar accent, "It would seem that we have a standoff at the moment. I can't come in and get you, and you can't escape your little room. I believe that time favors me, however."

And that might well be true, Nikko realized, feeling his wounded arm weakening. The loss of blood would, in time, render him unable to defend himself. He looked around for something he might use as a more effective weapon.

"Sadly, though fortunate for me, you are not carrying your sword," the man said. "You are very quick with the blade. It would not have been so easy for me."

"What makes you think it will be easy for you?" Nikko threw back. "And why me? Am I someone important enough to kill? I am merely the First Officer of this ship. I claim no power or authority."

"You are the hand of Gilbert Greybaird, and that is enough for me," the man hissed and tried a quick lunge that Nikko parried, though not without difficulty. "After you are out of the way, the young King and his bride will be easy enough to deal with."

"Out of curiosity," Nikko said, "are you working for the Captain? I don't seem to recognize your voice from among the crew. Have you been with us all along, or did you slip aboard tonight?"

"You won't be able to distract me," the hooded man chuckled, a nasty sound. "But no, I didn't slip aboard, I've been here all along. I might as well satisfy your curiosity since you won't be telling anybody."

"Who are you working for, then?"

"That's asking too much," the man said. "It is enough to know that I have powerful friends."

"But not locally, I'd bet," Nikko replied. "The Ranapui family has always been an avid supporter of the Windovers and the Monarchy."

"I have my plans. You needn't worry about me," the man laughed again in his evil-sounding way.

"May I at least know who it is that seeks my life?" Nikko asked.

The man seemed to consider his request. "Very well, I am known as Ramosa."

As he weakened, Nikko settled upon a desperate plan. Few knew that he was an expert at knife throwing. In fact, the technique of throwing a knife was not commonly practiced since it left the thrower in an awkward situation if the throw missed. Nikko's rigging knife was well balanced with a razor-sharp edge and tapered point, but he'd not drilled with it. He only needed a moment's inattention on his assailant's part to have a good chance of succeeding.

"At least let me know the face of the man who will kill me," Nikko said, making his voice sound desperate. "It would be a common courtesy among men of honor."

"I don't take much stock in honor," the man said, "but if it will ease your soul out of this world, then I suppose it is little enough to pay for a favorable petition to G'rama."

In the moment that the man reached up to draw back his cowl, Nikko launched his knife with all his strength. The blade turned once and buried itself in the man's exposed throat. The man coughed in surprise and shock. He staggered back, clutching the hilt of the blade, jerked it free releasing a great gout of blood, and then sank to the floor where he lay shuddering while blood poured from the wound. It was all over within a few seconds.

Nikko took a deep breath and staggered out of the communications room, sliding the panel closed behind him and concealing the keyhole. He retrieved his knife from the assassin's limp grip, shed his coat, and cut out one of the sleeves which he used to bind the deep cut on his arm. He was dizzy, but he managed to stagger to the bridge entrance, opening it to find Brennet about to reach for the latch.

"What happened to you?" Brennet cried out, steadying his First Officer and looking in horror at the blood-soaked shirt, the genuineness of his expression relieving Nikko's fear that the man was part of a conspiracy.

"Assassin! Quickly, take me to the King and Queen," Nikko urged. "The royal couple may be in grave danger!"

As frantic as was his haste, he stopped briefly in his quarters to arm himself. No telling what they'd run into. He'd not be caught a second time without his sword.

A Surprise with Dinner

"PLEASE JOIN US," Pem said to Captain Agkor.

Claire felt the reluctance of the Captain when he bowed before seating himself at the table. Chef Prandi appeared and read from the night's menu.

"A very special grazer tenderloin with fruit glaze, a salad featuring the finest dressing of oil and vinegar enhanced with special herbs and mustard, fresh baked loaves of seed bread, and a dessert featuring a citrus ice topped with honey and nuts."

Claire's mouth watered at the Chef's description. Even Agkor appeared mollified. He accepted a flask of wine after the King and Queen were served and waited until they had tasted theirs before he took a sip of his. Leandra was drinking water.

"This is very good," he complemented Prandi, who was hovering anxiously in the background.

"Yes," Pem said. "It is the last of a vintage laid down by my father and comes from the Queen's vineyards."

"Then, I salute the Regent for his good taste," Agkor said with all apparent sincerity.

"Ah, but regent no more," Pem noted without taking offense.

"Of course,' Agkor apologized. "I'm sorry if I offered any offense."

"Come, come, Agkor, there need be no such formality around this table. We are just four friends enjoying a pleasant evening. Isn't that right, dear?" Pem turned to Claire who was gazing absently into the distance. Leandra smiled enigmatically and kept her own counsel.

"Quite right," Claire said, coming to herself. She had been sensing something wrong somewhere on the ship, but she couldn't quite put her finger on the reason. She smiled at the others and offered a toast. "To a safe voyage completed," she said and raised her glass.

Leandra waited until Pem had raised his own glass before raising hers. "If I might?" When the Claire nodded, she said, "To a long and prosperous reign." Agkor joined with the sentiment politely and took a very small sip of the wine.

Claire was a healer and often could read the general state of mind of her patients by examining the pattern of the cloud of nanites creatures within the vicinity. Since the usual emotion of someone seriously ill was fear and uncertainty, she wasn't sure if her senses were telling her anything she didn't already guess. This time, however, she could read a fuzzy anger and uncertainty in the Captain's general demeanor. A vague sense of danger hovered over the table.

"What can you tell us about the Copper River," Claire asked Captain Agkor. She grabbed Pem's hand on the table. "None of us has sailed on the river. Tell us what marvels will there be to see?"

Agkor looked surprised. Pem said, "The Queen is correct, while I have visited the mines in Akren, I came there by way of Malbreck, not the river."

Agkor thought a minute before he answered. "The Copper River was so named because at one time the river ran copper-colored from the mine tailings of the deep mines. An ancestor of yours insisted that the mines no longer dump the clay into the water, and so the river has been returned to nearly its original state—which is a beautiful, clear-blue river winding among low sandy hills and rocky plains. While the land seems barren, it is rich not only in minerals but also in a special species of hardy plant from which a form of rare oil is extracted."

"What is this oil used for?" Claire wanted to know.

"It is the only known cure for a variety of poisons," Agkor returned. "It was discovered because scavengers who were poisoned turned to chewing on the bark of these plants and did not die from the poison."

"What is the name of this plant, and why were these creatures being poisoned," Claire asked. "It seems a terrible thing to do to an animal."

"Sorry, I do not remember the name," Agkor returned.

Leandra broke in. "I think those predators were raiding herds of livestock, and people cannot survive if they lose their grazers. That was why the poison was used."

"I thought the land was arid and mostly unproductive," Claire said.

"Indeed, but irrigation from the river produces beautiful and fertile fields. You will see this, especially near Akren."

I will find this plant interesting for many reasons, Claire thought. The nanite-creatures will have much to show me.

They paused while one of the kitchen servers brought in platters of tender glazed grazer fillets and bowls of fresh salad greens along with small pitchers of assorted dressings. There were also small platters laden with individual loaves of bread, each with its pot of honey and dish of butter.

"A fine dinner," Pem congratulated Prandi who had come to hover in the background.

"Although," Claire offered, "I cannot imagine where you managed to get these fresh greens. One would think that you wave a magic wand and these things appear."

The Chef clasped his hands behind his back and bowed in Claire's direction. "I am at your service," the Chef said, preening.

"Though I seem to recall that during my first voyage aboard the Rachael Ann, the fruit was overripe and the chops were a bit off," Pem added. Leandra frowned at the deliberate slight.

Prandi blushed at Pem's words. "Indeed, My Lord, I was new to the job, and I made mistakes." Claire could tell that underneath his obsequious exterior, the chef was both angry at and afraid of Pem.

Pem whispered to Claire, "If you flatter this man, he will become insufferable."

She said, ignoring Pem, "I'm sure everything will be perfect from now on, Chef Prandi. Tonight, at least, you have outdone yourself."

Prandi looked from Claire to Pem and decided that no comment was the best course. He bowed low and spoke before he withdrew, "I will see to dessert personally."

The Sage chuckled when Agkor said, "I can't stand the man, myself, but the Reagent seemed to think quite highly of him."

"I believe that was because he knew his wines and always laid in a good stock of the best," Pem said and laughed.

Agkor looked uncomfortable. "I wouldn't know about the quality of the wine," he observed. "I was never offered any."

Pem looked surprised. "I'm sorry for that. I didn't realize you were left out. The Captain of the ship deserves the best. At least you can look forward to that."

"I thank you for your kindness," Agkor said stiffly.

Claire noted that, if anything, the Captain was getting more nervous.

She was debating on whether to bring up the subject with Agkor when there was a shout and a disturbance originating on the main deck forward of the fantail. Nikko appeared with Brennet and three other crewman and descended the steps to the aft deck where their table was laid out. He carried his naked blade in his hand and was covered with blood spatters. Pem uttered an oath, reaching for a sword that wasn't there; Claire went for her special knife that she carried pinned like a brooch to her overshirt. Agkor grew pale and rose from the table. Leandra sat quietly, as if she already knew what was happening.

Nikko advanced on the Captain, who backed away while trying to look outraged but only succeeding in looking fearful.

"What is the meaning of this? Put away your weapons immediately," Agkor snarled.

"Yes, what are you doing?" Pem barked at Nikko. Claire noticed that her husband, not having his sword, had moved closer to her and was gripping the chair in case he needed to swing it in front of them as a shield.

Claire relaxed, realizing that Nikko's anger was directed at the Captain. She had been momentarily afraid that her friend had been taken in a fit of madness. She put a hand on Pem's arm to calm him.

Leandra decided to intervene. She said in a voice of authority, "Everyone calm down. Nikko, I want to know why you are threatening the Captain—and Captain, I would prefer that you keep your hands away from the inside of your jacket."

Agkor looked wildly from Nikko to the Sage and finally to Pem. "Very well, since Ramosa failed me, I will have to do this myself," he said, as if to himself. He pulled a small object from an inside pocket and tossed it in the direction of the dinner table where it landed in the dish of greens.

Pem laughed. "It is only a tattle."

Claire grabbed at Pem's jacket frantically and pulled him backwards causing him to trip and fall to the deck. Before he could get up, Claire shouted to everyone, "Get back! It's not a tattle! It's an attack!" A dense swarm of nanites was trying to contain the black sphere; it was like one of the dimensional bubbles which she had created and would consume everything it touched—beginning with the salad.

I never thought Prandi's berry dressing was that good, Claire thought as the salad, bowl, and then a section of table disappeared into the growing sphere.

"Will it consume the entire ship?" Nikko asked, backing away but keeping an eye on the Captain.

Agkor said, "No, only those it has been told to seek. I believe you would be one of those, Officer Nikko."

Nikko paled, but remained determined. He turned to Pem and Claire. "An assassin attacked me while I was on the bridge. He nearly succeeded, but I am here and he is not."

Not that that would likely remain so if the black sphere continued to expand and gobbled them up into its interdimensional maw. Claire sent out a command to the nanites to thicken the wall surrounding the sphere. She hoped to overload the interface. This tactic managed to slow its growth, but not to stop it. Billions of them poured into the interface every second, cast into oblivion the instant of touching the surface of the sphere. The drain on the interface was enormous. Claire wondered who was controlling it—surely not Agkor. She thought of Jallis Ruffin and her eyes narrowed. Surely this was Nikko's proof of a conspiracy that Gilbert expected him to find

Agkor must have noticed the slowing of the sphere's expansion. His eyes grew larger and Claire felt his fear. There was something that he knew that was frightening him.

Abruptly, Agkor turned and ran.

"Let him go," Leandra ordered Nikko as he started after the Captain. "Something is about to happen!" She instinctively threw her hands out in front of her causing Nikko to flinch. Claire shoved Pem back to the deck.

"There was a flash from the sphere and a white bolt of energy ripped through the space between the table and the fleeing figure of the Captain. There was the briefest of shrieks, and then only a fine cloud of white dust drifting over the railing of the Rachael Ann and dispersing across the harbor. The sphere had disappeared simultaneously.

The shock of what had happened paralyzed everyone.

"Failure is not an option," Claire murmured to herself, quoting a line from a movie about Apollo 13. Stars danced in her eyes where the bright flash had occurred.

"What were you saying?" Pem, who was still scrambling to his feet, wanted to know.

"Something I remembered," Claire said. "In this case, whoever was in control of the sphere realized that the attempt on our lives might fail and wanted to make sure the Captain wasn't around to reveal any useful information." An action that would fit perfectly with Jallis Ruffin.

Leandra nodded in agreement. "I think you have the right of it," she said to Claire. "Agkor had become too much of a liability."

Nikko looked in disgust at the white patch of powder on the deck and ordered the crew to "find a mop and clean it up."

"Yes Sir!" The answer came simultaneously from three mouths. Claire was sure that the crew was relieved to have something simple to do. Sailors understood the part luck played in the dangers of life at sea, and they even understood that their superstitions were reactions to these acts of Lady Luck, but this incident would seem magical in nature to them and therefore a part of their deepest and irrational fears. She wondered how the story would be told as it passed from mouth to mouth.

"They'll say that the Queen did a magical sending and caused the Captain to vanish in a flash of fire," Pem said, sounding disgruntled. Leandra chuckled, and Claire looked pained.

"It certainly looked that way," Nikko added.

"Take us immediately to the bridge," Leandra told Nikko. "You must tell us exactly what happened. Brennet may accompany us. I think he may have something to add to all of this."

Pem looked faintly embarrassed, but said nothing. Seaman Brennet, who had remained calm throughout the incident, bowed respectfully to the Queen and then to the Sage. If Pem or Nikko felt slighted at any omission, they were wise enough to remain silent.

A Conspiracy Uncovered

AS I SCRAMBLED to follow Nikko to the bridge, I suddenly realized that I had to quit waiting for Jallis Ruffin to come to me. I had to go to him. I realized that I had been entirely too passive. Thing is, I couldn't really say why. I'd have to consult Leandra on how to go about this. Everybody kept telling me I couldn't do anything about Lord Garrund or his minion Jallis Ruffin. Why not? Calantha seemed to operate independently, and look at all the trouble she had created for Gilbert—in a way, a whole lot more than her husband had. I needed to figure out a way to deal with Illaina, also. I couldn't allow Gilbert to put himself between his granddaughter and me. I had to come to terms with myself. I had declared that I wanted to be Queen, so I'd better start thinking like one.

When I reached the bridge, Pem tried to block me from entering, an action which irritated me even though I knew he was simply trying to spare me the sight of the dead assassin. I wasn't keen on seeing dead bodies, but there was a mystery to be solved and I was sure that I had better be the one to solve it. I pushed past him with Leandra, earning a knowing look in Leandra's eyes that the Sage carefully hid from my husband.

There were deep shadows inside the bridge and the unpleasant smell of death. Twilight had gone, leaving the forward windows on the bridge looking like black, sightless eyes. Through them I could see gas lamps strung along the docks and a few lighted windows in the waterfront warehouses. We gathered around the body while Brennet lighted an extra lamp on the bridge. Pem asked Nikko to make sure there were extra guards at the rail in case intruders tried to come aboard. He instructed that the town guards be advised of the murder attempt.

While Nikko was out arranging this, Pem reached down and moved the cowl from the face. He drew back and studied the features.

"He looks vaguely familiar," Leandra said, looking unperturbed by the bloody sight.

"Yes," I agreed with the Sage, swallowing an unexpected wave of nausea at the coppery smell of the spilled blood. I was fairly sure I'd seen the face before, but at the moment I couldn't remember where or under what circumstances.

Nikko rejoined us and cleared this up for me. "He said that his name was Ramosa. I remember now where I saw him. He was bending over the crewman who was killed in the engine room when the entropy shielding was damaged. He seemed most helpful at the time—though I recall that he disappeared shortly afterwards."

"Perhaps he was the reason for the shield breach as well as the death of the engineer's assistant," I remarked. I looked one last time at the sprawled figure before me. I decided that we'd probably never know. I extended my senses but detected nothing unusual connected with the corpse.

"Did the man say he was working for the Captain?" Pem asked Nikko.

"Not in so many words. He boasted that he was working for a powerful and influential group," Nikko said. "I have no doubt that he was at least working with the Captain's knowledge. I find it difficult to believe that Agkor actually planned our deaths."

I remembered that the Captain mentioned Ramosa's failure as he tossed the sphere on the table. "I think we can well believe that Agkor was going to arrange a convenient accident. I would give much to know what he planned."

"Perhaps Agkor was ordered to take action by someone," Leandra said. "He might not have guessed that circumstances would escalate so soon. I believe he might even have bluffed his way out of his predicament if he had kept his wits about him. Something scared him badly."

"Someone on the Council thinks to keep his hands clean by using a proxy," Pem borrowed the phrase from me when I had described the concept of conspiracy on my world. "I did not fully appreciate the evil of a conspiracy until now," he told me.

I nodded at my husband. Frankly, I was surprised that Pem remembered something I had said as he can seem a bit thick at times—or perhaps stubborn. If anyone had ordered our deaths, I figured it would be one of the Garrunds. The whole thing had the flavor of something the Garrunds would do—or was Jallis Ruffin acting independently.

"We must consider that the hand that could reach out so close to the Monarchy is powerful and not likely to be easily uncovered or deflected from its purpose," Leandra reminded us.

Nikko said, "Gilbert guessed that the captain was working for the Garrunds. He had me watching the captain in case he sent a message. I was supposed to find out who he contacted. I failed his trust." He turned to Pem and me, looking miserable. "Can you ever forgive me?"

It was on my mind that Gilbert could not have known the full extent of our danger or else he would have removed the captain instead of playing for more information. I found myself feeling vaguely uneasy. Gilbert had always kept everything under control. It wasn't like him to make this kind of mistake—or maybe he'd assumed that I'd be more alert. Suddenly I had the feeling that I had been coasting on the job, playing the part of the love-struck young Queen, while the machinations of the courts drew a cord tighter around our necks—my neck in particular. Oh, I had been nearly fatally foolish.

"We know that Counselor Garrund guides this hand," Pem said, waving his hand in the direction of the dead assassin. I couldn't imagine a more useless and dangerous assertion, but I wasn't going to contradict my husband in public.

However, Leandra had no trouble giving her opinion. "We do not know that," she said, causing Pem to frown. Pem didn't like to be challenged. I didn't want to offend my husband, and also I didn't want him to say something that might offend Leandra, so I said, "Both of us certainly have had strong suspicions."

I remembered what had taken place under the palace when Tess and I had been attacked. I also remembered that Pem had been slow to react to the threat. Really, I would have to watch for his tendency to act on what he wished to believe. I reminded myself that Gilbert had warned me of this and trusted me to act accordingly. Unfortunately, I had been slow to act.

"Even if you had evidence, you could not accuse a counselor of such a crime," Leandra said. "To do so would be to reveal a fatal weakness."

"I don't understand," Pem returned. I stayed silent because I was pretty sure what Leandra meant.

Pem plowed on, "Isn't accusing the Counselor of high misdeeds and sending him off to prison an adequate action? It would be the logical thing to do and show my strength."

Leandra said, "Even if you could get the judiciary to act against the Garrunds, and remember that the judiciary is an arm of the Eccollate and not at all inclined to go against the economic power of the High Council, you would be unlikely to succeed because the High Council represents the vested interests of the same people who ultimately control the purse strings of the King.

Unless you wish to become the Tyrant of Lunaria, the Eccollate will always choose what is more profitable for them—even if such choices wind up hurting the common people on which the King and the political stability of the land depends. In fact, the common people might even blame you for an economic downturn."

"But that is outrageous," Pem sputtered. "Are you telling me that I must use the same underhanded methods that Garrund is using against me? This is contrary to everything that I believe! I will not use assassination as a political solution."

"Nor should you," Leandra said. "Sometimes, though, the indirect action is far more effective than direct action."

She left so much unsaid—a habit with all Sages, I was beginning to understand. I tried to explain. "Pem, she means that people in our position cannot afford the luxury of high mindedness." My directness got a chuckle of appreciation out of the Sage.

"More like a difference between public and private persona," Leandra said drily. "It's always handy to appear to take the righteous position regardless of the outcome you wish to promote."

Leandra's mind was obviously more devious than my own. I wondered where misdirection ended and treachery began. I had much to learn, and I would have to move more quickly than I had been. For the first time, I began to have a true appreciation for what Gilbert Greybaird was facing.

A commotion outside the bridge drew our attention; one of the crew stuck his head in the doorway. He said, "Begging your pardon, but there's a gentleman here who would see you immediately and he won't take no for an answer."

"See here, man, I left orders that no one was to be allowed on board this vessel without my permission," Pem said sternly.

"Excuse me, Sire, I trust that that order might not apply to me," a senior officer with the star-and-crescent insignia of a Major appeared in the doorway, displacing the crewman.

"Ah, Major Lorence," Pem said. "Of course not. Glad you are here."

I recognized the name, if not the face, from my acquaintance with Captain Allain—now General Allain. Lorence was a distant cousin of his and the Commander of the garrison in Ranaputkin. I had looked forward to meeting him while we were visiting.

Part Four

Ranaputkin

<u>A Proper Welcome</u>

.AFTER A NIGHT .with little sleep and much speculation concerning the assassination attempt and Captain Agkor's degree of culpability, I welcomed the arrival of the Ranapui's carriage at the docks. I was grateful for the diversion, and I was tired of Pem's angry pacing back and forth across the floor of our stateroom. Sage Leandra stood next to me, arrayed in her judicial robes, and not talking to either of us. I suppose that I should have thought of her as Magister rather than Sage. She appeared to be lost in her own thoughts.

House Ranapui ranked as the third House on the Council. The Ranapui colors began with an orange on the left, yellow over white in the middle, and green over black on the right. From what I had learned since the time of the Great Ball and my long detour with Tess to the north, people respected both Lord Farold as well as Lady Sidra, a woman who was said to have a rare talent for numbers and whose reputation suggested that she actually ran the vast shipyards belonging to her husband's family. Many said that Ranapui's handsome eldest son, Faroldson, had at one time favored Illaina. I knew that Gilbert had been in favor of the alliance of Greyhaven with the House of Ranapui. However, Illaina's alliance with the Garrunds had placed an insurmountable obstacle in that path.

Farold Ranapui and his wife, Sidra, arrived in their sumptuous conveyance along with two footmen and a driver, and a small troop of guards, all of whom were arrayed in spectacular uniforms of black with green trim.

Farold and Sidra were dressed conservatively in pure white linen, a good choice for the tropical climate of their home. I stood at the end of the dock, damp and uncomfortable, and wished that

I had clothing as suitable as my hosts. Pem was also overheated, but Magister Leandra appeared cool and collected. Farold was short and blocky, but not fat. He looked more like a middle-aged weightlifter, and I guessed that he was probably quite strong. From his rough hands and the way he carried himself, I supposed that his family had insisted that he learn the shipbuilding trade starting at the bottom. His olive complexion contrasted with his brilliant blue eyes and gray hair. Sidra was elegant in her white linen suit, slender but not frail, and delicate only in the aristocratic reserve that she wore unconsciously. Her glossy black hair was gathered at the nape of her neck; her round, startlingly grey eyes seemed to see through me. The Ranapuis made room for Sage Leandra at their end of the carriage, leaving the forward-facing seat for Pem and me.

"We did not know that you were accompanying the royal couple," Sidra said to Leandra. "But you are certainly most welcome," she added with all apparent sincerity.

Leandra merely smiled in acknowledgement of Sidra's deference and leaned back into the comfortable cushions with a sigh of relief. "I believe I will have a permanent curve in my back from my tiny bunk aboard the Rachael Ann."

I suppressed a smile at the Sage's words. Leandra's bed was at least as large as mine and Pem's, and there was nothing uncomfortable about her cabin which had the same conveniences granted to ours.

"You must forgive us any lack of attention," Sidra said. "We have only returned from Lumminea. We thought your wedding was splendid!"

I was quite sincere when I said, "I'm certain your hospitality will be flawless." Sidra looked slightly uncertain at my comment—probably trying to detect in any sarcasm.

We passed through the streets with mounted guards ahead and behind. There were even a few citizens standing around on street corners waving at us. Pem nodded and looked regally gracious. I fluttered my hands a bit and felt silly. I suspected that the Ranapui had arranged a bit of publicity. The uncharitable thought crossed my mind that being seen with us was probably more benefit to them than to us.

Farold and Sidra took turns interpreting the sights of Ranaputkin, beginning with the origin of the name many generations ago. "I suppose you could say that the Ranapui and Putkin families had reached an impasse over who would control the city. Farold's family owned the shipyards and controlled much of the city's trade, but the Putkin heirs owned the large mines along the river to the north and are clever politicians allied with the Orumundi and Garrund families. Both the Ranapui and Putkin families decided to avoid the obvious collision course and have cooperated reluctantly over many hundreds of years—at least until recently."

"You mean, they divided the city between them," Pem observed.

"Something like that," Farold grinned. "Of course, we think we got the better end of the deal."

"Putkin doesn't openly favor the Garrunds on the Council." I said, considering the armed guards who looked more watchful than ceremonial.

Sidra shook her head. "They bide their time and talk politely with us. They did try to ramrod a tariff increase through the city council last year, a measure to protect their prices against the influx of metals from the volcanic islands to the east of Port Sulphur. The economic disruption of increasing tariffs would have bankrupted some of our smaller businesses who prosper on trading Lunarian goods to the islands, although the Putkins would have made a fortune from the increase in their metal and timber trade with Tieben. Farold persuaded them of the inadvisability of that course."

"How did he do that?" Leandra asked innocently.

"By pointing out that we'd be happy to build more gunboats for our friends in Port Sulphur who trade with the outlying islands instead of with Ranaputkin."

This trade with the islands was mostly new to me. In the western half of Lunaria, there wasn't much reason to be interested in trade across the Sea of Winds, as the ocean off Port Sulphur was named. That, of course, would change if the islands were to be developed to promote trade with Frangeria—something that Rissa would be more likely to know than I.

I had my personal doubts that Farold was the one who had done the persuading; Lady Sidra seemed far more tough-minded and better suited to that role, but I couldn't argue with a political power arrangement that sounded far more intelligent than that the Texas legislature had with the oil lobby back home.

We passed through some impressive parks and flower gardens and saw a lot of people walking about pushing miniature carriages with small children. Many of them stopped to wave at us in a friendly fashion. I wish we had their brightly colored parasols to shade us from the sun. I suppose it was the price we paid for being on display.

AWAY FROM THE river, the air was still and dry. Dust stirred up by our escort drifted over our fancy carriage coating everything. It was a condition of life in Lunaria, but I didn't have to like it. There were even annoying black flies that our footmen dispersed by waving fronds on poles over our heads. It all seemed a bit silly to me, but everyone else seemed to think it perfectly normal.

I took my handkerchief and dabbed at the unladylike beads of sweat on my face and noticed that the white cloth came away gray. What I wouldn't give for the air conditioning of my grandmother's Cadillac. I noticed that feminine, lacy fans had sprouted in both Leandra's and Sidra's hands. They fluttered like hummingbirds and were apparently effective in the heat. I wondered why Mags had not thought to outfit me with a fan—for that matter, did I possess such an object? I'd have to have a talk with my assistant; Nikko was taking up entirely too much of her concentration.

Farold's villa, for it was more than an estate and yet not quite like a palace, was just outside the edge of city in the foothills. As we approached the hill upon which the sprawling, white complex was built, I saw that it was surrounded by irrigated gardens with fountains and hedgerows of flowering bushes and trees that looked like the palms I remembered from my visits to Galveston. Except for the lack of mosquitoes, it might have reminded me of Texas if the hill country between Austin and San Antonio had been relocated south to the shores of the Gulf of Mexico.

We entered the grounds of the property through an arched gate in a low wall that was more decorative than it was a functioning security measure—unless the thorn hedge just behind the wall was the deterrent. I took a closer look at the unpleasant-looking growth. It reminded me of an illustration in Grimm's Fairytales—one of those evil pictures that inhabits a nightmare. I decided that they didn't need a wall after all.

The two guards in slightly wilted uniforms straightened up and saluted the carriage as we drove through, dipping the Ranapui pennants and raising our royal colors over the archway. We were officially in residence.

Hospitality

LEANDRA BUSTLED OFF to business of her own, taking only time to give me a short hug and saying that she would see me when time allowed. Lady Sidra herself showed me to a private area of the villa with our rooms while Pem went off with Lord Farold to do whatever it was that men did—smoke, shoot, or perhaps discuss the arts of war. I was still not used to the idea that men and women were separated by so many layers of convention in Lunarian society. It was something I'd planned on changing, but then had run into difficulties. While Gilbert took me seriously from the beginning, and Royard and Turlo had eventually come around, I still found Pem irritatingly patronizing from time-to-time. It was a work in progress. Of course, in the cases of Turlo and Royard, I'd had allies in Rissa and Tess.

Even if I were going to bring forth an heir to the throne— and we had agreed that we wouldn't give a formal reception announcing this until we returned from our Royal jaunt—I was determined to be considerably more than a broodmare for the loyal faction on the High Council.

Lady Sidra, seeming to sense something of what was going on in my mind, inquired if I'd like to have refreshments on one of the shaded terraces outside our rooms where we could have a nice chat. I could tell that she had something she wished to ask me, a favor, perhaps, and there were a few questions that I'd like to put to my hostess as long as we were alone in a relaxed atmosphere. I assured her that I'd be delighted to share some time with her. She excused herself for a moment and then returned, saying that she'd left instructions for us to be served on the fifth terrace, a reference that left me puzzled as to why it would be called the fifth terrace.

Were there third and fourth terraces? Were there sixth and seventh terraces?

I ask her about this when we'd settled in the cool shade of a large tree that looked like one of the giant blackjack oaks I remembered seeing at the base of the rose gardens in Ft. Worth. A nearby fountain not only provided us with a subtle mask for our voices, but a pleasant sense of coolness from the fine mist that rose around us.

"Yes, actually at one time there were nine terraces arranged along the hill," Sidra responded. "They were named after the Nine Paths to Love, and the older parts of the building were built around the original gardens which were said to be here even before Ranaputkin became a village. Now there are only three such places, but they are still referred to according to their original names. The second terrace, the path of Humility, serves as our private garden, this one, the fifth, the Path of Equanimity, is exclusively for the Royal Suite. Higher up the hill, the eighth, the Path of Compassion, is used for formal affairs and large parties."

"I take it that the Nine Paths refers to the teaching of G'rama," I said, raising an expression of surprise on Sidra's face. "What happened to the others?" I wanted to know.

"I do not know," Sidra returned. "I only know the story which supposedly dates back to the Peace of a Thousand Years, a very long time ago. Perhaps they were simply built-over or fell into decay."

"Then this is much older than it seems," I said, motioning to our surroundings and extending my sense to the stonework and the fountain, However, I found nothing with my query to suggest anything but a completely natural artifact, unlike the Garden at Greyhaven or in the Palace.

We waited while a servant set out the tea service and arrange some sweet cakes decorated with a variety of tiny animals sculpted in various colors of frosting. I commented on how pretty they were. Sidra looked pleased and relaxed. I could almost see her thinking that maybe this wasn't going to be so difficult after all.

While the older woman was making up her mind, I wondered how Mags was coming with getting our baggage up to the villa. I wanted to bring a few things in a bag, but Pem had assured me that our hosts would expect at least a wagon full of useless extras. "Even if you only wear one new dress a day, you should have three or four in reserve," he had said.

I hadn't pointed out to him that Mags and I hadn't gotten around to purchasing most of my wardrobe.

"I hope your stay here will be a pleasant one," Sidra said, breaking the short silence. "Is there anything that you would particularly like to see or do? You have only to suggest it, and it will be arranged."

"For your afternoon pleasure, we have scheduled a ride through the orchards in the hills where it is cooler. There will be an opportunity to observe some of the athletic skills of our young people, and there are a few neighbors whom you might like to meet as well. A picnic lunch and suitable refreshments will be provided."

The way she put it, I was thinking that these neighbors were locals with significant influence that they wanted or needed to impress.

"We have announced a dinner in honor of your visit for tomorrow night. If that is not your wish, then I can easily change the scheduling."

I managed not to groan. The Lady Sidra was only doing her job as hostess, and no doubt if I were actually suited to this job of being the Queen of Lunaria, my heart would quicken at the thought of a crowd of adoring subjects. But, I'd like to think I wasn't quite that vacuous, so I took the middle ground and murmured my pleasure and added, "I can think of no better way to strengthen the ties between our houses and at the same time demonstrate the support that your house has always shown the monarchy."

Sidra seemed to take me at my word and flushed with pleasure. She might have suspected that I was laying it on a bit thick, but since I was completely sincere, she had no reason to doubt me. She certainly knew about the Putkin's alignment with the Garrunds, so, in effect, I was telling her that I was in a position to grant her a favor in return for her loyal support.

Having perceived that I had opened the door for her, she said, "I have a great favor to ask. It concerns my daughter, Ribecah."

"Yes?" I encouraged her.

"It would be a great honor if you were to allow Ribecah to serve you. She has spoken of nothing else since she was at your wedding. Her desire to serve you is strong, and she is a sweet and reliable young woman. If she remains here, she will be doted upon by her brother and spoiled by her father. She will grow up to be a pampered pet of Ranaputkin society, and I believe that her spirit will wither and die."

Sidra flushed at her boldness and finished quietly, "I believe you could not find a more loyal companion."

I was quite taken aback by Sidra's passionate plea which seemed so unlike the sophisticated and reserved wife of a great lord who was at least twice my age. I had to admit that I was flattered also, because Sidra was treating me as if I were wise beyond my years, though I doubt that she intended mere flattery. Certainly Garrund's wife, Lady Calantha, would never have been so open with anyone. Calantha would have considered such openness a fatal weakness.

Her frankness moved me, having met so little of it at court, so I said, "I would be most delighted to consider your request. I must meet this young lady. Can you arrange for me to meet with Ribecah tomorrow morning?"

"Of course," she returned immediately. A loud noise interrupted us. Mags, a gaggle of porters, and piles of baggage were erupting through a service entrance.

"I should leave you to settle in," Sidra said.

I scrambled to my feet, remembering belatedly that Lady Sidra would not stand unless I did. I returned her bow by inclining my head, something that I had learned was what people expected of royal behavior, and wished her a good day, thinking that I would see her later for the ride in the hills.

However, that was not what happened. I pretended to supervise while Mags first received, then checked, and finally distributed our baggage amongst the several rooms under our royal control.

"Where did these trunks come from?" I asked Mags concerning a pile in the center of my room of dignified, travel-scarred wooden boxes with ornate carvings and rope handles at either end.

She put a finger to her lips. When the last of the porters had disappeared through the servant's entrance and the doors had been secured behind them, she giggled.

"They are filled with ship's ballast," she said, bursting into another fit of giggles.

"Rocks?" The surprise must have registered on my face because Mags burst into another fit of laughter.

"Forgive me, my Lady," she said, not at all contrite. "It would have been unseemly if the Ranapui's had seen the Queen traveling with only the two trunks." She pointed to the two familiar cases lying against the wall next to an archway giving into a dressing room that was about the same size as my bedroom back in Greyhaven.

I decided to ask, since I didn't see Pem's clutter of leather cases, crates with his favorite weaponry, and trunks with his formal wear packed in silk cloth. "Is my husband to have a different room, then?"

"Oh, yes, Lady," Mags returned. "Here in the East, it would be improper for you to share a room with your husband. It is not the custom."

"I see," I said, without seeing. "And do we send cards to each other when we desire to visit one another?"

I was joking, but Mags said, "Oh, I knew there was something I forgot." She fretted for a moment while I was still trying to figure out whether she was serious. "I know, I can mark up your standard calling cards and we can use those," she said.

I gave up for the moment and decided to address a more urgent question. "Do I have a riding costume?" I asked Mags.

"Yes, Lady Claire. I have one packed away. You must always have suitable riding wear."

I envisioned a comfortable pair of trousers, an overshirt, a vest, and a wide brimmed hat such as I might have used in Greyhaven when I was making my healer's rounds. There would be a more delicate pair of lady's gloves for the sake of propriety. Mags pulled forth an outfit that produced a decidedly unladylike response.

"I'm expected to ride in that?"

"Unless you wish to scandalize the locals," Mags suggested.

I examined the split skirt and the high-cut riding jacket with its suffocating collar. "I think I'd rather offend G'rama himself—herself—than to wear this thing," I said. "Besides, what am I supposed to wear under this thing for the sake of modesty."

Mags shrugged. "I think there is accommodation in the saddle design. I do not know. You are the queen. Whatever you decide will set the trends. Did you notice the pockets on some of the younger maids around here? Lady Tess told me that you invented them."

I started to explain that I hadn't personally invented them, that they were common on the world where I came from, but stopped myself. What difference did it make?

"Women do wear trousers here—just not riding horses," Mags offered.

I thought back to the barrel racing championships I'd seen on TV as a child and decided that Mags was probably right. I dredged up the memory of a young woman—probably about my current age—whipping around a barrel in a cloud of dust, glued tightly to the saddle, and hauling up her horse's head to keep her from stumbling.

"I think we will not ride side-saddle. I think we will set a new trend," I said.

Mags' eyes twinkled. I could tell that she approved my decision.

Afternoon Ride

.I WORE MY silver-grey trousers, an olive-green overshirt, and a dark green vest with silver trim that set off the red highlights in my hair. For good luck, I slipped the yellow egg with its *Silly Putty* into its special inner pocket; for added security, I fastened Nikko's knife to the inside of the vest and took up a pouch containing a salve to block the sun and a stick of wax to protect against chapping of lips. I thought about leaving my sword behind—after all we were only to take a civilized ride through the countryside, but decided that carrying it might be a wise precaution. I'd been caught napping when the Rachael Ann's captain had gone rogue. Maybe it was only a ride through civilized countryside, but you could never tell what you might encounter, and I was loath to surrender my personal safety into other people's hands again. I strapped my blade on my back, and, for the first time in what suddenly seemed like a long time, I felt fully alive.

I borrowed a jaunty green cap from Mags and pulled it down on my head and looked at myself in the mirror. I looked mismatched, but definitely trendy, even dangerous. Mags had sent word to the stables, so my escort was not entirely scandalized when she arrived to collect me for the afternoon's entertainment.

A dozen young men and as many young women were gathered in the cobbled courtyard, milling about in idle conversation. The ripe but not unpleasant mix of smells of horse manure and fresh straw suggested a well-run establishment such as Stable Manager Bender ran at Greyhaven. Talk subsided when I arrived, turning to quickly suppressed giggles as they beheld me in trousers rather than traditional garb. I saw a few frowns among the men—probably over my decision to carry a sword. I decided that

I had probably started another one of those unpredictable revolutions that made Pem so nervous.

Pem was already mounted on a magnificent-looking brown gelding that skittered about nervously at the edge of the group. A young man that looked like a smaller version of Lord Farold was astride a white stallion at Pem's side. Darcil, Farold's youngest son, had grown up since I last saw him in Lumminea. I smiled, waved at him, and received a snappy salute in return. Both men wore their swords pulled back along their side.

I explained to the badged Master-of-Horse, a taciturn, grey-haired man in his late fifties, that where I came from women rode the same as men. He hid his skepticism fairly well—I was the Queen, after all—and ordered my horse saddled accordingly. I decided that I had better perform up to the expectations that I had set.

When all the mounts had been brought out and Pem and I were side-by-side, he on his gelding, I on my beautiful and somewhat skittish roan, the rest of the entourage mounted. I saw that the women all wore the split skirts and used the sidesaddle, a style that guaranteed that their riding skills would be greatly curtailed. I wondered briefly at the idiocy of such a thing. We were then joined by four of our own men and a dozen of Farold's mounted guards with rifles. They formed up along one side in military fashion. More rifles. Did this mean that the locals were unaware of the vulnerability of powder weapons to a Magister such as Leandra who could manipulate the nanites?

Darcil walked his horse over to their captain and spoke to him—giving him instructions, I assumed. Pem went to advise the men from our ship who were wearing swords and carried bows. No one else seemed to pay any attention to our escort, but I thought it odd that we needed this degree of security. I supposed it was Farold's way of making sure that his son was safe and that at least he wouldn't be held negligent in case something untoward happened to us. Personally, I was glad of having four of Nikko's best men to ride with Farold's guards.

With the sounding of a horn and a great clatter we were off following a cobbled lane that spiraled down the hillside behind the villa. After a few minutes, Darcil turned aside and led us over a bridge that spanned a dry riverbed and we began climbing steeply to the ridge bordering the back of the main grounds of the villa.

The way was long and steep. The pace Darcil set was swift so that the horses and some riders were blowing when we reached the top of the ridge. I had expected to see more of the dry hills, but the landscape had flattened into gentle terraces of green pastures and pleasant orchards that ended in an abrupt ring of low mountains. Through a gap between two peaks I caught a glimpse of brilliant white that was probably the edge of the great desert beyond the highlands.

We had gained just enough altitude that the air felt slightly cooler. I could see the young women looking jealously at the ease with which I rode the traditional saddle. Some changes would come of today's outing—unwelcome, no doubt, to the more conservative of the young men who would cling fondly to their idea of chivalry and male entitlements. Pem, at least, no longer attempted to fit me into the traditional female role. I wondered how he was going to react when I told him that he was a father. I dreaded the confrontation, but I knew I couldn't put it off much longer.

Darcil pointed to a colorful pavilion alongside one of the fruit orchards not far beyond where we were gathered. "We will have refreshments and entertainment laid out for us," he said, addressing Pem.

Pem looked interested. I said, "I'm sure it will be very pleasant." I resisted scratching at an insect bite in an inconvenient location.

Darcil let us rest before he started out again along the curve of the ridge towards some ruined walls that straddled a narrow rocky mount about a stat away. I rode at Pem's side, letting my roan negotiate its place alongside the gelding. The rest of our group strung out behind us. There was little dust stirred up by our passage, the soil being some mixture of course volcanic sand bound together by a tough mat of short grass.

As we got close to the ruins, Darcil pulled up and let us catch up to him. I could see that he had something important on his mind—perhaps a favor to ask as had his mother, Lady Sidra. We eased alongside and he said to Pem, "My pardon, Sire, but I would speak with your Lady?"

When Pem nodded, he spoke to me for the first time.

"My sister, Ribecah, was unable to join us. The young women of our party are disappointed as she usually leads them about and they look up to her. My sister is considered to have somewhat radical thoughts about a woman's place in the community. She insists that women's opinions should be given equal weight in matters of policy. I approve of her ideas, though I do not always understand her motives. Others, especially the young lords, do not like what they consider a bad influence. I cannot say what is best to do, but I would consider it a great favor if you were to take our young women in hand. I think they will take courage from being with you. I'm sorry, I know it's a lot to ask."

Darcil's cheeks and neck reddened slightly at his boldness, but I thought I knew what he was about and answered him in the same spirit. Pem ignored us by watching a distant hawk circling over a pasture.

"If they will accept me, I'd be delighted to introduce them to a whole range of ideas," I returned, not really all that interested in spending my time with a bunch of spoiled society girls. I think I managed to keep my irritation from showing. "I won't corrupt them too much. We have a saying back home. One cannot afford to lose half the leadership potential in any community." I wondered what sort of radical reputation preceded me to Ranaputkin. I didn't want to make life more difficult for Pem.

Darcil looked slightly embarrassed at my bluntness; Pem continued to watch the hawk. I thought I detected a slight smile on his lips, but I could have been mistaken since I could only see his face in profile.

"Women have always been important leaders in our community, but not publicly. We need a policy that includes women directly in our council. It isn't the most popular notion," Darcil replied, "but it is one that I believe will be necessary if our land is to prosper."

"You would bring about such a dangerous revolution?" I inquired, trying to be serious.

Darcil cast his eyes beyond me. "I apologize, Lady Claire, if I have left the impression of starting a revolution. I merely wish to promote a policy that I think would be advantageous to my people."

And you are not the heir and have no power to make policy. I nodded, accepting his dilemma. After all, his brother was the heir and there was little Darcil could do to influence the future state of affairs in Ranaputkin. Certainly he could not ask me to speak with his brother. Pem turned his attention back to us and changed the subject to something less political. "Tell us, Darcil, why have we come to these ruins?"

Darcil's expression brightened at the question. "These ruins are very ancient and are said to predate the very settlement of our world, before contact with the nine worlds. We think they belonged to a castle or fort built to command the approach from the desert to the mouth of the river."

Pem looked bored; I found myself interested. Darcil turned back to the trail and we followed him single file up a narrow ramp that led between two enormous blocks of white stone with an unfamiliar script carved deeply into the surface. Our guards remained behind, taking up positions along the approach.

"Can you read this?" I asked Darcil, referring to the script.

"As far as I know, there is no one who understands what language this is," Darcil returned.

I allowed my senses to seek out the mist of nanites that form a part of the pervasive background of Lunaria. I rarely do this, and haven't for a long time. Normally I only interact with the nanites when I am called to heal someone or do something dire. I'm always reluctant to immerse myself too deeply in this cloud because it can be very disorienting and claustrophobic. The amount of unfiltered information, when taken in this way, can be overwhelming. However, if I am seeking something unexpected, I can't formulate a specific query and so I can't expect to get a specific result.

The first thing I discovered was that the density of the nanites was low—not as low as on the barren White Desert far to the north where our landship was attacked by Oul's men, but definitely lower than what I expected in a reasonably lush environment. This made things both easier for me and more difficult: more difficult because there were fewer data sources available; easier because it was not so difficult to pick out unusual patterns from the thin fog of competing information. However, I learned little other than the sense of great age.

"Claire?" Pem's voice penetrated my concentration and I withdrew from the phage-world.

"Sorry?" I said. My horse, on its own, had come to a stop beside Pem's.

"Are you all right?" he wanted to know.

I must have drifted off longer than I realized. Darcil was stopped ahead of us, looking back over his shoulder with a puzzled expression. Pem was leaning over from his saddle staring at me. I waved a hand in a shooing motion.

"I'm fine, just thinking," I said, feeling embarrassed. I looked around me and discovered that we had ridden to the top of the ramp and entered a flat area that might have once been the floor of a great hall. The flat stonework was polished clean and smooth by the action of wind and rain. There were low walls around the edge that had a melted-butter look that weathered masonry achieves after many millennia of exposure to the elements.

I let my horse pick its way through some broken stone, between the pillars of what might once have been an internal archway and reined up at the edge of what must have been a wall that separated the hall from an open courtyard. The remnants of the structure were scarcely two vars high, and the courtyard beyond was broken with ancient, gnarled trees scrabbling through cracked stonework. Still, I could see a few intact pieces of ceramic tile peaking from under a layer of dirt and the detritus of uncounted years.

"A lonely place," I commented. There was an overwhelming feeling of great sorrow emanating from what lay beneath me. I sensed layer upon layer of ancient works culminating in the surface we now saw. The nanites showed me buried stairways and crypts, a hearth and stonework long cold, the bones of some long-dead beast of enormous proportions, and a great tangle of what might have been the corroded remnants of armor and the heads of spears, their wooden shafts fallen into dust.

I fell deeper, through other times and places, a set of dishes buried on its stone tabletop, and then a vaulted hollow space and the drip of water, cold air and eternal night.

I looked closer to the surface where I was shown fallen blocks and blocked passages. There was a pallet and an oil lamp— and a rectangular black stone. I jerked awake, jarred back to the present by the image of a modern oil lamp and an ominous black stone fringed with a greenish glow. There was a sudden feeling of fluid softness, the kind I felt when I saw the images of people trapped in the black stones on the floor of the Plain of Glass. I felt the floor tremble slightly, though I think it was my perception, not an actual rumble since no one else seemed to sense any disturbance.

My horse was waiting patiently for me to command it to do something. Had I seen something in the present, or was my vision a product of a past memory stored somehow in the collective memory of the nanites of Lunaria? I shuddered and looked around, seeing that Pem and Darcil had dismounted and were examining animal bones scattered in one corner of the space. The rest of our entourage separated into male and female groupings and was spreading out over the site, chattering loudly and picking their way through fallen columns. The men seemed intent on the defensive aspects of the castle and were discussing the various approaches an enemy might take in order to avoid the worst of the defender's fire. Some of the men were passing flasks around. About half the women were exclaiming over finding some broken shards of pottery. I eased off the saddle and slid to the ground, slightly disoriented by my vision. I put the disturbing image of the large black stone firmly out of my mind.

Instead of joining Pem and Darcil, I wound my way, leading my horse, through a line of blocks set in rows upon the stone floor and joined a group of young women examining a collapsed archway and the remains of the fallen keystone with some writing etched in its surface. One of the girls was on her knees, running her fingers over the lettering, feeling the edges.

She was saying, "This stone isn't nearly as old as the rest of this stonework. The edges on the carving are still sharp and well defined." She was a pretty girl, about my age, with intelligent brown eyes, a mouth that was slightly too wide for her face, and cheeks that were pink from the fresh air and sun. Her dark hair was drawn back in a tight braid wound and pinned at the back of her neck. I thought she'd do well to wear a wide brimmed hat to protect her extremely light complexion.

"A new architectural element added comparatively recently?" I asked, both to engage her as well as to satisfy my curiosity.

She looked up at me, surprised, and shaded her eyes against the sun which was at my back and in her eyes. "Probably, Your Grace," she addressed me. Something in her manner made me think that she resented my presence.

"Claire will do nicely," I returned. "This isn't an audience room at the Court." I hoped she'd take me at my word. I had no idea what a real audience room entailed, nor had I ever held an audience—something else that I'd probably have to learn how to do. I didn't much like the idea.

She looked mildly shocked, an expression that was mirrored on the faces of the other girls in the group. "Yes, Your

Grace—I mean, Claire," she said, stuttering slightly as she tried to get her mind around the unfamiliar informality.

I smiled. "Please introduce yourself. In fact, I'd like to know all your names." Of course I knew that what I was asking simply wasn't done. Formal introductions were a way of life that served to separate a mere Lord or Lady from the King and Queen as well as commoners. It was a custom that I was determined to undermine when the occasion offered the opportunity.

Clearly the girl thought that I was not offering her a real choice. She rose up, curtsied in her split-skirt riding costume, and gave me her name. "Joella," she said.

"Well, Joella," I said, "why don't you introduce me to your friends?" I was making it easier for her and she looked grateful.

She went around the circle that had formed with me in the center. Each girl curtsied in turn as I acknowledged the name. Mari, Elin, Bren, Catha, Sashi, and Nyri were all fresh-scrubbed, polite, and pretty young women leaning toward the blond-blue-eyed, fair skin, and privileged look. From their unblemished complexion, I doubted that they took regular rides into the countryside, although Joella looked as if she used her hands more than the others—perhaps she had a more-than-passing interest in archeology. No doubt these girls were the cream of the local crop, innocently spoiled, vastly entitled, and ready to sell me out the moment I turned my back. They were perfect for the experiment I had in mind.

I said, "So, all of you enjoy a ride in the countryside, especially in hot weather?" Catha, at least, couldn't hide her incredulous look. In fact, she actually giggled, receiving an elbow in the ribs from Nyri.

Catha's porcelain cheeks had the flushed look of a blossoming sun burn. I turned to my horse and retrieved my pouch of supplies from where the groom had tied it under the saddlebag. I rummaged around in the leather bag while the girls looked on with curious expressions. I could almost hear them thinking, what was a royal person doing digging through their own luggage? Servants did that.

I finally found the sun ointment. "There," I said, prying out the tight-fitting cork and offering the hand-blown blue jar to Catha. "Rub a bit of this on your face before you ruin your beautiful complexion. It's only something to block the harmful effects of the sun and will sooth the dry feeling."

Catha accepted the bottle and sniffed suspiciously. The scent came from distilled lavender, and I used it to cover up the faint odor of less-than-perfectly-processed lamb fat which, along with some extract from finely crushed tea and mint leaves, provided a degree of protection. I wasn't sure how much because I only remembered my grandmother mentioning it when I was taking swimming lessons and had come away from the pool with a bad sunburn.

"Take some on the end of your finger and spread it on your cheeks," I suggested. "The herbs will feel good." I decided not to tell them that the base was lamb fat.

Catha applied a small amount to her face and smiled. I gave the surrounding nanites a slight push that repaired some of her irritated capillaries. I had thought as much. She was feeling the burn already. As soon as she commented on how good it felt, the others wanted to try some. I rationed it out as if it were precious; in a way it was, since the only way I had to get more was to send for it from my stock in Greyhaven.

"I'm so glad that you came to keep me company," I went on, keeping a straight face. I wondered who'd suggested their presence—perhaps every ambitious mother in the area? The occasion had to be impromptu since neither Lord Farold nor Lady Sidra had known exactly when the Rachael Ann would dock.

"I'm sure there are many other more interesting activities you'd rather be doing," I added.

"Oh, no, we wanted to come as soon as we heard from Ribecah that you had arrived," Joella, the titular head of the group assured me. "None of us have ever been to the Palace in Lumminea. Will you tell us about what life is like at the Court? It must be very exciting." she said shyly, if ingenuously.

I pretended to take her assertion at face value—about spontaneously wanting to ride with me in the countryside—while I watched the other girls gathering around me. I clapped my hands together, surprising them.

"I think we should all ride immediately to the pavilion where it's shaded and comfortable. Aren't you hungry after all this fresh air?"

Mostly the girls looked scandalized. "We have to wait for the men," Nyri offered.

"Who would lead us?" one wanted to know.

"We're supposed to be escorted," another said.

"What on earth for?" I returned, touching the hilt of my sword suggestively. "Aren't we perfectly capable of deciding on our own?" I drew my horse over to one of the stone blocks and hauled myself up into the saddle, looking down on their startled faces. "I would imagine that the men would be glad to be rid of our company," I said.

Joella grinned and led her mount out beside me. "I'd like to show you the new fruits that the growers have been developing." Her boldness seemed to catalyze a few others, and then suddenly all the women were mounted and milling about on the flat stone area. The dust we raise drifted towards the men. I heard some coughs and some roughly phrased complaints that were quickly suppressed. As we rode out, I caught a glimpse of Pem with his mouth open and Darcil who grinned and flipped a quick salute.

A Picnic in the Orchard

.OUR MEN SEPARATED .from the rest of the guards and made ready to follow us the moment they saw me coming. Farold's Captain was caught off-guard by our appearance coming down the ramp. I nodded at him as we thundered by, and he did the best he could do which was salute me and deploy four of his men to follow us. That was fine with me.

I let Joella lead the way along the ridge and when we turned to cross over to the pasture land which lay between us and the distant pavilions, I took the lead again, although Joella was close by my side. Her hair had come unpinned and was streaming back in the wind. Her eyes were wide with excitement, though I could see that she managed her mount carefully. My roan was surefooted, if somewhat headstrong, and I had to jerk him back to a canter when he wanted to stretch out in a full gallop. Once again I said a silent thank you to both Bender and Reyfort who had taught me my riding and fighting skills.

A quick glance behind me assured me that everyone was managing to keep together—a grand sight as we came up the lane which ran through a golden grain field. We crossed a low rise and followed the track along the edge of the orchard's canopy of white blossoms smelling sweetly of granapple fruits.

I led my little flock off to one side where I saw some grooms near a picket line. I let the girls mill around me before I slid to the ground and handed off my reins to one of the handlers. The Master-of-Horse was there to give me a look of disapproval, but I laughed and ignored his expression.

We crossed a short field to the first tent. I turned as I heard the loud noises of galloping horses and watched the men arriving like a gaggle of angry geese. Well, Darcil didn't look angry, and

Pem still looked puzzled. Some of the young men looked furious, some of them appeared to be laughing. I urged my little flock to go on ahead while I waited for Pem and Darcil to catch up. I saw Leandra off to one side, engaged in a conversation with someone wearing formal robes. I supposed she was present in her capacity as a Magister. I tended to forget that the Sage was a member of the Communicate's judiciary and had a great deal of work laid out on her own schedule.

One of the irate looking young men, a slightly overweight fellow about Pem's age, stalked in my direction. He called out for Catha to stop and I could see that he bore a family resemblance to the young woman. I glanced behind me and saw that Catha had turned around. She looked apprehensive, even frightened. When I turned back towards the man, I observed that he was carrying his riding crop in a threatening manner. Behind him, Darcil's grin had faded abruptly to an expression of concern. He started out after the young fellow who by now had pulled almost even with me. I could see that the young man's face was red, his breathing rapid, and the knuckles of his fist gripping the crop were white. He ignored me as he started to circle around me. Nikko's guards had started running in my direction.

"You should not disobey me," he shouted at Catha who stood rooted to the spot with tears streaming down her face and fear in her eyes.

She said, "Giles, no, please."

"Is Catha your sister?" I asked, trying to distract his attention.

He jerked his attention in my direction, finding a mere woman standing a few vars from him. His eyes were bright, almost feverish. Clearly he didn't recognize me. He came at me with his riding crop poised to slash me across the face. I heard Pem shout.

The next thing I knew, the man was lying on his back at my feet, still holding on to a stub of his quirt, white-faced, and with an imprint of the flat side of my sword turning red across one cheek. The needle-sharp point of my sword was not quite in contact with his chest. I hadn't even remembered drawing to defend myself. I was irrationally pleased that my reflexes were still good. I felt my cheeks redden, whether in anger or embarrassment I couldn't decide—anger seemed the most pleasing. It was certainly an awkward moment. A rather large number of people were standing around with their mouths open and a shocked look on their faces.

"I only asked you if Catha was your sister," I said, pleased to hear that my voice was reasonably steady in spite of the pounding of my heart. Darcil came running up along with the guards. I eased my sword to one side and Darcil bent over the fallen form, grabbed his coat collar, and jerked him to his feet. Before the young man could recover, Darcil planted a boot in his backside and shoved him unceremoniously toward his men-at-arms.

"Take Giles out of our sight and hold him at the house until we return," he ordered his captain who glanced at me with a measure of surprise. The men from the ship looked more amused than worried—they were Gilbert's men and knew me well. I slid my sword back into its sheath and allowed myself a deep breath. Pem arrived, took my hand and guided me away from the men, peering anxiously at my face. I was going to go to Catha, but I saw that Joella had her arms around the girl and was talking quietly to her.

"Are you all right?" Pem wanted to know. "That idiot—he'd been drinking too much. Didn't know what he was doing—Darcil says he's trouble."

"I'm fine," I told Pem. "I'm sorry if I've spoiled your afternoon."

He looked at me oddly. "Perhaps we will let Darcil take care of this and ignore the whole incident," he said. "The cooking does smell rather good, doesn't it?"

Indeed, the aroma of fresh bread and meat roasting over open coals did smell exceptional, and people were turning back to whatever they'd been doing. Conversations resumed. I laughed, if a bit shaky. "Yes, and I've built up quite an appetite."

Darcil approached us with a white face. "I'm so sorry, Sire, Lady Claire."

He bowed low, almost prostrating himself before us. "Nothing I can say will make up for this inexcusable behavior. To attack a royal person is a capital offense. I can assure you that the man will be dealt with."

I could feel Pem gathering himself to say something that would probably be unfortunate. I squeezed his hand very tight and got in first.

"Let us put this aside for the moment," I said to Darcil. "It will do no good to make more of this than has already been made. I don't know about my husband, but I am ravenous and the food smells good. Let everyone enjoy the afternoon. It would be better to deal with consequences later, don't you think?" I didn't want anyone executed on my account, especially a spoiled brat who belonged to the local social scene—though I might have been tempted had Catha's brother actually connected with his quirt.

Darcil looked surprised, but grateful to put off until later something that was bound to bring a load of trouble down upon his young shoulders. He motioned to one of the servants standing nearby and instructed him in a low voice. Soon after, the man hurried away, a merry tune was struck up by a band of musicians, and a rhythmic clapping began as some adventuresome couples pulled each other out on a dance area of straw strewn over compacted earth. I saw that in addition to the riders who had accompanied us, there was a large group of people, probably neighbors living in the surrounding area, who had gathered for the feast and entertainment. I marveled at how quickly Lady Sidra could have pulled such a thing together. In fact, how could she have known unless she had prior knowledge of our exact arrival time? Had someone contacted her? I had a vaguely uncomfortable feeling that there was something I was missing.

I stood around, feeling a bit awkward in a social gathering where none but a few men and no women were visibly armed. Darcil invited us to follow him and led us to our place reserved at a high-table of sorts mounted on a temporary platform that overlooked rows of tables and benches spread out over a part of meadow shaded by an open canvas pavilion. Faroldson was in earnest conversation with a small group on the edge of the activities. Daarcil begged that we forgive him for not joining us immediately, explaining that he was gathering several of the most influential people attending the luncheon that we might find these folks useful and even interesting. Pem nodded and waved him away. He settled back in his chair and stretched his feet out under the table. Out of the corner of my eyes I noted that our men were standing not far away and were alertly scanning the surrounding groups of people.

The dancing was off to one side where we could observe, if we wished, the participants. A group of musicians played beyond that. A nearby field on the far side of a low wooden fence featured red barrels and wooden barriers which suggested that a demonstration of horsemanship might be in the offing.

Pem gave a grunt of approval. "Perhaps we shall see something interesting, after all," he whispered in my ear.

I, for one, had had quite enough interesting things for one day. I looked around for the young women who had followed me from the ruins. I spotted Joella and Catha sitting together, nursing drinks and having a serious conversation. Catha looked considerably recovered and Joella had pinned her hair back in place. The rest of the group were gathering towards the end of the same table, as if giving Joella and Catha room for privacy. Some of the girls looked up towards me, and I nodded to acknowledge their presence. I could see well-concealed sparks of resentment among them—no doubt because they blamed me for what had happened between Catha and her brother.

I lifted my glass of red wine and sipped thoughtfully. It was good wine and I reached the bottom of the glass far more quickly than I planned. I asked for a refill and told myself sternly to slow down. I said to Pem, "So, what did you and Lord Farold talk about while I was with Lady Sidra?"

"Farold wants a commitment to enlarge the port and dredge the river channel," Pem returned. "Their mages are developing a new class of entropy engine that will power much larger ships with extended ranges, and trade with Port Sulphur is growing since the discovery of new lands east of Lunaria--more trade means more tax revenue. Faroldson appears to be supporting increased production."

"I hadn't heard that they possessed the skill of building entropy engines, "I said. "More power in the hands of the Ranapuis, I think. I suppose the royal coffers will aid in refurbishing the port?" Privately I thought that I'd like to meet these engineers who built such sophisticated engines. I suddenly realized that it was only a short step from building entropy devices to designing fearsome weapons. Once again I blamed myself for not seeing the obvious! This world could be courting a catastrophe, and I hadn't even given it a thought.

"Certainly. How else do you expect to purchase loyalty?" Pem asked, oblivious to my alarmed expression. "Besides, with the increase in tax revenues, I expect a good return on investment."

"Honor and blood ties were the old fashioned ways to encourage loyalty and is less costly." I said, feeling vaguely offended.

"I'm not so sure about cost. If Gilbert's daughter had agreed to a union with Faroldson, things might have been easier," Pem agreed.

I was reminded that in this world, as in my former world, most people were rather literal-minded. I sighed. Pem, for all that attracted me to him, could be discouragingly literal.

And that thought reminded me of my central dilemma— when was I to tell Pem that I thought I was pregnant. In fact, I realized that I couldn't even bring myself to think much about it. I found myself wishing for either my mother or grandmother. How was I supposed to cope by myself? I needed to go to Leandra at once, or at least tonight, I decided, and forced myself to turn my attention back to the table where we were sitting.

Darcil drew up before us and waited for Pem to acknowledge him. When Pem waved impatiently at him, he stepped forward. "I have two people who would like to be presented," he said. I figured this meant that, in one way or another, these people were important to Farold. He had probably chosen them rather than being asked by them.

"Of course, please bring them forward," Pem said. Each in turn bowed low as Darcil made the formal introductions.

Krel was a large man with an honest face and kind eyes. His hands were rough and callused and his face was weathered, but the cut and quality of the clothes he wore were expensive and tasteful. He turned out to be the owner of the largest foundry in Ranaputkin, and supplied many castings as well as forged fittings for the Ranapui's shipyard. He was also a member of the city council—an important member, I decided.

Amberson controlled a wide variety of agricultural interests—a kind of factor, I gathered. He owned the orchard and fields where we sat, and proudly confided that he was a sponsor of the day's activities. He had that same open, honest look about him that Krel projected. He was a most charming man, well past middle age, with white hair and grey eyes. Like Krel, he presented himself as a man of substance who was ready to offer aid and services to the Crown as a token of his loyalty to the Monarchy. Pem looked pleased. I thought the meeting spoke well of Darcil's family and the position they held in the community.

A few pleasantries were passed—the current outlook for crops and the fluctuations in the price of pig iron—and then the two gentlemen were dismissed to be seated at the table immediately in front of us. Amberson sat alone while Krel, the foundry owner, was joined by an elegant-looking woman of about his age whom I took to be his wife. Darcil later told me that Amberson's wife had died the previous year.

Activity picked up across the fence on the equestrian course. Pem began to look interested. I plastered a smile on my face, put a hand on his arm, and leaned close to his ear. "There's one of those black transit stones under the ruins we visited," I said in a low voice, though I didn't think anyone could hear me.

He jerked in surprise and would have called attention to us so I squeezed his arm hard. "Smile," I said. He took my cue and continued to look out at a group of horses and riders who had gathered near one end of the arena.

After Tess and I were attacked in the Palace and bumped all the way to the Black Tower in Tieben, Pem and I had discussed the subject of the black stone with Sage Leandra at some length— as we had talked about the "prognosticators" and the special gardens scattered about Lunaria. While Leandra had been cooperative, she really hadn't had much to add to what we knew. The subject hadn't come back up for some time. I knew it wouldn't be welcome in Pem's mind. He mostly refused to think about my world of nanites, though he acknowledged my mysterious healing skills even if it made him feel uncomfortable.

"Is it useable?" he asked.

I said, "I won't know unless I check it out. I think it would be a good idea to know since it's at our backdoor. No telling what might come through." I was thinking about otherworldly gates and what I had seen under Rissa's holding. I hadn't elaborated on the narrowly averted disaster in Boggrash or the portal I'd seen under the Palace in Lumminea. There were worlds within worlds, and I found the possibilities highly unsettling. After a lengthy discussion with Gilbert before Pem and I were married, he had advised me to keep most of this information to myself. "Young Pem, like most males, doesn't welcome competition when it comes to feeling special," he had said.

"We'll talk later about it," Pem returned. "Darcil or someone from the Farold family will probably know something about it."

"I don't think we should trust Farold too far," I advised. "I'm supposed to meet their daughter tomorrow morning. I can mention the ruins and try to find out if she knows if there's anything special hidden there."

What I didn't say had to do with my growing feeling of unease. Had I been led deliberately to this place in order to discover the Black Stone? I had already survived a number of attacks on my person, and I was beginning to subscribe to the idea that a Black Council, not a single Sage like Jallis Ruffin, was behind a conspiracy. If so, I'm sure they saw me as a danger to any plans to reduce Pem's power over the Council. What better way to attack me than by setting a trap with a Black Stone. They knew I would have to investigate, and that the presence of the Stone, or transfer stone as I preferred to think of it, would make it possible to attack me directly. If it were a trap, I decided I needed to spring it. I should have known that decision was an extremely foolish idea.

Pem must have thought that my suggestions were satisfactory. In any case, he was pleased to unload any responsibility onto me. "We'll talk later," he said. The thunder of a couple of dozen horses charging each other in a mock-melee attracted his attention. I sighed and took another sip of the good wine. Servants arrived with food, and we spent the rest of the early afternoon watching young men hacking at each other with blunt wooden staves. One horse was injured and the local veterinarian took care of her. Fortunately, none of the riders were hurt—I was not in the mood to patch up someone crazy enough to participate in such nonsense.

By the time we returned to the Ranapui's holding, I was too tired to do more than to see that my horse was groomed and properly fed. Although one of the stable boys would have done the job for me, I always insist on taking care of the animal that takes care of me. Pem went off with Darcil, probably to drink a toast to the success of the day.

Actually, as it turned out, Pem went with Darcil to see Major Arlen Lorence. It seems that Catha's brother had committed a Federal offense against a royal person and it wasn't within the Ranapui's authority to dispense—or not to dispense—justice. I didn't find out the details until later.

Mags was waiting to help me undress, bathe and slip into my night clothes. She tucked me into the sumptuous bed in my private night chamber. "Shall I leave the small oil night lamp burning?" The lamp was on the chest next to the wardrobe which was on the wall away from a window that opened out on a small, private garden connecting Pem's room with mine.

"I think not," I told Mags.

"I'll leave you, then," she said. "Shall I leave the door to His Majesty's room locked?" she added.

I thought about how tired I was and the fact that Pem had gone off with Darcil—and that I hadn't been invited. "Perhaps you'd better leave it locked," I said. "Besides," I said with a grin, "we haven't exchanged cards to make an appointment."

Mags looked suitably amused. "Well, then, it's good night,' she said again. Did I detect a note of excitement in her goodnight? Perhaps Nikko was waiting for her somewhere. Another late-night tryst. I reminded myself that I really needed to talk with Nikko about monopolizing my maid's time.

I lay in the darkness breathing in the fragrant scents of flowers and the lulling song of the fountains. A breath of cool desert air stirred the curtains in the open window and let slip through a hint of moonlight that cast moving shadows on the wall. I closed my eyes and felt myself drifting off into a drowsy state of awareness. Nothing seemed urgent. Tomorrow would be soon enough to engage my brain in some much-needed activity. I was drowsy enough that when I heard a slight scrape in the direction of the window I thought I was dreaming. I opened my eyes to slits and shifted very slowly in the direction of the faint light coming through the thin curtains.

And swallowed a scream. A man's shadow was clearly outlined in the window. He was coming in, one leg already across the sill, his hand reaching to part the curtains. I could see that he carried something in his other hand—a stout club perhaps? I couldn't make out what it was, and I didn't have the energy to summon a query.

I must have made a slight noise because the figure stopped and waited, motionless. Meanwhile I stealthily reached for my long dagger that I always kept ready under the pillow when I slept alone. For some stupid reason I decided not to call out for help. I could sort out this strange burglar—or assassin—quite handily by myself.

Apparently satisfied, the figure continued his silent entry until he (or she?) stood up behind the curtain with the cloth parted slightly. I wondered if he were peeking through the slit, searching the dark room for my shape under the covers on the bed. I decided not to wait in case I might get tangled in the bed clothes.

"Come one step further and I will skewer you," I said. My voice came out more like a squeak than a roar. I threw off the covers and sprang up ready for action. If I needed to, I could reach my sword which was leaning against the chest.

At the sound of my voice, the shadow figure jumped and dropped something. The sound of breaking glass was followed by a curse.

Assassin!

."NOW LOOK WHAT .you've done," Pem cried out. "I've dropped the crystal glasses!"

The sound of Pem's voice left me unable to decide whether to laugh or curse. "What are you doing, coming through my window?" I demanded, suppressing a rising bubble of hysterical giggles.

"I am your husband, am I not?" Pem asked lamely.

"I could have killed you thinking you were an assassin," I shot back.

"Oh. Well, I suppose...," he returned. "But your door was locked," he complained. "I had to use the window. And besides, I've got this great bottle of champagne, although I don't have any glasses, now," he complained.

I slid the dagger back into its sheath and felt my way to the chest. In a moment I was able to use the igniter to light the small oil lamp. In the sudden glow, I saw my husband standing barefoot and pajama-clad in front of the window curtain, bottle of champagne in one hand, and something wrapped in waxed paper in the other.

"Don't move," I cautioned him. "You'll step on broken glass. I'll get something to brush it out of the way."

He nodded. There was a fireplace in the room, no doubt useful at times during the winter. I found a small broom and scuttle behind the screen. Using this, I swept a path to him and wrapped my arms around him. We kissed and felt a warm glow. Pulling back to get my breath, I looked at the bottle in his hand. The cork was loose in the neck so I grabbed the bottle, popped the cork out, and took a swig of the liquor. It tasted wonderfully bubbly, sweet and refreshing.

He took the bottle back from me and pressed it to his lips. I watched him take several deep swallows, his Adams apple bobbing up and down. Such a curious male characteristic, I thought. I led him across the cleared area and we sat on the bed. I wondered if his heart was beating as rapidly as mine.

I cleared my throat. "Sorry, I didn't know the door between our rooms was locked," I lied. "After all, you didn't send me a card announcing your intentions."

After Pem stared at me for a moment, not sure whether or not I was joking, he offered me the waxed-paper package. I unfolded the wrapping and found two slices of sharp cheese, some sweet cherries, and two chunks of fresh-baked bread inside.

I divided the snack between us, using pieces of the wrapping for plates, and we sat taking bites of cheese, popping a sweet cherry into our mouths, and munching on the tough, sweet bread. I spit a seed out onto my "plate" and took another long swig of champagne, sighing as I saw how rapidly the bottle of excellent liquor was being depleted.

"Too bad you couldn't have brought another bottle," I said, stifling a yawn.

"Ah, but I have the answer to that," Pem said. He crossed the floor to the door between our suites, being careful to avoid broken glass, and slid back the latch. After tapping on the latch and rolling his eyes at me, he disappeared into his room, returning almost immediately with two more chilled bottles. "I believe this will help," he said.

I was tired, but I found that indeed two more bottles of champagne helped enormously. I decided that now was not the time for further discussions concerning the Black Stone under the ruins and certainly not to bring up my pregnancy.

Ribecah

"YOU HAVE AN appointment to see Lady Ranapui's daughter," Mags was saying while she prodded my ribs with one finger. I groaned.

"I thought the door was locked last night," Mistress Mags said. I opened my eyes to mere slits and noticed that the bolt to Pem's quarters was slid home. Mags must have done since my husband could hardly have moved the bolt from the other side. I could only hope that Pem wasn't trapped naked in my suite.

"There was a situation that demanded my attention," I claimed, lamely.

"Of course," Mags said brightly.

I blushed and sat up, sweeping the covers aside. Fortunately Pem was nowhere to be seen. I was briefly irritated that I wouldn't have an opportunity to talk with him about the cave under the ruins and what should be done about it. On the other hand, I was relieved that the subject of his fatherhood had not come up.

Sunlight streamed in through the sheer curtains across the window. Birds were chirping loudly outside. The sound of voices blended with the splash of the fountains on the terraces. "What time is it?" The Lunarian technology dutifully translated my intent.

Mags mentioned the sun's angle and I bolted upright, forgetting that I was naked. "Sidra will be here with Ribecah," I burped and tasted the sour aftermath of too much champagne.

"We'll get you fixed up," Mags said soothingly. "Perhaps you'd like to bathe before receiving," she hinted. I was suddenly aware of my condition and grabbed my robe from the foot of the bed.

"It was a very demanding situation," I said somewhat crossly.

Mags laughed. "Begging your pardon, Lady. And, I've already drawn your bath."

Mollified, I allowed myself to be led into the bath and handed into the steaming hot water. The scent of the day reminded me of roses and cinnamon. Mags took a scrub brush to my back and I felt almost faint with pleasure. I wanted to say more but soon she was dragging me out of the water and giving me a brisk rubdown with huge, fluffy towels. There wasn't a lot to do with my hair since I was wearing it unfashionably short. In practically no time at all I was transformed into a semblance of dignity befitting my station. I emphasize semblance, because Mags was never satisfied. She stepped back, sighed, and informed me that I would do for now; she would work with me some more before lunch which was supposed to be held outdoors in the company of a group of prominent society ladies. I prayed for rain.

The bell sounded at the door to my suite, and Mags went to answer it. She returned to tell me that one of Sidra's servants had brought the message that Lady Sidra and Ribecah could join us shortly—if that were my pleasure.

"I suppose I must," I said, trying not to burp again.

"I'll tell her to convey our great pleasure and anticipation," Mags said, not quite suppressing the sparkle in her eyes. I growled, but of course I didn't mean it.

SIDRA RANAPUI, A person who did not seem like one who would bow to anyone, not even the Queen, bowed low and then looked me straight in the eyes. I think she was trying to evaluate my reaction to her abeyance rather than challenging me, but I was reminded of the difference in age and experience between the two of us. I tried not to react to her forwardness and swallowed what resentment I might have felt. After all, I reminded myself, I am an ordinary girl from Ridgeville who is acting the part of a Queen. I was hardly born and raised to the position, and Lady Sidra knew it. Unconsciously I fingered the amulet around my neck and felt a burst of gentle warmth.

Whatever her reasons might have been, Sidra followed up with a smile that was kindly and without guile. I found myself liking this woman even more, though not in the way that I trusted Gilbert or Leandra.

She moved aside and her daughter stepped forward. "Your Grace, I'd like to present my daughter, Ribecah Ranapui."

I knew immediately that Ribecah Ranapui was very special. She radiated a kind of power that indicated a strong connection with the basic character of Lunaria, although she seemed completely unaware of her talent. She resembled her mother in many ways. She was fair of skin, with large, exotic green eyes, and glossy black hair pulled back and pinned up on the nape of her neck. She was slender, but not as delicate as her mother, with more of the figure of an athlete rather than one of the society girls I had observed yesterday. When she bowed low; I thought it was more from respect than from any desire to flatter me. In this I was reminded of Tess, who, while respectful, saw clearly that character was more important than title. I had been lucky with Tess, and I thought that perhaps I would be very lucky to have Ribecah with me. I wondered if Sidra was aware of how special her daughter actually was.

Ribecah had risen after her deep curtsy, looking slightly apprehensive—probably because I had been off daydreaming. I said, smiling, "You need not be so formal."

Ribecah brightened noticeably. She said, "I just love your hair. You see, Mother, I told you that short hair was the latest style. It is much more practical."

Sidra blushed and looked apologetic at her daughter's words. "She didn't mean to offend, Your Grace."

I laughed, delighted at the girl's frank comment. "I'm not at all offended! Yes, short hair is often more practical, especially if you carry a sword and ride for endless hours through dangerous country. So far, I have had to do much of looking after my survival and little of holding court."

Sidra looked vexed with Ribecah and said, "I'm sorry Ribecah, but you don't carry a sword, and you are not allowed anywhere dangerous." She looked at me closely. "My daughter is well educated for a young woman of Lunaria, though she rarely seems to show it. However, I don't want her going around with weapons and acting like a warrior."

I returned, ignoring the fact that Sidra was instructing me, "Have no fear in that regard, Lady Sidra. I would never knowingly put your daughter in any danger. I have more need for bold intelligence than for expertise in court intrigue—or sword play for that matter. Considering your reputation in business, Lady Sidra, I do not doubt your daughter's abilities in many capacities."

"I have had training in the arts of self-defense," Ribecah insisted. "I am not one of those helpless society girls!"

Her mother snorted. "You call that defensive training? Go talk to your brother. See what he thinks about your defensive capabilities."

Ribecah looked wounded by her mother's words. I looked at her aura of nanites closely and decided that Ribecah, with the right weapon and a little training from me, would be a force to be reckoned with. I didn't say this aloud, though. If neither she nor her mother were aware of her talents, it was probably best left unsaid at the moment. The question I was left with was who else knew? Surely there were people in Ranaputkin who were capable of sensing Ribecah's potential—which meant that Ribecah, in her ignorance, was in danger. What if the young idiot, Catha's brother who had attacked me, had attacked Ribecah? She might have inadvertently turned him into a lump of charcoal! Unfortunately, that idea was much too attractive. I put it firmly out of my mind.

This danger plus the fact that I happened to like Ribecah made up my mind for me almost instantly. "If you wish it, you will be a Lady Companion to me," I said.

The girl blushed prettily. "Oh Your Grace, that would be truly wonderful. It is what I most want," she returned enthusiastically.

Sidra looked uncertain. "You have decided much more quickly than I had reckoned," she said. "Don't you wish to think about this?" She blushed as she realized that she was talking to her Queen.

I peered deeper into Sidra's emotions and decided that Sidra was about to withdraw her permission allowing her daughter to accompany me. I couldn't let that happen in view of the circumstances.

"I have made up my mind," I said firmly, determined to act like the Queen that I was supposed to be. "It is in Ribecah's best interest. She will accompany me." I projected a small surge of power into Sidra's personal matrix. It wasn't something I did very often. In fact I'd only done it twice before. Once was inadvertently when I first faced Captain Dread as he was trying to run me down on horseback. The second time was when Oul had tried to come over the side of the landship and had nearly taken off Tess's head.

I was very careful about how I applied pressure. Sidra blinked and her eyes opened slightly as she felt my certainty block her intention to object. She opened her mouth, then shut it.

"Very well," she said. "It is as you say. I do not object." She looked slightly confused.

I inclined my head and tried to project warmth and well-being. The truth was that I had scared myself. This was far too much power for anyone to possess, and I promised myself that I wouldn't use it again unless life itself were threatened. I also decided that I needed to talk with Sage Leandra about this as soon as possible, perhaps even sooner than talking about what was to be done about telling Pem that he was a father.

While I was occupied with my thoughts, Sidra took Ribecah's hand between hers and looked carefully into her daughter's eyes. "Is this truly what you want?"

"Oh, yes, Mother, I think I have dreamed of this moment. It is like all of this has gone before. It is what I am to become." She stopped in confusion. "I'm not sure how to explain this, but something in my heart that tells me that this is right."

I stood back, mildly appalled. Did this have anything to do with Ribecah's talent? To be so certain was something I'd had little experience with. I remembered my mother going on about me not making up my mind. She called me wishy-washy and lazy. She'd probably have told me that I got what I deserved if she knew that I made up my mind so quickly and foolishly to follow Pem into Lunaria.

Ribecah turned to me, bright-eyed. "What is it that you wish me to do, My Lady?"

At that moment I had no idea what I wanted Ribecah to do. I finally got out, "Come to me tomorrow morning and I will explain your duties to you." At least I might have time to figure out what I was going to do with a bright young woman who obviously expected way too much from me.

Ribecah and Sidra bowed and backed towards the exit from my suite where Mags was waiting to escort them. I'd not had anyone back out of my presence before. It wasn't a pleasant feeling. I almost blurted out that I wouldn't stab them in the back if they just turned around and left. Belatedly, I realized that if I turned my attention elsewhere it would make their exit easier. I turned my attention to my leather writing case where it lay on a table under an ornate, ceramic lamp decorated with animals that looked like foxes. I rummaged around for my writing materials and brought out some paper, a pen, and a tiny inkwell—oh what I wouldn't have given for a plain ballpoint—and made a note to myself to scrap this business of backing away from my royal presence. I snorted at the phrase my royal presence causing Mags who was returning from the entrance hall to look up startled.

"Are you feeling well, My Lady," she asked, anxiously.

"I was laughing at myself," I returned. "Promise me that you will kick me in the rear if I begin taking myself too seriously."

"I can't promise to commit such a serious offense," Mags said, eyes twinkling. "Perhaps I might contrive to accidently bump into you in the event of a severe lapse in your behavior."

"I'm sure you will find a way to correct me," I said, remembering how Mags always seemed to manipulate me into doing my hair or dressing in something besides my ordinary, comfortable pants and overshirt.

"And now, My Lady, about what you will want to wear to the luncheon this afternoon," Mags said brightly. I braced myself.

A Change in Policy

I UNDERSTOOD THAT the luncheon in my honor was to be all-women, Ranaputkin's finest. What should I say and what should I do to impress and satisfy the ladies of Ranaputkin that I was a worthy successor to Queen Rachael? I found myself very nervous, a mood that Mags took to be most amusing while she was putting the finishing touches on my hair.

"After all you've been through, I can't see why this meeting should make you nervous," Mags said, obviously trying to keep the tone of her voice respectful. "Not a single one of them could take the head off a snow leopard or defend herself against a barbarian attack."

I couldn't explain why I was so nervous. Maybe it was because my mother, after my father's disappearance during the early stages of the Iraq war, withdrew from the company of her former women friends. I felt as if I'd rather have a sword in my hand and face Oul than fence with Sidra's friends.

I took a deep breath and looked at myself in the mirror. Mags had combed my hair until it fairly glistened with red highlights. She'd used some kind of soothing cream to cover up the recent results of too much wind and sun on my face. For luck, my battered little yellow egg with its *Silly Putty* was tucked into an inside pocket. My amulet with its stars and crescent hung about my neck on its golden chain. If I grasped it in my hand I could cross over into the world of the tiny nanites populating Lunaria and summon many different kinds of powers—none of which I should need or desired to reveal at a luncheon with the Ladies of Ranaputkin. At the moment, it felt cool against my chest. That was a good sign, I reminded myself. When the amulet heated up, trouble always followed close behind. The amulet was my hidden backup.

While Mags was fussing over me and making sure that I had my finest embroidered lace handkerchief and fastened my pendant (the one with the special little knife concealed in it) to my collar, I remembered how my often my grandmother—and my father— had been there for me when something was bothering or frightening me. I never remembered my mother comforting me.

My grandmother had exposed me to some important ideas, though I was too young to understand her at the time. Almost as if she had known to prepare me for events in my future, these ideas were now unlocking one by one in my memory when the occasion called for them. They were now guiding me in my role as Queen. Her lessons popped into my head as I listened to Lady Sidra explain to me about how I would be presented to her guests.

On a rainy afternoon, after an humiliating defeat in a poetry contest at school, I had been tearfully trying to explain to my grandmother how I would never understand why Robert, with his snobbish attitude and mean friends, always seem to win these popularity contests. What lesson had I failed to learn? I was a nice person, wasn't I?

My grandmother sighed. "In life, things are not so much learned as they are revealed. True education is more about accepting what is revealed to us than it is about filing away answers to questions that others have asked. For many people, learning a thing is too much like making a thing exist in our memory. If tomorrow turns out to be richer than today, it is because more is revealed to us, not that we have imposed more of our ideas on the world."

I remembered the lesson. "I should not have been looking for an answer to why Robert beats me, which is like searching for an excuse, but I have to accept what is revealed to me by my defeat in order to change why I lose."

And so I forgot about what I was supposed to say or how I was supposed to act and decided that it was really up to the good ladies of Ranaputkin to seek my approval for all the things that they were or thought to be. It sounded a bit arrogant, but I realized that it was the first step towards actualizing my own person as Queen.

When Lady Sidra and a special honor guard arrived to escort me to the luncheon, I made sure that I acted suitably impressed so that my hostess would be pleased.

Be all you can be. The phrase I remembered from a television commercial sprang into my mind. I'd best be all I could be if I were going to survive in this world as Pem's Queen. I took a deep breath and allowed myself to be led out of the royal suite and into the lion's den. I felt like a prize poodle at the dog show.

A Message to Ribecah

IN SPITE OF LADY Sidra's impeccable hospitality and my self-imposed pep talk, lunch turned out to be stressful. Rather than dwell on some of the unpleasantness, I decided that I had to pen a message to Ribecah. I wanted to ask her to accompany us to the ruins and bring Darcil with her. I was familiar with the way messages got passed around a household, a little like sending slow text messages back in Ridgeville.

I sat with my writing case and its tools at the desk, pulled out a scrap of fancy parchment, and tried to think of what to say that wouldn't be too revealing and yet would convey a sense of urgency. Finally, I wrote:

Lady Ribecah, it is my wish that you accompany the King and myself on a ride tomorrow morning. We wish to explore the ruins of the old fort that we visited previously. I desire to keep this little outing very informal, so there will be no need for an escort other than who we will provide. I would also request that Darcil accompany us if at all possible. He will feel more comfortable, as I sense that he is reluctant to let you go off riding by yourself. I say this without intending any slight on your abilities to take care of yourself. We merely want to keep the peace with your brother.

I would appreciate your reply along with any suggestions you may have that will expedite this matter.

I debated on how I should sign this message. Heretofore Mags had always signed as my Chief Corresponding Secretary for the Queen. She claimed that this was the proper way to conduct the Queen's correspondence. This time, however, I was trying to send a personal message to one of my Ladies. How would I sign a message destined for Tess? I wondered what she wouldn't laugh at: something formal, but not too stuffy; something dignified, but not arrogant.

Finally I decided on Claire R., the R. being for Regina or Queen. I wondered how it would translate. It was one of those odd pieces of information floating around in my head from when I had read a book about Queen Elizabeth—given to me when I was a little girl by my grandmother. My grandmother was wise in so many ways. Strange how I was always needing odd pieces of information that my grandmother had anticipated.

I used fine white sand to dry the ink and folded my message. I took out the red lump of my official Queen's Sealing wax and used the desk lamp to melt a drop or two. This time I remembered to take off my ring to make the impression without burning myself. I felt my cheeks redden, thinking of Mags' amused expression the first time I'd tried this.

"Where I come from, we have a seal that we lick to make it stick," I'd said, trying to peal the stinging, hot wax off my knuckle.

"What a strange and unsanitary notion," Mags had said.

Looking at the pretty red puddle of cooling wax with its imprint of the royal seal, I had to admit that licking an envelope sounded positively barbaric. Besides, this would be hard to steam open.

I pulled the purple cord above the desk and waited for someone to appear—they always did, as if by magic. I handed the message to the young page who appeared at my side, a boy dressed in the Ranapui's household uniform, and placed a small coin in his palm. He looked most grateful, bowed low, and ran off through the servant's door.

I tidied up my desk, found a comfortable chair, and dozed for a few minutes. I wondered where Mags was, thought about trying to find the Fifth Terrace and sit outside, and then finally decided to get a drink of cool lemonade. I remembered Mags saying something about a pitcher in the icebox in the pantry.

I was puzzling over where I'd seen the pantry when the same page boy startled me by popping back in through the servant's entrance. He was carrying a message with him, though this one wasn't sealed. I offered him another coin, and he place the paper in my hands, bowing deferentially. "Your Grace," he squeaked. I managed to keep from smiling.

Your Grace, I would be most honored to accompany you on your quest. I haven't yet spoken with Darcil, but I am certain that he will wish to join us. I know of several ways to explore the ancient passages beneath the ruins, having often done so myself. I think you will find them quite interesting. If it isn't too presumptuous, our pantry will provide provisions in case we get hungry or thirsty while we are on our adventure. I will await your pleasure in the morning.
Your most obedient Lady, Ribecah Ranapui

I wrote another message, this one to the Master of Horse, and sent it off. This time a different page answered my call. This one was older, and I thought he let his eyes linger on me a little too long. I gave him a frosty look and an even smaller coin than I had his younger coworker.

A DOOR BANGED and voices interrupted my thoughts. Nikko and Mags were arguing about something and had backed into the study without seeing me. I cleared my throat.

My two friends whirled around and both turned red in embarrassment. "Oh, my Lady, I'm so sorry to have disturbed you," Mags stuttered. Nikko seemed incapable of speech. I laughed.

"Well, you two are a merry pair," I remarked.

Nikko bowed low. "Forgive me, Your Grace, I must be off to tend to business," he said.

"I must lay out your formal clothes for the dinner tonight," Mags added.

A thought suddenly occurred to me. "How could I never have met the King's valet?" I wanted to know. "I have you, dear Mags. You are my valued companion, coconspirator, and an incomparable manager of my life. How does our Pem manage himself?" I was irked that I hadn't thought of this before.

"The truth be known, your husband forbid Lord Gilbert to appoint a man to that position," Mags informed me. "He said that the only thing the man could do for him was to be Gilbert's spy."

"But Mags, you are Gilbert's spy, and I welcome it. Having the attention of two such friends is very flattering," I teased.

A Confession of Sorts

IT WAS LATER in the day, after dinner, when I confessed to Pem, "I've never been so nervous in my life. That luncheon. All those fine ladies looking at me like I was some off-world barbarian. You should have seen how Lady Putkin was examining me. I overheard her making a derogatory comment about my hair to one of the other ladies, though I was pleased to see that many of the younger women had cut theirs fashionably short. And there she was tonight! Two servings of Lady Putkin in one day is about all I can take."

The guests at dinner had included the Putkins as well as an ambassador from Tieben. Neither Darcil nor Ribecah were in attendance. The Putkins were polite, but I could tell there was a certain amount of tension between the two families. The ambassador had offered several hints concerning Turlo that I had been careful to deflect.

"I'm sure it was dreadful," Pem said in reference to my luncheon fete. "Fortunately, you are my very-own, much-loved off-world barbarian. No one will dare to criticize you to your face."

"Don't be patronizing," I snapped.

Pem laughed. "You are truly a marvel of contradictions. You're the most self-assured woman I know—excepting maybe Sage Leandra—and yet you let yourself be put off by a bunch of provincial women who have probably been to the Court in Lumminea once in their lifetime. You have no idea what I put up with. Surely you can cope with Lady Putkin. I have the entire Council to deal with."

My husband could be exasperating without intending to be. I wasn't born to this task. I could have pointed out that such things as royal courts didn't exist in Texas, much less the town where I came from. After all, I hadn't been to Court all that much, either. How well would Pem stack up against one of our hardboiled county commissioners? I think he might have found that without the traditions of monarchy and assumptions of inherited power, Texans would be pretty difficult to deal with. At least the traditions in Lunaria didn't include Divine Right. That would be too much for me.

Pem smiled at me and reached out to brush a stray curl from my brow. We were alone in our suites after an exhausting day of social affairs crowned by a formal dinner in the not-so-modest ballroom, Mags having been banished to Nikko's company for the evening. For once, I was glad to be rid of her. We were relaxing on a couch in my bedroom, and the door was open between Pem's rooms and mine. He said, "Umm, no cards to exchange, no locked doors."

Pem let his hand wander lower. "I think I could find another bottle of that good champagne," he suggested. Memories of my hangover warned me against this course of action. I grabbed onto his hand and held it. Maybe it was the moment I had been looking for. I was so scared that I practically shouted at Pem trying to get the words out of my mouth.

"Pem I've got something to tell you. I think we are going to have a baby. That is, I think I'm pregnant." It all came out in one awkward rush—not at all how I had intended to say it. I had imagined a long, romantic conversation leading up to a few well-placed hints that would have gradually led Pem into the discovery that he was going to be a father.

Pem looked stunned. "But that's wonderful," he said awkwardly and somewhat late. He jumped up and began pacing the floor nervously. For a moment I thought he'd forgotten me and was about to shout at him when he bent down suddenly, swept me to my feet, and kissed me so hard that I had a hard time getting my breath back when we broke. "I mean it. It's wonderful," he gulped, this time actually seeming to be aware of what he was saying.

"You realize that this changes everything," he babbled. "We should return to Lumminea immediately. You can't ride horses, you know. You'll have to give up carrying your sword, and we'll need more guards. I'll write a dispatch to Gilbert right away. Should you have drunk that champagne last night?"

He looked stricken and struck his brow with the flat of his hand. "I shouldn't have insisted that we make love last night." He grabbed my hands and looked into my eyes like a big puppy about to lick my face. "Will you ever forgive me?"

I might have hit him if he hadn't made love to me last night. I couldn't help it; I laughed. "For heaven's sake, Pem, you didn't do anything wrong. Besides, I don't recall that you had to insist. And don't start talking about returning to Lumminea just yet. We have a long way to go and I want to see more of my new land. Nothing is going to change for quite a while." I'd need to talk with Leandra about that.

"Besides, we have to deal with the existence of the black stone I saw under the ruins, and there is something else we need to talk about," I said, trying to distract him from this annoying need to protect me.

"No, you can't go near that black stone. It's dangerous. I forbid it," Pem said.

I felt my amulet turn warm against my skin and took a deep breath. I decided that I had to nip this protective instinct in the bud. "My dear husband," I started out. "You must understand that, despite what you may have been told, women do not become suddenly soft and obedient wallflowers when they are about to have a baby. On the contrary, our sex becomes stronger and more determined." A picture of a famous sculpture, The Pioneer Woman, floated through my mind. It was my grandmother's favorite photographic plate in a well-thumbed exhibition book. She had told me about her visit to Ponca City, Oklahoma, to see the famous bronze. "So sturdy. So indomitable," she had said in awe.

Pem looked confused. "What is this wallflower? Is it some kind of vining plant?"

I realized that wallflower was not a word in his language. I often forgot that although we understood each other's speech, a large part of that understanding was due to the influence of Lunaria's underlying technology which rendered all speech into a sort of common tongue—one of many interesting phenomena that I wanted to study.

"A wallflower is a—no, never mind," I stopped myself. Explanations were not what were called for. A declaration would be better. "What I meant to say was that I don't like for you to be so protective. Your sudden concern is hardly flattering. Protecting the child, my dear Pem, is my job."

Pem looked rebellious, so I grabbed him around the neck and kissed him hard. When I felt myself being propelled backwards towards the bed by a very ardent husband, I broke off and stepped to one side, laughing.

"We still need to talk," I said, poking him playfully in the chest.

"What about," he remarked, gloomily. He returned to the couch and scooped up a handful of grazernuts from a crystal bowl on the end table.

Fateful Decision

As things turned out, Pem and I had very little to discuss. At least we decided against the champagne and stuck with watered wine. Even so, I failed to suppress a loud groan as Mags shook me awake.

"Lady, the Master of Horse had sent word that your mounts will soon be ready."

I tried to turn over, but Mags cleverly entangled me in the sheets so that I couldn't escape her. "The King also sent word that he is awaiting you on the Fifth Terrace where an early breakfast is to be served. I have been given to understand that you requested an early start."

I said an ugly word and sat up in bed, looking around wildly for something to cover myself. Mags was ready with my robe.

"What time is it?" I asked Mags. For once the nanites failed me.

My maid looked at me with one of those blank stares that let me know I had said something that did not translate. In a world where there were no wrist watches or quartz clocks, time, except on board a ship, was a very relative concept. . "I mean, what is the sun's angle?" I corrected myself.

"A bit before tea time." Mags nose wrinkled. "I think you will be able to bathe before going out. You need it," she said.

So, I splashed about a bit in the warm scented waters in the bath that Mags had prepared for me. She had my towel ready for me when I emerged, dripping, and gave me a vigorous rubdown that left my skin tingling and my spirits awakened to the possibilities of the day. My stomach growled. Hunger propelled me into my costume-of-the-day, trousers, overshirt, vest, and what I called my bandana but Mags called a ladies kerchief—something I remembered my grandmother saying.

The memory set off a chain reaction and brought tears to my eyes. Mags misinterpreted my mood.

"Have I done something wrong, Lady?"

"No, of course not, dear Mags," I put a hand on her arm. "Only a memory of other times and places."

"You were a Queen in your own land?" she wanted to know.

"Hardly," I laughed. I couldn't tell her that I had felt like an abandoned child, so I changed the subject. "Shall I wear my riding boots to the table? It would save time."

Mags scowled at me. "That would be decidedly unladylike," she said briskly. "I have your slippers for you." She produced my soft leather shoes, and I slid my feet into the supple leather. I was still embarrassed by so much personal service, but I was beginning to get the hang of it—surrender to Mags and put my mind to work on more important things.

As in, what I was going to do if I got to the black stone. I fought against the cold chill numbing my brain.

At the last minute Mags went to my chest and pulled forth the locked box where I kept the special pendant with its entropy-enhanced key. This exquisite piece of jewelry was never far from my side, though I hadn't had the occasion to use the key's special powers.

"You might need this," Mags said, handing me the pendant. I tucked it away safely in one of those hidden inside pockets that I kept Mags busy sewing into my clothing. I felt ready for anything, with my yellow egg, my amulet, the key, and my Sword of Training.

Mags led me through the reception room and under an archway that I hadn't noticed before. We passed down a short passage with older stonework and out a brass-bound door into a garden where I found Pem seated at a small table, feet stretched out to one side, popping a few glistening grapes into his mouth. He stood to greet me, earning my smile. A fountain played in the background and the day seemed clear and bright, although the sun seemed to be hidden beyond a tall evergreen hedge. I wondered if this was one of those special gardens.

I set my sword aside, leaning it against an extra chair. Pem and I sat across the table from each other; he passed me a platter of fruit with grazernuts on the side. There was a sweet plum with soft yellow flesh and slices of a melon that looked and tasted like an ordinary Texas watermelon. I browsed through the fruit and added soft scrambled eggs laced with tasty bits of mushroom. Pem kept his eyes on me but didn't say much except to comment on the weather.

"I had a long talk with Major Lorence about Catha Siegart's brother, Giles," Pem said. "I offered to be quite lenient with the man since no harm was actually done, but the Major pointed out to me that there was an automatic penalty imposed in such cases—execution. The best I could hope for was to commute his sentence to banishment from Ranaputkin."

"Really?" Of course I was curious, but I waited to see what Pem was going to tell me.

"Yes, a very unfortunate state of affairs since his family is highly influential and already disposed to support the Putkins. Farold is understandably unhappy, though he understands the circumstance."

"Did you?" I asked.

"Did I what?" Pem returned.

"Commute his sentence to exile," I said impatiently.

"Yes," Pem said reluctantly, looking closely at me. "Personally, I might have run the chap through with my own sword if he'd touched you with that quirt."

"That probably wouldn't have been necessary," I said drily.

"Umm, yes of course," he returned hastily. "As it is, he will spend at least a year on a voyage to Port Sulphur where he will be assigned a position as a crewman on a trading vessel that plies a few of the small ports in eastern Tieben. It will be a desolate assignment."

"And at the end of the year?" I wanted to know.

"He'll be allowed to return to Ranaputkin on parole. If he behaves himself, in time he will be allowed return to a normal life. It was the best I could do under the circumstances," Pem said.

"I fear that we have created some mortal enemies," I said. "It might have been better if he had hit me. At least things would be finished."

I could see that my answer made Pem feel uncomfortable. He continued to watch me as I slathered a piece of toast with butter and added some berry jam.

FINALLY, HE ASKED, "Is there no way I can persuade you against seeking out this black stone?"

I wanted to tell him that I could care less about that black stone—that I'd much rather go off on an afternoon ride, find a nice shady meadow by a clear brook, drink a bottle of wine, make love, and forget all the things that were preying on my mind. There were still thoughts of my father, lost somewhere in Iraq—presumably under the care of an old man. There were thoughts of my grandmother and how she would be wondering what happened to me.

I'd much rather go shopping in the market and buy some new clothes and feel Pem's eyes on me. I'd rather do a thousand things besides the ones that I hoped would someday allow me to return to my home world. I had to know everything I could. These were the thoughts that pushed me towards the black stone.

What was pushing me away? How could I return without Pem? I knew I was still falling in love with him. What had started out as a friendly as well as convenient necessity in the eyes of a girl was deepening into a true relationship between a man and a woman. Pem was precious to me in ways that I couldn't yet understand, yet I knew that time and a child would bring all the fruits of life to my door if only I could navigate the treacherous waters that lay ahead of me. I could feel tragedy brewing, and I wanted to run away.

My thoughts were interrupted by the arrival of a messenger who carried a bulky sealed packet wrapped in waterproofs. I was fairly bursting with excitement. Finally, a dispatch from Gilbert— only the second to catch up with us since we arrived at the Southern Beaches! The thick sheaf of sealed papers would probably carry messages, not only from Gilbert to Pem, but also to me from Tess. I found that I dearly missed Tess's insightful analyses and humorous observations.

Pem told the young crewman to wait inside as he might have a return answer for him to deliver. He broke the seal on the wrapping and sorted a series of packets with various colored seals before him on our table. He broke open the seals, and we discussed each in turn, most being items concerned with the daily reports of supplies, budgets, and personal requests.

We had save the best for last, the one with the blue seal that we recognized as a private message from Gilbert. I watched Pem's face darken into a thunderous scowl. Something was terribly wrong.

"Tell me, Pem. Is it bad? What is wrong?" I insisted.

Whatever Pem saw in my face caused him to come and lift me up and hold me. We held a long embrace, breathing together, lost in the moment. When we broke apart he said, "I will go tell the master-of-horse that we will be ready shortly." He collected all the messages except the one from Gilbert and left.

I said nothing. When he had gone, I picked up Gilbert's communication and read the few short paragraphs. I was livid with anger. Jallis Ruffin had dared to violate my home!

I scooped up my sword and slid it into its place over my shoulder with a sharp snick. Whatever today would bring, I would be as ready as I could ever be. As for later, I dreaded that I might never be ready.

Under the Palace

THE ANCIENT PALACE lay along the top of the rocky spine above the Ranapui's holding. We took another trail that dipped below the rim of that ridge and made its way along the edge of the canyon below the ancient ruins. We were a small party, just Pem, Nikko, and myself accompanied by Ribecah and her brother Darcil. There was no need for an escort, and Pem and I had agreed that we would keep things simple and private.

Nikko and Darcil rode on ahead while Ribecah followed. I was behind Ribecah and Pem was behind me. After a sharp descent, we came to a wider place cut back into the overhanging stone. We dismounted and left the horses to rest. A stone trough filled with water from a dripping clay pipe had been placed there along with a supply of hay. Each of us carried water and Ribecah wore a pack with some biscuits and snacks. The plan was that Darcil would stay behind with the horses, a kind of official presence to deter anyone else from following us.

Darcil tried to protest once again. "I prefer to come with you," he said. "My sister should not be alone."

Pem intervened as Ribecah blushed in anger. He said, surprisingly kindly, "She had demonstrated that she is well able to take care of herself, Darcil. I believe that this is the time to let go. Besides, she is now the Queen's lady, and the Queen has her under her protection. Nothing will happen to her, Darcil. You have my word on that."

It was quite a speech for Pem. Darcil seemed to accept Pem's word and bowed to me. "I see that things change. I can only hope that they change for the better. I am sure that I leave my sister in the best possible hands." He spoke to his sister. "Serve well," he said. And to the rest of us, he nodded and said, "I will guard your back. I doubt that anything more serious than a pair of lovers seeking privacy will test my strength." He grinned boyishly. "Perhaps something interesting will come along. In any case, I and our mounts will be waiting for your return." With that he excused himself and walked away, settling on a comfortable bench near the edge of the trail.

We waited a moment. "It's a popular meeting place," Ribecah took up. "From here, a path descends to the floor of the canyon where there is a constant flow of water and loose sand that contains small flakes and even, occasionally, a rare nugget of gold. Some people spend all their spare time in a fruitless search for wealth."

Instead of taking the canyon path which was the only one I could see that led from the shelf, Ribecah stepped around a boulder that overhung the sharp drop. I caught my breath and swallowed as she swung momentarily out into space before disappearing behind the stone.

"There's a handhold at the top of the stone that makes it perfectly safe," Darcil called in a nonchalant manner.

Pem said, "Go ahead, Nikko, see what is ahead of us."

I nodded at Nikko who felt cautiously for the hollow cup before launching himself into space. I heard a few words exchanged between Nikko and Ribecah. Moments later he called out, "All clear for you, my Lady."

"Be sure to hold on tightly," Nikko advised. "The trail on this side is rather narrow.

I stepped forward to follow him. Pem stopped me. "Be careful," he said. 'I'll be right behind you. I should be going first, but I can't leave you unguarded."

I reached back and touched my sword. "You needn't worry on that account," I said.

I swallowed, took one look over the edge, and reached for the handhold that Nikko and Ribecah had used. It turned out to be more shallow than I'd have liked. I swallowed a second time and let myself swing out into space and around to the other side of the barrier when Nikko was ready to grab me and steady me with my back against the cliff behind the narrow shelf.

"We're all set," I called out to Pem who appeared almost immediately.

Once Pem was settled, Ribecah turned and led the way across the face of the cliff until we reached a blind corner. "Careful, here," she said. "There's a crack that might catch your foot when you make the turn." Ribecah stuck her head out so she could see where she was stepping and disappeared. Nikko followed next. I edged up to the blind turn and tried not to look at the long drop to the rocks below.

Once I eased past the crevice that had opened up across the path, I was able to step onto a broad shelf that was cut well back under an overhang in the cliff. I estimated that thirty men could have easily stood on the platform—easy to defend, I surmised. Any enemy would have to approach one at a time.

On the cliff side, a pierced rock screen obscured the shelf from observation below and provided protection against weaponry launched from across the deep ravine, although, looking at the angle, I could see that it would be incredibly difficult to hit the shelf in any case.

Ribecah waved at the ink-black opening looming at the back of the space. "The entrance to the levels underneath the Palace," she said.

Debris littered the floor. Two huge metal banded stone slabs lay bent and broken along each side of the entrance. The door had been at least two vars thick. I wondered how much force it would take to blow them apart—a lot, I decided.

"Historians conclude that a massive explosion blew the doors out from the inside," Ribecah explained.

I thought that this was fairly obvious but held my tongue. Pem wasn't so polite. Ribecah pursed her lips.

"Even so, it had to be an enormous explosion to create this kind of damage," I said hurriedly.

"Sabotage," Pem said, and Nikko nodded in agreement. "If the Palace were under attack, someone blowing the entrance from the inside would be a betrayal of the worst sort. Otherwise, I don't think you could penetrate the slabs. It might take weeks with sledges and boring equipment."

Unless they had the skill to use the nanites. I didn't mention this thought, however.

I let my vision focus on the nanites and watched how their swarms ebbed and flowed through the gaping hole. "I think that there is more story to it than that," I commented, somewhat awed by the scale of construction.

Ribecah reached into her satchel and brought out a handful of candles and what I took to be a lighter. We moved into the shadows of the opening. A gentle stirring of cool air flowed outward indicating that somewhere another opening existed to bring in fresh air.

I look curiously at the tool that Ribecah held. "Where did you get that?"

She looked embarrassed. "Please don't tell my mother, but I took it out of her special cabinet. She keeps a lot of interesting stuff stored there. It's some kind of lighter. I once saw our sage use it to light the candles." She clicked on a small lever at one end of the tube, but the tube remained stubbornly inert. "It used to work," she said, embarrassed.

I looked more closely with my "sight" and saw why it was so special. In fact, Ribecah's simple tube she had seen a sage use was one of the nanite machines. It was designed to respond to someone who had the ability to launch a query.

"Try it again," I suggested. She pressed the lever and at the same time I gave the cluster of nanites a sharp nudge. A tiny amount of entropy was transferred and a blue flame popped out of the end of the tube almost causing Ribecah to drop the device.

"Oh!" she said in awe. "I didn't know I could do that."

No, you can't now. But you'll soon be able to do so. I saw the girl's aura of power flicker more strongly and a ring of nanites form around her. I had a worrisome thought that if Ribecah accidentally activated the device with too much power she could incinerate not only herself but Pem, Nikko, and me as well.

"Here, better let me take that," I said. "I've used something similar before."

It was a lie that Pem caught as he was looking at me from behind Ribecah. He rolled his eyes, but of course he didn't know of the danger.

Ribecah held up each candle and shield while I applied the flame to the wick. Soon we had four bright candles in their reflector housings beaming a surprising amount of light into the darkness ahead of us.

"The supports look like the columns under the Palace in Lumminea," I whispered to Pem. Fluted columns of great age rose from the bases on the litter-covered stone floor and disappeared into the shadows high overhead. A few birds flew about, blinded by our lights. One collided with a column and dropped to the floor, either stunned or dead.

Ribecah cried, "Oh!" She hurried to where the bird lay quivering and set her candle on the floor. She bent down and picked up the bird with great delicacy. I watched the concentration of nanites around Ribecah shift. A Healer, then, I thought. She doesn't know it, though. Shall I tell her? Maybe later. I decided that I needed to know much more about Ribecah and her mother and the Ranapui family before I began training someone like my young Lady. I could be creating a dangerous enemy, or I could be creating a strong ally. At the moment I was unsure what the likely outcome would be.

I was pretty sure that the bird had only been stunned, but I was gratified to see the little thing struggle to stand up in her hands. The creature cocked its head, looked around for a brief moment, and then took flight, aimed directly at the bright opening to the outside. The last I saw of it, the bird was arrowing its way confidently through the slots in the stone curtain at the edge of the cliff. I sighed. If only my own course were so simple.

Neither Pem nor Nikko had paid any attention to the small drama of our little scene. Instead, the two men were huddled in conversation over part of an inscription wrought in green stone inset into the floor. The bulk of the writing was covered by fallen debris. Nikko got busy kicking and scraping away a layer of detritus.

"What does this say," Pem called Ribecah over. I followed.

Ribecah examined what Nikko had uncovered. "I don't know," she said. "There are many such inscriptions in the area, and I have studied only a few of the scripts. This is one that I don't know. Somewhere there is a book containing translations of many of these messages. This is one that I believe has not been deciphered. Perhaps it is an ancient script from one of the Nine Worlds."

"I thought you had explored these ruins," Pem said a bit impatiently.

"There are many ways to explore," I said into the uncomfortable silence following Pem's remark. "I'm sure that Ribecah and Darcil were more interested in finding out where all the passages might lead. I know that I would."

"As to this inscription, I recognize it as the same language that we encountered on the river, and not even Gilbert could decipher its meaning."

Pem sighed "Then, lead on, Lady," he addressed Ribecah.

The girl dimpled charmingly at Pem's address. "Yes, Sire, if you will come this way, the path deeper into the labyrinth is marked for safety. No one to my knowledge has ever explored all the ways under the old Palace, but much is known. Even so, there is a danger of becoming lost as you move deeper under the mountain."

I visualized where I had seen the chamber with the black stone under the ruins and estimated that it lay far back and much lower than our present position. Still, the lamp and other signs of a recent visit to the stone convinced me that someone had found a way into the area and was able to come and go at will—though for what purpose I didn't know. Was the stone active? Was it another portal or entropy tube into the unknown ways beneath the surface of the planet? I needed to find out. We could find ourselves with a deadly enemy at our back.

Pem looked at me expectantly while Nikko quietly asked Ribecah a few questions.

"Yes, the black stone has been visited," I answered Pem's unasked question. "I don't know how recently. That is part of what I need to know. We must find out who has visited there and what they did," I said.

My husband shrugged. "As you say, we cannot leave this thing at our backs," he said in a low voice. He glanced over at Ribecah who was talking earnestly with Nikko. "Are you sure we can trust the girl?"

"Yes," I said. "I believe she is completely unaware of the stone's existence. Also, I doubt that she knows that her mother's Sage-friend might have the power to activate a stone."

Pem frowned. "I have found no reason to distrust either Darcil or his father," he said.

"I am inclined to agree with you," I returned. "Perhaps I am reading more in this than is necessary. I promise to be very careful. Nevertheless, I think we must go forward."

Pem nodded his agreement and reached for my hand, holding it tightly. "You must be careful though," he said earnestly. "I do not want to lose you as well as our unborn child."

I felt a warm glow. Pem did not often express his feelings toward me so directly. I squeezed his hand back.

"Yes, dearest, I promise that for all of our sakes I will keep a close watch!"

We looked over at Nikko and Ribecah. They had ceased talking and were looking at us—Ribecah with great curiosity.

"They are newly married. Newlyweds always think they have many secrets that no one else could possibly guess," Nikko explained to the girl, laughing.

He laughed again. "Are you two quite ready to go? The Lady has explained the way to me and I think we will have quite an interesting time."

His easy manner of talking to us scandalized Ribecah who, even by the light of our candles, could be seen to blush furiously. "We are ready," I said lightly, and pulled Pem along by the hand.

"We are quite ready to be awed and astounded by your underground palace."

After all, there was no need to tell Ribecah any of what had happened under the Palace in Lumminea.

"WHICH WAY DO we take?" Pem asked Ribecah after we followed a path over and around piles of debris and confronted a wall pierced with three dark archways looming like inky shadows. Pem held up his lamp, but the beam faltered after only a few vars. "The left is the largest and must have been the main route. The right one looks more dangerous with a fallen lintel, and the center seems to be the one with the most traffic." Pem referred to the piles of rubble swept to either side to clear a path into the darkness beyond the range of our lamps.

Ribecah hesitated. "The large arch leads to a blocked passage only a little way beyond this room," she returned. "You are right in assuming that it was probably the main route. There is an old map that shows a direct route descending from the surface down to this level. To my knowledge, no one has ever been beyond the collapsed roof. Someone tried to excavate there, but their tunnel under the great beams fell in and the people all died. Several have tried to follow, but all they ever found were skeletons crushed under fallen blocks and loose rubble that continued to fall no matter how much they dug out. I don't think it's been tried again in recent history."

"The center way is the popular way and leads through a series of spirals up to a hall that overlooks the back side of the ridge. From there you can see the river and all of Ranapui in the distance. Most of the young people go that way. It is a popular trysting place," Ribecah added.

I'd have given odds that Ribecah was blushing. Perhaps there was more that her mother didn't know? I suppressed a grin and hoped that this was the case. I needed a bold traveling companion.

"And the broken arch?" Nikko asked her.

"That way descends deeper under the mountain and is partially blocked in many places. I think that will be our way. You described a deep chamber," she turned to address me. "I know of no such place elsewhere."

"You haven't been there yourself?" Pem asked her.

"No, Sire, but I have been a little way down that path and I know that it is possible to penetrate into the lower levels."

I was pretty sure that Ribecah was correct because I'd checked on the density of the nanites in each of the three possible passages. The left one had hardly any of the creatures, the middle way hosted a steady stream of them moving through the opening, but the right-hand choice, the one with the dangerous lintel, was thick with nanites—almost as if they were trying to attract my attention. Any Sage able to see this would have guessed that a place of power might lie that direction.

Nikko said brightly, "Okay, right it is, then." His jaunty words lightened our mood considerably.

I loosened my sword in its sheath. "Lead on," I told Ribecah.

Pem said, "Nikko will go with Ribecah, I will bring up the rear, and Lady Claire will stay between us."

Nikko grinned at me in the half-light and I took Pem's orders in good humor. I said, "I'm sure that Nikko will be happy to have my sword at his back."

Ribecah looked from one to the other of us, apprehensive. "You don't really think that we will run into trouble, do you?"

"Of course not," I returned. "Nevertheless, it always pays to be ready."

"Where Lady Claire goes, trouble never seems far behind," Pem commented gloomily.

Ribecah looked skeptical, but she fingered the blade at her side. Nikko joked, "Please Lady, don't pull that blade and accidentally stab me in the back."

Ribecah jerked her blade free and whirled the tip in a complex defensive pattern. "I think not," she said with pride, slamming the blade back home in its sheath.

Nikko looked impressed, but I thought back to what Ribecah's mother had said. "Practice is not the same as using your blade to defend yourself." I still had my doubts, but I was pleased that my new Lady had impressed Nikko.

A Hidden Door

.RIBECAH HAD BEEN .correct in her assessment of the difficulties ahead of us. There were numerous tights squeezes where walls and supports had cracked or sagged. Fortunately, nothing looked as if it had moved in a very long time. The passage was clearly marked by those who had gone before, although the markings thinned out the deeper we penetrated into the maze of tunnels and levels. I was reminded of how Tess and I had threaded our way through the support pillars and tumbled blocks under the palace in Lumminea—there was even water dripping from overhead.

Finally we came to a point where an unmarked passage led down at a steep angle. I sent out a query and received a faint image of a large chamber below us. "We go down here, I think," I said.

We had been silent so long that everyone, including myself, jumped at the sound of my voice. Nikko took out chalk and marked on the walls indicating where we were branching from the marked trail and attached one end of the line on the spool securely to a bolt set into the wall. Whatever the bolt had secured had been looted long ago. I noticed that it wasn't rusted even though it was covered with beads of moisture. I wondered what kind of metal could possibly last so long without corroding.

Pem and I were in the lead now. I followed the trail of nanites deeper and deeper under the surface. Every time we came to a choice between two ways, I led the way downwards. I felt Pem and the others growing more nervous with each step. The floor became rough and cracked; the air grew colder and smelled stale. I began to worry about whether it was fit to breathe. I closed my fingers around my amulet and felt a trickle of warmth. Nikko, who was in charge of the line that marked our trail, commented that we had used up more than half the spool since we had left the main passage.

We paused for a break and Ribecah passed around a selection of biscuits. I was surprised to find an assortment of flavors ranging from tangy berries to earthy nutty. One reminded me of a sweet cinnamon roll rather than a biscuit. We washed these down with water from our bottles. Pem settled down on a rocky shelf, drew his sword and put it across his lap, and closed his eyes.

I started thinking about the marvelous candles that Ribecah had brought with her; they looked barely used. I asked her about the wax. Once again I felt Ribecah's embarrassment.

"The wax is very special," she said. "It is said that the bees that produce this wax feed only on the divine white flower called the Queen's Coat. Supposedly it is found only in certain places in the high meadows of the Fault Line Range."

I let a thin stream of nanites feed me a microscopic image of the wax candles. I discovered something unsettling. These were not candles at all, but an artificial construct designed to look like wax candles.

Tiny disks of a clear crystalline substance were stacked like plates, laced together with nearly invisible lines of something I perceived to be metallic filaments. The thing looked more like exotic circuitry that it did a fuel. In fact, as I scanned nearer the so-called wick, I was treated to the spectacle of filaments of nanites spewing from the metal threads, flaring up and disappearing in rapid sequence. I didn't understand how it worked, but I realized I was looking at some kind of self-consuming circuitry that was transporting energy along microscopic entropy tubes—far too clever to be the anything but ancient technology. I came away from the picture a bit breathless. It was as if I was being drained of energy while I was viewing the pictures. It was totally unexpected. Dangerous!

I thought about the whole thing and I almost laughed. The only way anyone would design something like an artificial candle was that it was part of a wicked toy designed to simulate a real candle—someone's idea of a decoration and maybe a deadly trap. Also, I realized with a jolt, the candles flame was not an accurate indicator of the presence of oxygen. I had to hope that at least one other person, the one who visited the stone, had passed here and had not perished.

"Yes, very special bees, indeed," I answered Ribecah, not wanting to cause the girl more discomfort. I was pretty sure that she'd stolen the so-called candles from the same cabinet as the lighter. Was the girl simply over-anxious to please me, or was I dealing with a darker motive? I decided it would all bear watching.

I sighed and pushed the bung back into my water bottle. Another thing for me to invent: screw caps for bottles. I hated this business of twisting corks out of bottle necks. Invariably I'd wind up pushing them too deep and being unable to get to the water when I was thirsty.

"Time to go," I announced, bringing an end to a whispered conversation going on between Nikko and Ribecah. Pem opened his eyes and yawned.

UNLIKE SOME REGIONS under our palace back home, there was none of the evil feeling that we had encountered near the damaged portal where the Captain and a few of Ruffin's men had been sucked into space.

So, before we left our little rest area, I asked that we extinguish our lamps. I wanted to see if there were lighted guide strips under these ruins. Unfortunately, if there were any glowing guides to be found here on either the ceiling or floor, they had failed long ago or were never installed. The darkness and silence, except for the dripping of water, was intense. I put a hand to the floor and felt for the faint vibrations that underlay all of the palace in Lumminea. All I detected was the shuffle of Pem's foot as he moved behind me. I supposed that somewhere in this vast ruin there were the same ancient machines, only these were cold and silent.

I wiped some slime off my hand using my britches and lit each of our lamps. As I shuffled forward, I let my senses extend outward and down.

After a while, Pem asked, "Sense anything yet?"

"Something," I said vaguely, distracted by a dim light that seemed to flicker ahead of me. "Oof! Ouch!" My foot caught in a crack and I stumbled into a support column that jutted out at an odd angle, twisted, and sat down abruptly knocking the wind out of me.

"There's something ahead of us," Nikko said, sounding excited.

"I see it, too," Ribecah said.

Pem was busy helping me to my feet. "I see it," he added.

Since I was the only one facing backwards, I had to turn around to see what everyone was talking about.

I saw some ghostly lights flickering ahead of us. There also appeared to be some figures merged into the shadows. One of them was stepping forward.

"Stop right there," I ordered Ribecah who was trying to move past me.

Ribecah stopped. The other figure halted, too. "Are they trying to meet with us?" she whispered.

Suddenly I laughed, startling everyone. "I think we have met these friends before," I said, holding up my lamp and moving forward. Ahead of me, one of the group obligingly moved to meet me.

"Hello," I said in a loud voice.

"Hello," came the return.

"That sounded a lot like you," Pem said behind me.

"That's because," I said, pausing before a dark shadow in front of me, "I am the one talking." I held my lamp high and my counterpart held hers high.

"It's a mirror," Nikko guessed.

Ribecah giggled. "I thought they were ghosts."

I tried to look around the mirror, but the corridor ahead seemed to have disappeared. "This may be blocking the passage," I said, approaching the mirror surface. I saw why our images were so blurred—the mirror was covered with a fog like a mirror in my bathroom back home.

"Surely not," Pem moved up beside me and put his hand out.

"Don't touch that," I snatched his hand back.

"Why not?" He asked me, looking puzzled. "It's just a mirror, after all."

"Not quite," Nikko said, also joining us. Ribecah came up and pressed close to Nikko, shivering. I wondered if she were going to hold his hand—and what Mags would think.

"What do you mean," Pem said, irritated.

"Look closely," Nikko said. "Which hand are you holding your sword in?"

"My right hand, of course," Pem said. He waved his sword and the image obliged by moving simultaneously.

"And which hand is holding the sword in the mirror," Nikko asked.

Pem looked puzzled; I decided not to answer. Ribecah jumped up and down.

"You are holding the sword in your right hand in the mirror," she exclaimed.

"So?" Pem returned.

Ribecah said, "It's impossible. If it were a mirror, you'd be holding the sword in your left hand. It's called a mirror image just for that reason."

Silently I applauded my new protégé.

"Oh." Pem was silent for a moment, then put up his left hand. Sure enough, the left hand in the reflection—or whatever it was—moved in the same way. "You are right," he said reluctantly. Nikko chuckled. I held my tongue.

"So, what is it?" Pem wanted to know.

We all backed up slightly. "Well, it's obviously some kind of mirror," Nikko said.

"I'd have to agree with Nikko," I returned. "Let's back off. I want to try something."

"Best to back off a lot," Pem growled. "When her Ladyship decides to test something, there is no telling what might happen."

I took on my healer's sight and attempted to analyze the mirror. To my surprise, the mirror was only a membrane of specialized nanites. I could look beyond the membrane and sense a dark space that formed a large room.

"Whatever it is," I said lightly, "it appears to be put here purely for the purpose of discouraging visitors."

"Can you tell us more?" Ribecah asked me.

"It's a kind of screen that projects our true appearance," I returned. "I don't know exactly how it works, but that is the reason why things are not reversed as they are in a true mirror." I would have said that a camera was being used, but I knew that the word camera wouldn't translate into Lunarian common speech.

"Can we get through it or around it?" Pem wanted to know.

"I believe so," I said, and walked straight through the apparition. There was a gasp behind me.

"Are you there?" Pem said in a worried voice. "We can't see you."

"Yes, Lady, you shouldn't have done that," Nikko said.

I saw a thin filament of energy connecting my ring with Pem's sword. I pushed a hand back through in their direction and wiggled my fingers. Ribecah pushed through boldly to stand beside me, giggling in delight. "It felt slightly wet and clingy," she told me.

I tried not to laugh. "Well, are you coming?" Ribecah and I looked at each other. Men.

There was some hesitation. "Stand back, please," Nikko said and came through with the tip of his sword first followed by Pem.

"We wanted to be ready in case there was a problem," Pem explained.

Although I appreciated the thought, we had our swords so that the men need not have worried about us women. I said nothing, however, but merely smiled at Pem and Nikko. "We are getting close," I said in a subdued voice.

"There's just one small problem," Nikko said.

"What's that?" Pem asked him.

"This!" He held up the spool of line. The end that had been unspooling was cleanly cut and dangled to the floor. "I just checked it," the first officer said. "There was nothing wrong with it before we crossed through the mirror."

I hadn't really paid much attention to the backside of the membrane after Pem came through. I turned my lamp on it, expecting to see the shiny surface. Instead, I saw a wall that looked like solid stone. The way was closed. My stomach turned upside down. Had I led us into a trap? If only I had gone back while the others were on the other side.

While I was staring at the wall, trying not to panic, Pem reversed his sword and struck the surface with the pommel. There was a solid ringing sound. I winced. Pem would always treat his sword as if it were ordinary metal. Sage Leandra had explained this by saying only that it was unlikely that Pem would ever develop the ability to use the underlying power in Lunaria as I did. I hoped that he didn't inadvertently trigger some unknown capability.

"That doesn't sound good," Nikko said and tried tapping along the edges of the tunnel with the same result.

"There must be some switch," I muttered to myself. I called up my healer's sight, but all I found was a rock wall covered with a film of nanites—interesting, but not very helpful.

"At least it's clean in here," Pem said.

I looked down at the floor. Instead of the layers of muck and shards on the other side of the mirror, the floor was swept clean down to the polished stone. It was so clean in the room that I was reminded of the armory in the basement of the Dark Tower. There had been an automated cleaning machine that kept the vault in immaculate condition. Could this be a similar device operating here? I had been assuming that the labyrinth under the ruins was dead, but something must be left which powered the machine. I hoped it wouldn't decide to come along and mistake us for trash.

"There's a door here," Ribecah called out. The girl had walked to the other end of the room and was standing with her lamp illuminating a massive, iron-bound door. For some strange reason, the surface was free of any nanites. I tried to project my sight beyond the door, but I saw only blankness.

Pem saw my frustration. "Perhaps your special key?" He suggested.

I had forgotten about the entropy-enhanced key. It might work, and the door appeared to be the only way out of the chamber. I silently thanked Mags for making sure that I had it with me and crossed my fingers.

What to do? I touched the key to the door and received no response—no image appeared to me as it had before when I touched a door. The hard metal seemed strangely rubbery when I prodded the surface with the key.

"Perhaps you might try the key in the lock," Ribecah said ingenuously.

"It's not really a key," I murmured. "It's a device that supposed to give me an image of what's on the other side." I wasn't going to admit it, but I'd never actually tried it in a lock since, the way it was explained to me, I hadn't thought of it as a universal key.

Why not? I focused my lamp on the large key hole and tried to peer inside. All I could see was a black hole. I was carrying some small tools that might pick the lock, but if that failed—or my key didn't work—we might be trapped here forever.

I put that thought firmly out of my mind and stuck the key into the hole, being careful to grasp it tightly. It seemed ridiculous. The tiny key was certainly too small to affect the mechanism— assuming there was a mechanism. I tried my healer's sight again, but in vain.

Nothing happened with the key either. Disappointed, I withdrew the tool and looked at my companions in dismay.

"You didn't turn it," Ribecah reminded me.

"Ridiculous," I muttered, but stuck the key back inside the oversized hole. This time I turned the key, pretending that there was a mechanism to engage with. "I wonder which way I should rotate," I said sarcastically.

As I turned the key, I felt the metal getting warm in my hands. There was a warning flash of heat from the amulet around my neck. I jerked my hand with the key away from the door just in time to avoid molten metal spraying from the keyhole.

"What the devil!" Pem exclaimed. The radiant heat was intense; all of us scrambled to retreat. The floor shuddered violently, the door seemed to bend in the middle, and then crashed outwards. A cloud of dust filled out chamber. Pem coughed. Nikko beat frantically at his coat where globules of the molten metal had started a fire.

"Well, that was a bit dramatic," Ribecah commented.

I caught my breath and sneezed.

Into the Void

.THE GOOD NEWS .was that there was plenty of light in the next chamber, though the dust kept things pretty dim and indistinct. Pem held me politely back while Nikko pushed cautiously through the opening.

"Let him do his job," he whispered in my ear. I leaned back against his shoulder and bit him gently on his ear. Pem yelped.

Ribecah caught this bit of play and turned beet red; I shrugged and smiled back at her. Pem rubbed his damaged ear and watched Nikko for any signs of danger.

Nikko had finished his rounds of the next chamber before I stepped through the former door frame. I marveled at the violence. Iron bars an inch thick had been twisted and melted at the edges of the slab. I promised myself that from here on out I would no longer take anything for granted.

"The good news is that there appears to be another way out of here," Nikko said, extinguishing his lantern. Light was no longer needed. The rest of us followed his lead.

Nikko's words were good news, indeed. I could see that the haze was clearing out. It meant that the other entrance was probably the one most used to access this chamber, and that the way we had come was an old way that the mirror was intended to protect by trapping the interloper in the adjacent chamber. I wondered if there had been bones—then I remembered the evidence of the cleaning machine—a nice, neat way to get rid of intruders. A draft from a ventilation shaft somewhere was renewing the air. Across the room I saw the rectangular black stone. I checked the area carefully, but failed to find any sign of a concealing screen or illusion.

I cautioned my companions to stay clear of the artifact. The concentration of nanites in the area was so high that I took one of Gilbert's tattles from my bag and located it on a ledge across the room from the black stone. Such high concentrations of nanites often preceded the appearance of a wild channel. After the attack on us aboard the ship, I was inclined to believe that someone was tracking either myself or Pem and was probably waiting for the opportunity to try again. The transfer stone would be the ideal place. If that person had planted a tell of his own, like the glass sphere at the Battle of Tribana, then we had advertised our presence across the world when the door imploded. I found myself wondering if my little entropy-enhanced key was the kind of thing used to force the door at the underground entrance to the palace. The thought brought me cold chills. I was carrying around a much more powerful weapon than I had imagined. Of course, I didn't know how to use it, so what good would it do me?

I had allowed these thoughts to distract me and realized that Ribecah had wandered across the room and had drawn close to the Stone.

"Come away," I called out. As young people are inclined to do, Ribecah seemed heedless of my cries and reached over to lay a hand on the oily black surface. Almost at once a man in black armor seemed to appear from nowhere and grabbed her wrist. Ribecah howled in pain and tried to pull away, but her efforts had no effect. She reached for her sword but was hampered by having the wrong arm free. For a moment, I was paralyzed with fear. Where had this man come from? Why hadn't we seen him?

Then I realized that the man was going to pull Ribecah through the surface and into the void beyond. He probably thought it had trapped me. I was the one who would be heedlessly interested in the transport stone. It had been waiting for the first person to touch the surface, sure that it would be me.

"Claire, no!" Pem cried out as I threw myself towards the girl. I was not going to lose Ribecah—not now, not ever, and even if misfortune ultimately struck, certainly not so soon. I couldn't face Sidra and tell her that I had lost her daughter. I thought about my grandmother and how she lost her son—my father. I couldn't hold back.

As soon as I approached Ribecah, I felt a powerful pull from the stone unlike anything I had felt before. Our enemy was already merging with the black surface. I grabbed Ribecah and tried to draw her back, but the suction was too great and my boots started sliding across the floor. I threw a despairing glance back at Pem who was dashing in my direction, sword raised, as if he intended to hew the man's arm and pull us free.

Fear nearly paralyzed me. I thought I knew what would happen if his special sword touched the man's armor because I now believed that it was not real metal but an energy field that was part of an entropy tube, a construct of pure energy tightly compressed by a surrounding probability field. How else could he have eluded my detection? If Pem's sword were to touch the boundary, without the ability to control the reaction, Pem would be consumed in much the same way the dark warrior had been consumed when he attacked me during the Battle of Tribana.

I screamed at Pem to stay back. I was going to muster my strength to cut off the connection between the man and the surface before we could be dragged in. Of course I'd never tried anything like this before, but I figured it would have dire consequences for the man half-way into the void. I saw a brief picture of the tortured-looking people caught in the black stones on the Plains of Glass.

Unfortunately, my mule-headed husband continued to charge. His sword starting to descend in an arc that would intersect the arm between the stone and Ribecah's arm. There was only one way to save Pem.

I stopped resisting the pull and pushed with all my strength, plunging the man, Ribecah, and me through the surface of the stone and into the void. The last thing I heard was the faint clang of Pem's sword striking the now-inert surface.

Instead of the limitless space that I had seen on the way through a stone into the Tower in Tieben, I was confronted by glowing coils of white tubing. The tangle looked disgustingly like intestines with a man in a suit attached to this end.

I had no time to think about such things. I didn't know whether or not I had an actual body in the void or whether I was only a coherent presence—a conscious set of instructions which would be used to reconstruct me at some other time and place.

Someone was using an entropy tube like a tether instead of a probe. I had no idea how this was possible since the tube operated on the principle that the ends were interchangeable and one could move between them instantaneously.

Think, Claire. There was physical armored hand that was holding on to Ribecah's arm. I felt the young woman struggling and jerking at my arm. Stupid. I realized that I must have some sort of physical presence. I might actually exist. Perhaps the entropy tube gave shape and substance to the void. Having this thought, hope sprang into my heart. I reached for the lighter in my pouch. I may be simply creating the objects as I went, but I didn't think it would matter to what I had in mind. What would happen if I siphoned off enough energy to burn in my torch? Perhaps this would disrupt the armor field and either leave the man stranded or banished to the entry point—somewhere else, I hoped.

I felt rather than saw the blue flame spring into existence. There was an immediate reaction from my surroundings. I had the impression of everything thinning out. It was like being inside a balloon that was rapidly deflating. My sense of physical contact with Ribecah became more tenuous. The tube thinned and became translucent, suddenly looking more like plastic wrap around a sausage-doll.

Although everything was silent, I felt something I could only describe as a loud POP as the tube sprang away into the void leaving the bubble with the man in it. I turned the flame in his direction and the membrane split open to reveal a man thrashing about. One arm was stuck into an armored sleeve with a mechanical hand at the end. His eyes went wide with surprise when he saw me. I felt a blast of hatred in the form of heat, though it might have been ice—I couldn't tell the difference. Meanwhile Ribecah had stopped struggling and was as still as death. I hoped that she had only fainted.

The man was Jallis Ruffin, the Dark Sage, the enemy that I had feared most. He must have existed in the tube at both ends, ready to draw me in if I came close to the stone. Instead he had got Ribecah and I had trailed along as a nasty little surprise.

I could see that he was speculating on how to attack, but the fact was that we were shrinking away from each other, growing further apart with each second. It was too late to reach for my sword, even if it might have been effective in the void—which I somehow doubted. We were returning, each to our original portal. Without thinking, I threw the tube with the flame as hard as I could. At first I thought I would miss as the thing curved out away from where I had aimed. Then, obeying some physics of its own, it arced back again, headed directly for him. Perhaps it was guided by my will power. Whatever the reason, he looked surprised, then recoiled as he grabbed the little tube to keep it from hitting him in the face. I could see him flailing about and trying rid himself of the thing. I think he was screaming, but the void was soundless. There was a flicker and part of his hand seemed to melt away. I was horrified.

Then Ruffin was receding at a rapid pace and I lost sight of him as he shrank to a dot and disappeared. All of a sudden space was intensely black pierced by pinpricks of light. I was so cold my fingers and nose were numb and I could barely think. I had to get us out!

I looked around, but of course there was no Stone behind me, if indeed there was such a thing as a direction in this void. All directions and distances appeared to be the same. I pictured Pem's face and grabbed hold of my yellow egg with its alien Silly Putty inside—something about the yellow egg and its contents almost always seemed to help protect me against attacks through the channels. Almost immediately I felt a comforting warm glow from my pendant and sense of location. I concentrated on moving there. Ribecah was dead weight in my hands. My fingers were numb and I was afraid my grip would break and leave her adrift. There was a flare of blinding light, a loud "uff" as I collided with someone, a short fall to a very lumpy landing followed by Ribecah falling on top of me. The second "Uff" was the air being knocked out of me.

The blinding light turned out to be my eyes adjusting to the overhead power strips. The next thing I knew Nikko was lifting Ribecah's still form off me. I took a deep breath and realized I was sidewise across Pem who was also sprawled on the floor. I felt the connection between my ring and his sword fading and realized what had pulled me back. "Sorry about that," I said, enjoying the look of consternation on his face.

"What's happened to Ribecah?" Nikko voiced his concern.

"Just fainted, I hope," I brought my somewhat addled attention back to important matters. "The shock of the intense cold in there probably caused her to lose consciousness." I wasn't quite ready to describe my experiences—not yet. I needed time to think about what had happened in the void.

Nikko had deposited Ribecah on the floor with his coat rolled up under her head. He was busy rubbing her hands and wrist. "She's terribly cold," he said.

I shivered. "Yes. It's only the second time I've experienced the void. I wasn't sure what to do or how to return." I wondered if the difference was the presence of the entropy tube. Perhaps it temporarily destabilized the transfer port. I looked at the oily surface of the Stone, but it was smooth and totally inert. I decided that it would be a long time before I ventured to experiment with a transfer.

"Your elbow is poking me," Pem complained.

I said, looking fondly at Pem, "You brought us back."

Pem looked pleased with himself.

"Glad to be of service," he returned.

I disentangled myself from him and went to kneel beside Ribecah. Pem joined me, brushing the dust off his clothes.

To my immense relief, my healer's sight told me that the girl was fine, if in mild shock. I saw her eyes flutter and she looked straight up at me.

"What was that thing?" she whispered.

I decided it was time to tell everyone what was going on. "That thing was Jallis Ruffin. He was in what I believe to be a special kind of armor that could prove to be very dangerous to us." Ribecah sat up with Nikko's assistance, and I described what had happened. "He thought he was attacking me but got Ribecah instead."

When Pem and Nikko looked skeptical, I added, "And I think we will have proof, this time." I related how I thought I had burned his hand away. "It was awful," I shuddered. "If there had been any other choice...."

Pem gathered me to him. "I thought I had lost you," he said, his voice betraying a slight hitch. "I shall get a dispatch off to Gilbert at once. I think when we return, we will have a long conversation with Lord Garrund and his Dark Sage." It was the most dangerous and determined tone of voice I had ever heard coming from Pem. I didn't think I'd like to be in Lord Garrund's shoes when Pem and Gilbert caught up with him.

As for that, I had my own score to settle with Jallis Ruffin. I felt like I was ready to confront the Dark Sage.

A Miraculous Recovery

RIBECAH SEEMED TO have miraculous powers of recovery, or a short memory of her horrible experience, because she was ready to get up in only a few minutes. She brushed dust off her clothes and looked around.

"I guess I lost my pack and the rest of my stuff," she said.

"Luckily that was the only thing you lost," Nikko returned. "A few biscuits, a candle-powered lantern, and some personal items is not a high price to pay for an escape from sure death."

"The lighter is gone," she said. "Now I must tell my mother that I took things out of her private cabinet." She looked more stricken by this idea than she had looked at the idea of death at the hands of Jallis Ruffin.

"Never mind, I will speak with her," I said, trying to reassure her. "After all, we still have all of the special candles."

Pem was standing from one foot to another. "Never mind about that. I think we should leave this place immediately," he said. "Darcil will be anxious, and I am not so sure that something won't appear out of that stone."

"Yes," I agreed, "and I think Nikko has found us a way out." I was looking at a fat stream of nanites that extended through the opening at the other end of the chamber. I fancied that I could even feel a breath of fresh air. I started forward, but Pem held me back.

"I'll check it out," Nikko offered before I could say anything.

"I'll come with you," Ribecah said brightly.

"Stay here," I told her. "You'd be in Nikko's way. In case something happens, I'd not have Nikko harmed because he was looking after you."

Ribecah looked rebellious, so I added, "Besides, I'd rather you stayed to help us in case something does come out of that stone." I said this knowing that it was highly unlikely that we would have any further trouble. Ribecah looked mollified.

As it turned out, Nikko returned almost immediately with a big grin on his face. "If we'd known, we could have saved ourselves all the trouble of the other passage and come here directly. This place has a cleverly concealed back door that someone has been using regularly."

Ribecah looked startled. "If there is another way to the passages underneath the old temple, I'm quite sure I've never heard of it," she said, defensively.

"Well, you've learned something," Pem said dryly. "However, we don't want you to share this with anyone else."

"Definitely not," I added my weight to Pem's statement. "We may be able to set a watcher on this entrance and find out who it is that has been here."

Since Ribecah seemed to see the sense of this, I wasn't too worried that she'd tell any of her friends.

It took only a few moments to reach the opening that Nikko had discovered. It was very cleverly concealed by a false rock face that was passed by crawling through a slit at the bottom. A narrow shelf on the other side allowed a person to stand—if they were careful. A series of handholds and footholds led upwards to a wider shelf that followed the contour of the ridge and emerged near the place where we had originally followed the path down to the clearing where Darcil waited.

I looked cautiously over the edge, once we'd all scrambled to the top, and couldn't see a trace of where we had been. "Very clever."

Nikko went down the other path to find Darcil. The two returned shortly with our horses. The ride home was uneventful—thankfully so. I dreaded having to face Sidra with the news that we'd lost her precious lighter.

Landing at Tieben

.RISSA AWAKENED WITHOUT .opening her eyes. She felt comfortable, warm and drowsy, and, for some inexplicable reason, entirely happy. A fleeting glimpse of a fading dream flashed by, too fast to be remembered, too slow to be ignored. Something wonderful, then.

Faint alarm bells were ringing in her head. Where was she? What was the last thing she remembered? Lunch at the Stew and Brew with Turlo. Turlo! Hauk!

Rissa opened her eyes. She didn't feel any particular anxiety. The ship rocked gently, under sail in light seas. She could hear the whisper of water rushing past the hull. The port was partially open and she could hear a seagull screeching. Not far out to sea, then. The delicious aroma of cooking mixed with fresh, salty air aroused her senses. Hungry. I'm very hungry, she thought. That idea brought her wide awake. She sat up in bed and swung her feet to the deck, drawing her gown around her. Gown? I don't remember putting on a gown—or getting back to the ship.

The cabin door opened and Turlo backed in carrying a tray of something that smelled delicious. He almost dropped what he was carrying when he saw Rissa sitting up on the edge of the bed. Rissa saw relief flooding his features.

"Mara said you'd be awake this morning," he said, averting his gaze. "I didn't know whether to believe her or not."

"What day is this?" Rissa asked him. Her throat felt dry and unused.

"You've been sleeping for two days. We brought you back to the ship after Hauk came and pronounced you okay. He said that you'd awaken in good time and that you would feel fine. He didn't offer any explanations, but he was smiling. We've—I've—been worried. What happened?"

Rissa cast her thoughts back. The scrap of dream that remained was a picture of Claire smiling and looking at her from across a gulf of deep blue space. She seemed happy and well. Was there something she was telling her? Rissa watched her friend's lips moving and strained to hear her words.

Suddenly Rissa collapsed back on the bed. Turlo bent over her in alarm, but found her smiling, her eyes bright with happiness. "Claire is with child," she said to Turlo. She grabbed him and pulled him down to her, spilling the breakfast on the floor. Neither of them seemed to pay much attention.

AFTER A SMOOTH crossing of the Bay of Terror, the Trader ship anchored in the waters off the south coast of Tieben about a third of the way between Timbermill and Boggrash. Rissa and Turlo stood arm-in-arm at the rail and scanned a line of low hills for signs of habitation. A hint of a shadow in the background was all that could be seen of the high mountains of the Fault Line range beyond the coastal hills. Between them and the sandy shoreline, a line of foam marked the reef that separated the blue gulf waters from the emerald green of the lagoon.

Forward of her position, crew members were making ready to launch the pinnace that would ferry their party and supplies to the beach. Rissa's mother joined them at the rail.

"Your journey should not be terribly difficult this time of year," Mara said to Rissa and Turlo. "The weather won't close in for some time, so the passes should be easy. You will have Hauk's journal to guide you. Your main danger will be through betrayal or mischance."

Turlo looked grim. "I think betrayal the more likely danger," he returned, patting his sword.

"I'm sure you are well prepared for the sort of banditry you might find along your way. Be certain to keep my daughter safe," Mara said, pinning Turlo with a grim glance.

"We will keep each other safe, Mother," Rissa returned gently.

"Yes, back-to-back, one for all and all for one and such nonsense that young people imagine will ward off danger," Mara said. Rissa might have told her that she was nearly quoting from a story from another time and another world, one which Claire had told her during a long evening on the landship out of Boggrash. It gave a voice to a sentiment that spoke of the kind of loyalty of which Mara would have approved.

The Garrison at Ranaputkin

THE LOW POINT of our stay with the Ranapuis was my conversation with Sidra following our return from our little expedition to the black stone to spring the trap that I had been fairly certain would be laid by Jallis Ruffin.

Sidra was furious that Ribecah had been exposed to such danger. I could have been imperial and forbade her to discuss it, but I thought it much more politic to let her get it out of her system and then to point out that Ribecah had handled herself well. After all, Ribecah was a Queen's companion. She'd come through without a scratch. Eventually Sidra seemed satisfied with this, and we returned to a cordial relationship—if not quite as warm as previously.

The high point of our visit was Sidra accompanying Mags and myself to assemble a new wardrobe, a task that had been sadly neglected.

It seemed that every dressmaker in the city not only knew Sidra, but also liked and respected her. We put together a superb wardrobe that included two new ball gowns as well as a variety of practical yet stylish daily wear and travel costumes—all with plenty of pockets. This time I didn't even need to insist on the pockets as the dressmakers were already enthusiastic about the new fashion. If anything, I had to curtail their creativity when they began putting secret pouches in uncomfortable places. Certainly I had plenty of places to conceal my yellow egg with its alien *Silly Putty*.

Lady Putkin's frostiness thawed considerably as a result of putting on a highly successful departing celebration for Pem and me. I didn't think for a moment that we had become friends, but I was surprised—and amused—that she had changed her hair style to the latest shorter cut.

At Lady Putkin's Ball and Gala, Lord Putkin, whom I had met in his capacity as a member of the High Council in Lumminea, turned out to be a surprisingly good dancer as well as a gracious host. In spite of the summer heat, he managed to remain impeccable in his formal coat and lace collar. His mask slipped a bit when he asked me some awkward questions concerning Pem as we whirled about the polished ballroom floor, but I remembered Sage Leandra's lessons on what to expect from these powerful men and managed to deflect his interest in my husband's plans by changing the subject to wine.

We found common ground on the subject of wine. He praised my wine, and if he didn't claim my vineyard to produce the very best in the land, then at least he rated it very high among the famous vintages. I thought that this bit of honesty was a most charming ploy to put me off-guard and shared our conversation with Pem a few days later.

Pem thought it less charming and more devious. "Gilbert thinks that Lord Putkin is deep in Torvall Garrund's council and is one of those set against us," Pem said.

"He didn't learn anything from me that he couldn't confirm in some other way," I replied. "I doubt that he believes that I am much more than what I seem."

"Are you?" Pem asked me in a teasing tone.

"I do not know, entirely," I answered him in all honesty. "Sometimes I think that the things I experience are an illusion and that none of this is real." I waved my hands about.

Pem pretended to look hurt. "I do hope you think that I am real," he said. "I also hope that you think this is real," he said, putting a hand on my stomach.

"Oh, that's real enough," I returned. "This morning when I was sick I was convinced that this is real."

Like everything else that had happened to me in Lunaria, my condition had arrived ahead of time. Leandra had told me that the common experience of pregnant women was a period called morning sickness that generally lasted from about six weeks into pregnancy until the twelfth week, when the condition usually disappeared.

When I complained, she laughed at me and told me, "This sickness does not have a timetable. It will come when it will and leave when it is ready." Since we were leaving soon, I was hoping to pass it off as a shipboard malady.

Today, however, I had to be ready for the long-awaited visit to the local garrison where we were to formally review the guard under Major Lorence's command. It was not something I looked forward to, though Pem was understandably enthusiastic.

Pem and I had both balked at the idea of arriving at the garrison in a carriage. By the time an honor guard in full dress uniforms led by a young lieutenant about my age arrived to conduct us to the garrison, our horses were saddled and ready to go. The lieutenant and a sergeant dismounted and approached us, bowing deferentially. When Pem acknowledged their presence, Lieutenant Helton introduced himself and then Sergeant Tinsmythe and we exchanged greetings.

Helton's eyebrows rose slightly as I swung from the mounting block to my saddle, but I detected more of a sense of amusement in his look rather than disapproval. On the other hand, the Master-of-Horse continued to radiate his disfavor at my riding style, though he was careful to appear pleasantly neutral in my presence. I reflected on how difficult it was for some people to accept change. I reminded myself to be sure that I didn't fall into that same trap someday.

The city was waking to its ordinary daily routines as we clattered through the cobbled streets. The sky was clear and the air was cool, but the day would be warm and I hoped the Major had cooling refreshments for us while we inspected the military facilities. A few citizens stopped to wave at us—a few bowed. If they waved, I waved back. If they bowed, I nodded.

Their generous and polite attitude reinforced my impression that the city was moderately prosperous and its people relatively happy to be living in a safe and peaceful place. Perhaps the war with Tieben had been far away. After all, Tieben's navy could hardly have mounted a major campaign so far south. What would have been the purpose of attacking a city so far away—not that Ranaputkin had no strategic value? The shipyards would be a prime target for a seafaring nation. The trade in mineral wealth would be another prize. Fortunately, Tieben fit neither of these profiles being essentially landlocked or icebound and rich in timber without an industrial base for using mineral wealth.

We turned at an intersection flanked by a large ship's chandler on one hand and an impressive inn to my right named the Star and Crescent. The structure was some six stories high and featured large windows looking east towards the river. The glass caught the rays of the morning sun and cast bright patches of light into the shadows on the street. The delicious smell of baking breads and pastries wafted from an open kitchen door from which I could hear the sound of someone whistling as they worked. The street was swept clean and flowers in boxes lined the walk along the building's front. Ahead of us, the avenue ended at an impressive gate into the walled enclosure that housed the city's garrison and armory.

We were riding to the right of Helton who had been commenting on the various sites along the way—mostly of statues of famous politicians and soldiers as well as markers commemorating civic projects. There was a tremendous amount of history represented here. Later, when I had the time, I would probably find the same thing to be true in Lumminea.

"The Garrison Fort is only about eight hundred years old," the lieutenant remarked. "The original was left as a heap of rubble after the Great War."

I assumed that he was referring to the conflict that ended in the Peace of a Thousand years, only recently violated by Lunaria's war with Tieben.

Helton continued, "When it was time to rebuild, all of the stone had been used in restoring the city. The architects of the new structure wanted more of a symbol of peaceful authority than a structure of obvious military purpose. Besides, it had been plainly demonstrated that no mere structure could withstand a modern bombardment."

I was constantly reminded of the difference between the way the people of Lunaria thought of time and the way the people in my home town defined history. There were no buildings in Ridgeville much older than a hundred years, and these were mostly flimsy things build of wood that were either impractical to preserve or lacked any significance. Most waited to be torn down and replaced with modern flimsies. The very foundations of my culture were fleeting, whereas Ranaputkin had real roots and a sense of permanence that I found *impressive*, though perhaps the people who lived here might say *confining*.

Here, the old was replaced carefully with great respect. In Ridgeville, I remember that the oldest tree in the area was cut down to make room for a parking lot so that students at the University wouldn't have quite so far to walk to class.

Of course it helped that Lunaria wasn't blessed with endless forests to plunder for the kind of building that went on back home. Here, the abundant material was stone. From my memory of how the Great Forest that began at the edge of Greyhaven radiated power, I didn't think that anyone would give serious thought to plundering those trees in order to build cheaply. Neither of the great forests in the north were approachable in this manner. I wondered what would happen if someone like Torvall Garrund loosed his machines on the trees—major disaster, likely. I shivered.

"Present arms!" The booming voice of Sergeant Tinsmythe startled me from my reverie.

"Daydreaming again?" Pem asked me.

My horse, as usual, had been smarter than I and had stopped obediently by my husband's gelding when Lieutenant Helton had turned to give the sergeant his orders. Immediately ahead of us, the same commands were repeated.

I was looking through the open gates at a path between two double-ranks of mounted soldiers resplendent in the dress uniforms of Lunaria. Four perfectly straight lines of shining swords were raised with their tips pointed to the sky, a glittering array that made my heart race. At the far end of the passage, Major Lorence sat astride his white stallion, his golden helmet polished and his arms crossed on his chest in salute.

I must admit that I felt very proud to be at the center of attention as we rode into the courtyard with Helton and our honor guard behind us. I thought about the delicate position that Pem was in—he the Head of the Communicate and in effect the chief law enforcer of the land with none but the special Palace Guard to back him, and Major Lorence in the Correlate, a man who answered indirectly to Pem but was in the military chain of command. It was a complicated political situation. I was suddenly aware that I had not asked Leandra just how she, as a Sage and Magistrate, was linked with this arrangement in which the Correlate was expected to enforce the commands of the Communicate. I had a flash of intuition about how Garrund might be able to use this to his advantage.

"Well met," Pem hailed the Major and returned the salute as we reined up.

"Yes, Sir," the Major returned. He inclined his head in my direction. "Our warmest greetings to you, my Lady."

"Thank you, Major Lorence," I said. "I look forward to our time together."

Lorence acknowledged my formality with a quick smile. "Yes, my Lady. If you will accompany me, then," he said and turned to Helton. "You may dismiss the men to their duties for the time being, Lieutenant Helton."

"Yes sir!" Helton turned to the sergeant. "Dismiss the men, sergeant."

Tinsmythe rode back between the ranks until he reached the gate, turned, and barked, "Dismissed to duties!"

I would have watched the display of the riding skills involved in breaking formation except that Major Lorence was telling us some of the history of the garrison. I'd met the Major at several functions during our stay and found him interesting, friendly, and someone who felt very solid. If and when we needed friends, I was pretty sure that the Major would count himself among them.

We walked our mounts across the cobbled yard and dismounted in front of the company headquarters. Two rankers waited to take the reins from our hands. I told them that our horses had been fed this morning, but that they might need water after our ride. They inclined their heads without seeming greatly impressed with my title—a business-like attitude that I felt was very much in their favor.

I was thankful that Gilbert had educated me somewhat in the organization and customs of the military. A mounted company was generally assigned to a garrison in a larger city. The military was adjunct to, but not in lieu of, the civilian guard which was under the authorities of the local government and, in times of unrest, acted like additional foot soldiers. Gilbert had told me that this force could be expanded, albeit somewhat slowly, during times of trouble to a regiment nominally composed of six companies. The extra men came from a pool of officers and men that were scattered throughout Lunaria in regional posts. There was no standing army as such. "There is no budget for a national army," Gilbert had said in response to my fumbling description of the military in my former world.

In peacetime, Major Lorence would have about 180 men and horse to call upon. Many of these would be out on patrols around the area. While the region around Ranaputkin was considered peaceful, nevertheless there were the usual lawless elements that managed to earn a living by nibbling at the margins of the civilized area. The patrols saw to it that such activities did not operate too close to the city. Darcil had described the lands to the south and west as being particularly troublesome.

Two orderlies saluted and opened the thick, polished double doors for us as we walked into the building. Inside, I admired the tile floors inlaid with battle scenes as well as the carved wood paneling depicting scenes of city life. The headquarters building was not at all like the austere military construction that I had imagined. On the other hand, the offices bustled with the feel of efficiency and purpose. In spite of the somewhat lavish surroundings, there was no lack of discipline.

Lorence spoke to a middle aged man with captain's bars who had risen hastily from his desk and saluted us. "If you will see to it that we are not disturbed," he said.

"Yes, Sir," the officer snapped to attention. His eyes moved past the major and widened slightly as he saw me standing with Pem.

I had to suppress a smile. I did not need to be introduced. I'd seen Captain Nyrin with Gilbert quite some time ago as he was delivering a report into Lord Greybaird's hands at the Palace. We were never introduced; he probably thought that I was a simple staffer. It seemed that Gilbert had his eyes everywhere.

"If it pleases you, we will go to my office where the men have laid out morning fruit and pastries along with fresh tarle and tea," the major said after introducing Captain Nyrin as his Executive Officer.

I pretended to be impressed. "Food sounds wonderful," I said. "The fresh air has given me an appetite. I'd love a bite to eat and a cool refreshment. Then you take us about and show us whatever you think we need to see."

"I think we can dispense with the formalities," Pem added. "I'd rather receive your verbal assessment of the situation before I read a report that will be padded by your Sergeant after it leaves your hands."

The three of us laughed and the major relaxed. "You have the right of it," he admitted. "A commander has less control over his budget than he'd like to believe."

We climbed two flights of stairs and walked past a ranker standing at attention outside a door with the simple inscription Major Lorence. His office was even more organized that I had expected. I observed that the books on the shelves looked worn with use, the desk was polished but scarred, and the windows were clean. There was little of the luxuries that one might have found in a similar office in Lumminea. The only personal touch was a framed portrait of a pretty woman squared up on one corner of his desk. The artist was quite accomplished, and I wondered who had painted it. I stepped to look through the window glass and caught sight of the Rachael Ann lying alongside the wharf.

"You have a beautiful view," I observed.

"Lately I forget to look," Lorence returned. "Our patrols have been busier than usual across the river. There have even been several incidents at the shipyards on this side of the river. When the patrols are busy, I get more paperwork."

I could tell that the major was chafing at being desk-bound and yearned for some time in the field.

"Directed against whom?" Pem wanted to know.

"Mostly against the Ranapui's operation," Lorence said. "It's nothing too serious. Some thefts of metals, one fire that burned some fuel stocks, and a crane that was sabotaged so that it collapsed in the middle of lifting a hull section into place. Fortunately no one was injured."

"What about the weapons shops?" Pem asked him. "Doesn't Lord Orumundi keep an operation going here?"

"One of the foundries across the river belongs to Lord Orumundi. He hasn't complained of any losses. His machine shops and finished weapons on this side of the river are safe from raiding."

"Who is your second in command?" I asked Lorence.

"Captain Stringer," he said. "Good man. Out with Third Patrol and Lieutenant Coolan to the southwest. He rotates his support between the two areas with Captain Nyrin. He figures Coolan and Sergeant Eudard lead the best patrol we have. "

"What is Lieutenant Helton's position here?" Pem asked.

"Helton is in command of First Patrol which is in rotation at the moment. He's young, but he's learning fast and Sergeant Tinsmythe is careful. I have hopes that Helton will live long enough to become a good officer."

"I meant to ask you earlier," I said. "Does Captain Nyrin have a daughter named Nyri?" I'd learned that sons and daughters were often named using variations of a parent's name.

"Yes," Lorence said. "Charming young woman. Maybe a bit spoiled. The Captain dotes on her, and her mother died a few years back."

"She is one of Ribecah Ranapui's friends," I returned. "She seemed like a nice girl. I just wondered if there were a connection."

"Our mess has provided our best fruits and pastries," Lorence indicated a table covered with a starched white cloth and silver dishes laden with sweet rolls and assortments of sliced fruits. "I will be most pleased to serve you myself. I apologize for the lack of service, but having an orderly with us would be like advertising whatever we talked about with the entire garrison."

"We will serve ourselves," Pem held up his hand. "In this room I consider myself a soldier on a campaign trail first, a ruler second. A politician not at all," he grinned.

If it had not been for the major's presence I might have hugged dear Pem for his naïve honesty. It was a moment like this when I knew that I had married the right man. The major also looked impressed.

"Queen Rachael said much the same thing to me," Lorence returned and looked pained. I could only surmise that Pem's mother had left the same larger-than-life impression with most of her people. Pem was obviously pleased to be compared with his mother.

"What happened to the young man who threatened me," I asked the major out of curiosity. I'd heard part of the story from Pem, but I wanted to hear it from the major because it would speak to local politics.

"Ah, young Giles Siegert," Lorence said with a pained expression. "The young fool has been sent off on a ship to start his year's exile. After his year onboard the cargo ship, he will be allowed to return, under parole, to this city where he will spend another year under our watchful eye."

"I appreciate the help and advice that Magister Leandra gave us. She was a witness to the incident when Giles attacked you, and she was the one to suggest the temporary exile. It was the least inflammatory solution we could apply. In particular, I thank you for your tolerance, Lady Claire. This is a volatile situation with his family who controls a great deal of the banking in the city."

"They didn't approve of the year's exile?" I asked.

"No, though of course they're relieved that we didn't just pull him aside and shoot him," the major said in a fashion that let me know that he was speaking tongue-in-cheek. "These people think very highly of themselves. I'm a mere major."

"But you are in the royal trust," Pem declared hotly, "and that is all that they should need to know."

"Yes, well it's not my place to say," Lorence said, hesitating, "but even kings need to borrow money, if you see what I mean." Pem may have colored slightly, but I don't think he took offence at what Lorence said. The major was simply being a careful politician in his home town.

"Poor Catha," I murmured, more for myself than for the others.

"Yes, I hear that the girl was shipped off to relatives in Akren in order to avoid what they considered to be a scandal," Lorence said.

I walked to the table with the food and picked out a pastry with a butter icing and fruit topping. The pastry melted in my mouth. I let the butter and berry-compote roll around on my tongue and closed my eyes.

"If I'd known that they cooked this way in the military, I'd have considered a career in the army," I said, opening my eyes.

The major looked amused while Pem looked worried. I laughed.

"Fortunately, I have a much better job," I finished my outburst.

"Perhaps a much more difficult one," the major remarked, saluting me in a respectful manner, but with humor.

Pem remained worried. I realized belatedly why and felt my cheeks redden.

"Not like your mother," I said hastily. "I have no pressing need to charge uphill into a line of tough, hill-country rebels bent on killing me."

"Queen Rachael was brave but foolhardy," Pem sighed.

She didn't have my sword, as well. I kept the thought to myself.

I picked out one last pastry and savored its flavor. I was enjoying the attention of the two males, but we needed to change the subject.

"What of your surveillance of the entrance to the labyrinth under the palace?" I asked the major. Pem had requested Lorence's cooperation that night when we returned from the chamber of the Black Stone. Neither of us had felt it necessary to reveal to the major exactly what was in the tunnel.

"I asked Sergeant Tinsmythe to place a man in a hidden position so that the entrance could be watched night and day. So far there have been no reports of anyone entering or leaving."

I was disappointed but not terribly surprised. "I suppose the person we encountered has finished their business and didn't find a reason to return," I said. I didn't believe my own statement, but it was useless to continue the watch and told the major that he might withdraw his men. He seemed much relieved.

"SHALL WE PRESS on, Major," I smiled sweetly at Lorence as I wiped my hands on a fresh steamed towel pulled from a basket.

"Certainly, My Lady," Major Lorence returned to a more formal mode—at least he didn't call me Your Highness.

Lorence stepped to the door and had a few words with the ranker outside.

"I sent for three men to accompany us. We should be ready in a few recips," he turned to us. Pem stuffed his last pastry, heavy with figs and dripping honey, in his mouth. He finished wiping his hands and caught the juice making its way down his chin. "Ready," he sighed.

We toured the barracks and viewed rows of perfectly-kept bunks—the kind that my father would have described as hard enough to bounce a quarter. The floors were polished to a mirror's finish, and the glass in the windows was so clean that I couldn't tell whether or not it was there. Pem kept nodding his approval while I thought about the spit-and-polish way that Mags kept my quarters in spite of my slovenly tendencies. I couldn't help but think about the dirty clothes piles in front of Mother's washer and the dirty dishes in the sink. Dad would have hated it.

This thought in turn led me to wonder if I'd really visited my father in a vision. Was the old man faithfully taking care of him? Surely he must long since recovered . Maybe all I had experienced was nothing more than a comforting dream. I pushed the thought firmly out of my mind.

We admired the perfectly groomed horses and the fresh straw-strewn stalls in the stables. Our own horses had been provided with separate quarters and were being spoiled with sweetened seed cakes. The Stable Master was an older soldier who reminded me of Reyfort—all business, but kindly in his attitude towards humans and horses. He was wearing a heavy leather apron over his uniform and was inspecting the shoeing of one of the animals.

"You can't be too careful," he said. "These horses are ridden on pavement for much of their time which means that shoes have to be constantly replaced. We are testing a new alloy shoe that wears better and is lighter than the old iron ones. The shipyards make them for us out of scrap shielding plate. The farrier complains that they are harder to size than the old ones, but I figure it saves us a lot of lame horses."

Outside the stables, I confessed to the major, "I've never given much thought to the shoeing of horses. A tougher, lighter metal makes sense to me. The horses would be faster and more agile in battle."

Lorence and Pem both looked pleased at my observation. "It is an experiment, Your Grace," Lorence said.

"If it is successful, we will adopt the practice for all our horses," Pem said enthusiastically.

I thought of the cost and Gilbert's probable reaction. I hoped Pem would have his budget proposal hammered out to the last detail before suggesting such a scheme.

"Yes, a wonderful idea," I murmured. We drifted across another courtyard at the back of the complex and arrived at the edge of a small grassy field backed by a low hill with the compound wall circling along the top.

A number of men were practice-fencing while a small crowd of off-duty officers and enlisted men were watching the action. Loud suggestions and guffaws accompanied each man's efforts.

"Higher, keep your guard higher!" a man who must have been a trainer was shouting at a young soldier. "No, not like that!" he yelled as the older man slipped under the younger man's guard and struck what must have been a rib-bruising blow to his body. The two combatants drew apart, breathing heavily, and planted their wooden practice swords in the grass.

I spotted Sergeant Tinsmythe engaging Lieutenant Helton on the other side of the field. I could hear the clang of metal against metal as the glittering blades wove a pattern with the green hillside as a background. From his easy manner, I could tell that the sergeant was playing with the lieutenant and that the lieutenant was growing angry. The less-experienced officer was trying too hard to penetrate the sergeant's defenses.

Tinsmythe moved into the envelopment, a fencing move I learned from Reyfort, which spun the officer's blade in a circle and sent the weapon spinning out of Helton's hands. It landed point first in the ground not far from the pair.

"He's very good," Pem observed, sharing my interest in Helton and Tinsmythe.

"Yes, the sergeant is an excellent swordsman, the best we have, and a sort of local champion," Lorence remarked.

I surprised myself by what I did next. "I'm out of practice," I began—which was true. Pem and I hadn't had a practice session in fencing since aboard the Rachael Ann between the Southern Beaches and Ranaputkin.

"Perhaps you would allow me and Sergeant Tinsmythe to practice for a short period? I'm sure I'd learn a lot from the sergeant."

Pem looked surprised; the major looked distressed. "Why would you want to do that, Your Highness," Lorence managed to get out.

I took his use of the formal address to be a measure of his distress.

"Not that I question your request," he added hastily, reddening slightly at the breach of etiquette. One did not speak to one's queen that way.

Of course, I wasn't the least offended. "Please forgive me, Major. I did not mean to be the cause of any distress. I was simply proposing a short practice session to loosen up my sadly neglected sword arm."

I couldn't have said, exactly, but I supposed that I was thinking about how we, the royal couple, appeared to the major and his troops. Major Lorence had exhibited nothing but flawless hospitality and an easy and friendly attitude towards us that spoke of trust and loyalty. However, in the rest of his men, I sensed an attitude, not of a lack of respect, but a certain resignation to having to deal with what they were bound to consider largely figureheads of government.

I suddenly had what I might have described, if I'd had time to think about it, a vision of our future in which it became very important, to ordinary soldiers as well as to the officer corps, that Pem and I be seen as the kind of leaders that were willing to be up front. Not, I think, in a foolish gallop headlong into danger, but in service and sacrifice in the same measure as they were willing to give for their families and their land. It was my land as well. I felt my blood flow hot and my heart leap. Yes, there was a purpose I had to seize, and this seemed to be the moment to seize it, here in this city of Ranaputkin, in this relatively obscure garrison, under the eyes of some of our friends and no doubt a few of our undeclared enemies.

So I smiled my best smile at the major and looked expectant while Pem looked suspicious and was puzzling over my sudden interest in exercise.

Friendly Play

.THE MAJOR MOTIONED .to one of the soldiers who accompanied us. "Tell Sergeant Tinsmythe that he should finish with the lieutenant and see me."

"Sir, yes sir," the man saluted and rushed off to get the sergeant.

Tinsmythe arrived with the ranker almost immediately. "Sir?"

"Her Highness would like to enjoy a bit of swordplay for exercise," Lorence said. "She was impressed with your workout with Lieutenant Helton."

The sergeant turned from the major and managed a surprisingly graceful bow in my direction. "Of course, Highness," he said courteously. As he looked up, our eyes locked momentarily. He seemed friendly enough on the surface, but his gaze was more cool and calculating. I felt a small thrill of anticipation that surprised me.

"Shall I get a practice sword for you?" he asked.

"I think that the one I'm carrying will do," I returned. "Surely both of us are experienced enough to cross blades without harming each other. It is only friendly play." Pem flinched and I saw a brief rise of the sergeant's brow.

"Of course," the sergeant responded, his voice hearty and his expression friendly. His eyes, though, were cold.

"See here, Highness," Lorence interrupted. "I'm not comfortable with the Queen of Lunaria risking crossing naked blades in my practice field. What if you are hurt? I don't want the responsibility."

"I am distressed that you lack confidence in me and the sergeant," I smiled coolly at the major. "We shall be exceedingly careful, won't we, Sergeant?"

"Infinitely so," the sergeant replied.

"Perhaps you are worried that I might accidently do you harm?" I asked the sergeant.

"No, Highness, I can take care of myself. Do not worry on my account." There was an air of self-assurance about the sergeant that grated on my nerves.

"Shall we," I nodded in the direction of the field.

"A moment if you please. I wish to speak with the Queen," Pem said. He put his hand out. "We will join you at the field," he said to Lorence and Tinsmythe.

The major and the sergeant walked over to the gate into the field. The noisy crowd quieted down as if they were aware that something interesting was about to take place.

"Claire," Pem whispered urgently, "this is dangerous as well as unseemly. I should be the one challenging the sergeant to swordplay."

"I know, and I'm sorry, husband," I returned. "I have just glimpsed a future in which it is important to do this thing. I do not believe there will be any slight of your honor. I promise it won't happen again without my first consulting with you. In any case, don't worry. I'm wearing my camisole which is made from Everweave cloth. I am well protected."

I don't think this, in any way, mollified Pem, but it did convince him that I was determined in my course of action.

"Well, if you must, be careful," he said heatedly.

Feeling guilty, I patted his hand. "Everything will be fine," I assured him. Unless he cuts my head off. I peeled off my short jacket and handed it to him and then added my hat to his load.

Pem looked around but there was no one to hand them to. I hoped that I knew what I was doing because the sergeant was a formidable swordsman and there was something about him that reminded me of Captain Dread. I slid my sword from its sheath, the metal ringing in the still morning air.

The small crowd of officers and men parted in front of me as I approached the gate to the open field. "Let us find a place and begin," I told the sergeant.

"As you wish," the sergeant bowed low to me. The men were whispering among themselves.

The grass still held drops of morning dew; the sun warmed my back through the thin cotton of my overshirt. The sergeant grinned as if he knew that I was taking the favored position with the sun in his eyes, but he gave no indication that he minded. He stood relaxed waiting for me to signal that I was ready.

When I extended my blade, he drew and held the tip out, almost touching mine, but not quite engaged. Everything was exactly as it should be. The Sword of Training fairly quivered in my hands, either infected by my excitement, or else expressing an emotion of its own. I remembered that the Sword had a life of its own, but I didn't understand how it worked or why. I believed that it drew power from me and substance from the world around it. I extended slightly and touched Tinsmythe's blade, signaling that we could begin.

I watched his sword, not his eyes—an elementary strategy. The eyes could and often did deceive. I felt him shift his stance slightly as we drew back to give the traditional salute. He would go for the quick thrust. I let my sword tip sag slightly, inviting the move. The sergeant grinned, evidently thinking that he was facing an amateur rather than someone who had removed the head of quite a few barbarians. "So much for respect," I muttered to myself.

I watched his move develop—the Sword gave me the ability to anticipate. I saw that he would stop short, playing with me. I was in no danger from his thrust. I surprised him by slipping his thrust and sliding his blade outside of mine, leaving him open for a move of my own had I been so inclined. I decided he was too clever an opponent to be taken in and had either used the opening gambit to gauge my skills or else he had a very good reverse backhand slash. I stepped back and gave him a small smile.

"Well done, sergeant," I said. I saw the flicker of anger in his eyes though his smile remained warm.

We went back and forth like this for several minutes, continuing to feel each other out. The men clapped and cheered each time I blocked one of the sergeant's moves. I didn't let myself be distracted. I knew I was playing a dangerous game.

Sweat trickled down between my breasts. I felt the damp circle under my arms. I saw the beads of sweat on Tinsmythe's forehead. From behind me I heard the mating call of the common blue-tailed hawk. A vision of the icehawk circling in Tieben flashed in front of me. The sword in my hand settled as well, as if listening for something.

"Have we warmed up enough?" I asked the sergeant.

"I believe so, Highness," he answered in a low voice and launched an all-out attack.

My defenses sagged briefly as I retreated under his strong assault. Tinsmythe had the longer arms and my sword was shorter than his. As we crossed blades, I felt the balance in the Sword shift slightly as the metal extended in length to make up the difference. A puzzled expression grew on the sergeant's face as he tried furiously to slash through my defenses, but I met him stroke for stroke, though if this were to continue for long, I would tire before he did. The crowd had gone silent and Lorence was yelling at Tinsmythe to slow down.

I stopped retreating and traded blows with the sergeant's blade. The sharp clang of steel against steel echoed from the hillside, from the buildings in the compound, and from the compound wall which circled over the hill behind me. I started pressing back, my blade flashing in a blue blur, as I regained all the ground that I had lost. The crowd was going wild now.

Suddenly Tinsmythe disengaged and backed away hurriedly. "Enough!" he cried. "I fear that I might hurt you."

My sword had stopped just short of his chest. The crowd jeered. "She bested you," someone yelled. I stayed focused on his blade, just in case he changed his mind.

"I ordered you to stand down, Sergeant," Lorence said forcefully.

"You might have hurt the Queen," Pem threatened.

"Gentlemen," I interrupted. "The Sergeant and I were merely learning each other's moves. Isn't this not so, Sergeant?"

The sergeant bowed low to me, and the major had nothing more to say. I retrieved my hat, jammed it on my head, and pulled my jacket over my damp overshirt. As we were behind schedule, we moved quickly through the rest of our tour. The rumors of my swordplay with Sergeant Tinsmythe had spread before me, and Pem and I got a lot of approving looks. Like casting a small stone in a large pool, what happened this morning would spread widely across the pond. I could sense that Pem was anxious to talk alone with me, but there would be no opportunity until we got back to our quarters at the Ranapui's Estate.

The major, who had behaved rather stiffly throughout the remainder of our inspection, looked relieved when I thanked him warmly for the chance to inspect the garrison. I said, "I foresee that our paths will cross again." I extended my hand, and he bent over it. Really, this kind of behavior was very flattering to an ordinary girl from Ridgeville, Texas.

Once again we passed between ranks of the Second Patrol, this time on our way out the main gates in company with Lieutenant Helton and his men. Tinsmythe was wearing a fresh uniform and trying to avoid looking in my direction.

I wondered if I'd see Major Lorence again. The problem with being the Queen, I was learning, was that my list of friends grew shorter every day as I moved on to the next set of duties and obligations. If I didn't forge strong bonds quickly, I would wind up isolated and alone with Pem. Under me, my little mare snorted and sidestepped a loose cobble. Beside me, Pem kept his eyes straight ahead and his reins pulled so tight that his mount pranced about uneasily. I wondered what was occupying his mind.

I rode on one side of Lieutenant Helton as he chatted on in high spirits while we wended our way back through Ranaputkin. His anger with his sergeant seemed to be forgotten for the moment. When we parted company at the Ranapui's Estate, I managed to lean in close and speak to him privately. "He's not that good, Lieutenant. Keep your guard higher inside and watch his sword, not his eyes. Let him make the first move."

Helton nodded, looking interested and thoughtful. "I appreciate your attention, Highness."

From the way the lieutenant looked at me, I thought he probably had other thoughts as well. It was mildly flattering to be regarded in such high esteem by a handsome young officer, but I reminded myself that his interest was probably motivated more by my position than by my person.

"What secret do you share with the lieutenant?" Pem wanted to know as we walked our horses up to where the Ranapui's Master-of-Horse was waiting, flanked by two grooms.

Did I detect a flicker of jealousy in his eyes? "Only how to handle a blade with his sergeant," I said. Pem dismounted and I let him help me slide from my saddle to one of the mounting blocks. The day had turned out as hot as I had predicted, and my hair hung in damp strings under my hat. Pem made a comment about the awful heat.

"We could try a cooling bath," I suggested, leering provocatively at him. Truthfully, the swordplay had left me keyed up. A little splashing around with my husband seemed a marvelous way to get rid of the extra adrenaline.

Pem colored, as if reading my thoughts. Perhaps he was remembering the day he spied on me while I was bathing in the stream after we'd escaped through the great gate into Lunaria. Men are strange that way.

He drew a deep breath. "Perhaps later," he sighed. "I have pressing business with Farold before we leave tomorrow. We will need to talk about your behavior at the garrison. While I think it was quite remarkable, I also think it was foolish."

In spite of his criticism, I could tell that Pem was proud of me. "Thank you—at least for the praise," I returned, trying not to bristle at his other words. "Later I will tell you what I think we accomplished at the garrison today, and then we will see what you think."

<u>Ordinary Things</u>

A WHILE LATER I was lying on a table padded with towels in the bathing room. Pem had gone off on business and Mags was rubbing some soothing oils into the muscles of my back and sword arm.

"Evidently my invitation to Pem was not attractive enough," I said gloomily to Mags. "He has such strong hands."

"Ouch!" Mags had gouged a palm into my upper back.

"Ah!" The tightness melted away leaving my shoulder feeling relaxed and marvelous.

"I'm sure his hands are strong," Mags said, "but does he have my skills?"

"There is that, of course," I admitted hastily.

Mags put a thumb on either side of my neck and rotated the pressure. I almost fainted with pleasure. "I think I will reserve Pem's skills for other diversions," I said.

"A wise move," Mags slapped my backside and dragged me upright while my skin was still tingling. "Now get dressed. You have an early dinner and I have to finish your packing. We leave early in the morning which means that your luggage will leave for the ship tonight."

"Someday I will say no to your orders," I protested feebly, and then broke out giggling, ending in hiccups.

Mags draped a soft robe over me and handed me a glass of juice. "It's granapple," she said.

The Last Supper

THE EARLY DINNER was a private affair with Lord Farold and Lady Sidra attending. Faroldson was out for the night, Darcil was off with Nikko preparing the ship for departure, and Ribecah was saying goodbye to her friends. Our conversation mostly turned around affairs in Ranaputkin, notably the Ranapui's shipyards and plans for increased trade.

Lord Farold managed to get in a subtle hint concerning dredging and improvements in the harbor facilities, and Lady Sidra slipped in a warning about sending Ribecah into danger. It was a pleasant enough time, but I thought the grazer steak was a bit overdone and the berry tart too sweet. I had to remind myself that we were here at the Ranapui's expense. Even if they were discharging their traditional obligations to the Crown, I had little reason to be overcritical.

The stories that my grandmother had told me about medieval hospitality suggested that visiting royalty often got rat stew in disguise. I'm certain that the Ranapuis managed to do better than that, but I did look suspiciously at the fish soup which neither Sidra nor Farold had touched.

"Where will you be visiting?" Sidra asked me politely.

"It was most kind to allow Darcil to act as our pilot and guide up the Copper River," I said. "I expect he will return with our ship from Akren while we make plans to go forward from Akren to Malbreck via a trader landship and escort. Trader Mara Ellendor has so kindly provided these for our use."

Both Sidra and Farold looked surprised. Sidra said, "Indeed, that is a great honor."

"Yes. Her daughter Rissa and I are close friends. We have shared several adventures," I returned.

"Who will you be visiting? If I may ask, of course," Sidra blushed.

I didn't blame her for asking. I figured that Sidra would be calculating who her possible rivals would be. Farold was occupied with a large mouthful of grazer meat.

"I'd be delighted to tell you," I returned.

"We will be visiting Lord Wetzar and Lady Alcinia in Akren," Pem interrupted me, having turned his attention to us for conversation. "House Hussani's mining and mineral interests are very important to Lunaria. After that, we will be the guests of Lord Emorie and Lady Juditha in Malbreck. Our land cannot do without the wood that House Lantrus provides. The timing is fortunate The Council is adjourned for the season, and all the lords of the Great Houses are in residence.

I said, "I do so look forward to visiting with the Durgaas family in Drieven. I have visited the city only once, and I find the White Tower and the stories fascinating."

"Lord Halex and Lady Uda are very wealthy," Sidra audibly sighed, unconsciously twisting the plain gold wedding band on her finger.

"They certainly enjoy the benefits of handling large sums of other people's money," Pem said with a straight face.

The barbed comment brought a fit of coughing from Farold, who was still trying to master the mouthful of meat he had been chewing. Serves you right for serving old meat, I thought.

"I don't get to travel very much," Sidra said wistfully.

Farold, who had finally managed to wash the gristle down with a glass of wine, grunted, "I'd be most happy if you'd travel with me to Lumminea and spend time in the capitol while I attend the Council meetings."

"Who would look after the estates while you are gone?" Sidra put forth.

I got the feeling that this was an old argument between them and that Sidra wasn't as keen on travel as she pretended. Perhaps Sidra desired another kind of freedom—one she couldn't attain if she were to accompany Farold to Lumminea. Maybe she was growing restless with taking care of a business that was supposed to be her husband's domain. Columns of figures and numberless reports could become dreadfully boring no matter where your talents lay.

"The children are grown. Our oldest son can take care of the place," Farold said.

"Yes, yes of course," she returned, but I didn't think she was actually listening to her husband. She turned to me.

"You must find it a relief to be away from the cares and duties at the Palace," she said.

"Actually, dispatches seem to arrive almost daily. Work seems to follows us everywhere," I returned.

"Of course, being the Queen must be terribly complicated," Sidra said without much conviction. I supposed that she thought that my life was like a continuous vacation.

"There never seems to be much spare time," I said, hoping in vain to elicit even a spark of sympathy. The voluminous amount of correspondence was enough make me want to scream. Mags was up late every night replying in my name to an endless series of invitations, thank you notes for gifts, and giving answers to solicitations that were marked urgent by one of more of the stewards that took care of the daily routines. I hadn't realized to what extent I'd be Pem's social secretary when I took the job as Queen—and this was on my honeymoon! I'd have to get Tess to organize me and hire some help when I returned. Thank goodness she was taking care of managing the vineyards! I still hadn't met all the new staff at my estate. All I knew is that Tess showed me a steady stream of figures that indicated a positive cash flow.

Eventually we made our excuses and managed to bring an end to our meal before Sidra could order out a third dessert.

On The Road Again

MAGS WAS GONE .with the luggage when I returned from
the dinner with the Ranapuis. Pem had stayed for another last-
minute conference with Farold—I wondered what they talked
about and then decided that it was likely that they were having a
brandy and talking about, well, whatever men talk about. I didn't
care for strong drink, so that was alright with me.

Also, I was relieved to have an excuse to avoid a discussion
of my behavior with Pem. There would be time enough on our trip
up the river to sort that out.

Mags had laid out my sleeping garments as well as my travel
clothes for the morning. She had left a note saying that she would
return before midnight and that all my possessions would be safely
aboard the Rachael Ann. It had been a long day! I snuggled under
the covers and never heard Mags come in.

Mags awakened me just at daybreak. "Time to get up, my
Lady," she said, yawning. I thought I caught the suspicious aroma
of wine on her breath. I couldn't help but yawn in sympathy and
swung my feet to the chilly floor. I dutifully accepted the cup of
strong tarle that she thrust into my hands. A few sleepy chirps of
a bird outside my window expressed my feelings exactly.

Mags stuffed a pastry in my mouth when I paused for my
second yawn and began pitching items of clothing at me. I dressed
hurriedly, leaving a few crumbs on the inside of my overshirt.
There was a knock on the door between my suite and Pem's.

"I suppose that is my husband," I said to Mags, asking her
to throw the bolt on the door.

"It isn't locked," Mags returned as Pem walked into my
bedroom. I finished tucking my overshirt into my pants and
fumbled with the button of my fly while Mags stood discreetly

between me and Pem until I had made myself presentable. I still
didn't understand these customs between married people, but
Mags was quite firm about appearances.

"I talked Farold out of any farewell ceremonies," Pem
informed us. "We can slip aboard the Rachael Ann and cast off
without any more of these confounded public appearances," he
added. "Sage Leandra will be joining us for the ride down to the
harbor."

I was a little surprised at Pem's lack of enthusiasm. He
usually liked public appearances as it gave us the opportunity to
present ourselves favorably to the general citizenry. Maybe I'd
underestimated his desire to be moving on. Lately I'd thought that
I had developed that same need to look over the next hill to the
valley beyond. It wasn't because I thought I'd see something
different. I believed that I had developed a taste for the journey
itself over the need to arrive.

Doubtless this would change over the next few months. So
many people had told me how children forced them to settle down.
I wondered if that were really true, or had this been their excuse.
After all, Granny Miller had raised my father while traveling from
place to place in—where? I couldn't remember her ever telling me
where her travels had taken her. As a child, I had always assumed
that her travels were around Texas which was a very large place to
me. She could have meant to include the United States or Europe.
Basically I had no idea.

I smiled to myself. No one I had known back home would
ever have adventures such as mine.

"Daydreaming again?" Pem aroused me from my
conjecture. The carriage that was to take us to the docks was
waiting in front of me. Our escort, six mounted guards, shifted in
their saddles. An overnight dew had left the air rich and heavy with

the smells of wet grass on adjacent fields. I accepted Pem's hand and mounted the step into the carriage, settling into the comfortable leather seats which someone had thoughtfully dried off.

Our driver inclined his head to acknowledge us. The harness jingled cheerfully as one of the pair of horses snorted and threw his head around to nip at a sudden itch. Pem joined me, a comfortably warm body by my side. Sage Leandra appeared and took the seat opposite us, spreading a light blanket over her lap and feet.

"Old people need protection from the chill," she said primly.

"Greetings, Sage," Pem said. "We have not seen much of you since we arrived in Ranaputkin."

"I have been busy with my own affairs," she waved her hands about as if her affairs were either nebulous or inconsequential—something that I very much doubted.

"Major Lorence was very complimentary of your help with the case of the young man who attacked me," I said just as our carriage lurched into motion. The metal-shod wheels of our transport clattered loudly on the stone paving. I had to lean forward to hear her comment.

"Young Giles is very lucky," she said tartly. "Many officers in Major Lorence's position would not have acted so wisely. They would have sought to curry your favor by having the boy executed."

I shuddered. "That would not have pleased me in the least."

The people of the city still lay quiet in the early hours, sleeping lightly in that moment before truly awakening, those who were lucky trying to hold onto their dreams of love and riches and those caught in the web of darkness and evil trying to escape into the light of day.

We reached the docks without incident and boarded the Rachael Ann. Nikko waited by the gangplank, saluted us when we came aboard, and bowed low to Sage Leandra. I wondered what he had done this time and whether Leandra would demand his confession.

I broke with this formality by grabbing Nikko and planting a kiss on each cheek, watching pink bloom across his suntanned face. Pem neither approved nor resented my affection for Nikko and gave the officer a hearty slap across the back, asking him if the ship were ready to sail.

"She's ready for her journey up the river, Sir. I'd be nervous because she's not shallow drafted, but having Darcil Ranapui as our guide and one of the Trader's pilots aboard, I think we need not fear any misadventure."

As we stood around on the foredeck, I let my thoughts reach towards Rissa and Turlo who were on their own urgent mission somewhere far to the north. The Crown, probably my life, rested upon their success. Without Tieben as our ally, the Council was sure to challenge the Monarchy—that is, Pem and me.

I hadn't been able to cast my thoughts widely and retrieve images from the great owls and the more intelligent hawks since leaving the vicinity of Greyhaven and the Great Forest. I would have liked to summon an icehawk to fly north to spy out Rissa and Turlo and allay my fears even as Pem had journeyed in a dream with the great raptor to find me in Trappers Haven. He had seen Captain Dread attacking me through the icehawk's eyes. He was able to do this because he had been traveling up the banks of the River Songris which flowed from the heart of the Great Forest.

I trembled as I recalled how, in glancing upwards toward the icehawk when I sensed Pem's presence, Dread had nearly taken my head off.

"Something wrong, dear?" Leandra asked me.

The image of a beautiful, grassy meadow filled with colorful flowers flashed before me. A dark cloud was looming on the horizon. A dire chill settled in my heart. On impulse I said, "I suddenly fear for Rissa and Turlo. I sense they are about to go into great danger that they do not guess at." I told the Sage of my vision.

"I know," Leandra answered back. "I saw it as well. I do not know what it means."

I rubbed my eyes as if this would blot out the brief vision I had experienced. I said, "I thought maybe I was troubled because of the uncertainties on the journey before me, but now I think it a message about the future."

The great engine of the little ship vibrated beneath our feet as the Rachael Ann slid back from the docks and swung her bow towards the main channel of the Copper River.

"The future is best left to itself," Leandra said and remained silent on the subject long afterward.

About the Authors

Charles and Lydia Frenzel, writing as L.C. Frenzel, share the caring side of their lives with imagination and humor to craft adventure and mystery stories based on hard science.

They have lived on a yacht near New Orleans and in the gold mining area of California, in Kentucky, Texas, and Pacific Northwest. Charles is an artist, a writer, and a scientist. He combines left and right brain styles of attention. As a young man, he was on President's Eisenhower's Science Advisory Board and invited to appear on the "$64,000 Question." His art appears from Australia to England. With the age of Google, Charles is quoted by everyone, including the Chinese.

Lydia, "Water Witch of the West," covered the oil patch of Southern Louisiana, coal mining in California and rust and paint on ships. Her favorite project was conservation of Saturn V rockets and the Titanic "Big Piece".

Our characters are struck from the die of real life. The young people who worked and sometimes bled with us in our oil-patch adventures were often brave and almost always possessing a keen sense of humor. They proved to us that the future of our world is in rather capable hands.

Visit the web sites at:

www.charlesfrenzel.com,   www.lydiafrenzel.com, www.lunarianepic.com,   www.enneachronicles.com

Readers Guide to the World of Ennea

Readers Guide: 6/10/2017

Contents

OverView

The Chronicles of Ennea depicts paradise lost and then reborn by people who are changed fundamentally in ways that they could never imagine by their encounters with each other.

Claire Fisher Miller, a child of twentieth century earth, is the product of parents that are incompatible, a father that is loving but driven to adventure, and a mother who sees virtue in ordinariness.

Claire feels unneeded – except by her grandmother, Wendy, whom her mother Guinn dislikes and mistrusts. When her father goes missing in Iraq, Claire feels lost. Two years later, her mother gives up on her MIA husband and takes up with her preacher. Feeling alone and relatively unwanted, Claire is ripe for a profound experience in life. She meets a boy her age who guides her through a mysterious Gate into another world.

In Lunaria, Claire is befriended by powerful Councilor Greybaird who senses that there is a new power in the land that will heal rifts, and bring a new beginning. Lunaria is an ancient and sophisticated civilization struggling against the return of forbidden technologies proscribed a thousand years earlier in a terrible war. The resources of the world have to be balanced against excesses of usage. Claire, who thinks of herself as an ordinary girl, is torn between fulfilling a destiny to change Lunaria for the good or to return to her own home to seek her lost father.

Map of Lunaria

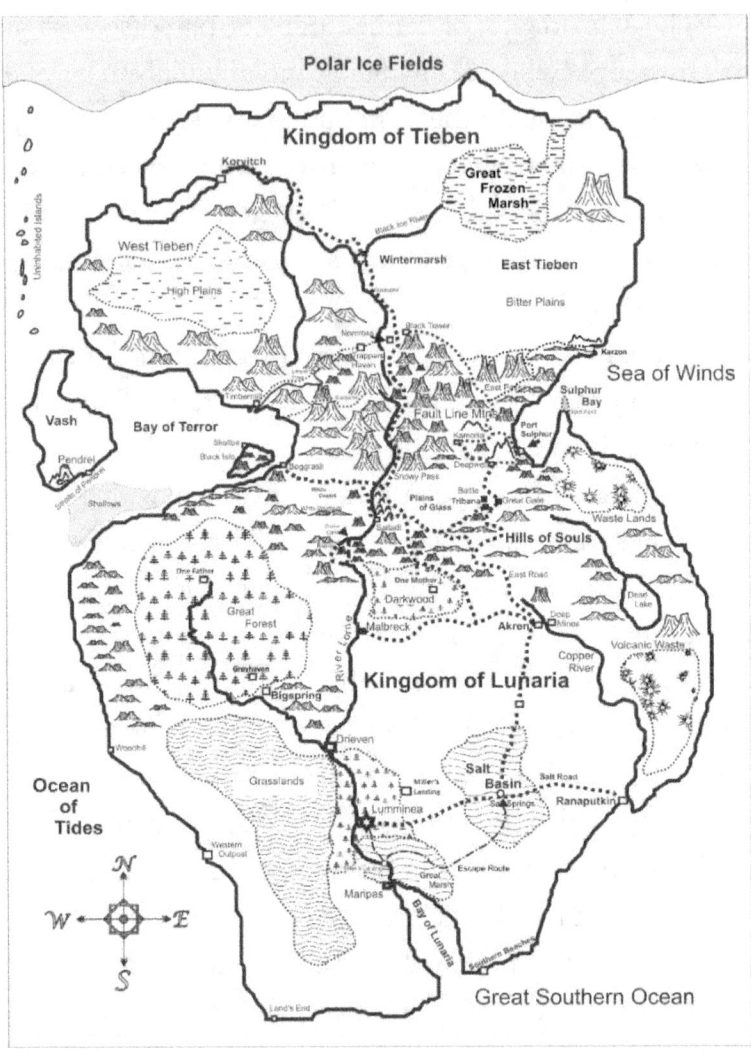

Map of Lunaria

Government

Eccollate

A powerful class of professionals who act as the judiciary as well as the tax collectors, trade and tariff regulators in Lunaria. The Eccollate generally answers to the High Counsel, though the Eccollate is also controlled to some extent by the presence of the Sages who form the judiciary arm of the Eccollate.

The Eccollate compares to the Department of Commerce combined with Social Security in Claire's home world.

The Nine Great Houses aspire to the centralization of wealth in their hands; The House of Durgaas is the principal controller of the Eccollate.

Correlate

The military arm of Lunarian society. Gilbert Greybaird, as the Privy Counselor to the King, is the nominal head of the Correlate as well as being of the Communicate class.

However, politics often mean the Correlate's standing army takes their orders directly from the Council. The independent Palace Guard is loyal to the monarch. For example, Lord Garrund, as First Family of the Council, issues orders and takes control of the Army when he comes under the influence of Jallis Ruffin. [Twin Scepters, Kamorian Gate]

Temporate

A Class of monastic professionals who claim to have the sole authority in spiritual matters. The keepers of the keys to ancient technologies and the disciples of G'Rama.

Delagus, as High Priest of the Temporate, must approve all royal marriages, e.g. the union between Pem and Claire. Claire's first act of defiance is changing the wedding Vows. [Claire and Pem]

Communicate

A mostly hidden class of people, who binds everything together, though old technology Communication Boards which are scattered throughout the Temples of G'Rama, various ships, and other sites.

A person belonging to the group of especially talented persons who can project an entropic channel—sometimes known as simply a channel. A wild channel is an event controlled by wild talent and the use of such is considered a crime against the Communicate. The King is the nominal head of the Communicate, even if he may not have the talent to project an entropic channel. (see channel)

Monarchy

The Lunarian monarchy is loosely devoted to populist trends. The King or Queen answers to the people, and shares power with the High Council composed of the Nine Great Houses. The monarchy in Tieben is more traditional.

Merchant Guilds

Class of professional traders, farmers, and craftsmen. There is continual balancing between the interests of the guildsmen and the Council of Nine concerning tariffs and trade rights and regulations. The Houses on the Council would like the majority of the economic benefits to come to them directly.

G'rama

The Spiritual Guide of the Nine Elder Worlds, eight that predate Ennea. G'rama is the name given to the path towards Balance and to the Nine Paths guiding all consciousness.

Sage

Essentially the same Class as Magister and sometimes known as enforcers of the Code or Balance, especially where forbidden technologies are concerned. Sages represent accumulated wisdom. They are sometimes seen as the conscience of the Temporate, though they operate independently. All Sages are also Magisters.

Magister

Local justices of the peace and judges of the courts. Many, but not all, magisters are sages. The magisters may follow the body of law recognized by the Council, but can also take appropriate action on their own to preserve the Code of Justice.

Council of Nine (High Council)

The Council of the Nine great houses and families is the closest thing that Lunaria has to an aristocracy. The Council meets every year; their power to set tariffs and to control the military is in constant strife with the Merchant Guilds who wish to retain more golds and the Magistrates who wish to control the courts and administer justice. For example, the houses own most of the mines, banking, shipbuilding, and other economic interests.

Garrund: 1st House

Torvall and Calantha Garrund have longed for control of Greyhaven and all of Gilbert Greybaird's holdings. Their Holdings are the richest agriculture regions along the Lorne River to the south of Greyhaven. The marriage of their son Griffin to Astora Greybaird ended in tragedy with the death of their son and grandson. Their plan to marry their grand-daughter Illaina to Prince Pemburton went awry with the arrival of Claire Fisher.

Garrund's anger was often fatal. He was reputed to care more for his hunting dogs than for a man, and his attitude towards his dogs was singularly pragmatic when it came to culling mistakes.

Calantha is Torvall Garrund's wife and powerful Lady of the Land. She covets the up-bringing of Illaina and is the power behind Garrund's household.

Garrund House Colors: dark blue over dark blue on left, yellow over white in center; violet over black on right

Hussani: 2nd House

Wetzar and Alcinia Hussani. The power of the Hussani Family House came primarily from mining and trade in rare gems located in Akren. Wetzer Hussani and Torvall Garrund are allies of convenience after Lord Wetzar could no longer count upon ties to the family of the deposed King Cornal Hushara of Tieben through his wife, Lady Alcinia. Daughter Lyra is introduced at Winter Ball [Twin Scepters].

As a favor to Garrund, Hussani attempts to assassinate the King and Queen during their visit to his gem mine. He blames the assassination upon the miners, much to the dismay of the miners. [Twin Scepters]]

Hussani House colors: yellow over yellow on left; sand over black in center; blue over white on right

Ranapui: 3rd House

Farold and Sidra Ranapui have three children. The power of the Ranapui family is their shipyards and maritime facilities. Their sons Faroldson and Darcil learn the shipbuilding trade starting at the bottom. Their daughter Ribecah, is determined to be unconventional. Faroldson is easily swayed; Darcil is more progressive and favors his sister's intention to break tradition. The Ranapui family is fiercely supportive of the monarchy as a fulcrum against the blatant greed of many of the Council members. They have an uneasy alliance with Putkin family who supplies the metal ores.

Ranapui House Colors – Orange over orange on left, yellow over white in middle, green over black on right

Farold Ranapui has a strong partnership with Krel who is the owner of the largest foundry in Ranaputkin, and who supplies many castings as well as forged fittings for the Ranapui's shipyard. Krel is an important member of the Ranaputkin city council.

Claire recognizes that Ribecah Ranapui is a healer. Ribecah wants to see the world and be more than a pawn in marriage. Ribecah goes with Claire to Lumminea as lady-in-waiting but also gets training in defense and arms and in her talent for healing. Ribecah travels to Greyhaven with Nikko Pizzar when Claire and Pem flee the Palace. [Claire and Pem, Twin Scepters]

Darcil Ranapui- youngest son of Farold and Sidra. Darcil encourages the destiny of Ribecah and is in favor of women being on the council, and women's rights. Darcil brings the Ranapui's troops to join Pem and Claire on their flight to Kamoria. He is killed at the Gates of Kamoria. [Kamoria Gate]

Faroldson Ranapui- eldest son of Farold and Sidra Ranapui. By birth, he would inherit the management of the shipyards, but he proves to be very easily swayed by outside interests. Farold recognizes this lack of skill and interest early in Faroldson's life, but doesn't know what to do after Darcil's death. Farold is still bound to the idea that the sons rule. Sidra recognizes her daughter Ribecah's acumen and intent to be more than a pretty thing. Sidra actively brings up Ribecah to be independent and to know no bounds upon what she can accomplish. This is ultimately the tragedy of this family.

Ranapui house colors: orange over orange on left, yellow over white in center; green over black on right

Lantrus: 4th House

Emorie and Juditha Lantrus have no children. Their power is their trade in timber and wood around Malbrec. The Lantrus family would very much like to harvest the Great Forest. Their ambitious and foolhardy nephew Bobberick becomes ensnared in a tree of the Dark Forest from which Queen Claire, with the Hands of the Healer, releases him. [Twin Scepters] Lantrus loyalty is uncertain and can be swayed to whomever promises them the most gold.

Lantrus House Colors are; brown over brown on left, white over grey in center; yellow over sand on right

Czarkas: 5th House

Camren and Belda Czarkas-reside in Port Sulphur. They do not have much influence on the Council, do not have immediate family, and keep their thoughts close to themselves.

Czarkas House Colors are: sand over sand on left, black over brown in center; red over violet on right.

Putkin: 6th House

Pross and Thyra Putkin along with the Ranapui family are cofounders of Ranaputkin. The very wealthy Putkins own many mines along the Copper River that produce copper and iron ores. Putkin is devious, even treacherous in his dealings. Putkin will change support to whomever brings him the most trade.

Lady Thyra Putkin is quick to criticize but also quick to adopt the changes in hair style and pockets which are introduced by Claire. At the Winter Ball, Lyra's beauty received great approbation making Pross is a very popular father.

Putkin House Colors are: violet over violet on left, yellow over white in center; brown over gray on right

Akrius: 7th House

Sorle and Lucinia Akrius are quite elderly with three married sons and one daughter Roesia. They own more gem mines than anyone in Lunaria and Roesia is an expert in precious gems. Roesia is the age of Pem, and exhibits elegant grace.

Akrius House Colors are: light blue over light blue on left, yellow over dark blue in center; white over sand on right

Orumundi: 8th House

Boden Orumundi is the arms and heavy equipment manufacturer as well as an arms dealer with machine shops and finished weapons on Ranaputkin side of Copper River. They own a foundry across the river. Orumundi monopolizes the arms trades. Orumundi favors business with Tieben where he exports arms for ore and rare minerals. Orumundi will be loyal to whomever purchases the most arms, and would favor any opportunity to eliminate competitive foundries. [Claire and Pem]

The Orumundi house colors are: green over green on left, brown over yellow in center; sand over black on right

Durgaas: 9th House

Halex and Lady Uda Durgaas live in Drieven. They are very wealthy, and specialize in banking and finance. Halex Durgaas knows how to avoid taxes, is the King's banker, and the nominal Controller of the Eccollate. Durgaas leans toward support of the monarchy as the Council Houses would take over all debt and finance if they could.

Durgaas House colors are: black over on left, dark blue over sand in center, yellow over light blue on right

The Shadow Council

A term describing a small group of the Council of Nine. Garrund, Orumundi, and Putkin are determined to control the Council of Nine and use corrupt trade practices to put more golds into their pockets. They mostly control the military standing army, and would control the Correlate through discrediting Gilbert Greybaird if they could. It is the Shadow Council who brings on the downfall of Pemburton Windover [Twin Scepters] They are ultimately fall under the control of Jallis Ruffin.

Main Characters

Queen Claire Ellen Fisher Miller

Believing she is an ordinary girl from Ridgeville, Claire Fisher Miller finds herself in Lunaria at the age of fourteen. She begins her odyssey to become Queen of Lunaria and the Great Healer. She meets and marries Prince Pemburton Windover, starts a family, and then must flee her enemies on the Great Council. Green is her house color, and she is very aware of the conservation of world resources

Queen Claire Fisher Miller house colors are: green over green on left, grey over grey in center, brown over dark blue on right

Wendy Miller

Name and persona adopted by Claire Fisher upon return and exile to her home world. Grandmother to Claire Ellen Fisher Miller. Wendy exposes Claire to self-sufficiency practices, and prepares her for the journey to Lunaria. The circle is completed.

King Pemburton (Pem) Windover-

Prince Pemburton Windover, reddish brown hair cut short in the military fashion and flashing green eyes in a striking, fair-featured face that reminded people of Pem's mother, Rachael. Pem has the characteristic impatience of someone who takes action before thinking and is certain that his actions are always correct and expected. Pem is very aware of his duty to his people.

Windover House colors are: brown over dark blue on left; yellow over white in center; orange over black on right

Queen Rachael Windover

Mother of Pemburton Windover, killed while leading a military action in the north against raiders. Pem strives to be as heroic as his mother within the eyes of his people.

Edward Godwyn

Consort to Queen Rachael, father of Pemburton Windover, Regent to the throne of Lunaria until Pemburton comes of age. Edward plays the role of drunkard fool at the court while becoming the secret spy master of Lunaria with contacts over the world. Pem does not realize or respect his father. Gilbert holds him in high regard. Claire recognizes that Edward Godwyn will support his son and the Windovers to his death.

Godwyn's informants keep popping up in the stories, mostly identified by the wine which they offer. They include Ironson in Tieben, Manjaros-Goldfind, Saharos- Jaga, Selvin Miller at Brown's Landing, Captain Winton at Black Tower, Trader Brey and Blossom Baker, Ka'Tara in Saitadi, Lumminea, Ka'Iiris in Timbermill, Karl Murten, Farkeel and Qinbow in Tieben. [Rissa and Turlo] and many others.

Gilbert Greybaird: Privy Councilor

Known as Lord Gilbert of Greyhaven. He is the father of Astora Greybaird Garrund, grandfather to Lady Illaina Estelle Greybaird *nom* Garrund, and the Privy Councilor to the Windover Crown. He is the last of one of the oldest families on Ennea.

Weathered wrinkles, round face, mane of grey hair, high forehead, intense, silver-gray eyes, oversized nose that is red with too much exposure to the sun and wind. He was a stocky man but not fat.

Lord Gilbert of Greyhaven is responsible to train Prince Pemburton Windover in the arts of diplomacy, ruling, and arms; sits on the High Council; and is loyal to, and defender of, the monarchy. Gilbert assumes custody of Claire Fisher upon her entry to Lunaria, and fosters her in Greyhaven, with his daughter Astora and his grand-daughter Illaina. He becomes Claire's *de facto* father figure, and protects Pem as he grows up. Gilbert eventually travels with Claire back to her world.

Greybaird house colors: grey over grey on left; brown over yellow in center; green over red on right

Gilbert Greyson

Gilbert Greyson is the persona of Gilbert Greybaird upon exile to Claire's home world. Gilbert keeps the objects of power concealed, and maintains his role of Privy Counselor to Claire.

Astora Greybaird Garrund

Gilbert Greybaird's daughter and widow of Torvall Garrund's son, Griffin. Astora is bound to the Great Forest at Greyhaven as Mistress of the Forest. Astora fosters Claire Fisher until time for Claire to go to the capital city, Lumminea.

Lady Illaina Estelle Greybaird *nom* Garrund

Daughter of Astora Greybaird and Griffin Garrund. Lady Illaina is to receive the equal honors accorded to the firstborn of the House of Garrund. She is the same age as Claire; they are raised together at Greyhaven for a few years.

Illaina, dark hair, delicate lips, prominent cheekbones, pale features, with eyes that were once gray now seemed to carry hints of blue and green. She is perpetually bored with everyday life; enthusiastic about fashion and new clothes, and desperate to leave Greyhaven and go to the capitol with her grandparents Torvall and Calantha Garrund. Illaina feels that it was her destiny that she was to be wed to Pemburton Windover, and thinks that her grandfather Gilbert abandoned her for the intruder Claire.

Illaina is ambitious for herself and hates it when Torvall Garrund weds her into the Ranapui family. Jallis Ruffin finds her to be a willing pawn.

Rissa Ellendor and Turlo Murten

Turlo Murten first shows up in Norcross where he plays the part of a guide to Claire and Tess on their way back to Lumminea. Turlo is a prince of Tieben and the First Heir to the throne. He is the nephew of Cornal and Veral Hushara, and the son of Karl and Maigret (Hushara) Murten. Turlo would rather be a wandering guide than face the marriage of convenience to a distant cousin arranged by his uncle Veral. When he meets Rissa Ellendor, all that changes. Turlo and Rissa are bound with, and are strong friends of, Claire.

Rissa has the gift of the Warrior's sight and the Shield of Balance from Cornal Hushara; and the Golden Acorn, a key to Heartwood, from Tiela Snowborn. Rissa is an X'tlan and has honey golden curls, exotic almond eyes, high cheek bones, narrow face, narrow waist, fullness of figure.

. Rissa protects and defends; Honor is her calling. The Warrior's sight allows her to perceive certain truths.

Turlo Murten has sharply angular, nearly oriental features. His dark-green eyes are wide-spaced, his hair a cinnamon-clay color, his face ruddy, and his skin fair. He thinks of himself as a rogue. Ultimately Turlo Murten becomes King of Tieben with the policy to avoid another war with Lunaria. Turlo and Rissa have a common vision—building trade between Tieben and the rest of the world that brings prosperity to the merchants, traders, and suppliers with reasonable support for the governments without onerous tariffs or trade barriers.

Jallis Ruffin

An Allele of unimaginable age; he is the mysterious Dark Sage and Magister who is determined to control all the known world, all trade, its people and governments. He covets old technology and has no regard for the Balance of world resources and the stripping away of the nanite population. Unbridled power is Ruffin's objective.

He is described as modest in size, with dark hair, a high forehead, cold black eyes.

Jallis Ruffin and Sage Leandra may have once been lovers a long time in the past. Jallis Ruffin and Leandra are by far the oldest remaining sages in Lunaria and were near-equals in the manipulation of these microscopic *implementers*, as Ruffin called the robotic nanites. It was fortunate for Lunaria that Leandra's ambitions were very different than Ruffin's.

In his greed, Ruffin takes the Shield of Balance from Rissa by striking off her hand. Ruffin loses a hand to Claire in a translation gate battle in Ranaputkin. [Claire and Pem] His impregnable stronghold, Karzon, is located in the wilds on the coast east of Tieben, where he is known as Lord Grandel Darkwood.

Jallis Ruffin standard is a black flag with the red figure of a gnarled tree upon it.

Tess of Tribana

Tess is the daughter of a cooper in Tribana who, by selection of Lord Gilbert Greybaird, becomes Claire's companion and Lady in Waiting. [Claire in Lunaria] Tess and Claire are fostered together at Greyhaven. Tess and Claire are abducted, but escape to the Black Tower. Tess receives the "Maker's True Sight" from Ayaba on their flight back to Lumminea. [The Sword of Training, Forgotten Garden] Tess and Claire are bound to each other.

Tess meets and talks with One Mother in Darkwood where she thwarts Jallis Ruffin's trap. Claire awakens One Mother in the Darkwood. [Forgotten Garden]

Tess has coils of blond braids. Tess is a math genius and becomes estate manager of Claire's holdings near Lumminea. She marries Fitz Royard, Captain of Palace Guard.

Tess and Fitz flee with Pem and Claire from the Palace. Baby Edward, twin to Burton, is placed with them as the two couples separate so that one twin can be brought up in secrecy. Tess and Royard raise Edward with the knowledge that he may serve the people even if he has to remain unaware of his heritage. [Twin Scepters]

Fitz Royard

Fitz Royard (called Royard all his life): curly hair, oversized ears, a little nanite talent, bashful. He becomes Captain of the Palace Guard and close friend to both Pem and Claire.

Tess and Fitz marry at the Palace. Tess resides at Merrick (Claire's estates near Lumminea) so that Royard has close contact, but can accomplish his daily routine for Gilbert and the Crown. Their son is born the same day as the princes. Tess and Royard are like brother and sister to Claire and Pem. Their loyalty, honor, and blood ties strongly influence Lumminea's future.

Support Characters

Reyfort

Reyfort was a survivor of the bloody campaign at Kamoria, and Gilbert had sought out the retired trooper at the beginning of the war with Tieben and made a place for him at Greyhaven and Bigspring where he served as the military advisory to Lady Astora as well as Claire's escort. [Claire in Lunaria]

It was Reyfort who befriended both Claire and Tess and was assigned to protect the girls. Reyfort was killed while defending Greyhaven when Torvall Garrund would have seized the holding. [Kamorian Gate] His adopted son Greylance became the defender of Greyhaven when Eberson, Nikko, and Ribecah sought shelter there.

Stable master Bender first taught Claire how to use a knife and sword on horseback. [Claire in Lunaria]

Reyfort taught Claire tactics and was with her in her first real battle test, the ambush on way to Gabron Taltson's farm.

Copius Ansel

Famous Scholar who tutored Claire and Illaina at Greyhaven. Ansel eventually goes to Garrund's household with Illaina. The Garrund household wants their glorious future to be chronicled, and so the Council, at the urging of First Councilor Garrund, creates the title of Scholar of Lunaria and bestows this upon Copius Ansel and his descendants.

Allain

Corwin Allain is the first military officer which Claire met when she enters Lunaria. [Claire in Lunaria] He has black eyes, hair in short braids. A handsome man except for the scar that slashed across one cheek. The scar was a scar of honor, but there was no honor left when Allain became the plaything of Jallis Ruffin.

Allain was protective of Claire and Pem as he was promoted through the ranks by Gilbert until Allain became commander of the militia. Allain betrayed the monarchy-Pem, Claire, and Gilbert-when he chose to be honor the Council edict and was instructed to bring Queen Claire before the Council to face charges of treason. Ironically, the Council was acting under the secret influence of Jallis Ruffin in his opening move to bring the whole of Lunaria under his control. [Twin Scepters]

Jallis Ruffin destroyed Allain and the Lunarian army in Kamoria so that he may march into Lumminea unopposed. [Kamorian Gate]

Guinn Fisher Miller

Guinn Fisher, wife of Burton Miller on earth, and mother of Claire Ellen Fisher Miller, desired a conventional life. When her husband was reported missing in action (MIA) in Iraq, she turned to Pastor Higgins Brownbottom for comfort as well as incessant prayer. Guinn resented that Claire turned to her grandmother, Wendy Miller, but Claire felt she was neither wanted nor loved.

Boy Prince Burton Windover, Burton Miller

The persona of Claire/Wendy's son, Prince Burton Windover, in her home world. Burton joined the military and was declared missing in Iraq war. Burton was unaware of Lunaria and his heritage, but Gilbert brought him up in diplomacy and arms training. As part of the endless Cycle, Burton is the father of Claire Ellen Fisher Miller; Burton Windover is the son of Claire and Pem. The Cycle is broken when the Queen returns to Lunaria with Burton Windover Miller.

Ka'Tara

Gilbert's half-sister and powerful ally in the Temporate as the High Priestess of the Temple in Lumminea; she also works closely as an ally of Edward Godwyn.

Ka'Tara rises to the top of the in the inner circles of the Temporate. She warns Gilbert that the Temporate Unity as well as the Correlate High Command is aware of a new power abroad in Lunaria when Claire came to Lunaria. [Claire in Lunaria]

Ka'Tara is a pretty, middle-aged woman dressed in a white robe with small red trim around the throat and at the bottom of the hem where it touched the floor. Her eyes were black but not cold and were set wide in a face that was rounded and peacefully composed. She wore her hair in long braids that wound over the top of her head in coils of black with streaks of white.

Nikko Pizzar

First encountered as First Officer on the Fortuna, and afterwards in command of the Rachael Ann until its destruction. Eberson, Captain of the Fortuna, recruits him to command the loyal forces in Greyhaven who are fighting against Jallis Ruffin. He marries Ribecah Ranapui. He brings up Naomi at Greyhaven when Ribecah must go to Ranaputkin. [Chaos in Lunaria-Beginning of a New Age]

Nikko, Claire, and Tess are all attracted to each other when they first meet. Nikko is often assigned escort duty.

Nikko is a genial rascal who is always around to aid Tess and Claire. Before Tess and Claire left Greyhaven at the end of their fostering, he gives them a pair of miniature daggers in green, jeweled cases designed to be pinned to a woman's clothing and look like jewelry. These special, miniature daggers played a saving role in more than one scrape.

N'Rat

N'Rat, an orphan, meets Claire in Trapper's Haven. He is enlisted to help her rescue Tess and Turlo who are jailed by Captain Dread and await possible execution.

N'Rat, as a boy, is described with a shaggy mop of brown hair and fierce eyes. He is a boy expecting much of the future. After N'Rat helps Claire rescue Tess and Turlo,. Claire recognizes N'Rat as someone with potential. [Forgotten Garden] N'Rat travels with them and is placed in the Trader's fleet, where he rises in the ranks, ultimately achieving command of the Trader fleet.

Mara Ellendor of the Traders

Mara Ellendor, head of an original trading Family, is an X'tlan descendent. Her daughter is Rissa Ellendor. Rissa meets and befriends Claire as she crosses the Plain of Glass. [Claire in Lunaria] Their meeting is fortuitous, and the girls become fast friends. The Traders, wth their powerful fleet, have long been the glue which holds the kingdoms together, as well as a defense against marauders. The Traders have the secrets of land and marine shipbuilding at Vash. When Rissa, her daughter marries Turlo

Murten, Prince of, and then, King of Tieben, the neutrality of the Traders becomes difficult to maintain.

Mara is wiry, handsome woman with piercing blue eyes, silver-streaked hair in a braid. Typically appears in the tailored jacket of Trader commander; she wears the Crescent of 9 emerald stars representing the Nine Worlds.

Saharos- Jaga, Valheart

The Jaga (or Jaga Un) is Sage and leader of the Saharos. Her Daughter Nani is part of Edward Godwyn's circle. [The Fall of the Council]

The Saharos are the mysterious desert people of central Lunaria. The *Saharos* reputedly means *people of the sands*. [Twin Scepters]

Valheart, Saharan Scout, is cousin to the Jaga [Kamoria Gate] Valheart comes to the support of Pemburton and Claire as they flee. Valheart's words at their final battle and parting: "My tribe is expecting me to bring back the full tale, the story of the legendary Queen Claire, the wizardry of the great Lord Gilbert— even the valiant heart of the King Pemburton—and how they escaped the wicked Council and saved their child, Burton, so that they might return to fulfill their promise to right the wrongs committed against themselves and their people." This is the Story of the Saharos—that Queen Claire and Prince Burton will return. The legend remains strong during the next 30 years as underground resistance continues to give Jallis Ruffin cause for concern. Jallis is vigilant for the return so that he is ever persecuting the Saharos and Manjaros people.

Manjaros

The mountain people, once widely known as the Manjaros, live along the northern slopes of the Faultline Range. They were named for an ancient mountain home whose existence survives only in myth and legend. Their lands are now much reduced. The ancient city of Minot is their capitol. Legendary names: Mt. Snowy, Snowy Pass, Callisfell, Stairs of Allorne. [Rissa and Turlo]

The mountain people are descendants from the valley where now the evil Captain Dread uses slave labor to work the mines. These people also know of secret ways to enter Tieben. Once they understand the Rissa and Turlo are friends with the old Cornal Hushara, they are willing to ally themselves to their cause.

Goldfind

A leader of the Manjaros, Goldfind is a much older man, with a mane of white hair and deeply wrinkled features that speak of great age.

The Manjaros and Saharos came from the same home world in the distant past, and work together in resistance to Jallis Ruffin. They simply seek to have a peaceful life without persecution by Dread or Ruffin's forces. The Manjaros and Saharos maintain a vigilant guard against gangs of thugs, raiders, and marauders.

Tiela Snowborn, Tiela Yellowleaf

Tiela is an allele of ancient age just slightly younger than Jallis Ruffin and Sage Leandra. She has olive skin, dark intelligent eyes, glossy black hair in a single braid, and a willowy body that is imbued with great strength. She is often seen wearing a pale green gown and carrying a sword. When Tess, N'Rat, and Turlo meet

Tiela, she is described by Turlo as an esteemed member of the court and loyal to Cornal Hushara. Tiela Yellowleaf gives the Golden Acorn to Rissa. [Rissa and Turlo]

Tiela Snowborn is the same Tiela Yellowleaf of Prince Redthorn's legend [Forgotten Garden], where Jallis Ruffin tries to forcibly wrest the secret of the Heartwood Forest from her. Tiela is key to the well-being of One Mother and One Father and is charged with bringing the Forests back to full sentience.

Alfred Watchman

Captain (Admiral) Alfred Watchman is an allele, once known as the Watcher; Ship's Captain in the powerful Ellendor Trader Family on the *Redclaw*. Watchman is a partial construct or allele, which is not revealed. Watchman comes to Pem and Claire's aid. [Kamoria Gates] Watchmen is often included in strategy sessions in the first 7 volumes as a matter of course when the Traders are involved.

Watchman has been an advisor to the X'tlans since Mara Ellendor's ancestors became First Family among the Trader Clans. He is as old as Tiela Yellowleaf and Jallis Ruffin. Watchman senses that his time draws near to an end.

Eberson

Captain of the Fortuna and close friend to Gilbert Greybaird and Edward Godwyn. He is a Communicate and introduces Claire to the secrets of the communication board. Eberson is in love with the Astora Greybaird Garrund. He is on his way to rescue her at Greyhaven when he learns of her death. Eberson's grieves and vows a great revenge upon Torvall Garrund.

He remains in Greyhaven and becomes acting Keeper of the Great Forest (Heartwood Forest) and a ranger, dedicated to the return of the One Father's alliance with One Mother. [The Fall of the Council]

Eberson recognizes that Timone represents a new template for intelligence created in Ennea. Eberson helps Claire understand her amulet is an object of power and what that means. Eberson is an important character who defines the ideas of blood, loyalty, and honor.

Ironson

Trader and spy for Edward Godwyn in Tieben. A irascible reprobate who works out Riversbend on the Darkfell River, Ironson provides escort between Norcross and Wintermarsh. Ironson is one of the few who has met the Manjaros Oracle.

Edward Godwyn is in league with Ironson to supply gold to the revolt. Ironson befriends Rissa and Turlo on their way back to Tieben. [Rissa and Turlo, A Journey]

Hushara- Veral, Cornal

Veral Hushara, Turlo's uncle, is Tieben's current ruler. He came to power by deposing his brother, Cornal Hushara. Veral caused the war between Tieben and Lunaria.

Cornal Hushara, former ruler of Tieben is exiled at the Black Tower by his brother Veral. Cornal befriends Claire and Tess and gives Claire the Sword of Training, and Everweave tunics to both girls. [Sword of Training] Cornal is tasked by Claire to undertake a future assignment in another world. Cornal is a fulcrum-in-time character. [The Fall of the Council]

Karl and Maigret Murten

Father and Mother to Turlo Murten. Karl is a Scholar and historian, a colleague known to Copius Ansel I, and author of books on the History of Tieben and Ennea.

Karl Murten: A man with intense brown eyes, almost black, snow white hair brushed straight back. Small, yet handsome and impressive. Olive skin.

Maigret Murten: Turlo's mother. Sister to Kings Veral and Cornal Hushara. Karl and Maigret reside in Wintermarsh. They are part of Godwyn's circle; they is well known and connected to everyone in Wintermarsh, Capitol of Tieben.

Mags Caar

Mags mischievous brown eyes have long been on Nikko Pizzar. She is Claire's assistant, a spy for Gilbert, and an operative for Edward Godwyn. Her sense of humor disguises a serious nature and strong sense of purpose and responsibility.

As Pem and Claire are preparing to flee, Mags brings Claire's all-important yellow egg, her amulet, the key, and the Sword of Training. [Claire and Pem, Twin Scepters]

Drott, a word of frustration that Claire picked up from Mags who explained that it was the name of a person in her home town who was forever doing the wrong thing.

Mags goes with Tess, Royard, Pem and Claire on escape to Kamoria. Mags travels with Tess and Royard, little Fitz and Edward, when they depart from Pem and Claire. Mags is part of the Eastern Islands Trading Company. Tess goes to Mags to enlist the aid of the Saharos to bring Edward and Fitz to the Garden of

Origins in the Plain of Glass. [Chaos in Lunaria- Beginning of the End]

Technology

Nanites

Nanotechnology; Nanophages, the building blocks of the world. The density of the nanophages was very high over fertile waters. Nanotechnology is at the heart and soul of Lunaria's ancient technology. They are the building blocks of the templates. Nanites can be generated by the Gardens, but are limited overall as a world resource.

Black Stone

Black Stone or Plinths are part of an ancient transportation network once connecting the various cities of Ennea; likely something like huge semiconductor chips in earth technology. They are also part of the Gate technology which once connected the Nine Worlds as well as the Seed Worlds.

Tattles

A Lunarian intrusion alarm and protection again a wild entropy channel or tube. A nanotech device designed to reflect the entropic energy back upon itself and destroy the source of a channel. Normally used as a defensive device when high energy flows are detected. A Guard Tattle is a safety device used to divert the unterminated end of an unanchored entropy tube or wild channel.

Channel

The deliberate propagation of an entrotherm between two points. Entrotherm: A term used to describe the nature of the virtual entropic path connecting two real events. Once, only the Communicate has the authority to generate and use channels.

A channel which is used outside the authority of the Communicate can cause a radical release of entropic energy (explosion) when it reaches its intended destination. Jallis Ruffin uses channels to blow up the entropy engines on the Fortuna. A channel for destruction requires the use of massive amounts of nanites.

Communication Boards

Advanced communication boards continue to work in only a few places; one is located on board the Fortuna and sometimes in G'Rama temples. A very select few know of their existence and are able to use them.   The knowledge needed to build a communication board died long before the War of a Thousand Years.

Household Prognosticator, Ayaba, The Oracle, Administrator, Executive

Electronic fragments of the nanite technology and intelligent machines which have maintain Lunaria and its world for many thousands of centuries. In current earth terms, holograms of artificial intelligence which were charged with terraforming, communication, weather control, template generation/evolution, and general well-being and development of the ninth world. The Administrator directs the total planning, supports the Garden of Origins and the sentience of One Father and One Mother who provide a living network of communication. The overall mission: Protect the Planet with Balance between the needs of the inhabitants and the resources of the world.

Accumulator, Amulet, Talisman

Amulet, Accumulator, talisman: A machine in the form of a jeweled pendant or amulet that aid in the interaction of the wearer with the underlying technologies of Lunaria.

The amulet which Rissa gives Claire [Claire in Lunaria] is 'the unconscious memory that lend speed and strength to our movements.' The amulet imprints on its host. Originally, a method of secure communications between paired amulets.

A communications channel is the technical process of launching a shielded probe carrying information along a null energy path between two points. Magisters possess this skill by virtue of a special amulet that works only with a unique individual. Not all individuals can operate a communication channel. Pem lacks the talent to see objects other than the physical, i.e. a ring is a ring; he can't see that it is a mutable object of power.

From historical sources: "Ancient history names a phenomenon known as the *Ripple Effect* in which there is always a possibility of finding a causal path or connection between two events no matter how remote from each other. This *Effect* is what the amulet is designed to control. The idea is not to disrupt the path by introducing real information. If you succeed in creating the connection, the intervening space is spanned virtually and instantaneously."

Everweave

Everweave is an incredible tough and durable cloth which is able to withstand and turn aside ordinary blades. Only special blades with enhanced molecular edges can cut the cloth which has chains of the microscopic organisms, nanites, woven throughout the Everweave.

Cornal has a bolt of Everweave cloth which he tailors into tunics and clocks for Tess and Claire. [Sword of Training]

Keys, Objects of Power

There exists a special key, an entropy-enhanced key, which grants the proper user a vision of what is on the other side of a locked door. The use of such a key is normally limited to either a Sage or a highly talented healer such as Claire.

Objects of Power are machines operating by ancient technology, nanotechnology. The current population of Lunaria do not understand their technology and surround them with mystery. They are neither magical nor mystical.

Sword of Training

As Hushara explained to Claire: "The *First Rule* is that the Sword of Training always goes with your accumulator/amulet. The amulet-sword combination is important in other ways. The amulet provides the unconscious memory that will perfect technique with the sword and lend speed and strength to movements. The amulet imprints on its host. The sword/amulet combination is unique to the person. [Sword of Training]

"The *Second Rule* of the Sword of Training is that the Sword can never be used against its owner. The importance of the *Second Rule* is that if I picked up the Sword and even pretended to go against you, I might well die from the shock. You need to be aware of the potential danger to your comrades. On the other hand, the danger should be kept secret because it could prove extremely useful in separating friend from foe. The owner of the blade carries the burden of responsibility."

Before Cornal gave the Sword to Claire, The Sword of Training last belonged to Cornal Hushara's mother. The Sword of Training goes with Claire into her home world and returns with Wendy Miller.

Sword of King/Ring of Queen

Each presented during their wedding, the Sword of the King and the Ring of the Queen are both objects of power. Claire feels her ring and the Trader Amulet flash fiery hot. The world about her seems to shatter into a swirl of bright sparks of energy that quickly joined together to reconstruct the image of Pem before her and the rest of the world around him.

The nanites have formed a thin entropy channel connecting her ring with Pem's sword. The power of the Monarchy is sealed by a fragment of the powerful black stones that were once part of an inconceivable transportation web connecting Ennea together. The Queen's Ring stays with her son Edward on Lunaria.

Qanna, Sword of the King, Shield of Balance

The sword as it passed from King Pem to Lord Gilbert in the Battle at Kamoria Gate, the name *Qanna* came unbidden into Gilbert's mind, was gifted with an edge that was as thin as a single point of light and as tough as the underlying matrix of the universe. Such an edge was so keen that it could slide between the very particles of reality that wove together the fabric of the Captain's armor and the nanite cables that sewed his sinews together. [Kamorian Gate] The King's Sword goes with Gilbert to Claire's world of earth.

Cornal gives Rissa the Shield of Balance, which is manifested as a gold band with a green jewel set into a crescent moon, and seals it with the *silly putty* given to him by Claire. Turlo just sees a pretty bracelet. Cornal says that it allowed a great warrior princess to win many of her battles without drawing her sword. Cornal was drawn to give it to Rissa when she came to the Black Tower. "It is for her," the Administrator whispers. The Oracle spoke, "The Shield will be only an outer manifestation of what is in your heart." The band changes to fit her wrist. An implanted command causes Rissa returns her piece of *silly putty* to Cornal.

The Spear of Glory (Eternity)

This object of power is transformed at the Garden of Origins upon the return of Queen Claire as it is the activated by the proximity of the Shield of Balance (Rissa), Edward Windover's Ring of Remembrance (the Queen's Ring), the Sword of Training (Claire, Wendy), and the King's Sword Qanna (Gilbert). The clan of cats which originated with Curly must also be present as representatives of the world-mass Gaia. The Spear has not yet been used.

Gardens

The Gardens are ancient technology. There are selected Gardens on Lunaria: Greyhaven, the Palace, the Dark Forest, the Garden of Origins on the Plain of Glass, and others which appear to be set out of time where transportation and communication can be accomplished. They are self-contained regions within themselves. The Palace Garden develops a recursive passageway and self destructs. They are maintained by the nanites under the direction of the Administrator, and can feel either welcoming or dangerous to those who would enter.

An impression in the Garden of Greyhaven: the colors of blossoms on miniature orange trees are florescent in their hue and heady in their perfume while the sky overhead seems lighted by an entirely different sun. There are *sweet autumn* blossoms. A house wren fusses and scratches in loose, rich loam under graceful arches of lacy ferns; a warbler fidgets on a lower branch of a fig tree and sings a song of welcome.

Golden Acorn

The template acorn for the sentient trees which make up Heartwood and Darkwood. The Golden Acorn must be planted in order for One Mother and One Father to become united and extend and repair the forest. Whomever plants the golden acorn will have some control over the Heartwood trees. Jallis Ruffin seeks that power, but cannot have it. According to legend, Tiela Yellowleaf has the secret of rooting the Heartwood sapling and planting acorns to become Heartwood trees. Tiela Snowborn extends that power to Rissa, but Rissa fails to use it wisely.

One Mother, Earth Mother, Darkwood or Dark Forest

An old and proud Heartwood tree standing alone upon a grassy hill at the exact center of the forest. Planted by Grandel

Darkwood with Tiels Yellowleaf's help, One Mother and Great Father once communicated across most of the world through their root-network system. One Mother worked through Tiela Yellowleaf, according to legend, to have new saplings and acorns planted.

One Father of the Heartwood Forest

The One Father and One Mother became cut asunder when Jallis Ruffin sought the secret of planting the Golden Acorn from Tiela Yellowleaf. It is part of the Administrator's plan that the two forests become united and sentient again as they help maintain the balance in the Lunarian world between the use of natural resources and sustainability.

Geography, Places

Greyhaven

Gilbert Greybaird's ancestral holding on the edge of the Great Forest or Heartwood. The Garden at Greyhaven is the garden of the Great Forest and the sentient One Father. Greyhaven is the site of great joy and great sorrow.

Greyhaven's entry ran between the ruins of two immense, gray stone keeps that had once supported a gate of iron-banded timbers of great thickness. The remains of a walled enclosure stretched in both directions. Tradesmen had scavenged the once-high crenellated walls through long years of peace so that only a row of smoothly dressed foundation stone remained. Beyond the open gate stood a large, well-fortified building built with the same gray stone as the gate keeps. The holding stood at least three stories high with towers, turrets, and iron-shuttered windows.

Lumminea

Largest city, the Capitol of Lunaria- site of King's (Queen's) palace; seat of the government. Most of the Council of Nine have holdings near Lumminea in additional to their ancestral homes.

Wintermarsh

Capitol of Tieben- Turlo Murten Hushara and Rissa Ellendor ultimately reside there. It is relatively cold, with the Great Frozen Marsh as the nearest major feature. Wintermarsh is dependent upon the southern region of Lunaria for most supplies.

Saitadi

Large city located near the White Mountains, Plains of Glass, and on the River Lorne. Saitadi is in the center of the land between Boggrash on the west and Port Sulphur on the east.

There are four districts of Saitadi built around a central area that features the great Temple of G'rama, the Temple University, the living quarters of the temple priests, and lands and parks belonging to the rich and powerful Temporate of Lunaria. We first meet Gilbert's half-sister Ka'Tara as chief Acolyte in the G'Rama Temple of Saitadi.

Port Sulphur

Port city on north east coast of the Continent of Lunaria, the southernmost port near Tieben or the northernmost port of Lunaria. Turlo's dream to build a land access to Port Sulphur through the Faultline Mountains is realized when Port Sulphur becomes a free port.

Boggrash

Free city of the Traders on the western edge of the Tieben-Lunarian border, near the Black Isle, Vash, and the Bay of Terror. As the home city of the Traders, Boggrash is the banking center of all trade. The ship-building industry at Boggrash gets supplies out of West Tieben where there is a surplus of wood, and tends toward landships and coastal trading sloops rather than "war ships."

The Trader Fleet and landships come under attack by rogue elements of the Lunarian Fleet as Jallis Ruffin tries to provoke a war between Tieben and Lunaria, and take over Boggrash with expansionist plans of the Lunarian Great Council.

Karzon

Jallis Ruffin's stronghold, hidden and isolated town in uncharted East Tieben, above the Faultline Mountains. Turlo Murten fortifies the border along the Faultline Mountain range, and supports the Manjaros traders to deny Ruffin an easy access to his stronghold. The stronghold is limited to access on the east coast through a small bay.

Eastern Islands; eastern Continent- Frangeria

Far east islands- there is little trade and travel. Tess and Royard make a import/export business at Newport. The Eastern Islands is the jumping off site for Frangeria, the eastern continent. Not much is known of Frangeria.

Towers

The Black and White Towers, once known as the North and South Apertures, are ancient transportation centers between the nine worlds, now largely abandoned. The White Tower is located in Drieven where the River Songris empties into the River Lorne and is surrounded by a blasted, empty, barren space. Few people visit there because of fear of a wasting sickness.

The Black Tower is in Tieben, south of Wintermarsh, and was the exile site of deposed King Cornal Hushara. The Guard at the Black Tower, Captain Winton, is part of Edward Godwyn's network, and aided Turlo and Rissa to escape from Captain Dread.

Rivers

River Songris

The River Songris, The River Without Troubles in the old language, is the joy of the land, for the Songris is cold, deep, and crystalline green—green only because of the verdant reflections in its pristine waters and joyful because it flows from unspoiled headwaters deep within the Great Forest.

River Lorne

The River Lorne is the tears of Lunaria, the carrier of salt from the high desert and silt from the rich farmlands. A great river which runs north to south, just to the western edge of the Darkwood and Malbreck, down to Drieven where it meets with the Songris, and then past Lumminea, to the Great Marsh and finally empties into the Bay of Lunaria at Maripas.

Copper River, Malbreck

Named for its red color, the Copper River travels in the northeast portion of Lunaria from the Deep mines in Akren south to Ranaputkin where it exits into the Great Southern Ocean. This is the launching river for the shipyards of Ranaputkin. Malbreck: Northern city in Lunaria noted principally for being the gateway from the west to the mining region near Akren in the east.

Antiphons and Liturgies

Antiphon describing the myth of Ennea

Antiphon from an ancient text written before the Peace of a Thousand Years. Though the context had been long forgotten by the people who live in the areas known as Lunaria and Tieben, those few who do remember understand its origin.

The Nine (From the Ennead)

Nine Worlds to rule the Heavens,
And Nine to Rule the Worlds.

The King to rule the Nine,
And the People to rule the King.

Nine Paths to Guide the People
To the mind and heart of G'rama.

The Pre-G'rama Antiphon known as the *Four* was written during the time of the First Empire on the Ninth World:

The Four

Reading: At the beginning, the Unnamed was being, and the Unnamed grew and became more, and all that became was similarity.
Response: This is the Truth.

Reading: At the ending, all that seemed different is indistinguishable. The Unnamed is the One name.
Response: This is the Truth.

Reading: Our beginning is renewal, and our ending is renewal. Nothing is lost and nothing is gained. There is only the balance between all things. This is the principle of conservation.
Response: This is the Truth.

Reading: Similation is the Unnamed in all it manifestations, which is the One made manifest in its many forms.
Response: This is the Truth.

The Meditations of the Ancients

The *Nine Meditations* were as follows:

1. *If my need is to be right, then I must beware anger. The world is not perfect, and I cannot be perfect.*

2. *If my need is to be needed, then I must avoid pride. Humility attracts true friends.*

3. *If my need is to succeed, then I must avoid deceit. Accepting failure will bring success. Accepting the truth will bring strength.*

4. *If my need is to be special, then I must avoid envy. Celebrate everyone's uniqueness. There is always someone who is better than you are at your chosen task.*

5. *If my need is to know more than my neighbor, then I must take care to share with him what I learn.*

6. *If my need is to be safe and secure, then I must find the courage to defeat fear. Fear is the enemy in my mind.*

7. *If my need is to avoid pain, I must take care to avoid gluttony. More often brings less.*

8. *If my need is to be against, then I must find compassion in my contention. A compassionate leader gathers many loyal followers.*

9. *If my need is to avoid commitment, then I must avoid being lazy, for what I do does matter greatly.*

The Ballads

They say of Queen Rachael that she loved her consort Edward and her child as well, but she was always drawn to action. She grew tired of her responsibilities at the court and made an excuse to quell a minor rebellion on the northern borders near Tribana. There, because of her overconfidence, she was drawn into battle and died needlessly leaving Edward to raise Pem as the Regent.

Queen Rachael

They say of duty that burns too bright
That madness finds its way to light.
The border raiders were grim and fell
And drew the Queen like flames to Hell.

Queen Rachael's anger was hot as fire.
The battle was fierce, bloody and dire.
And as she fought across the field,
There were none who asked of her to yield.

History says of those who bend
They do not break and drink the wind.
But Rachael courted death, not love.
And died by sword and chainmail glove.

Queen Rachael's hair was red like flame,
And where she fell, her blood became
A great red-flowering grove of trees
That bend like willows in springtime breeze.

The Gate at Kamoria

Honor and blood were both lost in that fight
When fire and blood ran red on that night
On the walls of Kamoria.

Brother struck brother without reason or right
When fire and blood ran red on that night
In the streets of Kamoria.

The Queen and her son were trapped in their flight
And brought to their knees before the dark knight
At the Gate of Kamoria.

The King with his sword polished and bright
Sought to hold for Right against Might
At the Gate of Kamoria.

Alas, Right could not keep that evil at bay.
The King shed his blood on his last living day.
Before the Gate at Kamoria.

No one knows where the Queen has gone
Of if she'll return with her son come along
Through the Gate at Kamoria.

Honor and blood were both lost in that fight
When fire and blood ran red on that night
On the walls of Kamoria.

A Desert Traveler

There are no paths on desert sand
Where roads themselves cannot diverge.
The only signs upon the land
Are stars whose nightly paths converge.

The Wheel is but a spiral constrained.
The Angle repeats but the dream moves on,
A Motion along a rim ordained
To give me purpose until the dawn.

Sunrise, I have no time to waste
To cast about for sure protection,
I seek a shadow in this place
That is not my own projection.

What is life but footsteps not prints?
Time erases all and leaves no hints.
The desert is the best place
To understand a trackless waste.

The River Songris

While deep with the Golden Vale
Where silence reins and waters glisten,
Astora heard the Heartwood's tale
When she paused to listen..

"The One, our Mother, wandered,
When our world was young and green.
The One, our Father, never heard
Of what she might have seen."

"The One our Mother, never returned,
And so we asked all passers-by
To ask our Mother if she's learned
That One Father was about to die."

Sorrow filled Astora's heart.
How terrible to be too late!
I would never stand apart
From my children or my mate.

"Please be our Mistress, Lady,"
The Heartwoods bowed before the maid.
"Don't ever leave us, Lady."
Crowns turned a golden shade.

"Oh yes," she clapped her hands.
"My life has been so gray.
I found no one in all these lands
Who needed me until this day."

Lord Gilbert heard Astora's thought
As he strode beneath his trees.
Here is the One heart I have sought
Through all the lands and on the seas.

The Mistress of the Forest
Was the Lady of his life—
In Greyhaven by the Songris
Where Lord Gilbert met his wife.

The Calendar

Illustrating some of the peculiarities of the calendar.

The Basic Lunarian Calendar

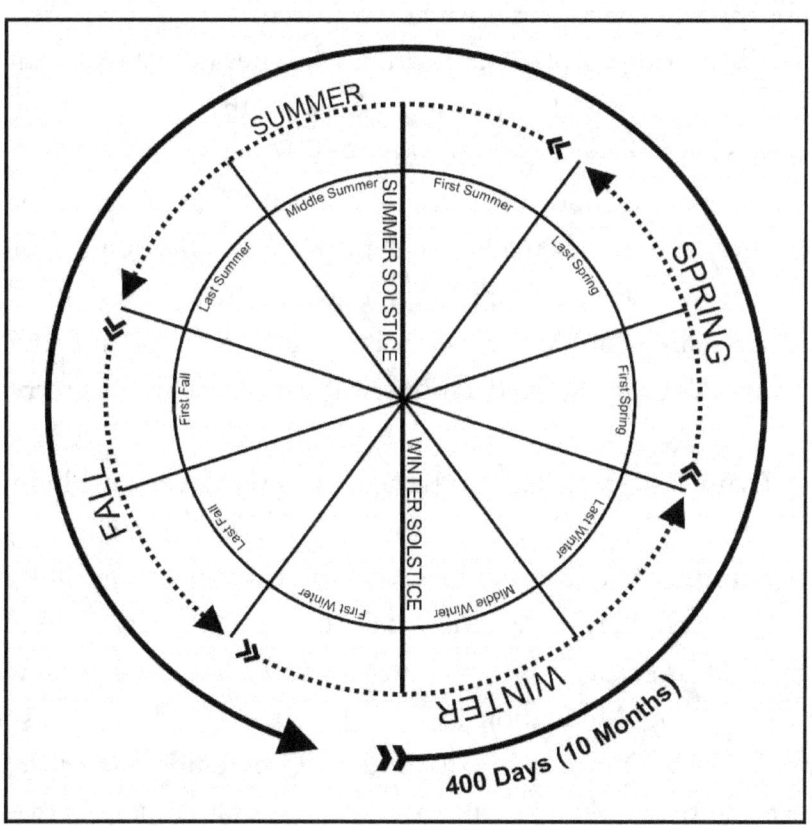

Some (very) Brief Notes on Lunarian History

Claire Miller, a clever and resourceful fourteen-year-old, desperately misses her father who has been lost in Iraq for four years; she is resentful of her mother's new boyfriend because she clings to the belief that her father will return. Her mother is determined that her daughter should find happiness by forgetting her past and becoming an ordinary child in an ordinary neighborhood playing with ordinary children.

Claire follows a boy named Pem and her neighbor's orange cat through a Gate and arrives in Lunaria on the world of Ennea. She discovers the boy, Pemburton Windover, is destined to be king. She is introduced to the powerful Lord Gilbert who immediately recognizes that she will profoundly change his world.

Ennea is an old world with a culture that at first appears medieval. Claire soon discovers this is an illusion hiding underlying nano-technology proscribed a thousand years earlier after a terrible war.

Claire's story appears to be a simple epic adventure, but the combination of failing ecosystems and forbidden technologies reveal a conflict between families, honor, and conflicting loyalties and what each may mean. The tale of people from different backgrounds is set against the nature of good and evil according to G'rama's "Nine Meditations." The Lunarian Cycle appeals to young adults who are seeking confidence, searching for wisdom, and earning trust; while starting to make difficult choices between personal integrity and security.

Claire in Lunaria, Chronicles of Ennea, Volume 1.

Claire Fisher finds herself on her way to Greyhaven. Along the way, she meets Tess a peasant girl of Tribana and Rissa, daughter of the Trader Leader, Mara Ellendor. The girls share a bond. Claire grows up at Greyhaven and starts to understand Ennea. Her actions begin to change the society, culture, and world of Lunaria as her talents as a Healer grow quickly.

As war threatens, Claire finds herself at the fulcrum of a struggle between powerful adversaries over forbidden technologies that were last used in a terrible conflict - will she meet her death on the river before she finds sanctuary in the cold stone of Lord Gilbert's Greyhaven? Claire is torn between fulfilling a destiny to change Lunaria for the good or to return to her own home to seek her lost father.

Sword of Training, Chronicles of Ennea, Volume 2.

The Two-Year War with Tieben has been concluded with compromise on both sides. King Cornal Hushara of Tieben has been deposed by his own people and exiled to the Black Tower where many think he plots his revenge on both Tieben and Lunaria.

With peace returning to the region, the great Winter Ball returns to Lumminea to heal the wounds from the war and usher in the beginning of a new era for the Kingdom. Claire looks forward with great excitement to the trip down-river on the Fortuna and to the festivities in the famous capitol.

Prince Pem secretly plans to fete Claire at the ball and announce their betrothal. In the excitement of the season, Pem unwisely reveals his secret to Sage Jallis Ruffin. The scheming Sage Ruffin discloses the Prince's plans to Lord Garrund, First Council member, whose utmost desire is that Pemburton unite the Windovers with the Garrunds by marrying his granddaughter, Illaina Greybaird Garrund. If the Prince marries Illaina, Garrund has the means of gaining control of the Monarchy as well as the lands and wealth of Greyhaven.

Claire and Tess of Tribana find themselves abducted and transported to the Black Tower with Cornal Hushara who turns out to be not the evil person they expected. Hushara gifts Claire with the Sword of Training. Claire and Tess flee to Trapper's Haven where they meet Turlo Murton, trader and guide and start back to Lumminea

Forgotten Garden, Chronicles of Ennea, Volume 3.

The struggle continues as the Ellendor Trader Clan aids Claire in her return to the Palace at Lumminea. While she is traveling across the White Desert, Pem sets out from the capitol, determined to rescue Claire and bring her gifts. He hopes, in spite of warnings to the contrary, to persuade her to marry him in order for him to become King. The rescuer becomes the hunted as Pem joins up with Claire and the Trader Landship in time to avert an immediate disaster. But it appears that death lies ahead on the River Lorne.

Claire and Pem, A Love Story, Chronicles of Ennea, Volume 4.

Claire and Pem marry and fall in love. They enter into the pleasures of marriage and together learn more about the dangers they are to face as the Royal Couple.

Their Wedding Day is greeted with great enthusiasm from the people, and not so great enthusiasm from certain Council members. Claire's small changing of the wedding vows send ripples throughout the land.

Pem and Claire leave the wedding festivities to begin their State visits to the Council members' estates around Lunaria while the Council is adjoined for the summer and the members are at home during the planting and harvest seasons.

Their honeymoon on the Rachael Anne is an opportunity to plan with Rissa Ellendor, Turlo Murten and Sage Leandra in relative seclusion. Tieben's King Veral Hushara and the Lunarian Council are seeking to form a monopoly that would create higher prices through artificial scarcity and tight government controls. The influence that the people have over the Council would be diminished, if not destroyed. The Monarchy, who represents the will of the people, is threatened.

Arriving in Ranaputkin, Pem and Claire's official visits begin with the Ranapuis and Putkins. There is time to relax. Slowly they learn more about who supports them and who is hostile.

Who is with them, and who is not?

Rissa and Turlo, A Journey, Chronicles of Ennea, Volume 5.

After the wedding, Rissa and Turlo leave Pem and Claire to their kingdom tour, and start to fulfill their own destinies. Rissa must secure trade agreements with Tieben before making public her intentions to marry Turlo. Turlo has decided to stop evading his Uncle Veral, King of Tieben, and goes to strike a deal amidst turmoil.

Taking a back way, Rissa and Turlo are captured by the Manjaros mountain people. The Manjaros seek trade and peace with the X'tlan but are being hunted by Captain Dread, who still terrorizes this region of Tieben with absolute power. Turlo and Rissa flee Dread, and find themselves with Turlo's uncle, exiled King Cornal Hushara. Rissa takes on the aspect of the Warrior's Sight with the Shield of Balance.

Turlo has to face Rissa's mother and disclose his true identity. In Wintermarsh, now it is time for Rissa to face Turlo's mother, Lady Maigret Murten, sister to the kings of Tieben.

Rissa learns that she is changing the world and begins to hear and see the underlying technology that Claire hears and sees. It is a great, and unsettling, revelation. Turlo, like Pem, is totally unaware of what Rissa can hear. When Rissa and Turlo finally meet with King Veral Hushara, Hushara seems to agree to Rissa and Turlo's plans for both trade and marriage. As Rissa and Turlo start their return to Mara Ellendor with the Trade Agreements, and thence to Lumminea with plans of peace between Tieben and Lunaria, they are kidnapped by Sage Jallis Ruffin, whose greed for power and desire to destroy Claire extends to her companions. Rissa and Turlo are set adrift on the Gulf without provisions in a small boat. Once again, the World changes.

Twin Scepters, Chronicles of Ennea, Volume 6.

The twins, Burton and Edward, are born to Claire and Pem. Claire and Pem's popularity with the people is overwhelming. Torvall Garrund, First Member of the Council, accelerates his plot to weaken the monarchy, unknowingly driven by Dark Sage Jallis Ruffin, who wants to rule the world.

Garrund takes control of the standing army with an arrest writ against Queen Claire that Captain Allain cannot avoid. Those who must flee: Claire and Pem; the twins, Burton and Edward; Tess, Royard, and little Fitz; Mags; Gilbert. They flee with the loyal Palace Guard through Lunaria to Miller's Landing, and the Badlands until a fateful decision for survival and separation of the twins is reached. Total power is within Ruffin's grasp.

The Kamorian Gate, Chronicles of Ennea, Volume 7.

The extent of Jallis Ruffin's betrayal of the people and the greed of the Council members arise again and again as Claire, Pem, Gilbert and baby Burton travel across the land to the Great Gate at Kamoria. Garrund enters Greyhaven to rape the Great Forest, and meets resistance from Reyfort and the Forest. The land itself rises to aid Claire, who misses her son Edward. Pem still clings to the thought that, with the aid of the Saharos, Ranapui's son, the Traders and the miners, he can yet rally enough of the people to overthrow the influence of Ruffin. Pem cannot accept the separation of his twin sons. At the final battle of the Kamorian Gate, Gilbert realizes the power of the Sword of the King and embraces the nanite world. Captain Allain's pledge to honor proves to be his fatal downfall.

Claire, Gilbert, and baby Burton return to Earth, one of the original seed planets. Gilbert looks after Claire who forgets her time on Ennea but manages to raise her son to someday be a ruler.

<u>Chronology of Stories</u>

Claire in Lunaria	Claire Ellen Fisher meets Pemburton Windover and crosses over into Lunaria. After the Battle of Tribana, Lord Gilbert Greybaird selects Tess as Claire's companion. X'tlan Trader Rissa Ellendor gives Claire a matching amulet. Claire travels to Greyhaven where Sage Leandra says she is to change the world. The Garden at Greyhaven is more than just a garden. Claire begins to use her Healer's Sight. Pem returns to the Capitol, Lumminea, in training to become the Monarch, but asserts that Claire is his true love. A war breaks out between Tieben and Lunaria
Sword of Training	Claire and Tess travel to Lumminea for the Winter Ball. Dark Sage Jallis Ruffin plots against the monarchy and Lunaria. Pem plans to announce betrothal intents to Claire. Abducted from the Winter Ball, Tess and Claire end up in Dark Tower with deposed King Cornal Hushara of Tieben, who gives Claire an object of power, the Sword of Training.
	In Norcross, Turlo Murten, as guide and trader, is hired to take Tess and Claire to Trapper's Haven.
	N'Rat aids Claire in releasing Turlo and Tess from captivity by Captain Dread. Pem has a nightmare where Claire is threatened by a swordsman who is running her down.
Forgotten Garden	Claire, Tess, and Turlo meet Mara and Rissa Ellendor at Timbermill. Rissa and Turlo realize that they are meant for each other. Turlo reveals that he is the intended heir to the Throne of Tieben.
	As Pem rushes to meet them, he finds himself with a Household Prognosticator, who relates the ancient story of Prince Redthorn.
	Pem and Claire, Tess and Royard, Rissa and Turlo leave on the *Redclaw* to return to Lumminea, when they are attacked. The band of companions separate. Turlo and Rissa are left to run the *Redclaw* through a burning fire on the river.
	Tess meets Ayaba the Monk on their way to Darkwood. Tess awakens the One Mother, and the Dark Forest begins to change. Tess receives the gift of True Sight
Claire and Pem	Claire Fisher and Pemberton Windover are married in Lumminea and fall in love. Their official reign begins as they leave on what they hope will be a perfect honeymoon with a tour of the Kingdom. On the Southern Beaches. Claire finds herself pregnant.

	Danger follows them to the city of Ranaputkin where sword practice proves to be more dangerous than Claire anticipates.
Rissa and Turlo	While Claire and Pem are on their Royal tour, Rissa and Turlo set off with ensign N'Rat to convince Turlo's Uncle that if Turlo Murten is confirmed as the King's successor, then Rissa Ellendor, will consent to marry Turlo and bring the full force of the X'tlan's Trader's empire behind the throne. In the Dark Tower, deposed King Cornal Hushara gives the Shield of Balance to Rissa. Rissa meets with an Oracle and accepts the Warrior Sight. Turlo's cousin, Tiela Snowborn, gives Rissa the "Golden Acorn", a key to the Heartwood. After meeting with Turlo's parents and uncle King Cornal Hushara, Rissa and Turlo are betrayed by Cornal's security agent to Dark Sage Jallis Ruffin. Rissa and Turlo are set adrift to die in a small boat.
Twin Scepters	The twins, Burton and Edward, are born to Claire and Pem. Tess and Royard have Fitz Jr. The three babies are inseparable. Pem, as King of Lunaria, supports programs that help the population, while the Council plot to gain complete control over the economy. Claire, with the aid of a local Magister, begins to set up schools based on merit, not privilege. First Councilor Torvall Garrund, spurred by the influence of Dark Sage Jallis Ruffin, sends out a warrant to arrest Queen Claire for treason. With Gilbert's help, Pem and Claire, Tess and Royard, flee with their three babies until a plan for survival can be devised.
Kamorian Gate	A long flight to safety. The fall of Greyhaven and death of Astora Greybaird Garrund. The loyalty of the miners at Akren, Ranapui family, the Traders, and Saharos. The awakening of the One Mother with the Great One in the Heartwood Forest. The Awareness of Gilbert to the nanite technology and the Administrator. The final battle at the Kamorian Gate. The betrayal and destruction of Allain's forces. Arrival on Earth to break the old cycle and begin the new cycle.